Shadows of Love

by

Gail MacMillan

This is a work of fiction. Names, characters, places, and incidents are either the product of the author's imagination or are used fictitiously, and any resemblance to actual persons living or dead, business establishments, events, or locales, is entirely coincidental.

Shadows of Love

Contact Information: info@thewildrosepress.com

Cover Art by *Tina Lynn Stout*

The Wild Rose Press, Inc.
PO Box 708
Adams Basin, NY 14410-0708
Visit us at www.thewildrosepress.com

Publishing History
First Historical Mainstream Rose Edition, 2014
Print ISBN 978-1-62830-194-6
Digital ISBN 978-1-62830-195-3

Published in the United States of America

"Well, madam, we meet again." The captain twisted my arm and held me so I could not move without causing myself pain. He looked down into my face, his gray eyes a mixture of smoke and ice. "You're proving to be more trouble than the few paltry pennies you paid for passage. Perhaps a good keelhauling would be in order."

"Do as you will, Captain," I said. "But I will not return to that hellhole alive until I've flushed my lungs of its stench."

"I see." He released me and thrust me away from him. I stumbled against the bulwarks. "Well?" He swept out an arm to indicate the star-dotted sky and lightly ruffled sea parting its surface as the great ship knifed through it. "Breathe deep."

Suspicion enveloped me. Everything about him told me Captain Barret Madison was not a man who easily acquiesced to the demands of others. Aware of his appraising gaze pinned on me, I turned to look out over the vast expanse of ocean.

Suddenly America seemed impossibly far away. As I stared out at the dark horizon, a lump rose in my throat. *Darcy! Darcy, wait! I'm coming!*

Praise for Gail MacMillan and…

HOLDING OFF FOR A HERO

"Great wit and humor start this suspenseful romance that keeps you guessing."

~Matilda, Coffee Time Romance & More (5 Cups)

"An incredibly entertaining read. The characters are great, the chemistry is there from the start.… It's one light, wonderful read I gladly recommend."

~Rain Hart, The Romance Reviews (4 Stars)

"Enjoyable read. The author did a great job of building background and character as well as suspense and mystery…. I recommend this as a good read."

~Marcie Oropeza, Siren Book Reviews (4 Siren Stones)

"Full of emotion, intrigue, and laughs….characters that have their good and bad traits and can grow on you."

~Storm Goddess Book Reviews (3.5 Lightning Bolts)

GHOST OF WINTERS PAST

"Entertaining and well written,…definitely worth checking out."

~Long and Short Reviews (4.5 Stars)

"A wonderful read….riveted me to it till the last page. This was a fast read but exciting."

~Daniella, Guilty Pleasures Book Reviews (3 Stars)

CALEDONIAN PRIVATEER

"A lovely story of romance and suspense with history thrown in…. I loved [this] story of love and piracy."

~Robin, Romancing the Book (4 Roses)

LADY & THE BEAST

"A sensuous, true romance if ever there was one…. Worth a look for the casual romantic."

~Megan, Night Owl Reviews (3.5 Stars)

Dedication

To friends, family, and fellow writers
who have always had faith in me.
Thank you.

Chapter One

My mother was five months pregnant with me, her first and only child, when she learned of the death at sea of her husband, Captain Morgan Reynolds. Her grief was overwhelming. For a time, she once told me, she wished to die also. Then, on the star-filled, wind-tossed night of May 17, 1827, I was born, and Rose Reynolds discovered a new reason to live. She named me Starr because my father had told her he charted his voyages back to her side by these suns of the night.

As soon as she recovered from childbirth, my mother took stock of her situation. My father had made no provision for his wife and child in the event of his death. His wealth had been his ship and the frequently illegal cargoes he carried in her. Although he never dealt in the highly lucrative commodities of arms and slaves, he had often circumnavigated tariff inspections and slipped through marine blockades to bring food and other necessities to people cut off by these barriers.

Because of the dangerous routes and suspected unlawfulness of his commerce, no insurance company would back my father's enterprises. He and my mother lived from cargo to cargo. When he had a good voyage, when he'd managed to elude customs officials or the blockaded people had been able to pay for his services, he and my mother would celebrate royally on his return to London. No gown was too expensive for his wife, no champagne too fine.

The poor of the great city benefited as well. Captain Reynolds readily shared his bounty with the needy. And when it was gone, he'd once again head back to sea.

But when the voyage had been unsuccessful or when his ship, the *Sea Star*, limped back into port damaged, his wife would gather up her finery and make for the music halls to replenish the family coffers. A popular singer and dancer, Rose Reynolds had, before her marriage, drawn sizable crowds. Later, as the wife of the dashing outlaw of the high seas, she became an even greater attraction. Londoners flocked to glimpse the handsome, legendary swashbuckler who sat at the rear of the hall to watch his wife perform, the man who was as colorful as any of the characters in the currently popular romantic novels.

Rumors also circulated from time to time that Captain Reynolds, because of his remarkable ability to slip through the tightest blockades, was frequently employed by the British government to perform certain acts of espionage. This suspicion explained the fact that while he was in port in London and might easily have been apprehended by authorities he was left in peace.

He was on such a clandestine mission for King and Country, gossip had it, when his ship was sunk off the coast of an enemy power. Because he was in waters unlawful to British shipping, the English government branded him a pirate and an outlaw in the press. My father, thus denied by those he had in all probability been aiding, died in disgrace.

As a result, no one came forward to help the family of a man declared a traitor by his own country. Even my parents' relatives turned a cold shoulder on my mother in her time of need. Morgan Reynolds' only real friends, the poor of London, were in no position to offer financial support. There was barely enough money to see my mother through her last days of pregnancy, her confinement, and recovery. Consequently, as soon as she was physically able, she was forced to leave me in the care of our landlady and return to work in the music halls.

Fortunately, she was in as much demand as ever. Her beauty and talent had not diminished, and as the widow of a famous outlaw, her presence exuded an aura of adventure and romance not to be found around other performers.

But the years passed and the legend grew cold. My mother had to search harder and harder to find employment, then work ever-increasing hours to keep us housed and fed. I remember awakening just before dawn as an exhausted sigh and a casting aside of shoes announced her return to our cramped rooms.

In the morning, I would awake early and amuse myself until near midday when slight noises from her room would tell me she was astir. Delighted, I would scurry to her and climb up onto her bed to snuggle close against her. Her hugs and kisses were constant reassurances that I was loved and wanted. Then she would laughingly draw me to my feet and together we'd go into the kitchen to share bread and tea.

In the afternoons, she'd read to me, then teach me to sing and play the guitar as she practiced for her evening performance. On Sundays we'd have an outing together—a picnic in season, or sometimes just a happy stroll through the park. I loved my mother dearly.

Childishly unaware of her exhausting struggle to ensure our survival, I simply believed she was the most beautiful, most wonderful creature in the world.

Then she met Sir Harry Blackwell, and our whole world changed. Smitten by Rose Reynolds' vivacious beauty and sparkling talent, he soon became her most ardent admirer. I was seven years of age when he began to call regularly at our London rooms and my mother dismissed the bevy of younger men who had become an eager throng around her.

I disliked him at once. Large and overpowering, Sir Harry, with his corpulent red face, ham-like grasping hands, fusty dark clothing, and brandy-scented breath, appeared a totally unattractive suitor in my innocent eyes. I was too young to understand the appeal a wealthy knight of the realm might have for my mother, who at thirty-two was growing weary of the constant battle to support herself and her child.

I hated the mornings when I awoke to hear stirrings in my mother's room that told me Sir Harry had been our overnight guest. I despised the retching cough he roared forth as he arose. But most of all, I abhorred the thought of him in my place in my mother's warm bed, his sweating obese body pressed against her delicately scented, lace-and-silk-clad form.

He had been coming to our rooms for over a year when the word "wife" began to crowd the conversations he had with my mother. He was not proposing to her, I soon understood; there was a Lady Charlotte who already held that position in his life. And it was my mother, not he, who constantly drew this lady into their discussions. Rose Reynolds wanted him to divorce Lady Charlotte and marry her. A clever woman, my mother realized that once her beauty was spent and the romantic myth of her past forgotten, London would cast her aside and find another darling. Married to Sir Harry, she would have established financial security for both of us.

"Sometimes one must do certain not altogether agreeable things to survive, my darling," she'd tried to explain to me when I questioned her. "Harry will never, never be able to replace your father in my heart, but I must think of us, of you in particular. If anything were to happen to me, you would be alone and destitute. But if I marry Sir Harry, you'll have security for life. Remember, Starr, many marriages of convenience become great successes."

"I hate Sir Harry, Mother!" I cried. "Please, please don't marry him. We can go away. To America! You told me Father and you planned to settle there when he retired from the sea. You told me Father said it is a wonderful place where everyone becomes rich. If we were rich, you wouldn't have to marry that horrid old man. Or anyone, if you didn't want to."

"America, my sweet, is far away and a great wilderness, not a place for two ladies alone." She'd gently ended my arguments. "It was your father's dream, a dream I shared with him. But the time for dreaming has come to an end. I must be practical. Marrying Sir Harry is the best way I can deal with the reality of our present situation. One day I pray you will understand, my precious little Starr."

Sir Harry proved unwilling to free himself from his wife. Although he often referred to her as a horse-faced nag and their grown son Charles as a milksop, he was not about to involve himself in divorce proceedings.

Divorce was a messy business, he declared, something to be avoided at all cost.

But Rose Reynolds was adamant. A survivor who wasn't above resorting to harsh means in order to stay afloat in life's tempestuous seas, she was ready to grasp at the most promising bit of debris floating about her. If he did not begin divorce proceedings at once, she told him bluntly, she would tell the London newspapers of their affair. Peering out of my bedchamber, I saw his rotund face become a beet-red portrait of outrage.

"Damn you, Rose!" he exploded. "Don't you realize what a divorce will cost me? It could put my seat in government in jeopardy! People will not support a man who's been shown unfaithful to established values like marriage vows. And you must be sufficiently astute to realize that most of my income is derived from Charlotte's holdings. With steam power the coming thing, those coalfields of hers are more valuable than gold mines. Using my influence in government to secure contracts for that commodity, I'm becoming a rich man, and I don't plan to let all that slip away for a bit of fluff like you."

"Then I must go to the papers." My mother calmly picked up her cloak and started for the door. "I'm sorry, Harry, but you leave me no choice."

"God damn you, Rose!"

Those huge, sweating hands seized my mother and threw her across the room. With a dull thud, her head struck the upper bricks of the hearth. Rose Reynolds gasped, shuddered, then moaned as she sank to the floor in a crumpled, silken heap.

"Rose!" Sir Harry rushed forward to kneel beside her.

I watched as he struggled to revive her. Sweat broke out on his forehead and trickled down his face as he chafed her limp wrists. For what seemed like hours, he kept muttering her name over and over again. Finally he must have realized his efforts were useless.

He stumbled to his feet, his breathing harsh and ragged in the quiet room. Frozen with shock and horror, I remained at the crack in the slightly opened bedroom door. The clock on the mantel tick-tocked in the shadowy firelight. Then a red liquid began to trickle from the heap of silk that had been my mother. And I screamed.

"Mother!" I rushed into the room and flung myself over her body.

Instantly I was seized and dragged to my feet.

"She's dead," Sir Harry muttered, his sweating face close to mine. A desperate glare lit his small, darting eyes. Cupping my face in a jaw-crushing grip, he forced me to look up at him. "She's dead, and you saw it all, didn't you, you little bitch!"

I started to struggle, to cry out, but one of those giant, wet hands hit me a numbing blow across the face. Dazed, I went limp in his grasp. Moments later he had swathed me in a bed sheet and carried my semi-conscious body from the flat.

Like a sack of dirty linen, I was taken away from my dead mother and thrust into one of the most brutal existences a child could face.

Sir Harry put me to work in his coal mines with dozens of other miserable, homeless children. I became his prisoner, incapable of voicing to anyone in a position to react in my favor the horrendous fact of his brutal murder of my mother.

In those horrible mines I was harnessed to other children and forced to crawl into tunnels barely large enough to admit our small bodies in search of the black gold called coal. Behind us we pulled a heavy cart. Cave-ins were common in the cheaply constructed mines; the idea of being buried alive in one of those hellholes haunted my waking and sleeping hours.

I soon discovered that in order to survive I had to be tough and strong. I learned to fight back whenever another child tried to rob me of my meager food or ragged blanket. I also developed an entirely new vocabulary, rich with invectives and laced with profanity.

Then, just when I felt I was becoming proficient at taking care of myself in the Hades to which my life had been reduced, Darcy arrived. Recently orphaned by his father's death, Darcy Pod had been commandeered on a London street, promised food and a home in return for an honest day's work, and then tossed, like myself, into the brutality of the mines. Blue-eyed and fair-skinned, with golden curls forming a soft halo about his finely featured face, he was a beautiful child. When he was thrown into the earthen-floored hovel that was our sleeping quarters, he was clad in a threadbare velvet suit and soiled, once-white linen blouse.

As we settled for the night after his first day in the depths, I heard him sobbing. The other children ignored him. None had the strength or spirit to mock or comfort the newcomer. Pity managed to overpower my exhaustion, and I crawled across the dark room's dirt floor to join him.

"Hush," I whispered. "If the overseer hears you, he'll whip you for keeping us from our sleep. We can't work our best if we're not rested, he says."

"They promised me a nice house and good food and warm clothes," he choked. "But the mines are horrible, and I'm cold and filthy, and the food is pig swill, and…"

"Hush," I said again. "We must be brave. One day we'll escape. One day"—I searched my mind for a dream—"we'll escape and go to America. My father was a sea captain. He told my mother America was a golden land, a land where everyone's dream could come true."

"Shall we go together?" The sobbing ceased. Interest entered the thin voice.

"Yes," I said. "You and I will go to America and be free and rich and happy."

Darcy and I were both nine years old when I fashioned the dream that would come to dominate our lives.

****

America proved to be an elusive reality. Our next five years were spent in a grinding, dehumanizing world of darkness, filth, and brutality. Chronically tired, cold, and hungry, we lived our childhood as slaves to a brutal master.

All that kept us alive was the hope of a paradise called America. Planning for the glorious day when we sailed to our Eden, Darcy and I did what we could to prepare ourselves for life as a gentleman and lady in the new land. We practiced what we believed to be a refined manner of speaking and the gestures we fancied befitted members of the gentry.

Darcy took advantage of the few daylight hours we spent above ground to teach me to read and write by scratching words and sentences in the hard-trodden earth floor of our hovel. Sometimes he composed poems and recited them to me as part of my education. A lady must be able to appreciate such things, he declared.

His father, he'd once told me, had been a man of letters. Like my mother, William Pod had been one of London's celebrated artists. Then his wife, Darcy's mother, died, and he'd taken to the bottle in an effort to kill his sorrow.

One night, as he returned home from a drinking bout, he staggered out into a street and was run down by a carriage. Abruptly Darcy was left to survive on his own. In spite of William Pod's astronomical success a few years prior to his demise, the man had died penniless, due to his excessive carousing. The only thing Darcy inherited was his father's penchant for the beauty of the written word.

One miserably wet day in November of 1840, Sir Harry's son Charles came to the mines. He was a pale, weak-chinned stick of a man with darting, furtive eyes and the clothes and manners of a London dandy. He slapped a slender black riding crop against his high, polished boot, his eyes raking over each of us as we stood in line for his inspection. When he came to me, I had to struggle not to fidget or stick out my tongue. I was relieved when he shrugged and moved on. Then his gaze fell on Darcy, who at fourteen, even dressed in rags and covered with filth, held the potential of becoming a handsome young man.

Charles Blackwell leaned close to the brutish overseer and spoke in his ear. He pointed the crop at Darcy, the man at his side nodded, and Charles

Blackwell left. That night the overseer came and took Darcy from the place where he lay wrapped in his ragged blanket beside me.

"You'll not be goin' inta the mine tomorrow, Mr. Pod," he said, wrenching Darcy to his feet with a giant hand. "Mr. Charles has other plans for you."

"Don't whip him!" I cried, leaping to my feet. "He's done nothing to deserve punishment!"

The overseer, known to us as Simon, was a brute who towered well over six feet in height and weighed more than two hundred pounds. His greasy hair hung in filthy strings about his unusually large ears to frame a drink-reddened and raggedly bearded countenance punctuated with rotting teeth and small black eyes. His clothing stank of unwashed flesh, stale liquor, and putrid food. I loathed and feared the man, but I could not let him take my only friend away without protest.

"You're getting to be quite a piece of a woman," he rasped, letting his gaze rove over my coal-blackened body while he held a terrified Darcy by an arm. "Some night soon I'll invite you up to me digs for a spot of wine."

"Vile-smelling cur," I spat at him. "I'd rather die."

A huge hand hit me across the face and I was sent tumbling back against the hard floor. Stunned, I lay as I had fallen, vaguely aware of Darcy's cries of rage and a scuffle as he was dragged away.

Simon came for me at dawn the following morning. The other children were headed as usual into the mines, but I was singled out and forced from the hovel before him. His huge, hairy hand, wet with hot sweat, shackled my thin arm in its filthy grip as he half pulled, half dragged me toward his coal-blackened cottage, a distance from the mine.

The single-room shack proved to be a pigsty, raw beamed, smoke darkened, and littered with the filth of months of habitation by a person content to live like a swine. The stench of spoiled food, dirty linen, and the overseer's own unwashed body mingled to make my stomach heave as he threw me against a wall and turned to shove the door closed behind him.

The room contained a bed blackened by coal and sweat, a scarred plank table piled high with rotting provisions and unwashed tin dishes, and a single ladderback chair with several of the rungs missing. Against the rear wall, on an unswept hearth, the fire that had kept the night's chill at bay lay dying. I looked up at my tormentor in the gray half-light of a miserable, rain-soaked dawn and felt the panic of a creature destined to be slaughtered.

"Come here, me girl," he leered at me over decaying teeth, his ugly face a portrait of evil intentions.

"Stay away from me, you great hairy beast!" I spat. "I'll die before I allow you to touch me."

"That can be arranged, missy," he snarled, the horrible grin dissolving into an expression of determined rage.

He started toward me, shoulders slouched, hands outstretched. I had only one chance. Gathering my strength and courage, I bolted for the door.

With a roar of triumphant laughter, he caught me by an arm and yanked me about. When I regained control of my feet, I was against his reeking body, my hands secured behind my back by one of his massive fists.

"Now, me pretty," he sneered, breathing the odors of stale tobacco, cheap whiskey, and tooth decay over me, "I'll have a little kiss."

Too revolted to struggle further, I went limp in his embrace. As his mouth drew close to mine, I retched.

"Why, you arrogant little slut!" he roared, throwing me against the table. A hard, deep pain shot through me as my shoulder hit its sharp edge on my way to the floor. "Try to vomit on me, will you? Well, by the holy saints, I'll teach you manners!"

He was advancing toward me, a murderous gleam in his small, savage eyes, when I saw the knife, an oversized bread saw with sharp, ragged teeth, at the table's edge.

I waited until he stood towering over me, legs wide apart, arms akimbo. As he drew back his foot to kick me, I seized the knife and lunged up at him.

My attack caught him unprepared. The knife slashed deep into his right forearm and ripped a jagged, blood-spewing tear down its length.

"Rotten little whore!" he roared and fell upon me.

The impact of his weight knocked my weapon from my hand. It clattered across the floor as he ripped open my bodice and wrenched up my ragged skirts.

"You'll pay for this dearly!" he snarled, as blood from his wound flowed over both of us. "I swear, you'll pay dearly!"

I couldn't breathe. Imprisoned beneath his great bulk, I was suffocating.

"Mr. Simon!"

From somewhere in the nightmare the voice of the overseer's simple-minded assistant echoed into my ears.

My attacker cursed and ordered the boy away. His free hand was fumbling with the fastenings of his trousers when the simpleton again sought to get his attention.

"But, Mr. Simon, there's been a cave-in!" the halfwit cried. "There's screamin' and cryin', and Sir Harry is callin' out for you. He's in an awful state!"

Simon roared a great oath that sent the boy stumbling back out of the hovel. Eyes glittering wickedly, he returned his attention to me.

The horror that followed would haunt me for the rest of my life. Fighting only spawned more violence, so I suffered his degradations and prayed for death. When finally he staggered to his feet, chest heaving, blood dripping from his wound, he glowered down at me.

"You're a rotten little piece of baggage," he snarled. "I can find better than you."

He grabbed up a rag, wrapped it around his wound, then turned and followed the boy at a shambling trot.

****

When I felt confident he'd gone, I struggled to my knees. I ached in every pore of my body; I was bruised and bleeding. The most unbearable feeling, however, was the sensation of utter filth. I must bathe at once, my disheveled mind told me. I could not bear another moment with that brute's foulness clinging to me. I forced myself to my feet and staggered out through the doorway he'd left open.

A thin, cold rain was weeping miserably from a leaden sky. I lifted my throbbing face into it and frantically tried to catch enough moisture in my hands to scrub myself clean.

Then I caught sight of a nearby horse trough. In a state of shock that surpassed common sense and the penetrating November cold, I ran crookedly to it and flung myself full-length into the icy water. As I scrubbed savagely at my body, the lines Darcy had once quoted from Shakespeare raced across my confused mind. Like Lady Macbeth, I would never be clean again.

The water began to numb my shocked body. Unable to care, I allowed my hold on reality to slip. I ceased to claw at myself, and let my mind and body go limp. I was drifting into unconsciousness, stretched out full length in the trough, when the halfwit came upon me. He dragged me from the wooden tub and carried me back to the empty hostelry I had shared with the victims of the recent disaster.

It was the following morning before I became fully lucid again. As I lay aching and ill in the eerie emptiness of the hovel, I vowed I would never let another man abuse me again. I would kill either him or myself before I would suffer a repeat of that body-and-soul-shattering experience.

There were no survivors from the cave-in that cold, wet November morning. For days I lay alone and ill in the bitterly cold hostelry and wondered what had become of my friend Darcy and what would become of me. Wrapped in ragged blankets left ownerless by the disaster, I huddled in a dark corner and wondered whether pain and illness or terror and despair would kill me first.

The possibility of a return visit from Simon haunted my every conscious hour. Even in sleep I could find no relief from the horror. In nightmares I relived his heinous assault time and time again. Often I awakened myself screaming or whimpering like a beaten puppy.

Two days after the cave-in, his half-witted assistant began to bring me food and water. My desire to survive returned. I forced down the stale bread and lukewarm water, determined I would not die—not here, not now. Somehow I had to escape and find Darcy. Somehow we had to escape to America.

****

Ten days later, Simon pulled open the door of the hovel and stood on the threshold, silhouetted against a blazing winter sun. A long black whip hung coiled about his shoulder. I shrank into a corner. Cold sweat broke out over my body. He was going to lash me.

"Bring them in here, lad, and be smart about it. The sooner we get this mine producin' again, the better."

A group of thin, ragged youngsters began to pour in through the doorway, the new workers for the hell Simon called a mine. The whip, I realized (and almost sighed aloud), was his way of cowing these novices. I was safe…temporarily.

The next day, harnessed at the front of his new group of slaves, I returned to that awful black hole in the earth.

I had feared Simon's return from his recruiting mission would bring him once more seeking me. It didn't.

Then I noticed one of the newcomers, a girl of about my age but more physically mature for her years, begin to absent herself from our hostelry at night. At dawn, when we returned to the mine, she would rejoin us. She always looked contented and smug, her workload less than half what was expected of the rest of us. Bold and saucy, she would swagger past us and settle to rest while we were herded into the mine. Simon and his halfwit pretended not to notice and harassed any of us who dared point out Sarah's leisure.

"You could have had it easy like me, dolly," she whispered one night as I was preparing for sleep. "Simon told me he once fancied you, but you valued yourself too high and mighty. He wants a willin' lass, he does, not a bitch what attacks 'im with a bread knife and don't know when to part her legs."

"Then Mr. Simon fancies whores like you," I hissed, and rolled away from her into my blanket.

"Bitch!" Like an enraged feline, the girl sprang at me. Kicking and clawing at each other, we rolled over the earthen floor. The others gathered around, glad for the entertainment, cheering on first one, then the other. Only Simon's intervention moments later stopped us from doing each other serious injury. Dragging us apart by the backs of our ragged dresses, he laughed harshly.

"Too late, missy," he guffawed at me through those terrible rotten teeth. "You had your chance. Now Sarah's me lass."

I wiped blood from my face and glared up at him in utter disgust. He had no idea what an immense feeling of relief his words cast over me.

****

As I was settling to sleep with the other children one evening when I was nearing my fifteenth birthday, however, Simon *did* come for me.

"Someone wants to see you," he said.

"Who?" I asked, getting to my feet.

"Never you mind!" he snapped, and grabbed me by

an arm to propel me out into a magnificent May twilight full of singing birds, blossoming greenery…and Darcy.

Impeccably groomed and dressed in the height of fashion, my friend stood in the last rays of a wonderful spring day. He'd grown tall and broad-shouldered. His fair hair, devoid of filth, was golden and curling. He was the most wonderful sight I'd seen in years; only the cruel bite of the overseer's fingers on my arm kept me from flinging myself upon him.

"Well," Darcy smiled, and there was a sense of final victory and relief in the word.

"Here she is, sir, although what a gentleman like yourself would be wantin' with such a bit of trash I don't know," the overseer said. With eyes unaccustomed to brightness after years in the mines, he'd failed to recognize his former charge.

"She's grown too big for the mines." Darcy affected a superior attitude. "We need a scullery maid at the manor. The two conditions coinciding, Sir Charles has decided she'll do nicely."

"Very well, sir." The overseer, satisfied with the explanation, shrugged and released me. "But mind. She's a spirited bit of trash. It might be well if you broke her to the bed first."

"I appreciate your advice, Mr. Simon," Darcy said, holding his head high. "Come along, young lady. I can see our housekeeper will have a sizable task preparing you for civilized duties. Thank you for your cooperation." He bowed slightly to the overseer. "I shall inform Sir Charles of your agreeable stance on the matter."

"A pleasure, young sir, a pleasure." The overseer

stood aside as Darcy put a white-gloved hand gingerly beneath my coal-blackened elbow and led me to where a horse and curricle waited.

When we were safely out of Simon's sight, Darcy halted the horse and turned to me. "Starr," he said, his voice trembling. "At last!"

"Oh, Darcy," I cried, and was in his arms, sobbing as I had not done since my first day in the mines.

"Starr, sweet Starr," he murmured against my filthy hair. "How I've longed for this day!"

"But how?" I pulled back to look up into his face. "How did you come to be freed? How did you manage to free me?"

"I've been made secretary to Sir Charles," he said. "When the scullery maid ran off with an itinerant peddler, I offered to find a replacement. I'm sorry I couldn't secure you a better position, but at least you're out of the mines, and we'll be able to see each other from time to time."

"I don't care about the position. To be out of the mines and with you is a miracle. Oh!" I gasped, noticing his smudged cravat and gloves. "Look what I've done!"

"It doesn't matter," he smiled down at me. "I've got a number of better ones at the manor."

At the mention of the mansion to which I was going, a chill of terror invaded my exuberant mood.

"But what of Sir Harry? Will he not be incensed when he sees me in his kitchens?" I'd told Darcy the story of my mother's death one winter's night as we huddled together for warmth.

"Sir Harry died last month," Darcy said. "Charles has become Sir Charles. Did you not notice when I spoke of him to the overseer? That was the major reason I thought it now prudent to attempt to secure your release. The availability of the scullery position merely facilitated a move I had already determined to make."

I looked up into his sincere, long-lashed eyes and murmured from my heart, "I love you, Darcy Pod."

"You mustn't say such things, Starr," he said, a cloud descending over his features. "I'm not worthy of your love."

"Of course you are. I love as I would a brother, a very dear, wonderful brother."

"Starr, please don't." Gently he took my hands from his coat front, kissed each blackened fist in turn, then picked up the reins and clucked to the horse.

I sat by his side, puzzled and hurt by his rejection.

During the drive back to the manor I told Darcy of the overseer's brutality. In the gathering gloom, his expression hardened and his jaw twitched.

"He'll pay for this," he muttered. "To think he'd do such a thing simply because you dared to try to defend me is to reflect on an atrocity!"

"But how can you hope to punish him? You've said you're merely Sir Charles' secretary. Surely…"

"Don't question me, Starr," he said, staring ahead between the horse's ears. "Just rest assured the man will pay for his actions if it's the last thing I do." He flapped the reins and sent the mare forward at a gallop.

Within a week of my arrival in the manor house, Simon was dismissed from Sir Charles' employ. Rumor had it he had been driven from Blackwell lands with the family hounds tearing at his heels.

When Darcy came to see me on the day following

Simon's departure, he was pale and gaunt. He moved slowly, as though in pain, and his voice was hoarse.

"Darcy, are you ill?" I asked, frightened. I could not bear the thought of sickness taking him from me, not when we had just found each other again. I put a comforting arm about his broad shoulders, but he flinched away.

"I'm fine, Starr. I've gotten you out of the mines and Simon's been punished. That's all I care about."

He looked up at me, his eyes suddenly filled with tears. "We're winning, Starr, we're finally winning." Triumph echoed through the rasping young voice.

"But how, Darcy? How are you managing to get all these things accomplished?" I knelt before him and took his soft, smooth hands in my work-reddened ones. A cold, nebulous fear wrapped itself around my heart.

"You mustn't worry about me, sweetheart," he said gently. "We're going to be fine, just fine. Wait and see."

****

I had been a scullery maid in the kitchens for nearly two years when the news flooded the house. Sir Charles was to be married to a wealthy merchant's daughter. Lady Charlotte, his mother, proud old matriarch of the estate, would be moving into the dower house across the river from Blackwell Hall.

In spite of this change of residence, Lady Charlotte was highly pleased, or so I was told by above-stair servants who had occasion to actually see the esteemed mistress. She had feared her only child might never marry. If Charles left no heir, the estate would go to distant—and undeserving, in her opinion—relatives.

Household rumor also declared Sir Charles had

been pressured into the engagement by his mother. Apparently he would have much preferred to remain a bachelor, enjoying the gaming houses and sporting clubs; the pleasures of having a demanding, overweight wife appeared, at best, dubious to him.

A fortnight before the marriage was to be solemnized, Darcy came into the kitchen gardens in the middle of the afternoon when I was harvesting carrots.

"We're going to America!" he burst out. "Our dream is to come true!"

"Darcy, how?" I gasped, catching his hand in my earth-soiled one.

"Sir Charles' fiancée is a wealthy woman," he said. "When they marry, all that is hers will become his. The daughter of a shrewd businessman and well aware of the fact, Maude Bell wants a servant of her own choosing close to her new husband, to watch over both him and her money. A personal secretary will fill her requirements. But since I now hold that position and she perceives me as 'his man,' she has ordered Sir Charles to dismiss me, replace me with her cousin, and send me away." He paused to catch his breath, then continued, "Apparently Maude's money and his mother's constant nagging for an heir have proven overwhelming. He's paying my passage to America. I sail within a fortnight."

"But you said 'we,' " I pressed, the glittering panorama of my imagined heaven wavering in my mind like a heat mirage.

"I must go alone first," he said, caressing my coarse hand. "Charles would not agree to pay two passages. But," he hurried on as my expression must have revealed my dismay. "America is a land of quick wealth. Within months, perhaps even weeks, I will be able to send your passage fare and you can join me. By that time, I'll have a home prepared for you."

Two weeks later, on Sir Charles' wedding day, Darcy sailed for America, and I settled down to wait, resolved in one matter of which he was unaware. When I got to America, I would marry Darcy Pod and make him the best wife a man could have. That was how I would repay him for all he'd done for me.

****

I made the most of the time I spent in service at Blackwell Hall as I waited for Darcy to send for me. As I had learned music and dance from my mother, and poetry and prose from Darcy, I set about to discover and memorize the social graces and skills of my employers.

Although seldom above stairs, I made the most of those rare moments to listen and observe. I studied the dress and mannerisms of Sir Charles' lady, the furniture and floral arrangements she chose, and even the table settings I sometimes managed to glimpse laid out for formal dinners.

When the master and his wife entertained lavishly, as they frequently did, I mulled over the menus and learned the names of the various dishes and wines. I studied the order of service, the correct method of offering food and drink to guests, even what cigars and port the gentlemen preferred after a hearty meal. Every possible minute I could manage was spent in preparation for the day when I would become Darcy's lady wife in America.

Letters from Darcy came as often as there were ships to transport them. Although they were never frequent enough to satisfy my constant need for news of him and the land to which he had gone, I savored each line as a connoisseur relishes a glass of rare wine.

He was in the British North American colony of New Brunswick, he wrote. He'd found work in the shipyards of a burgeoning young community named Pine. The village's main industries were lumbering for export and shipbuilding to provide the vessels to carry its timber products to England and the Caribbean. Fish, salmon in particular, was also exported, although "wood, wind, and water" provided the backbone of the young township's economy.

He'd bought a bit of land, he wrote later. He and a friend had begun to construct a home on it for us.

He had signed himself as usual, "most affectionately, Darcy." Then, in a scrawled postscript, he had continued that he hoped I'd like his friend.

He did not identify this person by name, and I was puzzled. Explicit writer that he was, Darcy Pod would not carelessly omit such information. I wondered over this only briefly before drifting off again into fantasies of Darcy and myself in the great green paradise called America.

Ten months after Darcy's departure, the promised passage fare arrived. I'd almost despaired of seeing him or America when one cool, sunny morning after a May shower I received the much-handled envelope.

I read Darcy's accompanying letter in the sprouting vegetable garden near the kitchen, beneath a clearing sky full of scudding white clouds. The paper fluttered in my hands and, as I finished reading, I flamboyantly blew a kiss in what I fancied to be the direction of America.

"I love you, Darcy Pod!" I cried. "And I'm coming to you!"

In America I would be reborn. In America all my past hurt and shame would be washed away and I would begin a new life.

The retreating clouds and warm sunshine that had marked the arrival of my passage fare were prophetic, I told myself as I returned to my work in the gray depths of the kitchen. My days in darkness and suffering were about to end.

I didn't then realize that one's apparent good fortune could change as swiftly and completely as shadows in the wind.

Chapter Two

Finally, I was on my way. One cold, foggy morning at the beginning of June I caught a ride with an itinerant peddler named Pattie O'Brien. Two years previously, he'd inadvertently facilitated my release from the mines by seducing Daisy, my scullery predecessor, into marrying him. Now, I drove with him in his creaking wagon to the Portsmouth docks.

I sat proudly on the plank seat behind the shaggy pony, a threadbare carpetbag clutched in my hands. In the satchel were two much-mended gray dresses similar to the one I wore, a change of undergarments and stockings, a cotton nightshift grown transparently thin from frequent washings, and the all-important paper that declared I had paid for and was entitled to passage from Portsmouth, England, to Pine, New Brunswick, aboard a vessel called the *Maris Stella*.

Behind me in the wagon were a sack of food and a cask of water. Old Wicks the gardener at Blackwell Hall had prepared these provisions for me.

"Them sea captains be dreadful mean with victuals," he'd told me as he stuffed my bag. "When I were a lad, I went to sea. I know."

I had smilingly thanked him for his kindness. Wicks lived in the past, I remember thinking. Modern ships' masters were not churls. As the peddler and I lurched along the pot-holed road, I caught the stubble-faced man perusing me quizzically.

"Do I interest you, Mr. O'Brien?" I asked.

"Nay, you puzzle me," the Irishman said. "Each time I stopped at Blackwell Hall these past years, I'd say to meself, 'Pattie, lad, there's a lass as has good sense, a lass who'll make some man a fine wife one day.' Then I discover you're off to America alone…and near penniless, I'll wager. Why, in heaven's name, girl, why?"

"I'm going to marry the man I love," I said proudly. "We're going to build a new life in America. We're going to be rich, and I'm going to be a lady."

For a moment he simply stared at me, then he burst out laughing. "There goes me theory about your common sense. A lady you're goin' ta be, is it? In a secondhand bonnet, a mended cloak, and a pair of lad's work boots? Girl, America is a land of possibilities, not promises. The country alone cannot make a silk purse from a sow's ear. You have to be willing to work and sacrifice and compromise to make your dreams come even partly true. Me young brother Kevin and me sister Bridgit went out there years ago, and they're still livin' in a log shack. I reckon that's the same kind of home your young man has in store for you. A lady, indeed!" He guffawed.

"Darcy and a friend are building us a real house," I said, sticking out my chin. "We'll live in style, and I will be a lady."

Pattie O'Brien's words proved to be only the first of many shadows that would be cast over the sunshine in my soul that foggy June day.

At the Portsmouth dock, I found myself crowded among people as poor and shabby as myself. We were herded into longboats and rowed out to a ship waiting at anchor a distance off shore. Each of us clutched bags and boxes that contained all the worldly goods we were able to transport to America.

But in spite of the cramped conditions of the longboat, the dreariness of the day, and the peddler's dire words, I experienced no sense of loss at leaving the austere gray edifices and backbreaking work that England had come to epitomize in my mind. Instead, I rejoiced in the vision of a beautiful, green America such as Darcy had described in his letters, and of being reunited with the kindest, most wonderful young man in the world.

As our long boat bumped against the ship, I glimpsed her name on the bow. The *Maris Stella* was a beautiful craft, freshly painted, and one of the finest ocean-going vessels about the Portsmouth docks that day. I wondered why such a ship was being used to transport poor immigrants, when British manufactured products would have been a much cleaner and more profitable cargo.

I had little time to speculate on the matter. I was prodded by one of the sailors who'd rowed us out to the vessel, and told to get aboard "smart and proper or be left behind." Having no desire to miss my one chance to America, I scrambled up the dropped rope ladder hanging against the *Maris Stella*'s sleek side and over her tall bulwarks.

As I stumbled onto the cleanly swabbed deck, my boot caught in the hem of my cloak. I pitched forward and would have fallen had not a pair of strong hands caught me and steadied me on my feet.

"Careful, young woman," a male voice iced with

annoyance ordered. "If you persist in stumbling about the deck, you'll soon find yourself in the water. And this ship cannot turn about for anyone foolish enough to fall overboard."

I looked up into eyes as gray and cold as hoarfrost. Their owner was tall, well over six feet, with coal black, curling hair and a face most women would have found breathtakingly handsome. Broad shoulders towered over a body muscularly lean and lithe as an athlete's in well-fitted tan breeches, white linen shirt, brown leather jerkin, and gleaming knee-high boots.

"Thank you, sir," I snapped, freeing myself from his hands with a swift, impatient shrug. "I wouldn't think of falling overboard. I might foul the wake."

"Sharp-tongued little wench, aren't you?" he said, as embarking passengers glanced furtively at the stranger and me. "And quite alone, I see. Luckily no poor, innocent man has fallen into your gentle clutches."

"I'm on my way to be married, sir," I retorted. "My fiancé is a fine gentleman who knows how to speak to a lady. You could take a few lessons from him, Mr…"

"Captain," he corrected. "Captain Barret Madison, master of this vessel. Mr. MacIntosh," he bellowed before I could recover from my surprise. "Take this sweet young thing below and show her the steerage quarters. Perhaps after a couple of weeks under the deck she'll be less likely to spew insults at her captain."

"Aye, sir." A burly seaman seized my arm and jerked me toward the open hatch through which ragtags like myself were descending to the bowels of the ship.

I glanced back at him as he stood against the boom of the mighty vessel. In the fog his silhouette stood out, commanding and virile before the framework of lofty masts and rigging. Then I was pushed into the darkness of the hold.

****

The stench was incredible. Even I, who had lived in the filth of a mining children's hostelry, found the odor in the depths of the *Maris Stella* overpowering. The wastes of too many people crowded too closely together, with facilities inadequate for healthy individuals let alone that of the many ill we now had among us, had fouled the dark cargo hold which had been our communal cabin for the past two weeks. To make the situation worse, one or more of the children always seemed to be crying, a man with an ugly cough retched and gagged constantly, and there was usually a woman seasick or sobbing.

I stood and went to peer up at a distant skylight. It was night. Through the opening I could see a sprinkling of stars. The *Maris Stella* rolled steadily forward, rising and falling with a life of its own. It must be beautiful and clean and fresh up on deck, with the tang of salt air and sea breezes.

I glanced about. In the dim light of the single dirty lantern swaying from a beam, all my fellow passengers appeared too engrossed in their own personal miseries to take any notice of me. I edged my way to the ladder in the darkness at the far end of our quarters.

Moments later, my heart hammering, I gained the top step. Hardly daring to breathe, I eased the hatch open a crack and perused the deck. It appeared deserted. I knew there had to be a helmsman at the wheel, but he would not be able to leave his post to chase after me. My heart beating a tattoo, I pushed the plank cover open.

I'd gained the deck and was pulling in my first lungful of fresh air when a hand seized me and swung me about. The sailor MacIntosh.

"And where would you be goin', me fine lassie?" he inquired.

"I needed air," I snapped, wrenching against him. "The stench below deck is suffocating."

"You know the rules," he said tightening his grip on my arm. "You're not allowed up here. You'll go back where you belong, at once."

"No!" I swung back on the man and sank my teeth deep into the hand that held me captive.

He yelped out a curse and weakened his grip long enough for me to pull free.

Tripping over ropes and stumbling around water casks, I made a desperate bid for a few more moments of freedom.

Then suddenly, seemingly out of nowhere, I was once more seized and flung against a man's body that on contact felt as hard and unrelenting as any of the barrels I'd been careening into. I looked up to see Captain Barret Madison holding me in a vise-like grip.

"Let me go!" I cried, kicking at him as he held my hands pinioned behind my back. "Let me go at once! I will not go back in that rotten hold…not until I've had my fill of decent air."

"MacIntosh, what's the meaning of this?" he demanded. "Can't you be trusted to keep our unwelcome passengers below?"

"I'm sorry, sir. She took me by surprise. She bit me, she…"

"Oh, she bit you, did she? So we have a little bitch

on our hands. Very well. I'll deal with this infraction. You get back to your post before any more of them appear on deck. But mind you, let one more escape, and you'll learn just how much such occurrences disturb me."

"Aye, sir." The seaman hurried back to his post.

"Well, madam, we meet again." The captain twisted my arm and held me so I could not move without causing myself pain. He looked down into my face, his gray eyes a mixture of smoke and ice. "You're proving to be more trouble than the few paltry pennies you paid for passage. Perhaps a good keelhauling would be in order."

"Do as you will, Captain," I said. "But I will not return to that hellhole alive until I've flushed my lungs of its stench."

"I see." He released me and thrust me away from him. I stumbled against the bulwarks. "Well?" He swept out an arm to indicate the star-dotted sky and lightly ruffled sea parting its surface as the great ship knifed through it. "Breathe deep."

Suspicion enveloped me. Everything about him told me Captain Barret Madison was not a man who easily acquiesced to the demands of others. Aware of his appraising gaze pinned on me, I turned to look out over the vast expanse of ocean.

Suddenly America seemed impossibly far away. As I stared out at the dark horizon, a lump rose in my throat. *Darcy! Darcy, wait! I'm coming!*

"Does he love you?" The question made me start. I whirled to face Captain Madison. He cut a charismatic image, silhouetted against a backdrop of wind-inflated sails and black, starry heavens.

"Of course," I managed, swallowing hard and trying to suppress the tremble that had come into my voice. "I'm going to marry him."

"Do you love him?" He came to lean against the rail beside me. His profile was perfect, like one of the heroes in books I'd secretly perused in the library of Blackwell Hall. His shoulders beneath his seaman's jacket must be broad and powerful.

"Definitely." My answer was haughty, self-certain.

"Then he's not simply a ticket to the land of promise?" He glanced over at me, skepticism in the sculptured planes of his face. "You wouldn't be the first young woman to manage her way out of bondage in England on the coattails of a naïve and newly affluent colonial."

"I'd never sell myself…not for money—not even for freedom." After what I'd suffered, after how I'd fought to survive without giving in, his suggestion incensed me. "How dare you say such a thing, you arrogant, despicable bastard!"

"What did you call me?" I was caught up in his arms, my hands pinioned behind my back in an iron grasp.

"I called you a bastard, an arrogant bastard!" My outrage surpassed fear. I knew only blind, reckless fury.

"You dirty little slut! Fresh off the London streets, I'll wager, any man's dolly for a bit of coin, and you dare to call me a bastard!"

"Slut?" Fighting with every ounce of strength I possessed, I determined to kill him, to rip him to shreds with my bare hands. "I'll have you know I'm a sea captain's daughter, a brave and famous sea captain's daughter. Captain Morgan Reynolds was a man of honor. I'd do nothing to sully his good name!"

His grip fell from my wrists so suddenly I lost my balance and staggered back against the bulwarks again.

"You're Morgan Reynolds' daughter?" he asked. "*The* Morgan Reynolds?"

"There was only one," I managed, although his sudden acquiescence left me as breathless as his attack.

"Prove it." His words were razor sharp, brooking no denial. "Name his ship, her port of registry."

"The *Sea Star*," I replied, my gaze fixed on his face for his next reaction. "She was registered in Saint John, New Brunswick, where she was built in 1818. She broke a number of records for speed passing through the Roaring Forties in the years my father commanded her."

"I'd heard he left a wife and daughter, but it was said the woman was dead and the child had disappeared." The words were a mutter of astonishment.

He grasped me by the hand and started toward the rear of the ship.

"Where are you taking me?" I cried.

"To quarters befitting the daughter of Captain Morgan Reynolds, if indeed you truly are who you claim to be."

Near the stern of the vessel he pulled open a hatch and urged me down the ladder beneath and into the gleamingly clean, lantern-lit companionway beyond. When we reached a door at the far end, he flung it open and thrust me inside.

The living quarters beyond the door astonished me with their elegance. Richly ornate woodwork gleaming with polish formed the backdrop for a fine mahogany desk covered with carefully arranged maps and navigational instruments, a matching captain's chair, a copper bathing tub, and a large built-in bed covered by more than one quilt. A single lighted lantern cast bewitching shadows as it swayed gently in time with the ship's subtle motion. After the dark stench of the overcrowded hold, the cabin was a small piece of heaven.

But why had he brought me there? I could think of only one reason, and the idea sickened me.

"What are you going to do with me?" I asked, backing away from him.

"Treat you as the daughter of Captain Reynolds deserves to be treated…if you are indeed who you claim to be." He started toward me, but when I leaped away, he merely smiled sardonically and reached past me to take a cigar from a box on the desk. "Steerage is hardly a place for such a lady."

He pulled a small penknife from his pocket, snipped off the cigar's end, then lifted the lantern's chimney and used its flame to light it. He took a long pull, blew smoke in a leisurely fashion, and hunched a hip up onto a corner of the desk as he fixed me with an evaluating gaze.

"What?" I asked finally, unable to stand his silent, caustic perusal. "Why do you study me so intently? Do you think I'm lying? Why should I lie?"

"Why not? It would most definitely prevent your being returned to the hold. Any respectable sea captain would treat you like royalty, if you are who you claim to be."

"Haven't I given you enough facts to prove who I am? Question me further if you're still not convinced.

My mother told me many stories of my father's exploits before she died. I can tell you whatever it is you need to know."

"I know enough to satisfy me for the present. I'm still not certain you aren't fresh off the London streets, of course. I've never known a decent lady able to fight the way you can. I'm thinking Morgan Reynolds' daughter could well have fallen on hard times and been forced to adopt an unsavory way of life in order to survive."

"Think what you wish." I swung away from him, head held high. "Just keep your hands off me."

"You can feel safe on that score." He headed for the door. "I'm not about to risk catching something from a waterfront doxy."

"Catching something…? Why, you…" I started toward him, hands balled into fists at my sides, my entire body clenched with outrage.

"I'd advise you to control that temper," he said mildly. "I'm a good deal bigger than you and a lot better versed in the arts of self-defense, I'll wager. At any rate, I'm about to do you an immense favor…just in case you truly are Morgan Reynolds' daughter. I'm going to let you use my cabin for the remainder of the voyage. All I ask is that you bathe in the water my men will soon bring for you. I don't fancy finding lice in my bed when you disembark."

He turned and went out. I heard him bar the door behind him, and I was left to fume over his last words in the complete luxury of his quarters.

Shortly, sailors arrived with hot water to fill the tub, while the ship's disgruntled cook, apparently awakened from sleep, brought me a tray heavy with a bowl of thick stew, hardtack, and a pot of tea.

I longed to hate the arrogant Captain Madison, but later, freshly bathed and with my belly full as I snuggled down in his luxurious featherbed, I found the emotion hard to come by. Instead, my drowsy mind wondered if he lay amid the quilts and pillows as I did when he sought repose. Did he sleep on his back or on his side, or stretched out full-length on his flat stomach…?

I caught my thoughts up short. I was on my way to marry Darcy Pod. I loved Darcy Pod. I buried my face in a pillow in shame and struggled to draw Darcy's image to mind.

But all I saw was a darkly handsome man, standing arms akimbo, feet planted squarely on the deck, virile and breathtaking against a backdrop of spars and sails.

Chapter Three

The next morning, I awoke alert and refreshed. Sunlight streamed in the cabin's skylight as the great ship lilted forward. I yawned and stretched like a contented feline. It was good to find oneself in a soft, warm bed, one's body and hair fresh from a thorough washing.

I arose and dressed. I could not risk lingering in my transparent old chemise, lest the captain decide to visit. One of the sailors had fetched my carpetbag, and I'd been able to don my nightdress after I bathed. Once fully clothed, I wandered about the room, searching for clues that might unlock the secrets of the master's enigmatic personality.

Most of his personal possessions had been removed by the man who brought my meal the previous night, but on a shelf above his desk was a collection of books. "A man is what he reads," Darcy had once said. With this in mind, I set about perusing the volumes.

Many, not surprisingly, were about ships and sailing, trade and world travel, astronomy and mathematics, but there was also a King James Version of the Bible and a dog-eared copy of Shakespeare's *King Lear*.

I leafed through the worn pages of the latter and wondered what intense attraction this story of a father's psychological blindness could have for the captain.

Certainly he did not seem the type of man to be impressed by the beauty of its poetry.

****

Although I was a veritable prisoner, with my door kept locked from the outside, I passed the remainder of the voyage in continuing comfort. A seaman came regularly to bring me food and see to my other needs; each evening another sailor brought bathing water and towels. But those were far from the most astonishing events of the voyage.

Every midnight, when most aboard the great ship appeared to be asleep, the captain himself would knock on my door, unlock it, and request I join him on the deck, where a single sailor and a helmsman carried out their duties.

Once on deck, we would stand by the rail and watch the winds frothing the sea as it filled the *Maris Stella*'s great ivory sails and pushed us closer to America and Darcy. We seldom spoke. I felt as if I were simply being taken out to be aired like so much dirty linen.

One night Captain Madison brought me up onto a deck shrouded with fog. The great sails hung limp in a windless calm. Darcy and America again seemed far away, an unreality on such a night.

"How long will this last?" I asked.

"A few hours, a day." He shrugged. "We're ahead of schedule, so I'm not particularly concerned."

We walked to the rail, and he looked down at me appraisingly.

"You've washed your dress," he said.

"Yes."

"You look much better in a clean gown," he said.

"Your hair has benefited from cleanliness, too. It's remarkably like honey, both in color and"—his fingers went to a straying curl—"in texture, rich and soft."

I looked up at him, my eyes widening in surprise. His hand moved to my cheek, cupping it slowly, gently. Intense gray eyes gripped me in an invisible hold. Mesmerized, I couldn't resist as he drew me into his arms. When he lowered his head to kiss me, I melted into the sensuous thrust of his tongue between my lips and the power of his lean, hard body.

His hand slid to the small of my back and thrust me full length against him. Drawn inside his open seaman's jacket, sheltered from the damp chill by his coat and body, I was overcome by a wave of erotic pleasure the likes of which I'd never experienced. Enthralled, I allowed his kiss to deepen. This devilish man was bewitching me with sensations I'd never known existed. My entire body came alive to his, and I was giddy with an overwhelming sense of ecstasy.

When he finally raised his head and brought his hand from my back to caress my cheek with his knuckles, I was breathless, awakened to a wonderful sense of intoxication that left me weak-kneed and lightheaded.

"I don't know your name," he said softly.

"Starr." The word came in a tremulous whisper.

"Starr." Astonishment colored his reply. "You're named as my vessel. *Maris Stella* means Star of the Sea, did you know?"

I shook my head as he looked down at me, his expression enigmatic. "Starr of the Sea," he muttered. "My *Maris Stella.* Morgan Reynolds' daughter. Strange."

"A coincidence." I struggled to find my voice. "Nothing more."

"It's cold and damp." He changed the subject. "I'll take you back to the cabin."

I nodded and let him lead me back down the ladder and into the companionway. At the door of his quarters, he paused.

"May I come in?" He leaned forward to kiss my forehead. I hesitated, then slowly nodded.

Will I regret this decision? Think of Darcy, Darcy who rescued you from the mines, who has worked to save money that you might take this voyage, Darcy who is building you a home.

The truth gushed out to shame me. I wanted to experience more of the wonderful sensations the captain had aroused on deck. Awash with conflicting emotions, I drew a deep breath and waited.

Inside, Captain Madison doffed his heavy jacket and went to a cupboard for wine and glasses. He poured us each a goblet, then went to sit in his chair at the desk. With a contented sigh, he stretched out in it, and I realized he must miss his cabin and its comforts. Softened by this insight, I seated myself on the edge of the bed.

"Your present quarters are perhaps less comfortable than these?" I asked struggling to keep the memory of that heart-throbbing kiss on deck from my mind.

"A trifle, yes. But, then, I'm no stranger to a hammock slung in the bow. No one begins a career at sea as a captain…as you should know."

"I'm grateful for your kindness." I caught the suspicion in his words but decided it best to let it pass.

"Are you?" He looked over at me, eyes narrowing.

"Yes, of course. You fancy Shakespeare." I changed the subject and indicated the worn little volume. "Darcy has told me the stories of most of his plays. I look forward to the day when I shall have access to books and may read them for myself. Why did you choose this particular tale?"

"The plot interests me," he said. "If art is a reflection of life, then this play is indeed just that, in its purest form."

"You think all fathers are blind to their children's virtues and vices, and are unable to recognize their own offspring for what they truly are?"

"Come here," he said. "I'm in no mood for a discussion of literature at the moment." When I stood beside him, he said, "You're very beautiful. Has your Darcy told you that you are? Has he told you how you can heat up a man's blood?"

He put an arm about my waist to draw me down onto his lap. I started to pull away, but when I looked into his eyes, his gaze caught mine in an invisible grip. Suddenly I was allowing myself to slip down onto his knee.

Slowly and sensuously he opened his mouth over mine. He tasted of wine and fresh salt air. I let my arms slide about his neck and gave myself over to the enjoyment of the moment. The excitingly erotic sensations I'd experienced on the deck moments earlier welled up from the pit of my stomach, enveloping me once again with the intensity of their impact.

Still in this state of euphoria I was only vaguely aware of his fingers on the fastenings of my dress. With a jolt of reality I felt his hand cup my breast. The horror of Simon's assault flooded back.

"No!" Pulling my dress shut, I leaped to my feet. "How dare you touch me like that! How dare you…"

"You invited me in," he drawled, reaching calmly for his wine. "You allowed me to fondle you. It was the next reasonable step."

"It was not!" I cried. "Darcy wouldn't have…"

"Then Darcy is less than a man," he said. He finished off his wine, arose, and reached for his jacket. "I suggest, my girl, you marry him as soon as we dock. You seem capable of satisfying only the effeminate excuse for a male your beloved must be."

He strode from the cabin and locked the door after him.

That night I prayed to be forgiven for my wantonness with the captain and to be kept safe from the dangerous attraction I'd experienced in those moments of dark magic on the deck of the *Maris Stella* under a star-studded sky. As an epilogue, I fervently restated my love for Darcy Pod and only Darcy Pod.

The captain did not come for me again during the remainder of the voyage. God had answered my prayers.

****

At dawn one morning about four weeks after we left England, Captain Madison aroused me from my sleep by pounding on my door and demanding I join him on deck. Clutching my shabby cloak about me, I stumbled from the cabin. He propelled me along the companionway and up into the fresh air.

"There," he said, holding my arm with one hand and pointing with the other when we came to the rail. "There is America."

Drowsiness fled. I leaned out over the bulwarks to better view the green line on the horizon. Separating the azure blue of the brightening sky and the charcoal depths of the white-capped Atlantic, the American coast appeared to be an unbroken line of virgin forests.

"It's beautiful!" I cried, as the wind caught my unpinned hair and flung it back from my face. "I know I will enjoy living there."

"Don't let appearances deceive you," he replied, cynicism heavy in his words. "Beneath its innocent façade, New Brunswick is as infested with opportunists, adventurers, and disreputable politicians as any colony in the Empire. Don't be seduced by its summer beauty. Keep in mind this is a land of long, brutal winters."

He turned and walked away. Undeterred by his pessimism, I returned my gaze to the strip of green thickening before me. Soon I would be with Darcy. Nothing, not even the captain's bitter words, could dull my joy at the thought of our reunion.

****

The *Maris Stella* nosed into a river's wide mouth and trimmed her sails. Barret Madison stood by the wheel to instruct his helmsman in navigating the bay's depths. I gazed about the shores for signs of human habitation and saw none. I was wondering if the land was a complete wilderness when the captain gave the order to one of his seamen.

"Mr. MacIntosh, return the lady to my cabin and see that she remains there until we've arrived at River Island. I'll have Randall check her for disease in my quarters."

I'd heard the other passengers discussing this quarantine inspection. Before the ship would be allowed to dock in Pine, passengers and crew must be checked for contagious diseases. If any were found, the vessel would have to remain anchored at River Island, a small bit of land in the center of the river near the village, until all traces of the sickness were gone. As I returned to Captain Madison's cabin, I silently prayed none would be found. I had to see Darcy soon!

****

The man who came to the cabin, escorted by the captain, was tall, well built, and in his late twenties. His dark blond hair curled softly about a face handsome yet surprisingly haggard for a person of his age. As they entered, I retreated against a far wall.

"Welcome to New Brunswick." The newcomer's words and smile were reassuring. "I hope your voyage wasn't too disagreeable."

"No," I replied, my apprehensions lessening.

"This will only take a moment," he said, putting down the small black bag he carried. "I'm simply going to look down your throat and check your neck for swelling, and then you'll be free to go. So far I've found no evidence of illness aside from seasickness aboard the *Maris Stella*, and you appear to be in perfect health."

Put at ease by his unobtrusive, kindly manner, I opened my mouth when he asked, and let him feel my neck. His fingers were cool and skillful, but I caught the smell of alcohol on his breath.

"She's fine, Barret," he said. He smiled at me again, picked up his bag, and headed for the door. "I'll see you in town later. Welcome to New Brunswick, mistress."

The two men went out. I was left alone to scrabble

my belongings into my valise. *Darcy, Darcy.* His name beat a tattoo in my heart and mind.

****

Captain Madison kept me locked in his cabin until all but a few of his crew had left the *Maris Stella.* When he did open the door and carry my case up onto the deck, I discovered I'd be the last passenger to disembark.

Undeterred, I gazed about the village that was to be my home. Sprawled along the frontage of a river that measured about three-quarters of a mile in width, the settlement called Pine lay basking in the warm June sun. Behind a series of crude, sturdy wharves and piers that were piled high with sawn timber, plank and log buildings lined the waterfront. At a number of locations farther downstream, several partly built ocean-going vessels stood in dry dock, while hives of workers swarmed over their developing forms.

Three or four dry, rutted lanes wound among the buildings, finally disappearing into the depths of the great green forest that surrounded the developing township. All of the structures were typical of a community founded a scant forty years previous by an itinerant Loyalist trader; all, that is, save one.

Overlooking the river and the village, the exception stood on a rise some distance beyond the shipyards. A massive white three-story structure, the house dominated the village below in the manner of a medieval castle dominating the homes of its vassals. With an ivory-columned verandah sweeping around its ground floor, the magnificent house was surrounded by wide, beautifully manicured lawns, a curving drive, and huge shade trees.

When I turned to ask Captain Madison who owned the marvelous dwelling, I discovered he'd left me alone. His attention on the task of seeing to the final docking arrangements for his ship, he appeared to have forgotten my lingering presence on his deck. I shrugged and returned my attention to the village.

On the wharf, my former shipmates were assembling their scanty possessions and reuniting families separated in the rush of disembarkation. I saw a buggy drive in among them, a man whose attire marked him as a clergyman at the reins.

"Is there a Miss Mary Constable among you?" he asked, clutching a Bible to his chest as he alighted. An elderly little man, he appeared to be in a state of nervous agitation as he looked about at the new arrivals.

"Here I am, Vicar."

A young woman about my own age, whom I'd met briefly and who I knew was also coming to America to be married, detached herself from the group and went hurrying toward him.

"Did Kevin send you?" she asked, her face bright with anticipation. "Are you to marry us at once?"

"I'm sorry, child." The shabby little man's voice shook. "Mr. O'Brien won't be coming for you."

A silence fell over the ragged group on the pier. All eyes turned in Mary's direction.

"What are you saying?" Mary clutched his sleeve, her eyes widening.

"He was killed yesterday, my dear, in a shipyard accident," he said weakly. "I'm so very sorry."

A shocked silence encompassed those near enough to overhear the clergyman's words. Then Mary screamed. And screamed.

One of the women with whom she'd traveled rushed forward and enveloped the hysterical young woman in her arms. Overwhelmed with pity, I picked up my case and hastened down the gangplank to join the pair.

"Mary, I'm so sorry," I said. "Is there anything I can do?"

"She don't need anything from a whore like you!" The older woman's eyes flashed with outrage as she addressed me. "Go peddle your false sympathy elsewhere, you two-faced bitch."

"What!" I gasped.

"Don't deny what you are." She held the sobbing Mary to her ample bosom. "You left the hold and never returned. Today, you come up on deck from the officers' quarters, fresh and clean and well fed. How many of those gentlemen did you have to satisfy to manage that state of affairs?"

"I swear I…" I began, but again she interrupted me.

"Whore!" she yelled. "Filthy sailors' whore! It should have been your young man what died. Then he'd have been spared taking trash like you as a wife."

"Ladies, ladies, this is no time for such talk." The clergyman ended the confrontation. "Mary, child, come with me. My wife and I will be glad to share our home with you until you can sort things out."

"Go along with the vicar, Mary." The woman released the young woman but continued to glower at me. "He'll see to it that a good, respectable girl like yourself is well taken care of."

Sobbing, Mary joined the clergyman in his decrepit buggy, and together they drove off the wharf. I was left with a pounding heart and clammy hands desperately gripping a shabby portmanteau.

The people on the pier began to disperse. As they passed me, many cast belittling or sneering glances in my direction. Stunned by the woman's vile accusation and the fact that most of my fellow passengers appeared to share her opinion, I stood rooted in place and watched them go. Only when I was alone on the pier, except for a few men engaged in further securing the *Maris Stella* and unloading her empty water casks, did I think again of Darcy and wonder where he was.

I looked up at the great ship, as her sails were furled away by deck hands, and sat down on a squared deal, one of the large logs now missing its rounded sides and ready to be safely stacked in a hold or milled further into planks, and prepared to wait for Darcy. The joy of my arrival in America had been muddied by the woman's vile accusation and my fiancé's tardiness.

"Your intended is late," Captain Madison said.

His ship safely laid up at dockside for the night, he'd come down the gangplank and stood before me, a canvas duffel bag slung over his shoulder.

"He'll be here," I said. "Darcy Pod has never made a promise he didn't keep."

"Ah!" he said. "Then, due to his elegant name, may I wish you all the happiness and intimacies of two peas in their natural confinement."

I was about to make an angry retort when a clatter of hooves made me turn toward the town. A young man wearing impeccable riding habit and mounted on a fine bay gelding was cantering toward us. He led another saddled horse, a huge, highly disgruntled black stallion that kept tossing its handsome head, snorting, and kicking up its heels.

What a beautiful creature, I caught myself thinking. In spite of its bad manners and ill humor, the horse was magnificent. My attention captured by the stallion, I took little notice of the young man on the bay until he spoke.

"Welcome, Barret. I trust you had a good voyage." The stallion snorted and half-reared. "Now, will you kindly take this black devil and come with me? Father is anxious to hear from you."

"Lucifer, my child." His face relaxing into a pleasured expression, the captain strode over to the prancing horse. "Come, my lad, what's the problem? Did you miss me? Has Colin been mistreating you? You look in fine fettle. Perhaps a good run is all you need."

He patted the horse's gleaming neck and took his reins from the young man. The great horse quieted. Docile as a kitten, he lowered his head and nuzzled the captain. Barret Madison gave a deep, satisfied chuckle and swung into the saddle.

"You are a problem child," he said. "You have to be tutored with a firm hand." He cast a glance filled with nuance at me, then swung the animal about and headed at an easy canter from the pier and up the town's dusty main street.

"Ma'am." The young man the captain had referred to as Colin touched his hat brim in courteous salute, then followed Barret Madison from the wharf.

I was left with an impression of a tall, handsome youth of perhaps twenty years of age, blond and athletically built, polite and decent in contrast to the captain's crude insensitivity.

****

The afternoon became a sun-scorched, dust-filled agony of waiting. Loads of squared timber and other lumber products were pulled to the wharf by sweating, hard-muscled men driving teams of foaming horses and plodding oxen. Some of the men were kind and offered me drinks of water. Others, their bodies glistening with perspiration and streaked with dirt, made obscene suggestions and leered at me as they worked.

With each lurid remark and sly, appraising glance, memories of the overseer and his brutality rushed back. Nauseous from fear as well as from the heat, I longed to remove my cloak and open the throat of my woolen dress, but I dared not. Such a gesture might be interpreted as an invitation to the crasser suggestions of the workmen. Some of them had heard me called a sailors' whore. Hot, weary, hungry, and confused, I huddled against a pile of deal near the *Maris Stella* and waited… And waited.

****

Dusk fell over the waterfront, and still I sat alone. The workmen had departed. A single watchman on the deck of the *Maris Stella* lit a lantern and, after giving me a cursory glance, settled down, his back against the bulwarks, to smoke his pipe.

Stars appeared in the hot, dark heavens; crickets and frogs began to lace the sultry heat with their creaking songs. The village appeared to have retired in preparation for another long, arduous day. Only from a tavern in the center of the township did light and raucous laughter give evidence of wakefulness.

I wondered if Captain Madison was among the boisterous gathering. Mosquitoes swarmed about me in a droning, stinging cloud. I slapped at them, looked up at the towering, naked masts of the *Maris Stella* silhouetted against the charcoal sky, and decided I couldn't wait there for Darcy any longer.

I picked up my carpetbag and, with my shabby woolen cape draped over my arm, started toward the inn. Captain Barret Madison, the only person I knew in the village, had to be there, had to help me find my tardy fiancé.

Cautiously I pushed open the door and blinked in the brightness of the hot, smoke-filled barroom of the Black Horse Inn. The stench of sweating, unwashed bodies gushed out to greet me. In an instant, I was back in Simon's hut. *Run! Get away while you still can,* a voice deep inside me urged.

I was about to obey when, at the rear of the room, beyond the sea of glistening, red faces, I saw him. Looking relaxed and unaffected by the heat, Captain Madison sat at a table in a far corner, playing cards, a cigar clamped in his mouth, a tankard of ale on the table near his left hand.

One of his two comrades was an attractive brown-haired man about his own age. From the fine cut of his clothing, I guessed that he, too, might be a ship's master.

Captain Madison's other companion, a woman, stood behind his chair, her arm draped about his shoulders. She wore a flame-red cotton gown that swept low over her curving breasts and molded itself down about her body to blossom out over shapely hips below a slender waist. Her shining blue-black hair was piled into an artistic swirl about her head, a few wayward curls hanging loose and alluring about her face. She was smiling smugly down at the captain, her long dark lashes spread out like delicate fans over the creamy complexion of her lovely face.

I couldn't approach him under those conditions. Turning to leave, I felt a hand on my arm. Startled, I whirled to face a huge brute of a sailor, his face flushed from drink.

My entire consciousness swirled into a whirling vortex. Oh, dear God, it couldn't be! But it was. Simon the overseer, turned sailor.

"Come in, missy," he leered over those rotting, tobacco-stained teeth I remembered with such horror. "We can always use another pretty wench, with two crews fresh in from sea today."

"Let me go!" I cried, terror rendering me so desperate I would have allowed my arm to be torn from my body to be free of the brute's grip.

"Come now, dearie." He laughed as a crowd began to collect about us. He appeared not to recognize his former victim in the woman I'd become. "What's one little roll in the straw worth to you? See"—he reached into his pocket and drew out a gold piece—"I have a spankin' new coin for a likely lookin' lass like yourself."

"Let her go."

Simon and I turned as one to face Captain Barret Madison. Like the Red Sea before Moses, the crowd had parted to allow him to pass. Now he stood before us in all his charismatic power.

"The lady is a friend," he said. His tone held undeniable authority. "Leave her be."

"As you wish, Captain." Simon was instantly submissive, as I recalled he'd always been in the face of his betters. His hand fell to his side. "I was only lookin' for a bit of sport, you understand, what with bein' fresh in from sea, much like yourself, sir." He glanced at the captain's barmaid, who'd followed him to the site of the confrontation and now stood behind him, hands on her hips, a knowing smile on her face. "I meant no offense, sir."

"Of course." The captain's reply reeked of sarcasm. "Now get out."

Shuffling and muttering, Simon left.

"The rest of you"—Captain Madison raised his voice and turned to the onlookers—"if you want to remain healthy, you'll leave this lady alone, understand?"

Muttering their dissatisfaction, the group dispersed. Captain Madison grasped my arm and drew me to his table. There he shoved me into a chair opposite his brown-haired companion.

"Meg, fetch me another pint, that's a good girl," he instructed to his companion in the red dress.

She cast me a belittling head-to-toe glance, then sauntered off with a hip-swinging gait.

"Jared, allow me to introduce Mistress Starr Reynolds, the most troublesome bit of baggage I've ever been forced to transport." He sat down, raised his mug, and finished off his ale before continuing. "Mistress Reynolds, this is Captain Jared Fletcher, my good friend and master of the *Maris Stella*'s sister ship, the *Linnet*."

Without rising, Captain Fletcher nodded. Obviously Captain Madison's scathing introduction had made him feel justified in foregoing the proprieties due a lady.

"Why did you come here?" Captain Madison asked. He stuck the cigar back into his mouth and continued through clamped teeth, "I had assumed that by now you would be giving Mr. Pod a sample of the wares he'll soon be enjoying on your wedding night."

"Darcy didn't come for me." I fought to ignore his crude remark. I needed his help. "I thought you might be able to direct me to the house he was building for us."

"I've been away for the past few months," he replied. "I can't help you on that score."

"What am I to do?" My will to fight was fast evaporating in the hot, smoky barroom. The possibility of being alone and penniless in this strange, feral land was becoming a stronger possibility with each passing moment. And somewhere outside in the darkness was Simon…

"I'll order a room for you upstairs," he said. "You'll be safe there until your intended decides to put in an appearance."

"I can't stay here." I gasped. "This is a tavern!"

"And the very best I can do for you." He shrugged and picked up the cards he'd left lying face down on the table. "Take it or leave it."

"I'll leave it, thank you very much. Darcy will come. Soon. You just wait and see."

"Fine." He returned his attention to his cards. "Then you're on your own."

Confused and desperate, I stood and headed for the door. Near the exit I collided with Meg, who was returning with the captain's ale. I looked into her painted face and stumbled away from her, backwards, out into the freshness of the night air. I knew what

Captain Madison had really been suggesting, and I'd made my decision. Better to die in the streets than to share a room with the belittling cur who'd brought me to this country, who'd called me a doxy fresh off the London wharves.

Keeping in the shadows, with tears of despair coursing down my cheeks, I made my way back to the pier, the heavy carpetbag a leaden weight in my grip, eyes furtively peering into the darkness for the hulking shape of Simon.

****

It must have been nearing midnight when I saw a man on horseback coming onto the pier. The horse's hooves clopped hollowly on the planking as the animal walked slowly forward, his rider unsteady in the saddle.

For a moment I thought it was Darcy, and I rushed from my hiding place among the lumber piles. As he drew closer, my heart sank. I recognized the rider as the handsome, blond young man who'd come to fetch Barret Madison that afternoon. He drew rein before me and slid rather than swung to the ground.

"Starr?" he asked, holding onto his saddle to steady himself. "Starr Reynolds?"

"Who is asking?"

"I'm Colin Douglas," he slurred. "My father owns the *Maris Stella*. And a great many other ships. And the shipyards. And that big, white house on the rise yonder. And this entire valley, for that matter." He waved an arm expansively. "I've come…I've come to bring you some sad…news…that is, if you are Starr Reynolds." He staggered, causing the horse to snort and shy as he stumbled against him.

"Perhaps you should sit down, Mr. Douglas," I

said, taking his arm and lowering him to sit beside me on a deal. Cold terror at what his news might be was washing over me.

"Yes," he breathed as he sat down. "I guess I'd better. I've been drinking, you see, and I'm not very good at it."

"You said you have news," I pressed, when he fell suddenly silent, and I feared he might be falling into a doze. "You can tell me. I am Starr Reynolds."

"Very well." He roused himself with an effort. "It's about Darcy Pod, my dear friend, Darcy Pod. He's dead, you see. My friend Darcy is dead. Dear God!" He broke down sobbing, burying his face in his hands. "He killed himself."

My world reeled. I stared at the young man and saw his image twist, then blur. The ground rose up and hit me in the face.

When I came to my senses, I found myself propped up into a sitting position against a pile of lumber. Colin Douglas, looking ill, chafed my wrists.

"Tell me," I breathed. "Tell me it isn't so."

But he couldn't. He could only explain how he himself had found Darcy near the cabin he and my fiancé had built for us. Darcy had put a pistol to his temple and taken his own life.

I listened mutely, still too shocked to react. I could not imagine my world without Darcy.

"Miss Reynolds?" Colin Douglas brought me out of my trance as he touched my arm and spoke in a shaking voice. "Will you be all right? I know it should have been a clergyman who broke the news to you, but suicide… No one wants to admit it happened, not even our own minister. They wouldn't allow Darcy to be buried in the church cemetery. His grave is out in the forest, all alone…all alone."

His voice broke and again he was sobbing, his face in his hands. Too horrified to care, I stumbled to my feet and staggered around behind the pile of lumber. There I wretched and vomited until my insides throbbed.

When I finally regained control, I remembered Colin Douglas's distress and returned to the young man who sat on a log waiting for me. He, too, had managed to quiet himself and stood when he saw me approaching.

"What am I to do?" Weak and totally confused, I stared up at him. "I don't know anyone else in Pine, and I have barely enough money for a meal. Where will I live?"

"Come." Colin took my arm and spoke reassuringly. "We'll go somewhere out of these God-awful flies and talk. We'll find a solution, don't worry."

With my new acquaintance leading his horse, his trembling fingers beneath my elbow, we left the wharf and walked into the darkness of the wilderness village. What was to become of me, I wondered, as I stumbled along the dry, rutted street. I knew only one way of earning a living, and the tiny village of Pine with its rudimentary homes did not seem a likely place to find work as a scullery maid.

I recalled Simon's crude offer, remembered the nightmare I'd experienced in his hovel years before, and knew I could not take up the profession of a harlot. I must find some other way to survive, no matter how bold or unscrupulous, my muddled mind decided.

****

"I didn't know you were his girl until Barret mentioned who you were waiting for," my companion said. "Darcy worked in my father's shipyards. That was how we came to meet."

He'd taken me to a fodder storage barn on the edge of the village, tied the horse in a corner, lighted a lantern on a bare place on the earthen floor, and seated me beside him in a mound of sweet-smelling hay. Then he drew a flask of rum from an inner pocket of his coat and offered it to me.

I barely hesitated. I'd never drunk liquor, but I'd heard it numbed the senses, and I needed anything that would help quell my pain and despair. The first drink burned, and I choked. Colin patted my back solicitously.

"Sip, don't gulp," he advised, and the mouthfuls that followed slid down more easily.

"One day while I was practicing at the piano, Darcy came to the house on an errand," Colin continued his story. "When I looked up and saw him, I was startled. Cap in hand, his shirt and breeches dirty and soaked with sweat, he was listening with rapt attention at the drawing room door. Embarrassed at having been noticed, he turned to go back to the entry, where all such messengers were told to wait. I stopped him. I asked him if he'd enjoyed the selection.

" 'Handel could move Satan to repentance with his sacred music,' he astonished me by replying. I'd never known any of my father's laborers to have a knowledge of classical music. We fell into conversation. By the time my father came to receive the message my new friend had brought, I'd learned a good deal about Darcy Pod, including his father's achievements and misadventures, his life in the mines, his own love of composing poetry and…you."

He glanced over at me, a sad ghost of a smile touching his lips.

"Please, go on." I wanted to learn all I could about Darcy, about what had driven him to that awful decision.

"We soon became boon companions. He composed lyrics for several of the pieces I've written, and I spent many evenings at his cabin as I helped him build it for you." Colin paused and took a drink from the flask before continuing.

"He seldom came to my home. Father does not approve of my socializing with his workers. Whenever he was away on business, I'd invite Darcy up to the house. I'd play the piano while he sang the words he'd written to accompany my scores. It was the best time of my life." He handed the flask to me as he wiped his mouth with the back of his hand. "It's damnably hot in here," he muttered, pulling out a linen handkerchief to wipe his forehead. "May I remove my coat and vest?"

"Of course." I slipped off my cloak and opened the top buttons of my woolen gown. "I'm uncomfortably warm, too."

"You're a very nice young lady." His words slurred as he threw aside his outerwear. "Darcy was fortunate to have known you. I didn't realize who you were today when I went to fetch Barret, or I would have seen to your needs immediately. It was only when we were dismounting before my father's house that Barret chanced to mention the young lady whose fiancé with the unusual name of Pod had been left waiting on the pier. I knew what I had to do." He paused and looked beyond me, then continued, "As soon as I could escape from the meeting with my father and Barret—I was ordered to attend and, as you'll learn, one does not disobey Abraham Douglas—I planned to return for you."

"That was kind of you."

"But for you the time must have seemed interminable," he said. "And I could have been here much sooner, but as I was about to leave the house, my courage failed. I couldn't imagine how I would tell you about Darcy's death. As a result of my cowardliness, I took a flask of rum from my father's liquor cabinet and went to my room." He shook his head in disbelief at what he'd done.

"It's all right," I told him gently. "You're not responsible for me."

"As Darcy's best friend, I most definitely am," he answered solemnly. "But it was only after I'd finished one pint and a goodly part of another that I found the strength to do my duty. Our fledgling community is not a safe place for a lady, especially a beautiful one such as yourself, to be abroad alone at night."

"Thank you." A sensation of relaxation began to slide over me. I took another swallow from the flask. "Now you really should be going home. Your family will be missing you."

"And leave you alone? Certainly not!"

His eyes were heavy-lidded as he took the flask from my hand and raised it unsteadily to his lips. Rum dribbled down his white shirtfront, but he appeared not to notice.

"But you must," I said. "You can't spend the entire night here with me. I'm grateful for what you've done, but now you must return to your family. I'll spend the night in this barn, and in the morning…"

"Don't be absurd!" He pulled himself to his feet and looked down at me as indignantly as his inebriated state would allow. "I won't desert you!"

"You must," I repeated. "Unless, of course, you plan to elope with me in Darcy's stead," I finished facetiously.

"Of course!" He seized my hand. "That's the answer. We'll get married! You need a husband and, Lord knows, my father is pushing me to take a wife. Come, we'll go to Reverend Prescott and demand he marry us at once." He tried to pull me to my feet, but I held back.

"I was jesting," I protested, my tongue thick from drink. "You barely know me… It would be madness…"

"Miss Reynolds… Starr," he said, dropping on one knee before me. "You need a husband and I need a wife. It's a perfect solution, don't you see?"

Through a haze of pain, fear, grief, and rum, I saw before me a handsome, probably wealthy young man who was proposing a way out of my miserable circumstances. I squared my shoulders and looked into the earnest face of the boy kneeling before me.

"Very well, Colin Douglas," I said. "We'll be married."

"Good, good." He led me to his waiting horse, hoisted me into the saddle, swung up behind me, and we were off at a trot to make our vows.

****

Reverend Prescott, the clergyman I'd seen on the pier, married us an hour later. At first, when Colin had aroused him and his gray-haired, motherly little wife from their bed in the small hours after midnight, he'd been reluctant to go along with our scheme.

"Mr. Douglas, are you quite sure?" he asked, blinking behind his spectacles, his nightshirt hanging to his heels, his tasseled cap askew on his balding head. "This is very sudden, and you've been…ah…drinking."

"Reverend Prescott, must I remind you my father is the chief contributor to your church?" Colin asked, his arm about my waist. ""He wouldn't be pleased to learn you refused a small favor to a member of his family."

The little man hesitated only a moment longer.

"Very well," he said. "But, mind you both, this ceremony will bind you legally and morally for life. Only death can end it."

"We understand," Colin said. "And we agree."

As we stood before the clergyman, I saw Mary Constable, who'd been summoned from her bed to act as a witness, staring at me, contempt mirrored in her swollen, red-eyed face. What would she do when she learned the man I was marrying was not the same one I'd crossed the Atlantic to espouse but a sudden, fortuitous substitute? Would she feel sufficiently vindictive to tell my soon-to-be husband about my voyage in Barret Madison's cabin? Distracted by the possibility, I nearly failed to reply "I will" at the crucial point in the ceremony.

She didn't. In what seemed a few short minutes, the ceremony was complete. Colin kissed me on the cheek, thanked the nervous little clergyman, his wife, and Mary for their help, and, catching my hand in his, drew me once more outside. In less than an hour I'd been proposed to and married.

****

His home was called Peacock House, my new husband informed me as he turned the horse toward the dark silhouette of the mansion on the hill. His father had named it after the proud, showy birds he allowed to roam the grounds in summer. Too full of rum to really listen or worry about the reception I would receive in my new home, I could only think of it as a refuge, a haven from my dire circumstances. Leaning back against my husband's hard chest, I let all serious considerations slide away into the sultry night.

We entered the stable furtively. I slumped into a mound of sweet hay to wait while Colin unsaddled the gelding and put him into his stall for what remained of the night. Then he joined me, and together we finished a second flask of rum he'd hidden in the barn.

"Now we must go to bed," he slurred, staggering to his feet.

I reached for his proffered hand, missed, and tumbled to my knees in front of him. Instantly he was kneeling beside me, his expression one of deep concern.

"Are you hurt?"

"No," I murmured. "But I think you will have to help me to my feet."

He did as I requested. Then, each with an arm about the other's waist, we started toward the big, dark silhouette that was to be my home.

After Colin had eased open the huge front door, we crossed a vast, tiled foyer that echoed with our booted footfalls in spite of our efforts to be quiet. We climbed a great spiral staircase to the second floor, but because of the darkness and my state of inebriation, I noticed few details of the mansion's interior.

"My room," Colin whispered, pausing at a closed

door halfway along a wide, upper-story corridor. "*Our* room now."

Inside, he crossed to a lamp burning low on a bedside table and turned up its flame. Standing just inside the door where he'd left me, I stared about the big, elegant bedchamber.

A huge, high-posted bed covered with a maroon velvet spread dominated a room furnished with gleaming mahogany pieces adorned with shining brass hinges and pulls. My rum-dulled mind did not further scrutinize the place but turned its attention to Colin.

My husband was throwing his vest and coat across the bed, tearing off his cravat, and opening his white linen shirt. In two strides, he was at the window, brushing aside heavy dark red draperies to reveal delicate lace undercurtains. With an impatient push, he shoved up the sash to let in the pre-dawn, dew-tinged freshness.

"Lord, it's hot in here," he muttered, looking out into the night and pulling off his shirt.

His bared shoulders were broad and rippling with muscles. When he turned back to me, he caught me staring at him.

"Oh, God!" he muttered, looking about for his discarded shirt. "I wasn't thinking. Excuse me…please."

"It's all right," I said feeling a flush spreading across my cheeks. I lowered my gaze to the carpet beneath my boots. "I'm your wife."

"Yes," he said. He stopped looking for his shirt and came to stand before me. "It isn't wrong, is it?"

I shook my head. My lowered eyes saw his hand go to the belt buckle at his slim waist and open it with a single abrupt jerk. The next instant he stood before me clad only in skintight undertrousers.

"Starr," he said, his voice shaking.

"Yes." I exhaled and began to unbutton my woolen gown. I was a married woman and this was my wedding night. I had a duty to accept.

My dress fell to the floor, and I stood before him in my mended chemise. Slowly I raised my gaze to my husband's face.

It was a pale mask of nervous tension.

When he put out a hand to touch my cheek, I felt the quiver in his fingers. Carefully I moved into his arms, against his rock-hard chest.

"Starr," he whispered, and lowered his head as if to kiss me. The reek of rum on his breath jerked the memory of the night at the overseer's hovel over me. Panicked I wrenched away and rushed to cower by a bedpost.

"Starr, I'm sorry!" His voice was full of compassion. "That was too sudden. Forgive me. Let me put you to bed. Tomorrow we'll talk and get to know each other. I won't force you into intimacy, I promise."

I looked up at him and saw sincerity in his troubled expression. I could trust this man. I controlled myself and allowed him to take my hand and lead me to the side of the big bed. There he threw back the covers and gestured to the spotless white linen exposed.

"Rest, my sweet wife." He touched my cheek with his fingertips.

"Yes." I sighed.

Exhausted and inebriated, I dropped into his bed. And fell asleep.

Chapter Four

"Colin, wake up! Who is this you've taken to your bed in *my* house? Speak up, boy!"

I awoke to find a tirade breaking over me. A towering, barrel-chested man about sixty years of age was shaking Colin and roaring. Outraged and demanding, he was centering his attention on my husband; apparently I was only the catalyst to the situation.

As I attempted to sit up, my head pounded. I fell back, cowering behind Colin's broad, bare shoulders. He came awake and struggled up on one elbow to face the angry stranger. Wearing impeccable business attire, his receding gray hair the color of his sharp, cold eyes, the stranger had long, thick sidewhiskers and a ruddy complexion.

"What is the meaning of this, sir?" the big man bellowed. "Have you so degenerated as to feel it permissible to bring a whore into my house for your pleasure?"

"She's not a whore, Father." Colin dragged himself to a sitting position but kept the covers to his waist. "She's…" He hesitated and looked down at me a bit incredulously. "She's my wife." He rubbed his forehead as if trying to clear confusion from his mind. "Reverend Prescott married us last night."

"Married you!" The man he'd addressed as Father

jerked backward as though struck. "Colin, are you saying this young woman and you spent the night together in your bed as husband and wife?" I was astonished to hear amazed pleasure entering his tone.

"Papa, please!" Colin flushed. "Starr is my legal wife."

"All right, son." He reached out a beefy hand and slapped Colin on the shoulder. "You and your…bride get dressed and come down to breakfast. We can talk later, while she rests. I'm sure it's been an exhausting night for her."

"Papa!"

"Very well, my boy." He held up his hands in a gesture of surrender. "I'll go." He patted Colin on the shoulder and smiled down at him. "I'll expect you at the table in half an hour, but if it takes longer, I'll understand."

Smiling smugly, he turned and went to the door. He paused at the threshold and glanced back at my husband.

"I'm proud of you, my boy," he said gently. "Very proud."

I was startled to see a mist of tears in his eyes. Closing the door softly after him, he left. I looked up at Colin and saw he was staring after his father, his eyes also moist.

"Colin?" I touched his arm.

"I've deceived him again," he muttered.

"What are you talking about?"

"I'm sorry, Starr." He ran a hand through his tangled blond curls. "It's nothing you need concern yourself about. Let me deal with my father."

He slid his feet out of bed and started to rise, but

fell back to sit on its edge.

"Ohhh," he moaned, grasping his head in both hands. "That cursed rum…"

He still wore his undertrousers.

With an effort, I pulled myself to a sitting position and felt again that painful hammering in my own head. Colin turned to me as I grimaced.

"You're suffering from our excesses, too," he said. "I'll get you a cold compress."

He eased himself from the bed and went into the adjoining dressing room. Through the door which he left open, I saw a copper tub and a washstand with a mirror, shaving equipment, and hairbrushes. Neatly folded snow-white towels were piled on a shelf against one wall. Colin dipped one of these into a basin of water, wrung it, and returned to me.

"Lie back," he said, pushing me gently down on the pillows. He applied the cool towel to my burning forehead. I flinched but almost immediately felt relief.

"Rest." He touched my cheek with his fingertips. "I'll excuse you from breakfast and have a tray sent."

"No, Colin." I sat upright to protest his words. "I must put in an appearance. I must meet your family before I have time to imagine their responses to your sudden bride and lose my courage."

"Very well," he said. "If you insist. But rest while I shave. As my father said, he'll understand if we're late."

The last sentence carried sardonic bitterness out of character for the man my young husband had so far shown himself to be.

"He was only assuming we'd had a normal wedding night," I said. "He couldn't know you married me out of compassion, that there was nothing more between us."

"He never understands anything I do." Colin arose and strode into the dressing room.

He shut the door after him, and shortly I heard the sounds of water. I assumed he began to wash and shave. From the lawn below, through the window Colin had left open all night, came the sudden, harsh cries of the peacocks he'd mentioned. They belonged here, I thought. They were like the master of this house: flamboyant, colorful, demanding, and loud.

I leaned back on the pillows, closed my eyes, and tried to relax. What would Colin's family say when they saw me in my shabby dress and work boots? My stomach, ill from the rum and apprehension, roiled.

My thoughts were cut short as Colin returned to the bedroom. Blood streamed from between the fingers of his left hand which he held clasped over his right forearm.

"Colin, what happened?"

"My hands are shaky from last night's drinking," he said, grabbing a corner of the bed sheet and wrapping it about the wound. "The razor slipped and I cut myself. Please don't mention it to anyone. It will only serve to suggest I was inebriated last night. I don't want to give my family reason to believe I was intoxicated when I married you." He smiled at me. "When, in fact, I'd do the same thing this morning, cold stone sober."

****

The previous night, darkness and inebriation had prevented my taking in the amazing ambiance of my new home. When we emerged from Colin's room that morning, I was astounded by the opulence of my surroundings. I found myself amid richly embossed wall coverings, thick Persian carpets, gleaming mahogany wood paneling, and shimmering crystal chandeliers.

Several maids were engaged in polishing and cleaning the bedrooms and upper corridor. For each, Colin had a word and a smile. They responded with dropped curtsies, blushes, and, in some cases, shy giggles.

One, in particular, caught my notice. Beautiful, shapely, and bright-eyed, she responded to my husband's greeting with a vivacious but still properly respectful reply I found charming.

"Marie, this is my wife, Starr." Colin paused to make an introduction. "Be her friend…please."

"Of course, monsieur." She bobbed a curtsy. "It will be my pleasure."

We went down the wide, curving staircase. Colin led me past several closed doors until we came to an open one toward the rear of the house.

When he drew me inside, the gleam of silver and polished crystal and china glistening in the June sunlight on the big mahogany table struck my eyes with the force of a sunbeam. I blinked in the sudden glare. Then, as my eyes adjusted to the sun-drenched dining room, I saw them seated about the table. My new family.

"Come in, come in." Beaming, Colin's father got to his feet at his place at the head of the table and gestured to us with alacrity. "This is Colin's family, my dear."

Two women, one elderly, the other young, and a man sat at the table. I tried to force a smile, but as my gaze fell on the latter my whole being froze. The handsome, well-dressed gentleman on my father-in-law's right hand was the doctor who had examined me aboard the *Stella Maris*. Startled, I lost track of the conversation and had to struggle to regain its flow.

"This is my wife, Starr," Colin was saying as he eased me into a chair. "I hope you will all help me to welcome her into our family. Starr, meet my brother Randall, my sister-in-law Caroline, and my grandmother Ida Douglas, whom we all call Gram. My father Abraham"—he hesitated before continuing—"you've already met."

"Welcome." Randall Douglas was the first to respond to Colin's introduction. He arose and came around the table to place his hands on my shoulders, stoop, and bestow a kiss on my cheek. Again, I smelled liquor on his breath.

As he paused before straightening up, he winked conspiratorially. I almost sighed aloud in relief. He wasn't going to betray me, at least not now.

"Careful, darling." His wife looked across at us, her beautiful violet eyes narrowing. "She's *Colin's* wife, remember."

"Never fear, my love." Randall turned away from me with a weary sigh. "You give me scant opportunity to forget my circumstance."

He returned to his place, his shoulders drooping beneath his fine coat. Caroline Douglas stuck out her chin. Raven-haired and breathtakingly beautiful, Colin's sister-in-law wore a soft summer gown of pale yellow, pearl eardrops presenting a perfect contrast against her dark curls. Beside her I must appear exactly what I was…a dowdy little scullery maid. I smoothed my threadbare skirts and tried not to let feelings of inferiority overwhelm me.

"So you're married, Colin," she continued, stirring her coffee daintily as she smirked at my husband. "I trust you weren't forced to wed in haste lest a bundle from heaven arrive before its proper time."

"That will do, miss!"

The gaunt little old woman introduced as Ida Douglas spoke for the first time. Surprised at her vehemence, I turned to look at her. Although she appeared frail and ancient in her black gown, a thatch of unruly white curls escaping from beneath her cap, Colin's grandmother's eyes revealed a personality far from delicate or spent beneath the matronly façade. Charcoal, nearly black, they snapped and flashed with vitality and, at the moment, anger. Clutching a gold-headed cane, she arose and started toward the door. She paused beside me and looked me over critically.

"I want to see you in my room after you've eaten, young woman," she said when she'd finished her perusal. "Have one of the servants bring you to me."

"Yes, mum," I murmured, and caught myself bobbing a curtsy. She stumped out, her cane thumping over the thick carpets. Out of the corner of my eye I saw Caroline Douglas purse her lips.

"Come, children." Abraham stood and beckoned to Randall and Caroline. "Let us leave the newlyweds alone. I'm sure they'll not miss our company this morning."

As he followed his son and daughter-in-law from the room, he paused behind Colin's chair and slapped a big, affectionate hand on my husband's shoulder. "Eat hearty, boy. You'll be needing all your strength in the next few days…and nights."

"Papa, in God's name…"

With a boisterous laugh, Abraham Douglas left the room, closing the door after him.

"I'm sorry," Colin avoided looking at me. "Please don't let my father's crudeness distress you. I'll get you some ham and eggs. The cinnamon buns are particularly good. You must have some. And coffee. Or perhaps tea?"

He stood and went to a heavily laden sideboard.

"Just coffee and a bun, please," I admonished. "My head and stomach are still a mite uncertain."

He glanced over his shoulder to grin at me. "Mine, too. Coffee and buns all around, then. Tomorrow morning we'll attack the ham and eggs."

****

"More coffee, Mrs. Douglas?" Colin picked up the silver pot and smiled at me when we'd finished eating. It was the first time I'd been addressed by the title, and I looked up at him, startled.

"It'll be all right." He refilled my cup. "They'll adjust to the fact that you and I met when Barret's ship docked yesterday and it was love at first sight."

"Is that the story we're to tell?"

"Yes, please."

"Colin, perhaps it would be best to make a clean breast of it and have this marriage annulled. We were both drunk and half-mad with grief…"

"No!" Colin set the silver pot down with a thump. "I plan to care for you as Darcy would have. You're my wife, Starr, and I want it to remain that way." He took my hand and continued, "We'll make it work. Just give it time. And rely on Marie. She was my mother's lady's maid. She'll be your friend and guide."

"If that's what you wish."

"It is." He released my hand and got to his feet. "Now I must see my father. If you want anything, ring the bell and one of the maids will fetch it for you." He stooped to kiss the top of my head and left me alone to finish my coffee in the colossal room.

I was taking a sip of the fine coffee my husband had poured for me when *his* voice, bitter and hostile, caused me to spill the hot, black liquid over my dress front.

"Well, madam, you seem to have a talent for maneuvering yourself into comfortable circumstances."

Brushing coffee from my lap with a napkin, I swung on my chair to face Captain Barret Madison. In a white shirt, neatly tied cravat, elegant tan vest and trousers, and gleaming knee-high riding boots, he looked every inch a member of the colonial gentry, far removed from his prior role as swashbuckling sea captain.

"So you tricked young Colin into marrying you, did you?" he said pulling out a chair and sitting down opposite me. "Village gossip already declares he was drunk at the time. The maids who live out and come in each morning have brought the news. Where did you get the rum to seduce him? Did you steal it from my cabin?"

"Who made such a vicious accusation?" I cried, rising.

"Mary Constable was aroused to witness your triumph, was she not?" He helped himself to coffee from the silver urn Colin had left on the table. "The poor little wench is bitter. She's already told her tale in the village mercantile for all to hear. She feels her goodness and virginity have brought her nothing but pain, while you, with your lax morals, have managed to marry the wealthiest young bachelor in the valley. It's not every day the son of the village's most prominent citizen elopes with a ragamuffin immigrant whose intended has been dead a scant two weeks. You must appear incredibly fortunate—and adaptable."

"Get out!" I ordered. "Get out of this house at once!"

"Playing mistress already, are you?" he mocked. "Caroline won't like that. You'd do well to tread carefully near that feline."

"Get out!" I repeated, bringing my fist down on the table with a violence that made the dishes dance.

"Most unbecoming behavior for a lady of the house." He clucked his tongue disparagingly. "And all in vain, I can assure you. You see, I live here."

"You *what*?"

"I'm commodore of Abe's fleet," he said. "He finds it convenient to have me close at hand when I'm in port."

"Well, you can't stay here anymore…not now." I couldn't live in the same house as the man village gossip was suggesting I'd seduced on my voyage to this country.

"Oh, but I'm afraid I must. It's our master's wish. As you'll learn, no one defies Abraham Douglas."

"Well, I do…I will."

"Not wise." He poured cream into his coffee. "I think you'll find it won't be an intolerable situation. I'm not a barbarous houseguest. I don't chew tobacco, I seldom use a chamber pot—I've known the path to the privy for some time and I'm not afraid of the dark—and it's only occasionally I come in under the influence and molest a maid servant or two."

Fuming with outrage at his brazenness, I could only listen in silence as he continued, "And, as you may recall, I defended your honor most chivalrously only last evening. Surely that entitles me to something more cordial than an order to vacate my current comfortable living arrangements."

"You said you couldn't help find Darcy, that your only assistance would be to share a room in that tavern with me," I raged. "That hardly constitutes a gallant rescue. When I fled because of your crude offer, you didn't trouble yourself to come after me. I could have been raped or killed in the streets."

"Hardly," he said, stirring his coffee with infuriating calm. "Once I'd ordered you left alone, you came under my protection in this village. You were as safe as you were aboard the *Maris Stella*. And I did not offer to share a room at the Black Horse with you. I merely said I would get you a room. Your female vanity read more into my offer than was intended."

"You have a smooth tongue! I wonder how long Mr. Douglas would allow you to remain under his roof if he knew you had tried to seduce his future daughter-in-law?"

"Or how long you would remain if he knew you'd lived in my cabin for nearly a fortnight? I have a shipload of witnesses to my allegation and a faulty reputation when it comes to celibacy."

I longed to throw what was left of my coffee into his smirking face, but I knew I could not risk the possible outcome of such a show of contempt. We would either both remain in Abraham Douglas' house or leave unceremoniously together. Angry and thwarted, I tried to make a haughty exit, but his mocking laughter followed me.

I was at the foot of the staircase, hoping to find a servant and ask direction to Gram's room, when Abraham stepped out of his office near the front door to confront me.

"Come in, my dear." He greeted me profusely and escorted me into the richly furnished room. Situated on the west side of the house and still untouched by the morning sun, it seemed cold and dark after the hot coffee and brightness of the easterly-facing dining room. I shivered.

In a corner Colin stood by a window, his hands clasped behind his back. He tried to smile at me as his father assisted me to a chair, but the gesture resulted only in a nervous tick. He returned his gaze to the view outside.

"Now, my child," Abraham addressed me pleasantly. "Before I go to my office in the village, I want to speak to you. I must admit you puzzle me. Captain Madison has told me you sailed to this country in steerage, but you're well spoken and decently mannered. That's not common among that class of people. Tell me about yourself."

I paused, wondering what more Captain Madison had told him or would tell him in the days ahead and trying to sort out what I should say.

"Come, come, child." Abraham's tone was genial. "It can't be all that bad. Are you perhaps from an aristocratic family fallen on hard times? Tell us your story. We shall be kindly and attentive listeners, won't we, Colin?"

"Starr, you don't have to..." My husband tried to intercede.

"Of course she must!" Abraham overwhelmed him. "She's a member of this family now. We must know all about her. Go ahead, child. We're listening."

His tone brooked no refusal.

I told him the story of my life as briefly and honestly as I dared. I did not tell him that the young village man who'd killed himself prior to my arrival had been my intended, that my father had been Captain Morgan Reynolds, or that I had been assaulted by a creature worse than vermin. I most certainly did not mention the events of my recent voyage.

"I still say you speak well for a child brought up mainly in the coal mines," he commented when I had finished my story. He appeared undeterred by my past as an orphaned miner or as a scullery maid.

"The man I came to America to marry...who died before I arrived...had a learned father, and he himself was a man of letters," I said proudly. "He taught me to read, write, and speak properly."

"Ah." He rubbed his hands together, a cat-in-the-cream smile crossing his broad features. "So all you lack is a first-hand knowledge of dress and the social graces. That can easily be remedied. Yes, you'll do nicely. Now you may go. I'm sure you wish to rest. This afternoon a seamstress and several other merchants will arrive to outfit you properly."

I got up to obey, then froze as I saw a crumpled pile of linen behind a side chair near the door. Red stains were blotted over what I recognized as our bed sheet. Horrified, I whirled on Colin. His eyes, desperately pleading, met mine. His face was tense and haggard, a nervous twitch afflicting his jaw.

"I'm sorry, my dear." Abraham said, becoming aware of the object of our mutual attention. "I had to have proof of your virginity. I had to be sure your child will be Colin's. I could not allow a whore with some sailor's bastard already in her belly to become my daughter-in-law. You're very beautiful. You could easily have seduced my boy into making an unfortunate choice."

"Father, please!" Colin joined us, his face flushed.

"Colin," I began, turning angrily on my husband. He had deliberately deceived his father into believing he'd become my lover and that I had been a virgin at the time. I was about to tell Abraham Douglas the truth when I saw Colin's desperate expression. Silently he was begging me to go along with the ruse.

The truth died in my throat. When I'd been in dire straits, Colin Douglas had come to my rescue. The very least I could do was to go along with his fabrication of our wedding night.

"You two have made me very happy," Abraham was saying. "Now run along and rest, my dear. I must talk business with your lover. Since he's seen fit to take on the responsibilities of a family man, he must also take on more of the responsibilities of running the Douglas business."

Ending his words with a fond, intimate chuckle, he slapped Colin on the back before propelling me out of the office and into the hallway. As the door shut after me, I was left alone to ponder Colin's strange deception and what had driven him to it—his father's shameless need for proof of my virginity at the time of our copulation.

****

"Sit here, near the window, in the light. I want to have a good look at you."

I crossed the carpeted room and took the straight-backed chair the old lady indicated. I'd obeyed Ida Douglas's order and come to visit her in her room as soon as Abraham dismissed me.

For a few moments she scrutinized me with shrewd, dark eyes until finally, as if satisfied with her findings, she grunted and settled back in her chair.

"You've been in service, girl?" She gestured at my work-coarsened hands.

"Yes, mum," I murmured, keeping my eyes downcast. "For the past three years, mum."

"And before that?"

"I was in the mines, mum."

"A hard life," she said crisply. "Much like my own early day. Do you love my grandson?"

"Not yet, mum," I replied. "But he's a good man. Love will come, I've no doubt."

"You're an honest lass," she said.

"I try to be, mum," I said, daring to meet her piercing gaze for the first time.

"Yes, I believe you do," she said. "You may call me Gram. Give me a kiss. Welcome to the family."

I went to plant a kiss on the soft, wrinkled cheek. As I began to straighten up, she caught my hand in hers with a strength startling in so elderly a woman.

"Be good to the boy, Starr," she said, her sharp old eyes bright and imploring. "His life has not been an easy one, in spite of his father's wealth."

"I will, mum," I said. "Never fear."

"Gram," she corrected. "You may call me Gram. Now run along. I'm sure you'd much rather be with that handsome grandson of mine than with a fractious old woman."

"As you wish…Gram."

I left, acutely aware of her shrewd eyes on my departing figure. Like Barret Madison's, they seemed to have the power to peer into my soul.

****

"So you've trapped yourself a rich husband."

As I started down the upstairs corridor to return to Colin's room, Caroline's voice made me turn. She stood outside a closed door near the end of the hall and glared at me with contemptuous violet eyes.

"What was your profession before you became Mrs. Colin Douglas, Starr?" She advanced toward me. "A scullery maid? A stable hand's whore?"

"How dare you! You don't know me. You've no reason to make such a filthy accusation."

"Look at yourself," she sneered. "Unless he was out of his mind with drink, as Colin was, no man of means would marry the likes of you. Poor lamb, he was led to the slaughter by a set of long eyelashes and a bottle of rum. Soon you'll be pregnant, I've no doubt, and he'll never be able to free himself from you. But until then, mind where you tread in this house. If Abraham discovers any reason to be dissatisfied with Colin's marriage, he's perfectly capable of finding a way to rid his son of unwanted baggage like you. Our father-in-law, in spite of the benevolent, charming façade he can so quickly and convincingly conjure, is as dangerous and ruthless as he is rich and powerful."

She turned and swept into the room behind her.

Enraged to immobility, I could only stare at the closed door behind which she had vanished, my breath coming in shallow gasps. At length I moved on.

Alone inside Colin's room, I shut the door, leaned back against the closed panel, shut my eyes, and let the tears trickle from beneath my closed lids. *Darcy, Darcy, why did you have to die? Why did everything have to go so wrong?* Caroline's brutal accusations had been like a whiplash across my tightly strung emotions, cracking open all the pain of the past twenty-four hours, pain I'd managed to keep contained until that moment.

With an effort, I regained my self control. Drying my eyes with the backs of my hands, I re-evaluated my position. Life had never been easy for me. I'd always had to struggle to survive. Caroline's insults and Captain Madison's blackmail could never hurt me as deeply as that awful day in the overseer's cottage.

On the positive side, I had a young husband who had all of Darcy's attributes of good looks, intelligence, and kindliness. My new home was an elegant mansion within which I had never in my wildest dreams imagined myself as being anything other than a scullery maid. I could cope, I told myself, and squared my shoulders.

My future decided, I began to wander about my husband's room. It was as though I were seeing it for the first time. The previous night I had been exhausted and inebriated. In the morning, before breakfast, excitement and trepidations had dulled my interest in its contents.

Large, clean, and fresh-smelling, the room was centered by the wide, high-posted bed where we had slept, its tall polished headboard against a wall between two long, narrow windows. Since we had arisen it had been made up with fresh linen and the burgundy velvet cover that matched the draperies on the windows. A thick maroon-and-tan rug covered the center of a polished hardwood floor.

The rest of the room's mahogany furniture consisted of a dressing table, a magnificent armoire, a settee covered with maroon velvet, a rocking chair, a full-length cheval mirror, and, in one corner, a finely carved desk with bookshelves above it reaching to the room's lofty ceiling. Remembering Darcy's axiom "a man is what he reads," I went to the latter.

Finely bound volumes of various sizes filled the shelves. The surface of the escritoire beneath was littered with papers. The only part of the room left unscathed by the maids' industrious cleaning, it appeared to be a very personal area Colin allowed no one but himself to disturb.

Curious to learn more about my husband, I moved to the writing table. A framed sketch of a beautiful blond woman in one corner immediately drew my attention. Fragile and elegant, she looked the epitome of what a refined lady should be. Was she someone important to Colin?

I looked at the scattered papers. They were covered with musical notes and words in a language I did not understand.

I turned my attention to the books on the shelves above the desk. Many were in a foreign language I suspected might be the same as that on the papers of my husband's escritoire. Learning about the man I had married would be a challenging experience.

At noon, as I sat curled up on the settee reading

one of Colin's few English books, Marie came to fetch me for lunch.

"You'll be eating alone with Monsieur Randall, madam," she said. "The others are otherwise engaged. Except for Madame Ida. She is confined to her room with a sharp bit of indigestion and does not wish to be disturbed."

****

As I entered the dining room, Randall Douglas stood and smiled.

"Good afternoon, Starr," he said. "Join me in a glass of sherry, won't you?"

"Yes, of course, sir." I took the chair he drew out and accepted the delicate crystal glass.

"To my lovely new sister-in-law," he toasted me. He took a long drink, then sat down opposite me, the decanter of wine close to his right hand.

"Mr. Douglas, why didn't you tell what you knew about me at breakfast?" I could not prevent myself from asking. "Why didn't you say you'd seen me in Captain Madison's cabin?"

"Why should I?" He shrugged. "You and Colin have obviously found each other. And before Barret took me to his cabin to examine you, he told me that you were only a child who could not bear the hold, that there was nothing between you and him. Barret's an honest man. I have no reason not to believe him. In fact, I had nothing to gain by telling stories…and much to lose."

"To lose?"

"Although I assure you, I'm trained as a doctor, my father prefers I don't practice medicine," he replied. "He wants me to concentrate on my other field of expertise, which is the law, politics in particular. He wouldn't be pleased to hear I've been acting as a medical examiner. I'm supposed to be the family politician, not to mention procreator of the dynasty. However"—and here he gave a sigh of relief—"now that Colin's married, some of the latter obligation will be relieved, thank God."

He looked over at me and smiled. A hot blush flooded up my cheeks, and he hastened to continue, "But enough of me. Tell me, how have you enjoyed your first morning in Peacock House? Have you seen it all?"

"No," I said, relaxing in his friendly, candid company. "I spent the morning reading in Colin's room."

"What! You mean you've seen nothing of this monument to free enterprise?" I caught the sarcasm in his tone. "We'll remedy that directly after luncheon. Since Colin is busy, I'll show you around the mansion and grounds this very afternoon."

"Surely you're also involved with the family business. Are you certain you have time?"

"As I've said, I'm the politician in the family." He poured himself another glass of wine. "Tomorrow I'm off to the provincial capital to try to further my father's interest through the province's House of Assembly, in which I hold this region's seat. Today I'm supposed to be with my wife, enjoying all the intimacy of a passionate farewell, but"—he raised a hand in mock resignation—"as you can see, my loving spouse has chosen to absent herself from my attentions. I'm therefore free and would enjoy giving a guided tour of the house and grounds to my beautiful new sister. And by the way, my name is Randall, not Mr. Douglas, and most definitely not Sir."

A maid brought our luncheon. As I looked over the sumptuous fare, I realized I was hungry. Recovered from my hangover and put at ease by my husband's kindly brother, I knew I could do this meal the justice I had not been able to afford breakfast.

"Try the salmon," Randall urged, indicating an attractively prepared, pink-fleshed fish on a silver salver. "It's from the river, one of the finest salmon streams in the world. Pour this sauce over it. It's Cook's specialty. Take some small potatoes. They're fresh from our garden, the first of this year's crop. And save space for dessert. Cook's strawberry tarts with cream are a delight."

Urged by Randall and a sudden, raging hunger, I set upon the fish, vegetables, and sweets with full enjoyment. Only when Randall arose to pour my coffee as I was eating a cream-topped tart did I realize I had neglected many of the table manners I had studied during my days at Blackwell Hall.

Embarrassed, I looked up at my brother-in-law. "I'm sorry. You must think me a hopeless barbarian."

"On the contrary." He smiled, pouring my coffee. "It's been some time since I've had the pleasure of watching a member of this family genuinely enjoy a meal at this table."

His smile faded as he put down the coffee urn and took my hand. "Be good to Colin, Starr," he said. "In spite of all this opulence, he's not had an easy life. Our father brought us up to be able to shoulder all aspects of his enterprises, from laborer to businessman. He never believed in sparing the rod or spoiling the child. But you've probably guessed as much already." He leaned back in his chair before he continued. "Colin and I are hardly built like pampered gentlemen. In our father's lumber camps, we developed muscles like great apes, and the accompanying strength. To this day, whenever he thinks he sees an ounce of fat or flabbiness on either of us, he ships us out to the bush to rebuild. But it's spiritually and emotionally that Colin and I have been most severely battered. You'll soon come to understand what I mean. I've resolved myself to my lot and found compensations, but Colin deserves better. See that he gets it, Starr."

****

That afternoon, on Randall's arm, I received a guided tour of the magnificent estate that had become my home. I also formed a deep and lasting affection for the unhappy, compassionate man who was my husband's older brother.

At four p.m. Randall left me outside Colin's bedroom door. He had a meeting with his father, he said as we parted company.

Until I returned to Colin's room that afternoon I had not been aware it was located directly over his father's office. Through a grate in the floor that allowed the passage of heat from the fireplace in the room below in colder seasons, I heard voices, Randall's and my father-in-law's. Although I told myself eavesdropping was wrong, I found myself drawn to listen.

"Now that you've had an opportunity to peruse my plans, you must begin to chart a course for bringing about their implementation in Fredericton," Abraham was saying. "It's imperative you waste no time in haggling or diplomacy. Those grants and loans must be approved at once. As for the mail contract, Barret's January voyage from Halifax to London with the *Maris Stella* will be all the proof we'll need of our ability to provide fast, dependable service."

"Father, the mail contract is impossible for Douglas and Sons to secure, no matter how well Barret and his ship perform." Randall's voice replied. "The Trans-Atlantic agreement will go to a steamship company, not a firm that deals in windjammers. The days of wooden sailing ships are numbered. Iron vessels powered by coal are more dependable. Steam ships and steam railways are bringing an end to the era when wood, wind, and water ruled the commerce of the world. You'd be wise to consider investing in these modern means of transport. And you must realize Barret will never agree to attempt what amounts to a suicide January run on the heels of your forcing him to carry that cargo of immigrants."

"Damn Barret Madison!" the older man exploded. "He's an employee. He'll do as I say or suffer the consequences. As for these steam conveyances, show me any iron tub that can outdistance the *Maris Stella* in a good wind."

"In a good wind, yes," Randall replied. "But how often are she and her sisters becalmed for days? Cargoes spoil and food and water run out during those lost hours. Steam is independent of the caprices of nature. Set Barret to the task of becoming a steamship captain, and you'll have a winning combination. He's clever and resourceful. He would do you proud."

"I own this valley, and I always will," Abraham said, regaining his self-control. "I'm king here. I won't be dethroned by a puff of smoke. I have friends in the British Parliament who'll guarantee my loans until this current fascination with iron boats and tin trains has passed."

"I wouldn't depend on money from Britain," Randall said. "Their Parliament has adopted the 'little England' policy, which means they've decided to reduce their financial responsibilities to the colonies. It's becoming too costly for them to continue pouring vast sums into their overseas possessions."

""Don't be a sniveling pessimist," Abraham snapped. "Go and pack your portmanteau. I want you on your way to Fredericton by first light. You're to convince the honorable members of the Assembly that Abraham Douglas and Sons can handle that mail contract with ease and guaranteed regularity. And tell the Governor I'm still awaiting those letters of credit he promised from London."

"I'd do a much better job being the doctor I've been trained to be." Randall's voice took on a bitterness. "This valley needs a physician a good deal more than it needs a mail contract and more debts."

"Only the strong deserve to survive." Abraham's voice had a bite in it. "The sick and weak must be weeded out if we're to create a viable society here. By nurturing lame ducks we only produce a community of the infirm."

"When you came to Edinburgh and dragged me away from my studies beneath some of the world's finest doctors, I should have defied you." Randall's tone moderated to that of a broken man. "Instead I allowed myself to be forced into one of the Inns of Court in London and converted into an attorney. Then I let you marry me off to that inhuman bit of British aristocracy. A titled lady would make a fitting mother for your grandchildren, you said. Fitting mother! The woman can care for no one except herself. There's not a trace of warmth in her soul. No child deserves to have her as a parent."

"Shut your mouth, boy. Caroline is a lady, born and bred. Her educational background alone is impeccable. She has an astounding knowledge of arts and speaks French and German like a native. Perhaps if you expended a little more energy in her direction and less on fish-shed sluts, you'd be able to make liars of those doctors who declared you sterile."

"I don't have to take this abuse." Randall's voice shook with suppressed emotion. "I'll go to Fredericton and fight for your demands. I will not go back to the bed of that succubus you arranged for me to marry! You may continue to rule my professional life, but I'll be damned if I'll allow you to tell me whom I may sleep with or love."

A slamming door marked Randall's exit.

"Damn you, boy! You'll do as I say or your fish-gutting floozy will pay dearly!" his father roared after him.

A second door, this time the one at the front of the house, slammed on his words.

I turned away from the grate, wondering who Randall's fish-shed floozy was, if he was her lover, and what Abraham would do to her if his son refused to do as he'd demanded.

Chapter Five

A couple of hours before the dinner hour, a seamstress and a milliner, both heavily laden, arrived. Chatting together and all but ignoring me, the two women were escorted by Marie into Colin's room, where I waited. They laid out the plans and fabrics of an extensive and elegant wardrobe I could scarcely believe was to be mine. Silks, satins, cottons, linens, woolens, velvets, laces, with ribbons in almost every color of the rainbow, were to be made up into a wide variety of the latest fashions. Coordinating hats and bonnets joined the designs and cloth samples on the bed to form a glorious collage. When I commented on the cost, the seamstress sniffed disdainfully.

"We're following the orders of the elder Mr. Douglas," she retorted. "He instructed us to outfit you in a style suitable to your new station in life. Your husband's family is prominent and wealthy, and your wardrobe must reflect their position. The cost will be a pittance to a man of Mr. Douglas's fortunes."

Silenced, I allowed myself to be measured and scrutinized from the size of my wrists to the color of my eyes. My outfits must be perfect, the seamstress told the milliner. Mr. Douglas Senior must be pleased. No mention was made of Colin's approval or mine.

The seamstress was holding a length of crimson silk against me when, over her head, I caught Marie frowning and shaking her head in disapproval.

"Not red," I said taking her hint. "Perhaps…"

"This soft peach is lovely, Madame." Marie picked up another length of cloth.

"Yes," I agreed, seeing the wisdom in her suggestion. Crimson did not suit me. It was important that I not allow myself to appear gaudy or tasteless. "The peach, if you please, Miss Byron."

The woman glared at Marie, but she complied with my request.

For the remainder of the fitting, Marie continued to advise me. She had excellent fashion sense, probably learned under the tutelage of Colin's mother.

As the two women were leaving, another village merchant arrived, and I was measured for boots, shoes, and slippers of the finest quality. It had become the kind of afternoon a young woman's dreams are made of.

After Marie had escorted the final tradesman from the room, I sank down on the velvet bedcover. *I had to be dreaming*. Suddenly I was the wife of a handsome young gentleman whose wealthy father appeared intent upon treating me like a prized possession. Was it because Abraham Douglas had been presented with what he believed to have been proof of my purity? Surely not. Rather, it appeared he was grateful Colin had taken a wife, any wife, at last. But why? Surely a man as rich and attractive as my husband would have had no difficulty getting any woman to marry him.

Puzzled, I got to my feet and went to open a clothespress near the door. I needed to know more about the man I had married. Inside hung a long row of elegant masculine attire. The floor beneath was littered with fine leather boots and shoes. My husband was apparently a man of taste who enjoyed dressing well. I looked down at my tattered dress and work-coarsened hands. Colin Douglas hadn't embellished his collection of finery when he'd married me.

I vowed then and there that I would do everything in my power to be the best wife he could imagine. It was the least I could do for a man who'd readily and uncomplainingly married his friend's ragged fiancée simply to provide her with a home.

****

Marie brought my supper to the bedroom that night. She explained Mr. Douglas Senior had thought that since Colin would not be home for the meal, I might prefer to eat in my room instead of joining the family in the dining room.

I flushed. I guessed the unspoken message in my father-in-law's instructions. I was to rest before another night of arduous lovemaking.

To keep Marie from seeing my embarrassment, I looked down at the tray she'd brought me. It was heavy with roast beef, vegetables, breads, tea, tarts, and even oranges and raisins. In the center was a bouquet of blue violets.

"The flowers are from Monsieur Colin," she explained. "He is working at his father's offices in the village today. He sent a message to say he will be late getting home."

"Thank you," I said. "He's very thoughtful."

"You may wish a bath before Monsieur Colin arrives," she continued. "After you have eaten, I will prepare one for you, if that would suit you." She turned to leave, but I stopped her.

"Thank you for your assistance this afternoon, Marie," I said. "I should have made some unfortunate mistakes without it."

"I enjoyed helping, Madame," she replied with a shy smile. "It reminded me of the time when Madame Christiana, Monsieur Colin's mother, was alive. She was a wonderful woman. We all loved her dearly."

Later, while I waited for Marie to prepare my bath, I strolled downstairs and out onto the verandah. The evening was warm and tender. I looked out over the village basking in the last rays of the sun and thought how peaceful it all appeared. Crude and rudimentary though it was, Pine represented a fresh beginning, offering a second chance to people like me. When its rough edges were smoothed away, this little village would be a fine new community free of the Old World prejudices of race, religion, and social position.

A number of ships rode at anchor on the river's calm surface; several more, including the *Maris Stella*, were tied up docksides. Five more partially built vessels lined the shore. No wonder Abraham Douglas was insistent on the success of his windjammers. He had a fortune invested in them.

As I was returning to Colin's room, I met Marie in the foyer.

"Your bath is ready, Madame," she said. "I scented it with violets. Madame Christiana always enjoyed their fragrance."

Inside Colin's room, I locked the door and unbuttoned my dress. Feeling uninhibited and sensuous, perhaps inspired by the perfection of the evening and luxury of my surroundings, I doffed my clothing and confronted my naked self in Colin's cheval glass.

I saw a shapely young woman with loosened, honey-colored curls falling over the smooth white shoulders of a body with an overall creamy complexion. Rested, clean, and well fed, I was not an unattractive woman.

Confident I would not repulse my husband and swinging my hips in an imitation of Meg the barmaid's sultry walk, I strolled toward the closed bathroom door. I pushed it open, sauntered inside…and froze.

Submersed in suds, a cigar in one hand, a drink in the other, Captain Madison sat in my tub staring unblinkingly at my nakedness.

"Good evening, Mrs. Douglas," he said. "This *is* a surprise."

For a moment I was too shocked to move. Then I snatched a length of toweling linen from a shelf and flung it about me.

"What are *you* doing here?" I spat out the words. "This is my husband's room."

"Unlike the rest of the Douglas clan, I don't have a private bath." He took a pull on his cigar before continuing. "Since sharing Abe's, or Randall's and Caroline's, appeared inappropriate, Colin and I decided I should have the use of his. You might say I have priority over you, since I was here first."

"Get out!" I cried, as outrage replaced embarrassment. "That's *my* tub and *my* water. Marie prepared it for *me*!"

"As you wish, milady." He started to rise.

"Oh!" I gasped and swung away to flounce back into the bedroom.

When he joined me a few minutes later, I wore my coarse woolen dress over my naked body and was sitting in a chair near the window. I pretended to ignore him, but he circled to stand before me, clad in closely fitting trousers, a towel draped over his broad, bare shoulders.

“Next time you feel the need to bathe, please inform me,” I said crisply. “If we must share our bath with you, you must give notice of your intentions.”

“That seems fair,” he replied with cordial civility. “We wouldn’t want to end up in that tub together.” His gray eyes twinkled wickedly.

“Get out! Just get out!”

“Of course.” He bowed and went to the door. There he paused and glanced back at me. “But I must tell you that, naked, you’re quite beautiful. Colin Douglas is a lucky boy.”

****

He’d said I was beautiful, “quite beautiful” to be exact. As I slid between the cool, fresh sheets of my husband’s big featherbed, I found myself basking in the implications of his comment. Perhaps I was attractive to men. Barret Madison was a man of the world. I was probably only one of any number of women he’d seen in a state of undress. Perhaps in time Colin might also find me “quite beautiful” as well.

I was still speculating on this aspect of my marriage when the door opened and my husband entered. In the light of the single lamp I had left burning on a bedside table, he forced a tired grin and began to open his cravat. I had been planning to question him about deceiving his father that morning, but when I saw his haggard face, his linen shirt stained with perspiration and grime, I could not find it in my heart to reproach him. Freshly bathed, my hunger sated by fine food, I sat ensconced in his luxurious bed, my mended chemise a poignant reminder of my recent past and only recently possible future. He was responsible for my comfortable state; he did not deserve to be interrogated.

"You smell wonderful," he said, bending to touch his lips to my forehead. "Marie knows I'm partial to the scent of violets. I'll wager she put some in your bath. I must thank her. And speaking of my favorite fragrances, did you receive my flowers?"

"Yes." I tried to forget the fact that Marie had had to scent a second tub, and why. "Both you and Marie are kind and thoughtful. Colin, are you unwell? You look exhausted."

"It's been a long, hot day, and I'm still trying to shake a deuce of a hangover," he replied. "Don't concern yourself."

"There's a tub of water prepared for you," I said, still struggling to push the earlier presence of Captain Madison from my mind. "Once you're bathed, you'll feel better."

"Perhaps," he said with a wan smile.

Stripping off his shirt, he went into the bathroom and closed the door.

Twenty minutes later he emerged freshly shaven and bathed. He wore a maroon silk dressing robe, below which his feet and legs were bare. His muscular, naked chest was visible through its half-open front. As he paused to look out the window into the balmy night, I thought, *Tonight we will be lovers.*

But when he turned and came to the bed, his expression was grave and strained.

"Starr," he said sitting down on its edge and taking my hand. "We must…talk. I…I can't consummate our marriage."

"Why?" *What is he saying? What have I done? Captain Madison said I'm quite beautiful* "Am I…that repugnant to you?"

"Sweet Starr." He touched my cheek. "Of course you're not. You're one of the loveliest women I've ever seen. Most men would risk life and limb for the privilege of making love to you. But I…can't. You see, until recently, there was someone else…and it's still too soon…"

He lowered his head, shaking it in confusion. I swallowed hard. I should have guessed a handsome, wealthy young man like Colin Douglas would not have been unattached.

"It's all right, Colin." Tears blurred my image of him. "I understand."

"Thank you," he breathed, raising his head to look at me, his eyes also moist. "Even though you don't. Not really."

For a few moments we sat in silence. Then I could hold back the question no longer.

"Why did you perpetrate that hoax with our sheets this morning? Why didn't you simply tell your father the truth? Surely he'd understand."

"You don't yet know my father, Starr," he said, his expression hardening. "He thinks a man can assert himself with a woman as easily as a stud stallion covers a brood mare. Forgive my coarseness, but I cannot think of a better analogy."

"You could never be coarse, Colin." I looked up into his sensitive young face. "You're a gentleman like Darcy."

"You really do smell wonderful," he repeated. His

tone was once more warm and gentle. “That fragrance reminds me of my mother.”

“Marie told me it was her favorite scent. She’s taking care of me, just as you asked.”

“She’s a good person,” he said. “I’ve been fortunate in the women who’ve come into my life.”

“Who is the girl in the picture on your desk, Colin? Is she another woman you’ve been fortunate to know?”

“Yes,” he replied. “She was an Austrian opera singer, perhaps one of the finest in the world, until she married my father and gave up her career to come to live out her life as another of his chattels.” The bitterness arose again in his voice as it always seemed to when he spoke of his father. ”She died last autumn.”

“Your mother,” I breathed. “Colin, I’m sorry.”

“She taught me music and German and any other worthwhile accomplishments I may possess.” There was a catch in his voice.

“Those books on your shelves…they’re written in Austrian?” I asked.

“German.” He managed a shaky smile.

“And the music on your desk?”

“I play piano and guitar.”

“You’re very like Darcy, talented and sensitive.” I touched his cheek with a growing sense of sincere affection. “I could love you, Colin Douglas.”

“No, Starr.” He caught my fingers and kissed them. “Don’t.”

“But, Colin, we’re married! We must give ourselves a chance to…”

“My mother allowed my father to consummate their union,” he retorted, turning away. “All it brought her was two disappointing children and a possessive, ruthless husband who had no time for her except in bed. For years he kept me from her, from music, from all we both loved. He sent me away to school in Scotland, along the Clyde River, that I might learn shipbuilding as well as academic subjects.

"When I returned, he put me into his lumber camps, chopping trees for fifteen hours a day, and freezing in subzero temperatures." He got to his feet and went to stare out the window, his back to me. "Finally I became so ill he was forced to bring me home.

"It was early spring. I had fallen into a half-frozen river during a log drive. I could barely breathe when they brought me back to this house. My mother, who had never been strong herself, nursed me. She moved out of my father's room and put a cot in mine, to be near me." He paused and drew a deep breath before continuing.

"They had a terrible row over it, but for once she stood up to him." He turned back to me, his face bright at the memory. "She wouldn't let anyone, not even Randall, care for me in any way. She exhausted herself." His tone softened.

"When I was finally back on my feet, she fell ill. In September, she died. If Barret hadn't taken me to Vienna after her funeral and let me submerge myself for a time in the musical community there, I believe I would have died of misery myself."

He covered his face with his hands. I jumped to my feet and went to put a comforting hand on his arm.

"Colin, I'm sorry, so very sorry."

"Thank you." He dropped his hands and looked down at me. "I know you are." He put his hand over mine and bent forward to kiss me lightly on the forehead. For a moment we were silent; then I broke the spell and moved away.

"You said you went to Vienna with Captain Madison?"

"Yes," Colin said. "He knew I needed to escape. Defying my father's repeated orders to return home, we spent nearly six months there." Colin squared his shoulders and led me to the bed to sit beside him.

"When we came back, early in April, Barret shouldered the blame for our escapade. As a reprimand, my father ordered him to carry immigrants aboard the *Maris Stella* on his next return voyage from England. It's a cargo Barret despises, but refusing to do it would have resulted in his losing his position as Commodore of the Douglas Fleet and, quite possibly, his Master's Ticket. My father is the magistrate for this area and, as such, holds considerable sway with the Court of Vice-Admiralty. On the day Barret sailed for England to carry out his penance, I met Darcy." He took both my hands in his and smiled reassuringly. "But enough of me. Tell me about yourself, Starr."

I hesitated. I had to decide what I could tell him now and what I'd best save for later when our relationship stood on firmer ground.

"Starr, please. I'd like to know more about my wife."

"Of course." I drew a deep breath and began.

He listened attentively, but when I told him of my mother's death and of the overseer's brutality, my voice breaking over the words, he drew me to him, against his broad, naked chest.

"No one will molest you again," he murmured

against my hair. "As God is my witness, no one will hurt Darcy's girl again."

To change the subject and not have to continue my narrative, which would have to include the story of my voyage, I recalled Caroline's brutal accusations and decided I must ask Colin the reason for her attack.

"My father has made a strange but specific and legal will," he explained. "His entire estate will go to the son who produces his first grandchild. As long as I didn't marry, it appeared Randall and Caroline would be the winners. Quite frankly, I didn't care. Then you came along, and suddenly Caroline has competition—competition she isn't able to deal with. She and Randall have been married five years and there's still no sign of an heir apparent. Although I know it's difficult, please try to ignore her. She's a grasping, nasty creature not worthy of your concern."

He sounded so weary as he finished speaking that I looked up into his face.

"Have you had supper, Colin?"

"Supper was well past when I arrived home," he said. "Father has a cardinal rule in this house. If one is late for a meal, regardless of the reason, that person goes hungry. Abe Douglas doesn't tolerate tardiness."

He grinned resignedly down at me, but I guessed he must be hungry. He'd eaten little breakfast and, since he had not come home at midday, probably no lunch.

"Then we'll raid the kitchen." I jumped from the bed and tugged at his hand. "Come on. It'll be fun."

"I don't know, Starr. Mrs. MacDonald, our housekeeper, keeps a tight inventory on foodstuffs."

His hesitation did not give me pause.

"Oh, come on, Colin! Where's your sense of adventure? If we're caught, I'll defend you to the death."

"Well… Oh, all right." He stood up, tightened his robe about him, and grinned. "Let's go."

****

Shortly we were back in the bedroom, a tablecloth filled with bread, fruit, and cheese slung over Colin's shoulder. As soon as we'd closed the door behind us, we looked at each other, eyes bright with the comradeship of a shared mischief, and burst out laughing.

"We did it!" Colin laughed, flinging our booty onto the bed. "And look!" He drew a bottle of wine from inside the top of his robe. "I filched this while you were looking for a knife. Lord, I haven't had such fun since…" His words trailed off, and he was suddenly solemn.

"Since when, Colin?"

"Since Darcy was alive," he breathed. "Oh, dear God, why did I have to remember…"

"We'll never forget him," I said, a thick lump forming in my throat. "Remembering him isn't wrong, but we mustn't recall him with sorrow. He would want us to remember the happiness and laughter we shared with him, not the tears."

"Yes," he agreed. "Of course. Now"—he forced a smile—"will you honor me by cutting the bread and cheese for this elegant repast, while I open the wine?"

"I would be pleased to, sir." I dropped him a mock curtsy.

"I need a corkscrew," he said. "There's one on Barret's dressing table across the hall. He's not in yet.

I'll dash over and get it."

Picking up the bottle, he eased his way out of the room. Soon he returned with the corkscrew. His distracted shove at the door as he reentered, working at the bottle cork, failed to make it shut completely. I recall thinking I would close it when I had finished cutting the cheese, but I forgot a moment later when Colin pulled the plug from the bottle with a mighty pop and wine fountained out over the front of his robe.

"Oh, God!" he breathed. "Champagne." We burst out laughing.

"Sweet Jesus!"

Our mirth ended as we whirled to the sound of his voice. Barret Madison had shoved the partly open door wide ajar and stood staring at us.

"Drinking again, Colin? Is making love to her so difficult you have to dull your senses to get to the business of it?"

"Damn you, Barret!" Colin's face grew red. "Get out! You have no business in my…*our* bedroom."

"Of course, young master," Captain Madison favored him with a mocking bow. "A word of advice before I do. Don't allow yourself to become inebriated. A man can get rough and crude, or at worst, unable to perform. Get your lady drunk; she did no less for you last night. A bedmate with a bottle of wine inside her loses all her inhibitions."

"Get out, Barret." Colin advanced toward the captain. "Starr and I aren't impressed by your vulgar talk." In front of Barret Madison, he stopped and sniffed. "Why do you smell like…?"

I caught my breath, horrified lest Colin recognize the violet scent of the bath the captain had stolen from me.

"Like a woman's perfume?" Captain Madison interjected. "A most indecorous question, sir, but if you must know, I've been visiting Meg at the tavern. I daresay a bit of our evening lingers about my person. Now, I'll take my leave and permit you two children the opportunity for a similar time of intimacy."

He touched his forelock and withdrew.

"Blast him!" Colin exploded, banging the bottle down on his desk. "Sometimes he can be such a…"

"Bastard?"

"Starr!" My husband swung to face me.

"Well, he can be, can't he?"

Colin paused for an instant, then as he caught the gleam of mischief in my voice and eyes he burst out laughing.

"Aye, lassie, that he can." He mimicked a Scottish sailor. "Come, let's forget the bastard and get on with our evening."

****

"I never knew how well wine and cheese complement each other." I settled back against the big bed's headboard, a glass of champagne in one hand, a piece of cheese in the other.

"Then I shall make certain you have them every night." Colin grinned.

"No." I laughed in reply. "Only on special nights …when we're alone…and happy…like this."

"Agreed," he said, and fell to munching on his bread and cheese.

****

"Don't get up," Colin said when I started to rise with him shortly after dawn the following morning. "I have to be at the shipyards at six, but there's no need for you to be disturbed. I'll not be home for lunch." He pulled a shirt from the armoire. "Father has promised to give me the day off tomorrow if I complete my work today. I'm looking forward to spending time with you, Starr. We need to get to know each other." He looked over at me, his expression serious.

I nodded, and he went into the bathroom to shave and wash. Snuggling back into the big, warm featherbed, I let a sigh of contentment escape my lips. It was wonderful to be permitted to lie abed as long as I chose.

Three hours later I got up. I washed, dressed, and stepped out into the corridor to go down to breakfast.

The door to Captain Madison's room across the hall stood ajar. Inside, the captain, naked to the waist, was shaving before a mirror and washstand while Marie smoothed fresh sheets over his bed.

The man has no shame. Disgruntled by his relaxed half-nakedness before the servant girl, I was about to go downstairs when Marie abandoned her task and sank to the bed sobbing.

Captain Madison in an instant was beside her, drawing her into his arms. To my astonishment, she leaned against his bare chest.

The captain spoke to her, much to my surprise, in French. I'd heard the aristocrats at Blackwell use the language when they didn't want the servants to understand. She quieted sufficiently to reply. I could not understand what she was saying. She also spoke in French, but the expression her words brought to her companion's face told me they had shocked and enraged him.

He swore softly. Then Marie noticed me and struggled from his embrace. Wiping her eyes with her apron corner, she rushed out of the room past me and down the stairs.

"Good morning, Mrs. Douglas." The captain stood and addressed me, his words bitterly cold. "Eavesdropping? I'd have thought that was beneath the dignity of a person of your newly achieved position."

"How could I be, when I don't understand French? And if we're discussing improprieties, you might either clothe yourself or shut your door."

"I don't see why my state of undress should bother you." He snatched up a towel and sauntered toward me, wiping the remaining shaving soap from his jaw. "It's not as if you're seeing anything you haven't looked at before."

"Hush!" I glanced around the corridor to make certain no one was near.

"As you wish, my lady." He leaned against the doorframe, his gaze raking over me. "You haven't yet thanked me for explaining our similar fragrances to your husband last evening."

"Argh!" I stifled the word "bastard" and turned to follow Marie down the stairs.

The pretty French maid must be another of his mistresses. I remembered Meg at the tavern and the woman's possessive attitude toward him. Probably Marie had found out where he'd spent his first night ashore and they'd had a lover's spat.

I stumbled over a small wrinkle in the carpet. *Whore master!* I screamed inwardly, as I jolted to save myself from falling. The man had an insatiable sexual appetite and was no better than Simon.

****

Late in the afternoon, I grew restless and decided to go downstairs in search of either companionship or adventure. I had breakfasted alone and then spent a largely solitary day except for occasional glimpses of servants as they went about their duties. I had the distinct feeling I was being avoided by Caroline and that she was keeping Randall with her to further isolate me. Gram, I guessed, was unwell, and Abraham busy with his various enterprises. I didn't speculate about Captain Madison, content not to encounter him again.

As I was coming downstairs, the beauty of music issuing from the drawing room stopped me. Someone had put their fingers to the keys of the pianoforte and burst into a rapturous cascade of rippling, masterful melody.

I listened, a smile tipping my lips. I'd missed music since my mother's death. But this was well beyond the realm of dance hall tunes. Eager to see who was producing the delightful sounds, I tiptoed down the remaining steps and across the foyer to the half-open drawing room door.

My husband sat at the keyboard, his fingers gliding over it, his expression one of rapt concentration. A narrow ray of sunlight crept through a crack in the draperies to fall across him and turn his rich blond hair to gold. In that moment he appeared an angelic wizard, weaving an ethereal spell with his music. Entranced, I eased myself into the room without his noticing, since his back was to the door, and into a dark, recessed corner to listen.

The notes filled the still, late afternoon air with an aesthetic cadence. In those moments, I realized that my husband was a master musician.

"Here you are!" Abraham Douglas's voice, harsh with annoyance, brought Colin's recital to an abrupt end. The music ended in a tangled crash as my spouse whirled to face his father.

"Father…" Colin tried to speak, but was again interrupted.

"What's wrong with you, boy?" Abraham's face was livid with anger as he crossed the room and flung open the drapes to let in the harsh reality of the sun's wilting rays. Startled, I slid behind a tall wing chair. "I send you to the docks to see to the *Winsome Witch*'s outfitting, and half an hour later I find you trifling with this confounded music box. Either you're an incredibly swift worker or you've entirely failed to do my bidding. Well, speak up, boy! I'm waiting."

"Please, Father, I…I had this sudden inspiration." Colin was stammering, flushed and sweating as he tried to justify his actions. "This melody sprang almost full-fledged into my mind. I had to capture it before it was gone, possibly forever. I had to rush home for a moment, just a moment, to…"

"To play with a cursed bit of wire and wood!" Abraham's voice rose in outrage. "Now you listen to me! You've a man's responsibilities in this family. Try to live up to at least some of them."

"Yes, sir, I'm going, sir." Defeated, Colin started to move past his father, but Abraham caught him by the arm.

"I've said you have a man's responsibilities in this family," he growled, his voice lower but retaining its bitter ring. "That means producing my grandson. Starr's a lusty little piece of heather, if ever I saw one. She's capable of bearing you a dozen children. Thus, my lad, if you fail to become a father within the year, we'll know who's lacking, won't we?"

"Father, I…" Colin, distraught and perspiring, fumbled for words.

"Don't dare to tell me you can't," Abraham barked. "You're a man. Act like one! Now get to the *Winsome Witch*. I'll expect a full report about her progress on my desk tonight."

Colin wet his lips and went out. With a disgusted grunt, his father followed him. I huddled behind the chair's high back with clenched fists, anger forming an ugly knot in my stomach.

****

The following morning Abraham gave Colin his promised day free to spend with me. After overhearing what had transpired between father and son the previous afternoon, I understood the reason. And after the understanding Colin and I had reached on the first day of our marriage, I knew we would not fulfill the purpose of my husband's holiday.

I had another idea of how we might spend the time. As I waited for Colin to shave, wash, and dress in the privacy of our bathroom, I ventured to make the request that was burning in my heart.

"Colin, may we visit Darcy's cabin and grave today?"

For a moment there was silence behind the partly closed door. Then he replied, "Of course, Starr. I should have offered to take you. I'll order a carriage. We'll drive out after breakfast."

****

Darcy's cabin was about a half-mile beyond the

edge of the village. Situated in a grove of softly murmuring white pines, through which the river was visible, the little structure was a well-built log structure with glassed windows and a small stable at the rear.

Emerald green ferns and a soft bright carpet of moss provided a groundcover about the small house. Its freshly peeled log walls, not yet weathered, provided a stark reminder of how recent Darcy's passing had been. The peace and serenity of the setting made it seem all the more incredible that the horrendous act of suicide had, only days before, taken place there.

"It's the setting of a beautiful dream," I murmured in awe as Colin halted the carriage. "Or the subject of one of Darcy's poems."

"Darcy loved this place," Colin said softly. "He was happy here."

"I would have been also," I said, entranced by the hushed, sensuous atmosphere of the place.

"I know." There was a catch in his voice.

"Oh, Colin, I'm sorry!" I put a placating hand over his. "I didn't mean I'm unhappy at Peacock House. I only meant…"

"I know what you meant, Starr." He wound the reins about the whipstand and leaped to the ground. "Come," he said, holding up his hands to help me alight. "I'll show you where I buried Darcy. I think you'll approve."

****

The beautifully carved cross stood at the head of a still-brown mound beside a gently flowing stream, hidden from the cabin by a stand of young cedars. Sunlight streaming through an opening in the delicate patterns of the foliage cast a golden lace of light upon the grave and its polished mahogany marker.

I moved forward alone to kneel beside it.

"Darcy Pod. A man who fashioned dreams with words," the inscription read.

Tears trickled down my cheeks.

"Dear, sweet, wonderful Darcy," I whispered. "I shall always love you." I bowed my head in prayer.

When I stood and turned to Colin, I forced a smile across my wet face.

"I'm ready to go home now, Colin."

"Yes." His eyes were tear-filled, too.

"Oh, Colin!" I went into his arms to hold him to me. "Don't ever die and leave me—I couldn't bear this kind of pain again!"

****

As Colin and I prepared to drive away from Darcy's cabin, he gestured with his whip down the trail that led deeper into the forest beyond the log house.

"Bridgit O'Brien lives about a quarter mile farther along this trail," he said. "Her brother Kevin used to live with her. He was killed several days ago. He was also expecting a bride aboard the *Maris Stella*. He and Darcy would often talk with great excitement and anticipation about their ladies who were 'coming out' together. They frequently expressed the wish you and his Mary would become friends. Now, they're both gone. Mary is living with Reverend Prescott and his wife, and poor Bridgit lives alone and works in my father's fish sheds, gutting salmon. She used to be Caroline's personal maid, but when my sister-in-law discovered Bridgit had become Randall's mistress, she had her sent away."

"Randall has a mistress?" I recalled Abraham's

crude reference to Randall's dissipating himself with fish-shed sluts.

"Try not to be too shocked, Starr." Bitterness tainted his words. "We're a troubled family. You'll find you must stretch your powers of compassion in order to forgive us our sins."

As we drove slowly back toward Peacock House, I ventured to ask Colin the question that had burned in my mind like a firebrand the past few days.

"Colin, why did Darcy kill himself?"

"I can't tell you, Starr." He clucked the horse into a fast trot.

"But surely you must have some idea. You said you were good friends. Was he unhappy? Was it because…because he'd met someone else and no longer wanted to be obligated to me?"

"No!" Colin reined the horse to an abrupt halt. "No," he repeated, his tone moderating as he turned to me. "He wasn't unhappy. He was eagerly awaiting your arrival. Dear God!" His voice rose and broke as he raised his eyes to the blue sky above us. "When I found him lying beside the brook, his face blown apart, the gun clutched in his hand, I thought I would go mad!"

I gasped and put a hand over my mouth in horror at the scene he described.

"Take me home, Colin. Please take me home at once."

****

We had left the horse and carriage at the stable and were walking toward the house when I made a confession.

"Colin, I heard you playing the piano," I said, avoiding mentioning the particular occasion. I did not want to embarrass him by letting him know I had also been an eavesdropper to his father's angry sarcasm. "You were wonderful."

He paused and turned to look down at me, his face brightening for the first time since he'd described Darcy's brutal death.

"Did you enjoy it, truly?" he asked eagerly.

"Yes. I should enjoy hearing you play again."

"Of course. I'll play for you now! I'm delighted you share my enjoyment of music. There are few people left in that mansion who appreciate my enthusiasm."

In the drawing room, Colin seated me in a wing chair near the French doors, which stood open to catch a late morning breeze.

The next half hour was filled with magic. Relaxed and inspired by my joy in his music, Colin allowed his fingers to dance over the keys to produce rapturous cascades of sound. I closed my eyes and let the music envelop me. As I submerged in the depths of its beauty, the pain and degradation that had been an integral part of my life for so many years washed from my soul, and I was reborn to an ecstatic state of nirvana I had never dreamed existed. Colin Douglas was a magician, a good warlock who had the power to erase spiritual scars and heal old wounds in an aching soul.

When the last note had drifted into oblivion on a soft summer zephyr, I opened my eyes and looked at the young man at the keyboard.

"That was magnificent. You soothed my aching soul."

He turned to me and smiled, his expression bright.

"Thank you, my darling wife. *You* have soothed

my aching soul with your caring presence."

****

That evening fate decreed I was to have dinner alone with Barret, Colin, and Randall, whose trip to the legislature had been delayed. Gram, Caroline, and Abraham had gone to the Reverend Prescott's home for a meeting concerning church repairs and the enlarging of the village school.

"Will your trip to Fredericton meet with success?" Barret asked as soon as we were seated.

"God knows." Randall shrugged. "They will listen politely and then suggest I give proof of our ability to offer dependable, year-round mail service before they make a final decision. The wheels of government and bankers revolve with painful caution."

"Damn it, man, you have to push them into a decision," Barret snapped, as Marie offered Randall the wine that would accompany our meal. "You know how badly Abe needs that contract."

"I'm not as forceful as you." Randall poured me a glass of the ruby liquid.

"Perhaps if you drank less and spent more time doing your father's bidding, you'd be able to live up to his expectations."

"My father's bidding?" Randall swung on the captain. "I've done his bidding all my life! I've cajoled and flattered until I'm disgusted with myself."

"I wasn't referring only to your position in government," Barret retorted. "If you gave up that pretty little whore from the fish sheds, you'd have the strength and desire to bed your wife properly, and Abe would get the grandson he wants so badly."

"Bastard! Ignorant, foul-mouthed bastard!" Randall

brought the wine bottle down on the table with a crash. "You can dress yourself like a gentleman, but under those fine clothes you're still a piece of fatherless trash!"

"God damn you!" Barret was on his feet, facing Randall, eyes bright with rage.

"Randall, Barret, please!" Colin had risen from beside me.

"Sit down and shut up!" Barret exploded. "Your own conduct in Vienna left much to be desired, boy!"

"Barret…" Colin's voice broke, and he sank into his chair. He rubbed a hand over his forehead as if it suddenly ached.

"Colin, what is it?" Randall was instantly solicitous of his younger brother. "Did you get into trouble in Europe? Was it a woman? Did you father a child?"

"No, no." Colin kept his head bowed. "I didn't…I…"

"It's all right, Colin." Barret went to place a hand on my husband's shoulder. "It's over and won't be mentioned again. Randall, pour the wine. We've squabbled enough for one night."

"You're right." Randall acquiesced. "Starr, try the ham. Cook claims it's one of her best."

We began the meal as if nothing untoward had occurred, but inside I was seething with a question. What *had* Colin done in Vienna?

****

The first of my new wardrobe arrived on a rainy Saturday morning, six days after I'd married Colin. The drizzling gray skies could not dampen my pleasure as I examined the silks, linens, cottons, and laces, the delicate gowns and beribboned undergarments, the hose and night shifts, the bonnets, cloaks, and gloves, and even two riding habits I did not recall being previously mentioned. I would be attired as the wife of rich, handsome Colin Douglas should be, I realized as I preened in one outfit after another before the mirror in our room.

Marie helped me dress my hair to suit each outfit, and together we giggled and exclaimed over it all. We were becoming friends. I liked the young woman and was grateful for her assistance in helping me adjust to my new way of life.

Chapter Six

The following day proved to be as strange and unsettling as its weather. Hot and humid, with a heavy cloud cover, the morning was pregnant with a foreboding sense of repression.

Ignoring the uneasy atmosphere, I delighted in the fact that I looked well in the full-skirted white muslin gown, trimmed with hand-embroidered pink roses, chosen from my new wardrobe.

"You shall accompany us to church, my dear," Abraham informed me at breakfast.

"Of course," Colin agreed as Caroline sniffed her contempt. "I want to show the village my beautiful bride."

"You're a Presbyterian, I assume?" Abraham asked, signaling Marie to bring more coffee.

"I don't know," I said. "My mother and I never attended church. But," I hastened to add as I saw his appalled expression, "she did teach me to believe in God and to pray."

"Then we'll assume you are of our faith." He added cream and sugar to his freshly poured cup.

"Perhaps she's a Roman Catholic," Barret Madison, impeccable in white linen shirt and dark frock coat, vest, and trousers, interjected from his place beside me.

"A papist like you?" Abraham scoffed. "No

daughter-in-law of mine will ever kneel to false idols or bare her soul in confession to some supposedly celibate creature in black robes. She'll never wear a crucifix about her neck, as I've been informed you do at sea, to ward off evil spirits."

"Your grasp of the Catholic faith never ceases to amaze me, Abe." The captain shook his head.

"Mind your smart tongue, or not even your shipboard icon will prevent my pulling your command from beneath you," my father-in-law warned. "Now come, family. The carriage is waiting. Reverend Prescott won't start the service until the last Douglas is seated in the pews." Patting his mustache with a snowy linen square, he got to his feet.

"Barret," he continued as he turned to lead us from the room. "You may ride to that log temple in the bush, the place you call a Catholic Church, on the back of that brute Lucifer. I'll not have a Douglas carriage seen before a pagan place of worship."

"Aye, Master." There was a taunting tone in the captain's voice. "I'll say a prayer to the blessed Saint Anne on behalf of Colin and his bride. Perhaps she will intervene and see to it their union is blessed with fertility."

"Damn you," Abraham muttered. "I can only thank God you've never proven *yourself* capable of breeding. The last thing this village needs is another French Catholic. Come, family, let us proceed to church before this man makes me further blaspheme on the Sabbath."

He flung his napkin onto his plate and strode from the room.

"Miserable old cur!" Randall muttered. "Barret, I'm sorry about…"

He did not get a chance to finish. Marie, who had been waiting to clear the table, sank to the floor unconscious.

"Sweet Jesus!" Barret knelt beside her, Randall close by his side.

"Don't touch her until I make certain she's not broken any bones!" Randall stopped the captain as he started to gather her up in his arms.

"Right." Barret moved aside to let Randall get closer. "She took a bad fall."

I moved to Colin's side and looked down at my new friend. Her face was deathly pale, and there were dark circles under her eyes.

"Well, well," Caroline taunted as she joined the assemblage about the maid. "Morning fainting spells. I hope none of you gentlemen have been trifling with her."

"For God's sake, be quiet, Caroline," Randall snapped. "The girl is ill. Barret," he said as he completed his cursory examination and arose, "take her to her room. As nearly as I can ascertain, she had a simple bout of lightheadedness. Working in this cursed humidity is enough to make anyone ill."

As Barret gathered the young woman up in his arms and stood, her eyelids fluttered open. She stared up at him, confused at first, then distressed. She gasped something in French and began to struggle from his arms. He stilled her effort with soft words in the same language and a gentle kiss on the forehead.

"Rest, Marie," Randall advised. "Let Barret take you to your room. I'll look in on you after church. Don't worry. We'll see to it everything is all right."

He smiled reassuringly at her, then nodded to

Barret to take her away. When they'd gone, he slammed a fist into his other palm, his face filling with outrage. "Damn!"

"Darling, such vehemence," Caroline purred, going to slip her arm through his. "One would think you were in some way responsible for the little French girl's illness. You weren't, were you, my love?"

He shot her a belittling look before striding from the room, his wife trotting in mock obedience at his side.

****

In the small but well built and decorated church on the edge of the village, I became the object of interest for the entire congregation.

"They're admiring my beautiful bride," Colin whispered, leaning close and squeezing my gloved hand.

His words did not reassure me. I knew the truth. This was the villagers' first opportunity to view Colin Douglas's sudden wife. How had I managed to seduce the most eligible bachelor in the valley into marrying an unlikely creature like myself, they must be wondering.

****

After the noon meal that followed our return home from church, Colin asked if I would object to his going riding with Randall and Captain Madison.

"Of course not," I said. "Perhaps I'll look in on Marie, if she's feeling well enough to have visitors."

"I'm afraid you won't be able to do that," my husband surprised me by replying quickly. "She's been sent home to her parents. Randall thinks she needs complete rest for a few days. One of the grooms drove her there while we were at church."

"I hope she's well soon," I murmured. "I shall be quite lonely without her."

"As soon as I can find a suitable horse for you, we'll ride together." Colin had changed the subject. He kissed me on the cheek and hurried off to change into riding clothes.

****

As I sat in the side porch swing later in the afternoon, I heard their yells and the drumming of their horses' hooves. I joined the servants and grooms who had gathered in the stable yard to watch their approach.

Taking fences and brooks like steeplechasers, the three horsemen thundered across the long expanse of cleared fields behind the mansion and its outbuildings at full gallop. I recognized the big black animal in the lead. Lucifer ran flat out, setting a tough pace for the chestnut and bay at his heels.

Caught up in the excitement, the servants and stable hands cheered them on, each supporting one or the other of the three. Their exuberance was contagious.

"Faster, Colin! Give him his head! Let him run!" I yelled.

I was seized by an arm and spun about to face an enraged Abraham Douglas.

"Do not support this nonsense!" he roared.

"I'll do as I please," I snapped back reflexively, then immediately was aghast as I realized what I'd done.

"How dare you stand there, arrayed in finery my money paid for, your belly stuffed with my food, and defy me!" he bellowed. "You'll do as I say, missy, or be sent packing like the baggage you truly are."

Before I could reply, Randall, Colin, and Barret

thundered into the yard in a cloud of dust.

"Get back to work, the lot of you," Abraham yelled at the servants. "Don't ever let me catch you encouraging those boys' debauchery again!"

They hurried off like a pack of beaten dogs.

"Get down!" Abraham turned to roar at the horsemen as they milled about on their prancing, foaming horses. In his hand he carried a riding quirt, slapping it against his high leather boot. "Get down, God damn you!"

They dismounted and stood holding their sweating, blowing horses in check. Clad in riding boots and breeches, with shirts open well down over their chests, they were a handsome trio.

"Have you taken leave of your senses?" my father-in-law bellowed, cracking the quirt in outrage. "You could have gotten injured or killed…especially you, Colin, you young idiot! And you, Barret and Randall, encouraged this madness? Damn you both, I should have Burt and Harry whip a little sense into your stupid hides!"

"Father…" Colin began, but he was cut short as his father walked up close to him.

"You reek of cheap ale," Abraham spat. "You were at the Black Horse Inn, I'll wager, and on the Sabbath. Barret, if you introduced him to one of your whorehouse sluts, I'll see you tarred and feathered!"

"Take it easy, Abe." Barret turned his attention to loosening Lucifer's girth. "We only had a couple of tankards of ale. Colin's as pure as he ever was."

The quirt flashed out and cracked across the captain's shoulders as a single bolt of lightning rent the dry, dark sky. The blow tore the linen shirt and left a fine, red cut in the exposed flesh beneath.

Barret whirled as an explosion of thunder filled the hot, heavy air. For a moment I thought he'd strike my father-in-law. But he didn't. He simply faced him, gray eyes smoldering as the sound lessened to a disgruntled rumble.

"Don't ever do that again!" The threat in his voice sent a shiver up my spine.

"You deserved it!" the older man snarled. "I don't care if you break your own neck or end up crippled by some whorehouse disease. You're the best commodore I've ever had, but you *are* replaceable. My sons are not. I've been too tolerant, allowing you to eat at my table and sleep in my house. You've become too familiar with my boys and the family in general. Get your gear. You'll be joining the stable hands in their quarters above the carriage shed."

"Abraham, don't talk like a fool!"

I turned to see Gram stumping down the back steps of the house, her black eyes flashing fire.

"This boy"—she pointed to Barret with her cane—"Provides the only decent conversation at the dinner table each night and helps me up to bed with a great deal more compassion than you or any of your cowering servants. He'll leave this house over my dead body."

"Mother!" Abraham looked at her in exasperation. "He had the boys steeplechasing and debauching at the tavern. He…"

"Quiet!" she snapped. "Barret, come with me to the kitchen, my boy. I'll make a poultice to keep that wound from festering."

Barret hesitated only a moment. Then, a wicked

grin spreading over his face, he swept Gram a deep, gallant bow and moved forward to offer the little old lady his arm.

"I always did like the smell of horse sweat and ale," I heard her say with a chuckle as he helped her toward the house. "Reminds me of Abe's father, the swashbuckling pirate. Made his fortune privateering in the War of 1812, didn't I tell you? But Abe's too respectable to admit that now."

Silence reigned until the pair disappeared inside the mansion. Then Abraham turned to the two remaining riders and myself.

"Well, don't stand there gaping. Randall, get those horses tended to before they become ill. Colin, go bathe. You, young lady, help him. Perhaps once he's clean and sober, if he has any strength left, he'll act like a husband and not a drunken fool. Damn it, why doesn't it rain and get it over with?"

He turned and strode off toward the mansion. Randall, with a resigned, good-natured shrug, gathered up the reins and led the three wet horses toward the stable.

"Starr, I wasn't with a woman." Colin's face was grim and nervous beneath dust and sweat. "We were just letting off a little steam. I only had a couple of tankards of ale at the tavern, I swear."

"I know," I said, taking his arm. "Let's go get you a bath. Your father was right about one thing. You do reek."

At that instant it began to rain, a great, drenching downpour.

"You're good for me, Starr," Colin grinned, looking down at me, water streaming down his face.

"We'll have a fine life together, wait and see."

But as we ran to the shelter of the mansion I noticed mud soiling the hem of my elegant dress.

****

Later, as Colin was bathing and I sat alone reading in our bedroom, I heard Reverend Prescott and his wife arrive, with Mary Constable. I'd overheard Caroline telling the cook to prepare for supper guests and now assumed they were the minister and the two ladies. Caroline and Gram took the ladies to the library while Abraham drew the clergyman into his office below me. I found my attention straying from my book to the conversation rising through the floor grate.

"Adam, I have a plan I wish to discuss with you," my father-in-law began. "A plan I believe will prove beneficial to both of us."

"That sounds most intriguing, although I cannot imagine what it could be," the vicar replied.

"The young woman you have living with you, Mary Constable, she's still unattached?"

"Why, yes. She's been here but a short time, and she still mourns her young man."

"But she can't live with you and your good wife forever," Abraham said. "Another mouth to feed is always a burden, even when it's done in the spirit of Christian charity."

"What are you suggesting?" The clergyman's tone was suspicious.

"A solution that will benefit both of us, Adam." I heard booted footsteps cross the room. "Would you care for a drink?"

"No…no, thank you. Please continue."

"One of my captains, Jared Fletcher, has been

showing a good deal more interest than I deem healthy in my daughter-in-law, Caroline," Abraham startled me by replying. "He needs a woman. Since I don't intend to allow him to upset Randall's marriage, I propose to marry him off to Mary Constable. Respectable young women of marriageable age are few and far between in this valley. A marriage between these two would solve both our problems."

"You mean use poor, innocent, little Mary to satisfy a sailor's lust?" The clergyman's voice rose in disbelief.

"Calm yourself, Adam." Abraham's tone was placating. "She could do a deal worse. Jared is a captain, second in command of my fleet. He's handsome, well-to-do, intelligent, literate, and, more importantly, a good Presbyterian. I might have suggested marrying her to Barret Madison, a raving papist. Think, man! You'd be bringing her securely back into your fold. She was about to marry that Irish Catholic Kevin O'Brien and become a member of that pagan sect."

"I cannot agree to such a match," the reverend stammered. I guessed it was taking all his courage to stand up to Abe, and I admired him in spite of his faltering words. "I couldn't force that innocent child into the bed of that big, experienced sailor. She needs someone gentle and kind…and Kevin O'Brien, for all his papist faith, was just that. He and his sister Bridgit are…were fine people, full of love and compassion. Bridgit spent every free moment she had nursing my wife over her last illness. Religion was no barrier to her. She…"

"Don't talk to me about that fish-shed slut!"

Abraham roared. "She's a whore who satisfies men with her body as easily as she guts salmon with her knife."

"I will not have that good, kind girl defamed!" Reverend Prescott startled me by barking back. "She's already solved Mary's problems. Tomorrow Mary Constable will move in with her. Bridgit feels that Mary, as her brother's intended, should be her responsibility. Mary will not be a financial burden to Bridgit. Captain Madison has given her a job as clerk in his shipping office in the village. He's so often at sea, and such a great number of new vessels are being produced in your yards, he says he needs someone to keep up with the paper work—the insurance contracts, the cargo lists, the destination of each Douglas ship, registry papers, and the like. Mary is literate and good with figures. She'll do admirably."

He paused for breath, then continued more slowly, measuring his words. "And since Bridgit's cabin is small and allows for little privacy, I doubt your son will have many opportunities for intimate visits—if indeed such they were—to Mistress O'Brien."

"My son? I said nothing of my son," Abe huffed. "My sons both love their wives. I'm shocked, yes, horrified that you, Adam, could even suggest such a thing. And as for Barret Madison's giving Mary Constable a job—"

"Supper is served." A maidservant interrupted Abe's tirade to make the announcement.

The men fell back into their roles as host and guest.

"Shall we join the ladies, my friend?" Abraham said. "I'm sure Cook has an excellent repast waiting for us. We'll continue this discussion later."

"Of course, of course," Reverend Prescott murmured, and I heard them leaving the office.

I leaned back into my chair, astounded by the lengths to which my father-in-law would go to control his family. If he had known of the encounter I'd had with Barret Madison, would he also have found that captain a wife, or, as he'd threatened that afternoon, sent me packing?

****

That night, as we were preparing for bed, I told Colin about his father's verbal attack on me in the stable yard. I expected my husband to agree with my outrage. I was appalled when he sank down on the edge of our bed and slouched forward, elbows on his knees, to stare at the rug beneath his bare feet.

"Don't defy my father, Starr," he muttered. "He's not a man one can trifle with."

"Colin, he raised his voice to me!" I cried. "He grabbed me by the arm. He had no right—"

"Listen to me, Starr." My husband was on his feet in front of me, his expression pleading. "Don't antagonize my father. He's a dangerous man. Believe me!"

"Colin…?"

"Please, Starr! Do as I ask."

"As you wish, Colin," I said, touching his tense cheek. "I did promise to love, honor, and obey."

At my reassuring words, he let a smile twitch at his lips.

"Thank you, sweetheart." He brushed my forehead with a kiss before he released me and went into the bathroom to prepare for bed. I was left alone to puzzle what could make a son so fear his father.

Chapter Seven

Three mornings later, a shaved and fully dressed Colin aroused me from my sleep.

“Come to the window,” he said, his face bright with anticipation.

I allowed him to draw me from the bed and turn me to look out the casement at the left of the headboard.

Below, one of the grooms held a beautiful doe-eyed mare whose shining coat was the color of dark burnished gold. Her full mane and flowing tail shone silver-white in the sun and set off four ivory-stockinged feet. When she tossed her head, her snowy forelock flew aside to reveal a perfect five-pointed star.

“She’s magnificent!” My sleepiness dissolved into admiration.

“She’s yours.” Colin grinned. “A belated wedding gift. I had a deuce of a time finding a mare with a coat the color of your hair and a star on her face. Her name is Lady. Now you can ride with me.”

“Oh, Colin, I couldn’t accept such a present. She must have cost a fortune.”

He shrugged aside my protest and opened the window.

“Michael, saddle her, will you? And get Bach ready. My wife and I will be riding after breakfast.”

****

I took to riding as the proverbial duck to water.

Within a week I was able to acquit myself well enough in a sidesaddle to accompany Colin along trails into the bush, sometimes for sheer enjoyment but more often to get away from his father's constant badgering and the pressures of the work he hated. Sometimes we rode out to fish in one of the many fine trout streams near the village.

My husband loved to fish. I found my elegant riding habits ill fitted for pushing through alders and wading into streams. An excursion to the Douglas Mercantile was in order, I decided. Under the scrutiny of Ben Smith, Abraham's store manager, I purchased boy's breeches, shirt, and cap.

"You'll look like a young man in that get-up," the white-haired gentleman said, his eyes twinkling as he bundled up my purchases. "But it's what you'll need for fishing. And young Colin does love to fish. I used to take him myself, before my knees started troubling me."

"Didn't Colin's father take him fishing?"

"Abe is always too busy settin' the world on fire," Ben Smith replied, handing me the bundle of new clothes. "He has little time for pleasure…or his sons."

****

"Your fishing companion, sire, fittingly attired at last." I swept Colin an elaborate bow when I joined him at the stables later that morning.

"Who put you up to this?" Outrage hardened his face. Seizing me by an arm, he shook me violently. "Tell me, damn you, tell me!"

"Colin, you're hurting me," I gasped. "No one put me up to anything. I wanted clothes that would be suitable for fishing. I purchased them at your father's store this morning. Colin, let me go!"

His hand fell from my arm.

"I'm sorry, sweetheart," he mumbled. "Forgive me. Please forgive me. Did I hurt you?"

"No." I backed away from him and rubbed my arm where he'd seized me.

"Forgive me," he begged again, his voice breaking. He adjusted the cap covering my curls. "I've had a rough morning in my father's office, but you didn't deserve to suffer as a result."

"It's all right, Colin," I murmured against his chest. "I understand."

But I didn't, not at all. My knees were still weak from his frightening behavior.

****

A half hour later, we were enjoying one of Cook's excellent lunches on the bank of Colin's favorite fishing stream.

"Ah, what a perfect day," Colin sighed, unbuttoning his shirt and stretching out on his back to gaze up at the clear July sky. He was once again the kind, thoughtful young man I'd married. The incident in the stable yard seemed only a bad dream, a hallucination of some sort.

"Yes, it is," I agreed, stooping to take a handful of water from the stream. "But we've got serious trout fishing to do. I won't allow you to get lazy."

I tossed the cold water onto his bare chest. With a yelp of surprise, he bolted upright, then lunged for me, intent on revenge.

I jumped sideways to avoid him, slipped, and both of us plunged into the shallow stream. Laughing uproariously, we struggled to our feet and stumbled, thoroughly soaked, to shore.

"Witch!" Colin yelled as we sank down on the grass beside our picnic basket.

"Bully!" I taunted back. "Big, blond bully!"

"Foul-mouthed wench!" he cried, and grabbed me as though to throw me back into the stream.

Laughing and wrestling, we fell to the ground and rolled about for a few moments before Colin, on top, halted and looked down at me in sudden seriousness. My wet clothing clung to me; since I'd had no feminine undergarments that would fit under my boy's outfit, my naked body beneath was clearly outlined.

"Starr," he said softly, "you know we must try to have a child. My father has ordered it. If we don't, I'm afraid I might lose you. He's a dangerous man. Starr, sweetheart, will you let me…lay with you…as a husband?"

"Colin." I reached up and touched his tense face.

"I'll be gentle, Starr. As God is my witness. Please, Starr."

I put trembling fingers to his belt buckle and released it. His fingers shook as he began to unfasten my trousers.

"Please, dear God, please!" I was startled to hear him praying as he moved to lie on me.

He was carefully easing my legs apart when he was wrenched from me. I stared up to see a big, black silhouette blanking out the hot sun and hauling Colin to his feet by his shirt collar.

"God damn you, Colin! A boy in a meadow? Have you no common sense?"

As I struggled to close my clothing, I recognized Captain Madison's voice.

"That's no boy, you idiot!" Colin roared, struggling in his grasp. "It's Starr. We were…making love. Damn *you*, Barret Madison! Damn you, you've spoiled it for us again."

He turned and ran to his horse. He scrambled into the saddle and slapped the gelding into a mad gallop.

"You insensitive cur!" I cried as my husband thundered away. Pulling off my cap to free my hair, I stumbled to my feet. "You miserable brute! Are you blind?"

"Sweet Jesus!" he muttered, his bravado dissolving. "I had no idea… What are you doing in those clothes? Did Colin ask you to wear them?"

"No, of course not. I bought them for fishing. That's what we were doing here. Why did you come?"

"Abe wants Colin at home at once. I came to fetch him."

"Well, once again, you've done your master's bidding," I snapped. I turned and started toward my mare, curls flouncing over my shoulders. "Now you can feel free to visit your tavern wench. I'm sure she'll amuse you for the remainder of the afternoon."

"Damn you!" He caught up to me, grabbed me by the arm, and spun me about to face him. "Do you think I enjoyed coming upon you with that boy sprawled over you? Climb aboard that little yellow horse and get away from me before—"

He flung me in the direction of Lady and strode off toward the waiting Lucifer. I was left with a pounding heart and the frightening knowledge that the strange alchemy that existed between the captain and me was intensifying at an alarming rate.

****

After Barret Madison left me that infamous noon hour at the trout stream, I mounted Lady and was trotting her back toward Peacock House when I saw a carriage stopped ahead of me. Half hidden by the summer foliage, it might have escaped my interest had I not recognized the pair of bays harnessed to it. They were from my father-in-law's stable. My curiosity piqued, I reined my mount off the trail, dismounted, and stifled her whinnies to her stablemates with a hand over her nostrils.

I didn't have long to wait. Within a few minutes the carriage moved back into the road and stopped again. I recognized the driver as Caroline Douglas. My breath caught when I saw her companion was Marie. What could that pair possibly have to meet about?

I had not seen the young maidservant since the Sunday she'd taken ill at breakfast. While I watched, Marie got down from the carriage and followed a path into the trees. Caroline observed her for a moment, then clucked her team to a trot and drove off in the direction of Peacock House.

I rode back to the mansion's stable yard, my mind a turmoil of confusion. Was Marie perhaps, as Caroline had hinted, pregnant? If so, who was the father? Randall had been deeply distressed by her illness, and now here was his wife clandestinely meeting the girl. Had Caroline perhaps been attempting to secure her silence about an affair with her husband? Randall had had at least one affair during his unhappy marriage. Had he perhaps had several?

And then there was Captain Barret Madison, who seemed a confidant of the serving girl and whose morals with women left a great deal to be desired. Was he her lover?

Finally there was Colin; Colin, my handsome young husband who could not make love to me because he had loved—perhaps still loved—someone else.

I left Lady with a groom. As I walked to the house, Marie's distressed words when she'd regained consciousness on the Sunday morning of her illness came back into my mind. The words had been unintelligible to me but understandable to Barret and Caroline, who counted a knowledge of French among her accomplishments.

Two days later, Captain Madison had an opportunity to revisit his wrath on me. It was one of the few days Colin had had no time for me. I'd missed our luncheon ride and his presence by my side at supper.

Caroline and Gram had gone to a church meeting directly after the evening meal, and Abraham had ridden out on business. With Randall at the House of Assembly in Fredericton, I was alone in the mansion, save for the servants. Restless, I ordered Lady saddled and went for a short ride alone along the river.

It was a beautiful summer's evening, calm and quiet, like the backdrop for one of Darcy's poems. An urge to share it with him enveloped me, and I headed down the trail to the cabin that was to have been ours.

When I entered the clearing where it stood, I was surprised to see Captain Madison, mounted on Lucifer, perusing the little log house. In the deepening shadows of the tall trees, he and his horse cut a darkly handsome yet ominous image. My heartbeat quickened.

"Good evening, Captain." I reined my mare to a halt and tried to assume the detached, lofty air of a lady.

Before he could reply, the stallion snorted and

made a bolt toward Lady and me. The captain proved an excellent rider, quick and agile. Although the thwarted animal had risen on its hind legs, shaking and bellowing, in a matter of seconds he'd brought him back under control.

"Easy, my lad." He surprised me by chuckling as he brought the horse to a pawing, snorting stance. "These ladies belong to Colin and are both off limits to us. Good evening, Mrs. Douglas. My apologies for the lad's behavior."

"Of course," I said haughtily, ignoring the obvious double meaning in his words. "One must excuse *an animal*."

Unfortunately Lady chose that moment to respond to the stallion. With a soft whinny, she tossed her snowy mane and sidled toward him.

"Stop it, Lady!" I jerked on her bit.

"It appears your mare is not unaffected by my lad." The captain grinned, holding the snorting stallion in check. "I think we'd best return them to their stable before they fall more deeply in love."

"Don't you mean lust?" Annoyed, I swung Lady about and started back toward Peacock House at a brisk trot.

Captain Madison brought Lucifer into step beside me. For a time we rode in silence. Finally the question I'd been longing to ask bubbled from my lips.

"Why were you at Darcy's cabin?"

"It's a nice little property," he said. "I've been looking for a place to call my own. I thought perhaps you might want to sell it."

"Me?"

"It's yours, I understand. Your fiancé had the good

sense to register a deed in both your names with the county clerk. That means, even if your young man left no will, the property is yours. Weren't you aware of the fact?"

"I had no idea. But why this sudden interest in acquiring your own house? I thought you were quite comfortable at the mansion. Or did my father-in-law's anger the other Sunday strike a responsive chord?"

He burst out laughing.

"Hardly. I'm accustomed to Abe's ranting and raving. I know when to take him seriously and when to dismiss his threats as dramatic posturing."

"Then you're not afraid of him?" I asked, recalling Colin's and even Randall's submission to their father's will.

"Afraid, no. But I don't take him lightly, either. I'm fully aware of his ruthlessness and ambition. Now about your property, are you interested in selling?"

"You haven't given me a satisfactory reason for your desire to purchase," I said. "You say you don't believe Abe means to evict you from Peacock House."

He halted his horse and caught Lady's bridle to bring her to a stop beside Lucifer. Then he faced me, gray eyes intense.

"It's no longer wise for me to lie in a bed across the hall from you," he said, gray eyes piercing in their intensity. "I'm not a stallion. I don't have anyone to jerk my bit when I feel certain urges."

We sat staring at each other in the deepening twilight, his words sending strange tremors through my body. Then I came to my senses, struck his hand from Lady's bridle with my quirt, and galloped away. I was flushed and trembling.

****

The following afternoon Colin and I found ourselves alone in the house except for a few unobtrusive servants. Since it was too hot to go riding, we opted to retire to the drawing room, where Colin could practice at the piano. I curled up in a wing chair near the open French doors to listen and enjoy.

That afternoon he played as a master of the keyboard, the pianist without peer I had heard on my second day in the mansion. My husband was a magician, a spellbinder who had the power to whisk his audience into an enchanted world of awesome beauty.

When he paused for rest, he looked over at me and smiled. “You make that pale green gown beautiful. You should always wear your hair down, tied with ribbon and falling over your bare shoulders.”

“Nothing could be as beautiful as your music,” I said.

A muffled giggle from the hallway made us both turn toward the open door.

“Rose, Jenny? Is that you?” Colin asked. “Come, show yourselves.”

Crimson-faced and furtive, the two young maidservants appeared on the threshold.

“We wasn’t eavesdropping, Mr. Colin,” Jenny the scullery maid stammered. “We was only enjoyin’ your music. Please don’t tell the master. He’d dismiss me, sure, if he found out I was in this part of the house.”

“You know me better than that.” Colin smiled at the pair. “Come in, come in. It’s not often I’m granted an audience. What would you like to hear?”

The two young women exchanged glances, then Rose, the parlor maid, spoke.

"Would you be knowin' any Irish jigs, sir?"

"But of course." Colin grinned, flexed his fingers, winked at me, and broke into a rollicking piece. His mastery and joy flowed into the bouncing tune and set my feet tapping. Jenny and Rose, enthralled, clapped their hands in time. When he had finished, all three of us burst into hearty applause.

"Oh, sir, if Michael the groom and Patrick the stable boy could only have heard!" Rose breathed. "They're both dreadful homesick, and to hear the music of the old sod again would soothe their achin' hearts."

"Go fetch them," I exclaimed, caught up in the gaiety of Colin's devil-may-care tune. "We'll dance and sing and have a grand time. Go, go!"

Spurred by my enthusiasm, the two dashed off.

"We'll have a party, Colin," I cried, whirling happily about the room. "Rose and Jenny and Michael and Patrick and you and I. It will be such fun!"

"Starr, they're servants." Colin turned to me, a frown creasing his forehead. "Father doesn't allow servants and family to fraternize. If he comes home…"

"But he won't. He's gone with Barret Madison on a fleet inspection for the entire day. And after all, isn't this America, where there's supposed to be no class distinction?"

He hesitated only a moment longer.

"Very well, Starr. Let's have a little party."

****

Michael was swinging me gaily about while Colin pounded out a polka when *his* voice halted our dance and froze my husband's fingers.

"Dear God in Heaven, what's going on here?"

As the groom's arms sprang from about me, I

whirled to face the enraged countenance of my father-in-law. Behind him in the doorway stood Barret Madison, his expression inscrutable.

The four servants shrank away from him in horror. Colin stood and turned to his father, his countenance blanching.

"Get out!" Abraham roared at our four guests. "Get back to your posts! By God, I should dismiss the lot of you. Indeed, I may even yet, after I get to the bottom of this debauchery!"

Stumbling in their haste, the quartet scrambled from the room. Abraham turned his wrath on Colin.

"I left this house to you and your wife today for one purpose only," he said his voice trembling with repressed rage. "I had silk sheets put on your bed and a bottle of champagne placed on ice in your room. Now why in God's name aren't you upstairs getting her with child?"

"Father…" Sweat beaded Colin's forehead "I… We… That is…"

"Get out!" Abraham roared. "Get out and don't come near me again until you need to inform me of your wife's pregnancy!"

Colin hesitated a moment longer, glanced from his father to me, then dashed from the room, his expression one of excruciating humiliation.

"How could you!" I gasped, confronting my father-in-law. Fear held no place in my fury at his outrageous treatment of my husband. "How could you speak to Colin like that, especially in front of *him*!"

I pointed a finger at Barret Madison. The mocking bow he bestowed on me in return made me want to fly into his face like an enraged feline.

"Barret knows what I expect of Colin." Abraham regained his self control. "But what about you? Why this debauchery with servants? Why didn't you take my son to bed today? Your eyes, your expressions, the way you move… They all tell me you're a sensuous, earthy little creature perfectly capable of giving a man a deuce of a good time. Why don't you seduce my son? He's a good-looking boy, keeps himself clean, is well educated… I can't believe you find him repulsive."

"We're getting to know each other," I said, drawing myself up to my greatest height, struggling to keep from becoming an incoherent, incensed fool before the smirking captain. "Love and intimacy take time. Colin has been in love with someone else, and…"

"Dear God!" Abraham smacked one white-knuckled fist into his other hand, his face turning beet red. "He told you?"

"Yes," I managed to reply calmly, although his distorted countenance was weakening my bravado. "He didn't tell me with whom, but I believe it was recently. Therefore, I can't expect him to…desire me…yet."

The relief in Abe's expression was as startling as his outrage moments earlier.

"Quite right," he breathed. "Of course, you're quite right."

"Come on, Abe." Barret put an arm about the older man's shoulders. "Let's get a snifter of brandy. Leave the laying of Colin to this girl. I'm sure if anyone can teach the boy how to perform in bed, she can."

Abe allowed himself to be led away, but soon Barret Madison returned to where I'd crumpled into a wing chair in the hot drawing room.

"Does he have a problem in bed?" he asked. "Isn't

he able to perform?"

"None of your damn business," I cried, and rushed, tear-blinded, to our room.

A short time later, as I sat alone in our bedroom, I heard a group of men entering the office below. From snatches of the conversation, I gleaned it was a meeting of Abe's captains.

My anger melted into curiosity, and I dropped on hands and knees to listen through the half-closed grate in the floor. It allowed me partial view of the room below. Like a poisonous but mesmerizing snake, my father-in-law frightened and fascinated me; I knew I had to learn all I could about him if I hoped to survive in his house. I might one day find myself mother of the child who would inherit the Abraham Douglas legacy.

"Please be seated, gentlemen," Abraham said pleasantly. Not a single trace remained of the outraged man who'd left the drawing room less than an hour ago.

All of the nearly twenty men found places on the chairs Abraham had ordered brought into the room to accommodate them. His fleet must be much larger than I'd imagined, for whatever number was at home in Pine at any given time during sailing months, there were as many at sea, Colin had told me.

Within my field of vision, I watched as Abe sat down behind his huge mahogany desk near the window, Barret Madison on his right, Jared Fletcher on his left.

"Gentleman, as you're no doubt aware, Douglas and Sons has made a bid to provide a year-round transatlantic mail service between this province's government and Her Majesty's government in London," he began. "My son Randall has managed to bring our governor to the brink of signing with us.

There is, however, a small stipulation which we must first meet. These ugly iron steam tubs are providing the problem. They don't depend on the caprices of nature to do their job, some would argue. I say"—Abraham slammed his fist down on his desk—"show me the lumbering bit of tin that can outrun any of your ships in a good breeze, and I'll condemn myself to Hades!"

A heartfelt murmur of agreement issued from the men.

"The stipulation," Abe continued, "is proof that we can do what we promise—provide a dependable year-round mail service. Therefore, one of our ships must sail out of Halifax on New Year's Day and reach London within three weeks. Captain MacDonald, I've chosen you and your vessel for this task."

I suppressed a gasp. Hadn't I already heard him tell Randall that Barret would make the crossing?

"Put my *London Lass* to sea in January?" The big, bearded man jumped to his feet, astounded. "Mr. Douglas, she's swift as a eagle, but she's also delicate as a swan. I shouldn't have to remind you of that fact. She was built for the West Indies trade, not a North Atlantic run. Icy seas will split her apart in a matter of hours!"

"Are you defying me, Captain MacDonald?"

"Aye, sir, that I am." Captain MacDonald stepped to the desk to confront his employer. "I'll not send my men and ship to the bottom in a mad attempt to prove you right. Send one of your pretty lads. Captain Madison and Captain Fletcher both have ships equipped for speed and the North Atlantic in winter. Or are they too young and fine to risk on such a suicide mission? Perhaps you can best spare an old seadog like myself, one whose dissenting from blind obedience to your every wish has been a thorn in your side these many years?"

I held my breath, expecting my father-in-law to erupt into rage. Abe Douglas, as always, was full of surprises.

"Andrew, Andrew," he said, his tone placating. "Can't you see the reason I've chosen you over these…boys? You've more years before the mast than both of them combined. You know the winds and tides like your own hands. And when we get that contract, there will be a handsome extra in your pay, you can believe."

"No! I'll not risk my men on such a foolish mission for all the tea in China. You can dismiss me, you can take my command, but I'll not put my men's lives in jeopardy."

"Then consider yourself dismissed from your position." Barret Madison got to his feet and stood beside Abe. Tall, handsome, and powerful, he was an impressive figure in a room full of strong men. "I'll not tolerate insubordination to the owner of my fleet."

"Damn you, Madison! How dare you presume to take my ship from me? You're nothing but a piece of trash from a Caribbean gutter!"

"I'd advise you to leave this house at once, *Mr.* MacDonald." Jared Fletcher came to his feet, and I saw cold, hard rage on his face. "Otherwise I'll be obliged to invite you outside. I cannot countenance insults to my commodore's good name."

"Good name!" MacDonald was striding toward the door. "I doubt he has any real name at all. Bit of whorehouse leavings, if you ask me. Good name, indeed! Lusting after young Colin's wife and layin' that barmaid Meg all in one breath—the bastard!"

The door slammed and he was gone. A static silence fell. Finally Abe spoke evenly, as if nothing untoward had happened. "Any more dissenters?"

No one replied, but several shifted in their chairs. They might not like Abe's plan, but they were not ready to risk losing their commands as Captain MacDonald had.

"I'll make the January run, Abe." Barret startled me by speaking up. "Since my reputation has been besmirched," he continued sardonically, "I have little choice if I wish to command any respect among these men."

"Barret…" Jared Fletcher tried to intercede, but Abe drowned him out.

"Then it's settled. Captain Madison will make the run. And may God have mercy on all your cowardly souls if he doesn't return." Then his tone lightened. "There are refreshments in the dining room, gentlemen. Eat, drink, and be merry."

Chapter Eight

As I came down to breakfast the following morning, I heard Barret and Abraham arguing in Abe's office, situated between the foot of the stairs and the front entrance. With its door slightly ajar, their voices carried into the hallway.

"And I tell you, sir, you will go after that cargo of guano!" Abraham's words burned hot with anger.

"And I tell you, I won't." Barret's reply, cool and controlled, held no possibility of acquiescence. "I'm just now getting the stench of that human cargo you ordered me to carry as ballast on my last trip from the holds of the *Maris Stella*. I'll not foul her again. My crew are good men. I won't have them demeaned by ordering them to scrape bird shit from rocks and shovel it into the holds."

"A respectable captain does not use foul language," Abraham barked.

"A respectable captain would not be asked to transport bird droppings on a ship like the *Maris Stella.*" The captain's response was as cold and final as the snap of steel handcuffs on the wrists of a condemned prisoner. "I've already agreed to make that crossing from Halifax to London in January. Be satisfied with that foolhardiness. Don't expect degradation as well."

"Must I remind you, Captain Madison, you work

for me? You'll do as I say!" Abraham bellowed. "Remember that ship you're so proud of is mine!"

"Partly yours." Barret Madison maintained his calm, controlled tone. "I own a good piece of her shares. By next year I'll have the controlling interest."

"In a pig's eye you will!" Abraham snapped. "If you persist in refusing to carry out my orders, I'll not sell them to you."

"You have no choice," Barret said. "You'll recall the agreement you made when I became her master. I obtained the right to purchase her shares from you over the next four years; if I managed, in that period, to afford them all, you would have to sell. It's in writing and perfectly legal."

"Damn you!" Abraham muttered. "You're too clever and resourceful by a half. You should have been my son, not those two milksops I'm forced to acknowledge as blood kin." Strength returning to his voice, he continued, "Little did I know, when I took you in as a ragged sixteen-year-old and gave you a place on one of my ships, what a tough, smart devil you would turn out to be. I recall you worked like a thing possessed to become a bo'sun, then second mate, then first."

"And, at twenty-two, master of one of your ships, albeit the poorest in your fleet, a veritable floating coffin," Barret interjected. "But I kept her sailing, and you turned a nice profit with me as her captain."

"I don't doubt your ability, but I'm not unaware of your vices, either." Abraham's tone moderated. "You're shrewd and tough, and you don't let any ridiculous Sunday School morality block your way to what you want. We're a good deal alike in that respect, laddie, but don't ever forget who's the master and who's the servant in this relationship."

"Or who you're depending on to deliver up that mail contract. If I refuse to make that January crossing, you'll be hard pressed to find another who'll attempt it."

"All right, forget the guano. It's a highly profitable cargo just now, but if you want to forego your share of it, that's your foolhardiness. Now, there's another matter I wish to speak to you about. You gave Mary Constable a position in my shipping office without consulting me. That was highhanded of you. I have other plans for that girl."

"Plans to marry her off to Jared? Or, at least, letting him bed her?" Barret's reply held sarcastic amusement. "That won't placate Captain Fletcher. Only one woman can satisfy him, and we both know who that is."

"Don't talk nonsense!" Abraham barked. "All cats are gray in the dark. Fletcher will take what he's offered and be glad of it. Or"—his tone became nasty and smooth—"perhaps you have an eye for Mistress Mary yourself. Perhaps you're already bedding her and don't want to share with your friend. Well, hear me, and hear me well." His tone picked up. "I'll not allow you to thwart my plans with your lusting. I'm ordering you to discharge that girl immediately. Destitute, she'll have to marry Fletcher to survive."

"Sorry, Abe. I promised her a secure position for just that reason. I didn't want to see her forced to marry some man she didn't care about, in order to avoid starvation. Both your sons will tell you there's little joy in such arrangements."

"How dare you comment on my boys' marriages in such a demeaning manner! God damn you, you never did know when to keep either your mouth or your trousers shut."

To my surprise, I heard Barret chuckle. "Come now, Abe, let's not fight. It never gets either of us anywhere. Only when we both pull in the same direction do both your family and your enterprises prosper. Forget the girl. She's an asset to the office, but of no sexual interest to either Jared or myself. She's where she's most useful to Douglas and Sons."

Abe muttered something derogatory, but his mood was mellowing. Barret Madison had won.

A chair creaked, and I knew the meeting had come to an end. Not wanting to be caught eavesdropping, I slipped into the room across the entrance hall and out of sight behind its half-open door.

"And one more thing." Abraham spoke as the two men emerged into the foyer. "Stay away from Colin's wife. I've seen the look in your eyes when she's about, and I'm ordering you to stop any ideas you might have concerning her. I want to be sure the child she's going to bear will be my grandchild beyond any doubt. Do I make myself clear?"

A hot, outraged blush of anger flooded over my body. *Say something, Captain Madison. Defend both of us.* My heart pounding, I listened with clenched fists and drawn lips.

"There's no need to worry," I was chagrined to hear the captain reply lightly, almost mockingly. "I can assure you, no matter what I do, any child Starr Douglas bears will be your grandchild. You're letting MacDonald's innuendoes get to you, Abe. You know

I'm not really so great a whoremaster as he'd have you think."

"As long as we have an understanding," Abraham's reply was astonishingly congenial, as I'd might have expected from someone who had just struck a good bargain. "I know she's a tempting little piece, and you're forced to sleep across the hall from her. All the same, it's important to me you stay out of Colin's marriage. And his wife."

His vulgarity made me want to rush out at them screaming I was no common whore nor piece of baby-producing machinery whose body could be bartered between two ruthless men for the purpose they deemed best.

I managed to control myself with an intense effort as they went off up the hall to breakfast, talking companionably of other matters.

****

That night I found sleep difficult. Glancing over at Colin slumbering beside me, I reflected on the unnaturalness of our marriage. We'd married each other for reasons which were neither love nor desire. Now we must live with the consequences.

Yet we did love one another in a way. We cared for each other as a brother and sister might. I could not bear to see Colin hurt or unhappy, and he, I knew, would do all he could to make my life pleasant and comfortable. It could have been a much worse situation, I tried to comfort myself.

At times like these, however, when I awoke in the middle of the night with a strange, unquenched longing within me, I had to be stern indeed to make myself see the positive aspects of my marriage. Colin's warm body stretched out beside mine awoke feelings in me which aroused both fear and excitement. I never again wanted a man to try to take me in violence and lust, I would tell myself, as memories of the time in the overseer's cottage washed over me. Then Colin would stir in his sleep and roll against me.

The broad chest and lean belly of his long, muscular body would relax against my hips and breasts, and I would shudder with a nebulous mixture of sensual pleasure and heart-stopping fear.

Troubled and unhappy, I got out of bed. Without disturbing Colin, I slipped on a silk robe. A glass of milk from the kitchen might help me sleep. I eased open the bedroom door and was closing it carefully after me when a voice from the darkness near the top of the stairs made me start.

"Restless, Mrs. Douglas? Stealing out for a carouse while young Colin sleeps?"

I whirled to see Captain Madison silhouetted in the moonlight pouring in through a tall window at the end of the hallway. His shirt was open to the waist, revealing a hard expanse of chest. There was a distinct odor of rum about him.

"I'm on my way to the kitchen for a glass of milk," I whispered. "Please keep your voice down. I don't want to awaken Colin. Now, if you'll excuse me…"

I had to get away from the man. The sudden quickening of my pulses at the nearness of his blatant virility appalled the rational side of me, titillated the natural side.

"Milk? Or a man?" He moved closer. The giddy sensation I remembered experiencing with him that night on the deck of the *Maris Stella* washed over me.

My heart began to beat an incessant tattoo, my entire body lighting up with a wild tingling.

"You're drunk," I accused, feigning disgust in a vain effort to still the rush of feeling threatening to overwhelm my common sense.

"Ah, *oui*," he slurred. "Drunk and about to die and take a lot of good men with me."

"Die?"

"Don't let the idea distress you, my love." His words reeked of sarcasm as he reached to run a finger slowly down my cheek. A shock that set my senses reeling glanced down through my body from the point of contact. "I may survive that January run with only minor frozen appendages. The chances aren't great. So how would you feel about granting a condemned man a last wish?"

My breath caught in my throat. I could only stand staring mutely up into those charismatic charcoal eyes. In the dark shadows of the moonlighted hallway, Barrert Madison was a mesmerizing phantom lover, drawing me like a helpless moth into the flame of his desire. It was wrong, so wrong, and yet…

Colin pulled open the door behind me, breaking the spell as lamplight fell out over us.

I whirled to face him. Blinking sleepily, my husband ran his fingers through his tangled blond curls as he squinted out at us.

"Starr, what's the matter?" he yawned.

"I…I was on my way to the kitchen for a glass of milk," I stammered. "I couldn't sleep."

"That's right, Colin," Captain Madison said, fingering one of the tousled ringlets which fell about my shoulders, his words thick with sensuous innuendo.

"Your wife was restless."

Their implication brought Colin fully awake. He moved to my side to put his arm about my shoulders. "You've been drinking, Barret," he said with amazing calm. "Go to bed."

"Aye, aye, sir." Captain Madison stepped backward away from us and saluted. "A thousand pardons, young master. I thought perhaps *you* were inebriated again and had failed to satisfy this lovely little creature."

He turned and strode into his room across the hall. As soon as the door had closed behind him, Colin drew me back into our room.

"Colin, don't you want an explanation?" I asked as he started to get back into bed. "Aren't you angry? He was crude and vulgar and…"

"And very drunk." He turned to me in the moonlight and spoke gently. "I understand him, Starr. He's a strong man, but yesterday my father forced him into what amounts to a suicide mission, not only for himself but for his crew. Tonight he's alone and probably seeing death as a very real and immediate possibility. Don't judge him too harshly. Sober, he never would have behaved as he did just now. He's a truly good man at heart. And my best friend."

He lay down, pulled the quilts over his shoulders, and turned on his side, prepared for sleep.

****

I had spent the first days of my marriage buffered from the world, within the fold of the Douglas household. As a result, I had had no opportunity to meet the residents of the village and learn how the working people regarded the wealthy, powerful clan of which I had become a part.

My curiosity on this matter peaked as I came out of the dining room after breakfast one morning. When I saw Abraham at the front door, pulling on his gloves in preparation to leave the house, I decided to begin finding the answer.

"You're going out, Mr. Douglas?" I asked.

"Yes, my dear, on a tour of inspection," he replied. "Tell Colin I want him to examine the keel my men are laying for that new vessel today. I'll expect a full report no later than noon."

"Very well," I said. "Perhaps I'll accompany him."

"That wouldn't be prudent. The docks are not fit for a lady."

"But…"

"Come, walk me out." He ignored my attempt at protest and smiled down at me. "I enjoy a pretty woman on my arm."

He crooked his elbow. I accepted his invitation and accompanied him out onto the wide verandah. At the foot of the steps waited a pair of burly, mounted riders, one holding a big gray saddled and ready.

"Business associates." Abraham dismissed the necessity of an introduction by waving at the pair. He kissed me on the cheek in a fatherly fashion before he mounted the magnificent stallion with an ease surprising in a man of his years.

At the sudden weight, the animal began to prance and shy. Abraham yanked on the bit and kicked the animal in the ribs. The horse snorted and half-reared, then gave up the fight and stood, conquered and docile, while his master made himself comfortable in the saddle.

"Don't test me again today, my lad," he warned, triumph in his voice. "You know I can be unpleasant when annoyed."

His tone lightened as he addressed me. "Starr, my dear, don't forget to give your young man my message. Burt, Harry." He turned to his rugged companions. "Let's go. And mind you keep your eyes open."

He was about to ride away when a man in shabby homespun came running up the drive. Painfully thin, his long frame little more than a skeleton with a leathery cover of skin, the newcomer pulled his tattered straw hat from his balding head as he approached my father-in-law. Halting his shambling half-run he stood gasping in front of Abraham's mount.

"Mr. Douglas, sir…" He struggled to get out the words. "I must speak to you. Some of your men came to my farm this morning and ordered me and mine off our land. They said you'd foreclosed on our mortgage. I said you wouldn't do such a thing. You're not such a cruel man as to force me and my family from our home. You must tell them it's a mistake. Mr. Douglas, sir, please! You must—"

"It's no mistake, Jacob," the big man on the gray horse replied coldly. "You failed to hold up your end of our arrangement. In default, your farm becomes mine. You can have a job in my shipyards—I need laborers just now a good deal more than I need farmers. Your family can remain in the house, my house, for a percentage of your wages in rent. Now get out of my way."

Abraham gave the stallion a sharp crack with his quirt and sent him forward at a full gallop. The farmer jumped aside to avoid being trampled. My father-in-law cantered off down the drive, Burt and Harry closing ranks behind him.

"Miserable old bastard! Blood-sucking cur!" the man yelled as the three ranged out of earshot. "Take a man's home, will you? I'll see you burn in hell for this one day!"

****

"Colin, take me with you," I said.

I'd re-entered the house and found my husband in the foyer. He was preparing to leave for his appointed round of duties. After what I'd witnessed in the front yard, I knew I must see my husband at work. I had to know if he were as remorseless and hated as his father.

"Starr, it's going to be hot and dusty at the shipyards." He took my hand, raised it to his lips, and kissed it. "And I'll be walking a great deal. You'd get tired."

"No, I won't, I promise," I begged. "Your father said you were to inspect the keel of his newest vessel. Surely that task won't take much time. Colin, please! I get so lonely here all day without you."

A slight sound on the stairs behind us made us turn. Barret Madison, handsome and virile in well-fitted tan trousers and a white shirt open well down over his powerful chest, stood watching us from halfway down the curving stairwell.

"Would you rather I stayed here with *him*?" I whispered.

My husband's gaze met the captain's slow grin.

"Get your bonnet," he said.

****

"She'll be straight and clean, Mr. Douglas," the shipyard foreman assured Colin as my husband inspected the long, smooth keel and skeletal ribs of a burgeoning hull.

Other workers feigned absorption in their individual tasks, but all, I realized, were watching for Colin's reaction to their product. Some of the glances were interested and friendly, but a few were sly and hostile. As I waited for Colin to finish his perusal of the bow, one rough-looking bystander caught my eye. I suppressed a gasp of dismay. It was Simon.

"Young Douglas got himself a likely-looking wench, even if I hear she were a piece of steerage trash," I heard him mutter to another man as he caught my glance. "She's small at the waist, but with proper hips for gettin' laid and bearin' the results."

Trembling with outrage and fear, I hurried to my husband's side and clutched at his arm. Colin looked down at me in surprise.

"What is it, sweetheart?" he asked. "You look positively ill."

"Please take me home, Colin," I begged.

"Yes, of course," he agreed readily. "You see, I told you this day would be too much for you."

As we were about to leave the shipyard, a young man approached us. Thin and nervous, he wore the ragged, wet clothing of a steam pit worker.

"Mr. Douglas, sir," he addressed Colin, fingering the worn cap he clutched in his hands. "I was wonderin', sir, if I might have a wee advance on me earnin's this month. Me wife is near due, and I'll be needin' cash money to hire a midwife."

"Congratulations." Grinning, Colin extended a hand to him. "Don't worry about money. I'll have my brother Randall tend your wife when her time comes."

"Thank ya, sir. God bless ya, sir. A real doctor! Sure, and Heather will be thinkin' she's a genuine lady, with such treatment. We'll be namin' the child after you if it's a boy. And"—he looked shyly at me—"after your good lady if it's a wee girl." Then he turned and ran back to his job in the steam pit.

Colin grinned down at me. "There goes a happy man."

"And what about you, Mr. Douglas, sir? Does this pretty little thing make you a happy man?"

Turning, I saw Simon and several burly companions sneering at us from only a few feet away.

"Come, Starr." Colin took my arm and started to lead me away.

Seeing the wisdom in his actions, I hurried obediently along beside him. Simon blocked our way.

"I asked you a question, Mr. Douglas," he leered over those awful rotting teeth. "Does this piece of fluff make you happy? Does she warm your bed all well and proper? I'll tell you true, sir, she could visit mine any night of the week, and I'd use her as a beauty like her deserves to be treated by a man."

"Get out of my way," Colin grated over clenched teeth. "Go somewhere and sober up before I'm forced to terminate your employment."

"Ah, now, is that any way to talk to a man who's complimentin' you on your choice of whore?" Simon taunted. He shoved Colin with a dirty, hairy hand. "I understand your father's good Captain Madison broke her seal for you, too. Thoughtful of him, wasn't it? Saved you all the fuss and mess."

"God damn you!" Colin swung at the man, but he ducked, laughing, and rose to sink a hamlike fist deep into Colin's middle.

As my husband doubled up in agony, Simon brought up another fist to hit him squarely on the chin. In swift succession then, as Colin hurtled backward, he caught him twice in the groin with his heavy work boots.

Colin roared in pain and fell on his back, writhing in agony in the dusty wagon road. Simon drew back his boot and kicked him again and again. My husband's cries became pain-maddened bellows. I could stand no more.

"Leave him alone!" I screamed and flung myself at the brute. My fear of the man had melted into red-hot rage. I kicked and clawed like an incensed feline.

My efforts were futile. A huge beast with apish strength, hc threw me from him as easily as I might brush a fly from my sleeve. I was sent sprawling into the dust a few yards from my moaning husband.

"Son of a whore!"

A hand suddenly and seemingly out of nowhere grabbed Simon by the shoulder and spun him about, just as he was about to kick Colin again. In a split second a fist had connected with the brute's jaw and he was sent reeling back against a shed. His head crashed into a corner post. With a grunt of pain, Simon sank to the ground unconscious.

For a moment there was absolute silence. As I struggled to my feet, I saw Barret Madison standing over our assailant, rubbing damaged knuckles.

When he turned on the crowd of gaping workers which had gathered to watch, his expression was fierce.

"Get back to work!" he barked. "And pray to God when I tell Abe about this incident I don't decide to name the names of those of you who watched without so much as raising a finger while his son and daughter-in-law were being beaten!"

The ring of spectators dispersed. The captain, after a swift glance in my direction, turned his attention to Colin. I scrambled to my feet and followed him. My husband lay doubled up in the dust, clutching himself and moaning.

"Colin, oh, luv, oh, God!" I dropped on my knees beside him. His face was ashen, a thin trickle of blood running from a corner of his mouth. He rolled from side to side in agony.

"Starr, go home!" he choked. "Get away from here! Now!"

"Don't worry about her, brother." Kneeling beside us, Barret Madison took a small flask from a pocket of the loose vest he wore.

"It hurts…hurts," Colin moaned, his face contorted in agony.

"I know," Barret said. He screwed open the little bottle and held it to Colin's lips. "Drink this. It will make the walk home easier for you."

Obediently my husband opened his lips and let the captain trickle reddish-brown liquid over them.

"Laudanum," Captain Madison explained when I looked questioningly at him. "A captain often needs it to kill severe pain when one of his crew is badly injured. I was on my way to place it aboard the *Maris Stella* when I heard the commotion."

"Thank God you were nearby," I breathed.

"Colin." Barret put a hand on my husband's shoulder. "I'm going to pick you up now. It will hurt, but I have to take you home."

My husband's only response was a groan.

The captain lifted his semi-conscious body into his arms and, although my husband was nearly as big as he was, began to carry him back toward Peacock House.

Once, during that seemingly endless walk beneath a scorching sun, Colin rolled his head groggily and muttered, "Take me home, Barret, please take me home. I don't want to stay in Vienna any longer."

"Never fear, brother," Barret assured him. "I'll always take you home."

****

It was late afternoon when Barret, Abraham, and Randall finally came downstairs from Colin's room. I heard their muted voices in the hallway and rushed to join them. The hours I'd spent waiting in the drawing room had left my nervous system raw.

"How is he?" I asked.

"Very ill," Randall said, his expression grim.

"Why in God's name did you insist he take you to the shipyards with him?" Abraham barked at me. "Caroline overheard you pressure him into it. Common sense should have told you that was no place for a decent woman. If you hadn't been there, Colin wouldn't have gotten into a fight over insults hurled at you. I want you to arouse him in bed, not to fighting. for God's sake! Getting involved in fisticuffs is not what I meant when I said I wanted him to act like a man."

"I didn't think…" I tried to defend myself.

"Oh, but you do think, my dear," he snapped. "Perhaps too much. Perhaps you're even afraid that if he does act like a man with you, you will become pregnant and lose that slender figure. Perhaps you married my son for his money and hope to keep him too spent from fights and debauchery to give you a child." His tone softened to a smooth, dangerous glide like the slither of a deadly snake's easy approach. "Have you had a monthly cycle since you've been sleeping with Colin? Do you know when you're fertile?"

"Father!" Randall stopped him as tears of outrage filled my eyes. "This isn't a matter to discuss in an open hallway. As for blaming Starr for Colin's accident, all she wanted was to be with her husband. That's hardly a crime, especially when you're hoping for a pregnancy."

"When I want your opinion, I'll ask for it," Abraham roared. "I've given this girl everything she could desire, and now she'll do as I say! That means she'll either produce a grandchild for me or be thrown from this house as ragged and penniless as she entered it." Then he turned on me. "Go to your husband, girl. Wipe the sweat from his face, and hold his head while he vomits. I'm weary of the sight of you."

****

"This is all my fault, Colin," I said, as I knelt beside his bed and took his cold fingers in mine. I was trembling, my head throbbing with a dull, incessant ache. "If I hadn't taunted you into taking me with you… And that awful man—he was the one I told you about, the man who…who attacked me when I worked in the mines."

"Dear God, Starr, are you sure?" Colin started and tried to rise.

"Lie still." I eased him back onto his pillows. "Yes, I'm sure. One does not forget such a creature."

"No, no, I'm sure," he muttered. "Filthy brute! Pig! Did he recognize you, do you think?"

"No, I'm certain he didn't. His eyesight is poor

from years in the mines and…I've changed."

"Yes," he breathed. "Still, we must be careful. I must make certain you are safe and that no tales get to Father that will jeopardize our marriage."

"Colin, don't distress yourself. I can look after myself. As for your father…"

"Starr, you promised not to antagonize him," he rasped over fever-cracked lips. "Please, please obey me in this. You don't know him. He can be dangerous and cruel."

I looked down at my husband and knew I could not deny him this one request. In the sultry, drapery-darkened room, he lay among snow-white sheets and pillows, his legs bent awkwardly. Beneath a single light cover he was naked; the weight of even the finest of bedding upon his injuries caused him severe pain. His face was haggard and drawn. Sweat beaded his forehead and chest.

"Is it very bad?" I asked, my heart aching with concern.

"No." He tried to smile up at me. "In a couple of days we'll be out riding again."

Then the pain struck and he began to toss and moan.

"Dear God!" he moaned, pulling up his legs and rolling to one side. "Oh, dear God!"

"Colin." Barret Madison was suddenly with us and taking my husband in his arms. "Breathe deep. That's it. Try to relax. Think of your music. Imagine you can hear it."

Slowly Colin quieted and fell back among his pillows, sweating and spent.

"Barret, I need…fresh linen," he choked. "Starr,

please leave. I'm not much of a gentleman today."

I arose and walked from the dark, hot room. On the threshold I turned and looked back to see Captain Madison removing the sheets from my husband's battered body.

****

For two days after the incident in the shipyards, Colin lay desperately ill. Randall or Barret was always at his bedside. My husband vomited and moaned; sometimes he was delirious. When he raved incoherently, my heart ached with fear. *Dear God, help him,* I prayed over and over again. *I cannot bear to lose him.*

On the evening of the second day, as I was returning to Colin's bedroom after a late supper in the dining room, I overheard Barret and Colin talking softly in the darkening room. I paused outside the door and listened.

"I know you'd never touch Starr, Barret, but when that barbarian made that remark about…" Colin was speaking.

"About my breaking her seal?" Barret finished when Colin paused. "I overheard. Colin, I'll tell you the God's truth. I gave Starr my cabin for the crossing. She couldn't bear the hold. That was the extent of our relationship. That son of a whore must have learned of the situation and decided to make gossip of it. At any rate, he'll think twice before he kicks a man in the groin again. Your father, in his capacity as magistrate of this valley, put him in jail to await trail for attempted murder when the circuit judge comes through."

"Barret, that man, the one who attacked me," Colin's voice dropped to little above a whisper. "He once attacked Starr…when she was a child in the mines in England. As yet he hasn't recognized her, but I'm afraid he will, and…"

"Sweet Jesus, are you sure?"

"Yes. Barret, please watch over her until I recover. I'm afraid he might try to harm her again. She says he didn't recognize her, but I'm not so sure. I can't enlist Father's help. You understand why."

"Don't worry." Barret's tone was cool and reassuring. "It will be taken care of. You just rest and get well."

****

The following afternoon I went to the Douglas store in the village for oranges, for which Colin had developed a sudden craving. As I was about to leave the building, Abraham summoned me to his office at the rear of the huge mercantile establishment. As I entered, I was surprised to see Jared Fletcher and Barret Madison already there. A business meeting had been in progress, it appeared.

"Sit down, my dear." Abraham indicated a chair and returned to his seat behind his massive oak desk. As I took the proffered place, Jared and Barret, who had arisen at my entrance, resumed their seats.

"We were discussing Colin's beating." Abraham reached into a humidor on his desk and drew out a long, slender cigar. "I would like you to explain again how it came about."

"Why?" I asked, hesitating as I watched him snip an end off the rolled tobacco, then use a small lamp burning on his desk to light it. Something was afoot here, something that gave me an unpleasant feeling in the pit of my stomach. "I've already told you all I witnessed. Captain Madison was present for a good deal of it. He can give you details."

"I want Captain Fletcher to have a first-hand account of how it began." He leaned back in his chair and blew smoke. "I also want to make certain you omitted no details in your first, highly emotional account. Now, please. I'm sure you don't want to be kept from your husband any longer than necessary."

"Very well," I said haughtily, catching the nuance of a demeaning threat in my father-in-law's softening tone.

I finished my story a few minutes later with the understatement, "And then the sailor began to kick my husband."

"The brute disabled Colin and then tried to cripple him with kicks to his privates," Barret said impatiently. "It's as simple as that. I've seen a good many fist fights in my life, but this was the first I've witnessed that was purposely designed to sexually incapacitate a man."

"But why?" Abraham faced the captain. "I know I have enemies, but they're mine, not the lad's. Why would anyone try to disable Colin in that despicable way?"

"Someone who knows how much a grandchild means to you; someone who wants your dream of a dynasty destroyed."

"But this Simon fellow? He's merely a sailor, a sea tramp. He only recently came to this valley aboard the *Linnet*, as a replacement for one of Jared's men who contracted yellow fever in Haiti. He has no reason…"

"He was simply the instrument used." Barret arose and went to lean against the mantel of a massive fireplace against the back wall. "Someone paid him to do their dirty work."

"Barret's probably right." Jared Fletcher spoke for the first time since my arrival. "The man is scum. I wouldn't have hired him if I hadn't been in desperate need of a hand. He's lazy, drunken, and foul-mouthed. As soon as I docked in the village I discharged him."

"I must know who is behind this infamy!" Abraham banged a fist on his paper-covered desk. "Barret, you and Jared pay a visit to this fellow Simon in jail. Convince the guard to take a little fresh air while you *talk* to his prisoner. I want the name of the despicable cur who would disable my son and destroy my hopes of a grandchild."

"Of course." Jared Fletcher stood. "We'll wring a name from the scum tonight, Mr. Douglas, never fear."

He nodded to me and left. Barret straightened up and rubbed a fist into the palm of his other hand. The gesture was crude and suggestive of the brutality Abraham had authorized. Violence was breeding more violence.

"Mr. Douglas, isn't there some other way?" I got to my feet. "Having two of your employees beat another man hardly seems…"

"Go home, Starr." Abraham's words were an order. "Go home and care for my son. Leave justice to me."

Recognizing the futility of protesting further, I started toward the door, but my father-in-law stopped me with another command.

"You'll not travel about alone any longer," he said. "Barret, I appoint you my daughter-in-law's bodyguard while Colin is ill. I'll not have my hopes of a family further impaired."

"Mr. Douglas…" I tried to protest, but he hushed

me with a decisive flourish of his hand. "The matter is settled. Take her back to the house, Captain Madison."

He clamped his cigar between his teeth and turned his attention to paperwork on his desk.

The walk back to Peacock House was silent, the captain seeming no more delighted with the prospect of being my guardian than I was.

****

Simon had disappeared from the jail. I overheard two of the maids discussing the incident when I passed them on my way to breakfast the next morning. Someone had broken him out of his cell, they whispered. Perhaps, they speculated in even softer whispers, someone had disposed of him for harming Mr. Colin. It would save Mr. Abe the trouble of having to bind him over for trial when the circuit judge arrived. As the valley's magistrate and the victim's father, he would have been in an awkward position, they speculated. When they became aware of my presence, they scuttled away.

With a churning stomach. I continued on into the deserted dining room and, with trembling hands, poured a cup of strong, black coffee. The scene in Abraham's office the previous afternoon flashed like lightning bolts across my mind. "We'll wring a name from the scum tonight," Jared Fletcher's voice echoed across my reeling thoughts.

"I see there's another tardy riser in this house."

In the quiet room, his voice startled me. Coffee splashed down the front of my blue linen gown as I whirled to face Barret Madison. Perfectly groomed and dressed in tan coat and breeches, cream-colored vest, and spotless white shirt and cravat, Barret Madison was the image of a refined gentleman. His appearance infuriated me. He might at least have had the good grace, like Simon, to look the brute he really was.

"You killed him!" I cried. "You and Jared Fletcher took the law upon yourselves and murdered him. I overheard Colin telling you who Simon was and asking you to take care of me."

He strode past me and poured coffee as I scrubbed at the front of my gown with a napkin. Cup in hand, he went to stand by a window and look out into the fruit orchard beyond.

"Jared and I didn't kill him," he said. "He was gone when we arrived at the jail. The jailer will confirm my story. When Jared and I entered the lock-up, he'd just discovered Simon missing. The person or persons who released him did so while the guard was outside watching a ship navigating the river at low water."

"I don't believe you," I snapped, flinging the napkin aside, overwhelmed with anger and loathing. "I hate Colin's father's ambition! I hate your ruthlessness! I hate…"

"This house, the gowns, the food, that fancy mare in the stable, the leisure to do as you please?" He looked over at me, a sneer curling one corner of his mouth. "No, I thought not. Well, my lady, all this elegance has a price. Sometimes that cost is high and cruel in human terms. You must either learn to accept that fact or get out."

Chagrined to the point of being unable to respond, I whirled and left the room, my stained gown rustling over the thick carpets. I felt unclean and mercenary, soiled by the truth I had found in the captain's words.

****

That afternoon, news arrived at the mansion that horrified me more than the possibility that Jared Fletcher and Barret Madison might have murdered Simon. Marie had died, as the result of a miscarriage, at her father's house downriver.

The emotional scene I'd witnessed between Barret Madison and the young French woman took on poignant new meaning. They had been arguing about *her* condition, *their* predicament. That poor, innocent girl who had become my trusted friend had died losing Barret Madison's bastard.

Incensed to the point of irrational action, I pulled on the boy's clothing I had bought as my fishing outfit and rushed out to the stables. With shaking hands I put a bridle on Lady and led her from the barn.

"Where do you think you're going?" As I stood on the mounting block about to straddle the bare back of my mare, Captain Madison's voice made me whirl.

"Away!" I cried. "Away from you, you remorseless brute!" I scrambled onto the startled palomino and slapped her to a fast trot as I headed out of the yard.

"Starr, wait! You can't go alone!" he yelled, but I nudged Lady into a canter in an effort to get beyond the sound of his voice.

Nearing a favorite fishing spot of Colin's and mine, tears streaming down my face, I heard hooves pounding up behind me. I turned to see Lucifer and his master charging after me. Angered at the captain's temerity, I kicked my mount to a run.

I rode madly, wildly, the pain in my heart driving me. The thunder of Lady's hooves drowned all other sound from my ears. In an instant I was swept from my mount and onto the bare back of Lucifer, his master's powerful arm about my waist.

As soon as he was able, Captain Madison reined to a halt and let me slide to the ground. Lady went pounding off on her own.

"Have you no common sense, riding bareback at that speed with as little experience as you've had with horses?" He turned on me, his face contorted with anger. "You could have been killed!" The elegant outfit he'd appeared in at breakfast and which he still wore was coated with dust and horse sweat. I was glad he'd ruined his finery. He deserved much worse. I swung at him with my flattened hand. It connected with his clean-shaven jaw.

Before I realized what was happening, I was seized by the wrist and my arm twisted behind me. I was forced to turn against him, my back held against his flat, hard belly and powerful chest.

"That's no way to treat your hero," he breathed against my ear.

"Hero?" I cried, tears of chagrin and rage coursing down my cheeks. "Whore master, you mean. You don't care that Marie and your baby are dead! You don't care that you made her pregnant and—"

"Stop it!" He spun me to face him, his eyes bright with anger. "I didn't father Marie's child. She was my friend, nothing more." He released me, and his hands fell to his sides. "She was a good girl," he muttered. "She didn't deserve to die."

"You weren't her lover?"

"No, but it would have been better if I had. I would have taken care of her."

The emotional stress of my wild ride and the following confrontation hit me in a rush. I staggered.

He caught me in his arms and eased me down to sit on the grass with him.

"I thought…I thought…"

"I'm sorry," he said, with a tenderness surprising in the face of my accusation. "I understand how you might have come to such a conclusion. My reputation isn't good when it comes to women. But let me tell you, it's also exaggerated."

"But you must know who the father of her baby is," I said.

"No," he said. "I don't. She simply told me she was in trouble, the kind of trouble that can only come from a man."

"He must be made to pay."

"He will, rest assured," he said. "Just as soon as I find out who *he* is."

He stood and pulled me to my feet to stand beside him. "I was on my way to pay my respects to Marie's family when I saw you at the stables," he said. "I think you should come with me. That is, if you truly were her friend." There was a definite challenge in his last sentence.

"Dressed as we are, as I am?" I looked down at my fishing outfit.

"Marie's family are poor people, Acadian fisherfolk. To go there attired like a pair of London dandies would be the greatest faux pas of all. Now will you come, or was your concern for her only lip service?"

"Of course not. Marie was my friend. Certainly I'll come."

"Good." He pulled off his filthy coat, vest, and cravat, opened the top buttons of his shirt, and whistled for Lucifer. When the great black horse trotted up to him, he threw the clothing he had removed over the animal's back. "They're only fit for saddle cloths now," he said. "Later, we'll both need a good bath." I turned away and pretended to ignore any suggestive implication in his remark.

Gripping the animal's mane, he vaulted onto the stallion's back. Then he held down a hand to me.

"Get up behind me," he said. "Dressed as you are, you don't need to be held in front of me. At any rate, I'm taking you to the LeBlancs' as Starr, my friend, not as Mrs. Colin Douglas. Abe's people are not considered *amis* among the fishermen and their families. And it's reputed that Barret Madison's women don't ride like ladies."

I grasped his proffered hand and scrambled up behind him.

"Hold on," he said, and nudged the big horse to a canter.

As the horse forged ahead, I had to clasp the captain's waist to retain my seat. I should have been outraged, but once again I became overpowered by those intense feelings that close encounters with the man always brought rushing over me. Our thighs were pressed together, moving hard and fast in harmony with the horse's gait.

I tried to fight down the sensations coursing through me, but my hands were splayed out over his chest, enjoying the ripples of his muscles, the solidness of his ribcage. I wanted this man. I needed him.

Fortunately we did not have far to go. Shortly, the rutted wagon road we were following emerged into a clearing on the edge of the river. The captain slowed the horse to a trot, while I fought my racing desires back under control.

The small settlement into which we'd arrived consisted of weathered shacks and cabins scattered along the waterfront. Nets, traps, and small boats along the shore marked this as a fishing community. Beside the shabby houses, ragged vegetable patches struggled to grow. Ill-clothed, barefoot children paused to stare at us as Barret walked the horse among them.

The wretchedness of the place brought back memories of my life in the mines and the sudden realization that these were the people who provided my father-in-law with the fish he packed and shipped abroad for handsome profits. Did Abraham Douglas and Sir Harry Blackwell have more in common than I wanted to recognize? Were he and his family, which included myself, living in luxury at the expense of these fishermen and their families just as Sir Harry and his family enjoyed the income provided by the coal harvested by enslaved children? The thought sickened me.

At the last ramshackle structure, which had, like all the others, a stovepipe chimney and badly weathered shingles, Barret Madison halted the stallion.

"Get down," he said.

Beneath my hands, he expelled a breath. Had he also been affected by our sensuous ride? Perhaps the experienced Captain Barret Madison had gotten more than he'd bargained for, I suggested to myself, and found bitter comfort in the idea.

I swung my leg over Lucifer's rump and slid down the horse's side. The captain dismounted as well, his clothing we'd used as a saddle falling into the dirt. As he bent to retrieve the garments, one of the children who had been staring at us broke ranks and ran to him. Babbling in French, tears streaming down his little sun-browned cheeks, the child flung himself at the captain. Barret knelt to take him up into his arms. The little boy buried his face against Barret's neck as he babbled and sobbed. Somewhere in his tirade I caught Marie's name.

Stroking the child's unruly curls and speaking softly in French, Barret soothed the child. Then, wiping the small, dirty face with his handkerchief, he picked him up in one arm and stood.

"This is Claude," he said, turning the child to face me. "Claude is Marie's brother."

"Hello, Claude," I smiled at the little boy, but he cringed back against Barret.

"He's not accustomed to English," Barret explained. "Marie was the eldest of a family of fourteen children. These people are French Acadians and adhere to their Catholic faith, which denounces all forms of contraception and emphasizes the sanctity of a large family. Marie worked for Abe to help repay the large deficit her father had run up at the store over the years buying fishing gear and family necessities."

"But Randall told me his father makes a handsome profit from the fish these people catch and his Irish workers process in his shed. Surely he must pay these people a fair return for their catch, surely—"

"Surely he does not," Barret retorted. "Look around. Abraham Douglas has made veritable bondsmen of these people. He pays them next to nothing for their catch, gives them credit at his store instead of money, and forces them into debt to him by charging exorbitant prices for the necessities of their trade, which are available in this valley only at his mercantile. Add to these conditions the large families, no schools to improve their education, and you have a desperate cycle of grinding poverty."

The door of the shack opened and a bent man with a weather-darkened face and thinning gray hair came out, his gaunt body clad in a threadbare white shirt and dark trousers. When he saw Barret, he paused a moment. Tears trickled down his leathery face. He limped toward my companion, a gnarled hand extended.

Barret put the child down to seize it. The older man lost control and embraced the captain, sobbing.

When he regained control of himself, he moved out of Barret's embrace and squinted at me. Barret spoke softly to him in French. When the captain had finished speaking, the man extended his hand to me, struggling to force a smile over trembling lips.

"Starr, this is Michel LeBlanc, Marie's father," Barret said.

As I accepted the older man's greeting, I was amazed at the strength in his grip. Thin and gaunt though he might appear, Marie's father was a man as rugged as his weathered skin suggested.

He spoke to me in French, then limped back toward the house.

"He wants us to go inside and speak to his wife," Barret said. "He wants us both to say goodbye to Marie. I've told him you were her friend also."

I nodded and accompanied the two men into the cottage. What I saw inside brought a host of unpleasant memories gushing back. The place reminded me of the mining children's home, except that this shelter was clean and as well maintained as lack of money would allow.

The walls were of rough planks; small, bare windows allowed insufficient light to dispel the gloom of the overcast day. The floors were of earth, pounded hard by years of use. In one corner, a huge iron cooking stove gave off an overpowering heat into the already muggy afternoon. An enormous pot of what smelled like fish chowder bubbled on its top.

The only other furnishings were a big plank table and several rough benches. Shelves along one wall held a collection of pots and crockery. Nevertheless the little house was clean and neat.

A half dozen people sat silently around the room, faces sweat-streaked in the heat, eyes dull with sorrow. They, like Marie's father, bore the gauntness and raggedness that branded them his confreres.

Barret went to a pale, obese woman seated near the stove and dropped on one knee before her. He took her work-raw hands in his and spoke softly. Tears filled her eyes at his words, and she lowered her head. Barret leaned forward and kissed the damp, bloated cheek. Then he arose and, speaking again, indicated me.

The woman looked up at me and put a hand self-consciously to her graying hair in an attempt to force a stray length into the bun at the back of her head. Her brown eyes were large and beautiful. Most likely she was Marie's mother. In her youth, before poor food, too many children, and hard work had ravished her, she must have been quite lovely.

Suddenly I saw myself in the self-conscious, worn-out woman. But for Darcy and a rich, young husband, I might already be on the road to such a fate.

Impulsively I went to her, knelt as Barret had, and took her hands in mine. "Tell her I'm sorry, so very sorry to hear of her loss, Barret," I begged, looking up at her. "Tell her I was Marie's friend, and that I shall miss her deeply."

****

At the insistence of Marie's parents, we ate a little of the fish stew, went into the other room to view the pine box that contained Marie's remains, said a prayer for her immortal soul, and left.

"Those people are remarkable," I said as we returned to Lucifer, waiting in the dooryard. "In spite of their pain and loss, they welcomed us and extended the best of their hospitality."

"Yes. They accepted me when I first came to this valley as a ragged teenager." Barret surprised me with his answer. "I lived with them between voyages until I became a captain and could afford lodgings at the tavern. I took up space they needed, but they adamantly denied it. When I had a bit of money, I tried to repay their kindness." He paused beside the stallion and stood looking pensively back at the shanty. "Michel refused. He's a proud man. All I could do for the family was get Marie a job as lady's maid at Peacock House. And look what that led to. I wouldn't blame her family if they turned against me. But as you see, true to form, they have only warmth and love in their hearts. Sweet Jesus, how I'd like to get my hands about the throat of the man who killed that girl as surely as if he'd strangled her!" He slammed a fist into the open palm of his other hand, his face tensing with rage.

Then, cupping his hands to form a stirrup, he held

them down beside the horse. "Put your foot in my hand. I'll hoist you aboard. You'll ride back to Peacock House, and I'll walk. I don't think our being together on Lucifer again would be wise. He could very well carry us both into damnation."

I paused, wanting to be able to refute his words, to tell him I could ride to Hades and back with him on the stallion and it would mean nothing to me. But the words stuck in my throat.

I put my booted foot into his waiting hands, caught a handful of mane in my fingers, and vaulted upward as he lifted me.

Chapter Nine

For the next three weeks, I spent most of my time within the walls of Peacock House. Colin recovered steadily, but he needed care, and I was determined to be the person who administered it. He had become my dearest and most trusted friend.

On the day Colin planned to return to work, the *Winsome Witch*, the vessel whose construction he'd been overseeing when he was injured, was scheduled for launching. Abraham, proud of this fine, new vessel, declared it to be a worthy sister for the graceful *Linnet* and the beautiful *Maris Stella*. To mark the occasion, he decreed there would be a gala launching celebration in the afternoon. The entire family was expected to attend. Declaring the heat had given her a nasty headache, Caroline begged off.

When the carriage carrying Gram and myself arrived at the slip, I saw long tables laden with food and drink laid out in preparation for the festivities. The laughter and eager anticipation on the faces of the workers and their families told me this largesse was intended for their enjoyment once the *Winsome Witch* was safely in the water.

Abraham made a speech with Colin alone by his side. Randall was again in the provincial capital, with Barret Madison accompanying him. The captain had gone to learn the specifics of his January voyage to

London. Jared Fletcher, it appeared, had not been asked to stand in for his commodore. In fact, he didn't appear to be present at the gathering.

"A beautiful ship deserves to be anointed by a beautiful woman," Abraham finished his speech, beaming good-naturedly down upon the crowd from a platform erected at the ship's bow. "I therefore call upon my daughter-in-law to christen her the *Winsome Witch*."

As I was helped from the carriage and led to join my husband and his father, shouts and cheers went up from the crowd. When I passed among the people, I glimpsed hard, bitter hatred in many of the eyes above the smiling mouths. These people were as adept at role playing as Abraham Douglas. Today he might slap shoulders and banter with them, but they weren't deceived. Tomorrow he might as easily seize their homes or dismiss them from his service.

Later, Gram and I sat beneath a spreading maple to one side of the shipyard and watched the festivities. The *Winsome Witch* floated majestically in the calm river water, a hot, late summer sun beating down on her freshly painted decks. With fiddle playing and dancing and much eating and drinking, the party in her honor had been continuing for over two hours.

Eating our favorite foods as we watched the festivities, Gram and I were enjoying ourselves. Colin, acting as host with his father, was too busy to join us. The thought that he might overdo, in his weakened physical condition, cast the only shadow in an otherwise happy afternoon.

Ben Smith, the congenial manager of Abraham's mercantile, joined Gram and me. Smartly dressed in a white shirt and a vest, his cravat and trousers of a summer shade of cream, he wore a straw hat on his white hair and carried a frock coat over his arm. As he sat down by Gram, he mopped his perspiring face with a snowy handkerchief.

"Dickens of a hot day, Ida." I was surprised to hear him address her familiarly. "Too hot for an old man like me. Mrs. Douglas…" He turned to me. "You're looking pretty as a picture."

"Thank you," I replied.

I liked Ben Smith, and as I glanced over at him, I realized he must have been a handsome, powerfully built man in his youth. Tall and barrel-chested, he still cut a fine figure.

"Who's old?" Gram demanded. "You and I are of an age together, Benjamin Smith, as you well know, and I certainly don't consider myself old."

"Sorry, my dear." Ben took her hand and, to my amused delight, raised it gallantly to his lips. "I'd never think such a thing of one as lovely as yourself."

"Did you ever hear such stuff and nonsense, Starr?" Gram turned to me, but I saw she was basking in his attention. "Never trust an Irishman, my girl. They've all kissed the Blarney Stone. "But," she continued more gently, "this one is special. Did you know he founded this town over forty years ago?"

"I thought Abraham had." I was astonished.

"That's a natural assumption," Gram grunted. "My son does appear to be the beginning and end of everything in this valley. No, my dear, Abraham didn't settle here first. Nor did he establish a trading post for the Indians and the French Acadian refugees. It was this gentleman who first tied his trading ship to a huge tree overhanging a deep pool in the river; it was this gentleman who christened this village Pine in honor of the mighty and tenacious old tree that first held him fast to this place; and it was this gentleman who built the first store and sponsored the first English settlers. Starr, before you sits the true father of this village. And if it weren't for my son's ruthlessness and money-grubbing ways, Ben Smith would be magistrate and chief entrepreneur here yet."

"Ida, Ida…" Ben Smith tried to hush her, but she would not be stilled.

"My son came here after his father's death. With the money my Josh had made privateering during the war of 1812, Abe proceeded to buy up everything he could. He even persuaded the governor to take the post of magistrate from Ben and give it to him. Then, with the power of the law behind him and money in his pocket, he proceeded to gobble up everything in his path."

"Ida, please!" Ben tried to stop her.

"Hush, Ben. The girl has a right to know what she's married into." The old lady waved aside his protests and continued, "Finally he controlled almost everything in the valley, from shipbuilding to lumbering to the fisheries. Almost everything, that is, save Ben's fine mercantile. As luck would have it, Ben's wife fell ill about that time. Ben wanted her to have the best care, so he shipped her off to England. On a doctor's advice, he later sent her to an expensive clinic in Switzerland, where she lingered for months before she passed away. By that time Ben had been forced to borrow heavily from Abe. When Julia died, my son foreclosed on Ben's store. Thus, he had it all."

"Ida, enough!" This time Bed was adamant. "Abe is the child's father-in-law. I won't allow you to further defame him before her."

"I'm only speaking the truth, and you know it, Benjamin Smith!" Ida Douglas's dark eyes snapped fire. "She must know what manner of man may someday be grandfather to her children."

Then her tone moderated, her voice becoming old and weary. "Fetch me a cup of that punch, will you, Ben, my dear? And slip into it a dram of that rum Abe pretends he doesn't know Burt and Harry are spreading about."

"Ida, you're a wicked woman." Ben laughed as he rose with difficulty. "There's no one quite like you. I'll be right back."

I was silent after he'd gone, reflecting on what I'd learned. Was Ben Smith another enemy? Surely, if all Gram had just told me was true, he had good reason to hate my father-in-law.

"Starr," Gram interrupted my musings, "Would you be a good girl and do a small errand for me? I have a sharp bit of indigestion. At home, on my bureau, you'll find a flask of a remedy an Indian once gave me for such a malady. Fetch it for me, will you?"

"Of course, Gram." I scrambled to my feet. "Are you sure that's all I can do for you? Would you like me to send the carriage to fetch you?"

"Of course not!" Gram dismissed me with a flutter of a wrinkled hand. "I'm enjoying myself. And I've learned, over years of living in this country, if an Indian remedy can't help, nothing can. Now run along, that's a good girl."

Obediently I started off. She and Ben Smith wanted

a little time alone together, I was sure. I smiled to myself.

****

Anxious to return to the festivities, I hurried to the house and on soft-soled slippers dashed up the foot-hushing carpeted stairs and down the hallway to the room which, in my haste, I thought was Gram's.

I pushed open the door. And froze. Jared Fletcher, stark naked, lay stretched out on the bed. The woman kneeling beside him in a diaphanous silver-gray robe, her shining black hair forming a waist-length halo about her white shoulders, was Caroline Douglas. I had mistakenly entered her room, not Gram's.

In the shade-darkened room the man lay clutching the spools at the top of the bed while Colin's sister-in-law massaged a light, glistening oil over his chest with slender, long-nailed fingers. A pungent aroma of incense rose from a delicate, thinly smoking silver disc on the dressing table. Its heady fragrance made me giddy. I was dreaming. This couldn't be reality.

The shaft of light I'd let in startled the couple. Caroline whirled toward me, her gauzy wrapper spreading out about her like a spider's web. Eyes blazing, she leaped to her feet to confront me. Jared sat up, drawing a corner of the sheet about his hips.

"Why, you interfering piece of baggage!" my sister-in-law hissed. "Prying, filthy, gutter trash!"

With a snarl of rage, she flew at me. I dodged and managed to escape from the room before she could reach me.

Heart pounding, I raced down the stairs and was about to rush out of the house when I tripped on a scatter rug and fell headlong on the polished foyer floor. I tried to scramble to my feet, but I discovered I'd turned my ankle.

I heard someone rushing down the stairs behind me and turned to see Jared Fletcher, wearing only breeches, descending.

"Starr, it's all right. No one's going to hurt you." He dropped on one knee beside me and placed a hand on my arm.

He helped me to my feet and supported me as I hobbled beside him into the parlor, where he seated us both on the settee.

"I'm sorry you had to witness what you just did," he said, looking into my eyes. "In spite of the fact you're a married woman, you're little more than a child. It will be difficult to explain. You're not old enough to understand the desperation of impossible love."

"Are you saying you *love* Caroline?" I rubbed my throbbing ankle.

"Yes." He wet his lips and lowered his gaze to his bare feet. "Randall and Caroline aren't in love. They married under pressure from both their fathers, who'd struck a deal. Abe would bail Caroline's father, Lord Newton, out from under his gambling debts in exchange for Caroline marrying his son and producing an heir."

"That's no excuse—"

He cut me off. "Do you think Caroline's alone in seeking ways to assuage her unhappiness?" His tone and expression hardened. "Her husband turned to alcohol and other women early in their marriage in an attempt to ease his misery. Caroline remained faithful and suffered for years, until she and I met. Starr, I'm asking you to try to understand, not forgive or accept."

He looked at me with beseeching eyes. When I didn't reply, he arose and went to stare out the window. None of the appeal of his earthy virility escaped me in those moments. Reluctantly, I had to admit I could somewhat appreciate what Caroline's feelings might be for the handsome master mariner, as an image of Barret Madison flooded my thoughts.

"Perhaps I was in error when I said you wouldn't understand," he said, after a static hiatus punctuated only by the ticking of a clock on the mantel. "After all, you, like Caroline, have found solace in the company of one of your father-in-law's captains."

"Don't be absurd!" I cried, but the accusation had made my heart pound and sweat break out over my body. Had he read my mind?

"Don't try to feign innocence," he said, turning to me, his brown eyes narrowing. "People gossip, and while they might fear to suggest to Abraham Douglas that his daughter-in-law has taken his commodore as a lover, they don't hesitate to tell the man who's second in command of the Douglas fleet."

"And that's all it is…gossip!" I snapped.

"Oh, I think not." His tone became smoothly menacing. "I've seen the way Barret looks at you, the way you preen whenever he's about. You understand the feelings Caroline and I have for each other and appreciate the need for none of us to speak out of turn." He walked slowly toward the door. "Now, I'm going upstairs to finish dressing and then to the launching party. I have to put in an appearance in spite of the fact that Abraham chose not to include me in the ceremonies. Rest your ankle. It will feel better shortly.

And while you're resting, consider all I've said and do as wisdom dictates. I wouldn't want to be forced to tell Colin his beautiful little bride is his best friend's lover."

He bowed in my direction, then straightened and went out, letting the door slam behind him. The pain in my soul was much worse than the ache in my ankle. I must keep Caroline's duplicity from my brotherly friend Randall or risk losing the husband I had come to love with a deep and lasting affection.

****

Feeling heartsick, I hobbled back to the party with Gram's indigestion medicine. It had taken courage for me to go back upstairs, pass Caroline's closed door, and proceed to Ida Douglas's room for the small bottle, but I had. Returning without it would have aroused questions I couldn't answer. When I resumed my place beside her on the grass and handed her the flask, she looked at me sharply.

"What is it, child? What's happened? You're white as a sheet."

"I twisted my ankle. It's aching a bit."

Gram's keen, dark eyes told me she wasn't satisfied with my explanation. When she returned her attention to Ben Smith, I breathed a sigh of relief. At least for the present she wasn't going to question me further.

I was spreading my gown out about me when a splash of something ice cold hit my bare shoulders and trickled down my back. Whirling and coming to my feet, I faced my smirking sister-in-law, an empty punch glass in her hand.

"You witch!"

I sprang at her, taking her to the ground with me as

I'd once attacked Sarah in the mining hostelry. In a split second, we were rolling about on the grass, kicking, clawing, and slapping as Caroline shrieked for help.

Then I was being dragged to my feet as a pair of big hands seized my shoulders.

"What in God's name do you think you're doing!" Abraham Douglas's face was crimson with outrage as he held me before him. "How dare you humiliate my family before the entire village!"

"She attacked me, Father!" Caroline sobbed as Jared Fletcher helped her to her feet. "For no reason!"

"She threw punch over me!" I yelled, wrenching against my father-in-law's grip as Colin came running up to us.

"What happened? Starr, what have you done?"

"Your wife has taken to beating her sister-in-law at fisticuffs." Abraham shoved me from him, into Colin's arms.

My hair hung about my face, my beautiful gown was grass-stained and ripped, but to my satisfaction Caroline looked worse.

"No!" Colin's tone mirrored his distress.

"Yes." Abraham came to stand in front of us. "And she'll be fittingly dealt with, never fear. There'll be no repeat of this villainy, you can rest assured. Take her home, boy. I'll not have her shaming me a moment longer."

****

I learned my sentence later that afternoon. When Abraham returned from the festivities, he demanded Colin and I come to his office. As we stood before his massive desk, the scratches from Caroline's fingernails still smarting on my cheek, Abraham Douglas decreed that I was to be sent to a finishing school in Halifax for the winter.

"I'll not have a repeat of today's infamy," he snapped when Colin tried to protest. "Much as I want a grandchild, I don't fancy his having a socially unacceptable wildcat for a mother. Mrs. Lambert's Academy for Young Ladies will put an end to such a possibility. Now get out of my sight, both of you. I can no more tolerate the sight of an ungrateful guttersnipe than I can stand to look at a man who is incapable of controlling his wife."

****

Three weeks later, it was time for me to go to Halifax and take up winter residence at the academy, the colonial equivalent of a finishing school for young ladies. By spring, Abraham declared, I would have acquired all the social graces necessary to be a proper wife to Colin.

In March he would send Colin to Halifax on one of his ships bound for the Caribbean. I would join my husband aboard and sail with him to one of the French islands, where Abraham maintained a house. There we would honeymoon. He had our lives neatly planned, I realized, as I helped Rose pack my new winter wardrobe in chests. Colin and I were powerless against him.

Then I heard my husband at the keyboard. I gave the maid instructions for finishing our task and, clutching my skirts, ran to be with him. Since Abraham had informed us of my leave-taking, every second I could spend in Colin's company had become precious.

Enchanted as always by the spectacle of my handsome young husband enthralled in creating his unique brand of magic, I paused on the threshold of the drawing room to listen. That afternoon, the French doors were thrown open to catch the last warmth of a beautiful autumn day, the room dappled with the shadows of the yellow, orange, and red leaves of maples and birches beyond the verandah.

Colin had been working in the shipyards earlier in the day and still wore the crimson homespun shirt, rust-colored riding breeches, and dusty knee-high boots he'd donned for the task. With the rays of the declining sun in his blond curls, he looked startlingly familiar… Darcy as a shipyard laborer must have looked much as my husband did at that moment. A lump formed in my throat.

As I moved to stand beside the piano, he paused in his recital, looked up at me, and smiled.

"You're beautiful," he said. "Cream-colored lace must have been invented with you in mind." He took my hand, brushed aside the thick Italian trim that decorated the wrist of my golden-brown gown, and kissed my fingers.

"Sweetheart, what is it?" he asked, concerned, when he looked up at me again. "You look pensive and decidedly sad."

"I was thinking how very much you look like Darcy," I couldn't disguise the catch in my voice.

"Ah, sweet little wife," he breathed. "You yourself said we mustn't think of him with sadness."

"With sadness, no. But it's wrong to try to spare ourselves pain by pretending he never existed. I want to know about his life here in America. I want to know about your friendship with him."

Colin paused, then released my hand with a heavy

sigh.

"Very well," he said. "Perhaps the best way I can do that is to play one of our favorite songs for you. We composed it together. I'm not a fine singer, but I'll do my best with Darcy's words."

He put his fingers to the keys and began to play. The melody was hauntingly beautiful, the words tenderly plaintive. Deeply moved, I went to stand behind him and put my arms gently about his shoulders.

As the piece reached the magnificent climax in its tale of forbidden love, the words caught at me with a whiplash of ambiguous meaning:

"And my soul, afraid of dying,
Fears to face eternity."

Those were not the words of a man contemplating suicide. As the song ended, confused and frightened at the possibilities the lyrics had raised in my mind, I put my tear-streaked cheek against Colin's soft curls, my fingers tightening on his shoulders.

Colin took my hand and held it against his cheek. Frozen in our grief, we failed to notice the man who entered. Only when his shadow cast its darkness in the dappled sunlight did we become aware of his presence.

Turning to face Captain Madison, I was as nonplused by his expression as by the words of the song. His jaw flexed with a nervous tick and his gray eyes were strangely bright.

In the autumn hush, the static hiatus that followed seemed to stretch into infinity. Finally the captain broke the spell and moved toward us again, slowly. Colin got to his feet and put his arm about my waist.

"Was that a song you and Darcy Pod composed together?" the captain astonished us by inquiring when he stopped beside the piano.

His fingers tightening about my waist, Colin nodded. “Barret, don’t hit me,” he said, his voice shaking. “Not in front of Starr.”

“Hit you?”

“Like you did in Vienna when…”

“I’ve had opportunity to reflect since that night, and since my unwarranted behavior in the meadow that day I found you and your wife…together. Believe me when I say I’m trying to understand.”

He turned and walked away.

“Colin…” I began.

“Don’t ask, Starr. Please don’t ask.” His face crumpling into an agony of emotion, my husband hurried out of the room.

Barret Madison had once again proven to be an enigma. That same evening he further puzzled me when I overheard a confusingly intimate conversation between himself and Gram.

Sitting alone in the deepening twilight on the side verandah swing, I heard them come out of the front entrance and take chairs around the corner from where I was waiting for Colin. Unaware of my presence, they began to talk with a familiarity I had never known them to exhibit in the presence of others.

“You’re sailing with the morning tide, my boy.” Gram’s words reflected an intimate fondness. “Behave yourself and don’t take any mad risks to please Abraham. Remember, I hold your life especially dear.”

“Yes, Gram.” His form of address astonished me. “You know I always heed your words.”

“Huh!” The old lady grunted in pretended disgust. “You heed about as well as my dear departed Joshua did. He obeyed only his conscience."

"Your husband was a remarkable man," Barret said. "I should have enjoyed knowing him."

"I wish you had," she sighed. "Now go and prepare for your voyage. You need rest more than the company of a fractious, senile old woman."

"Fractious? Senile?" Barret chuckled. "You're as stable as Gibraltar and as shrewd as a fox. You'll never be fractious or senile, my love."

"Come, come, enough of this sentimental drivel," she replied, a sudden catch in her voice. "Kiss me good night and get to your bed. I don't want to hear of your being lost at sea because you weren't properly rested."

"Yes, Gram. Good night."

A moment later I heard the door open and close.

"God speed," I heard Gram murmur, "and bless you, my special boy."

****

I had not thought to inquire the name of the ship on which I would be travelling and was therefore appalled when we reached dockside the following morning to see the *Maris Stella* tied up at the pier, taking on supplies for immediate departure. When I'd overheard Gram and Barret discussing his sailing in the morning, I should have foreseen that Captain Madison's ship would be my means of transport.

As we alighted from the carriage, the master himself appeared out of the crowd of men busily engaged in loading his vessel.

"A fine day to start a voyage, Barret," Abraham said with alacrity. "A good stiff breeze and clear skies. I wish I were accompanying you. There's nothing to equal the feel of the wind at your back and the taste of salt spray on your lips. I believe it would make me feel young again. And to see those exotic Caribbean islands once more would be to glimpse heaven. When I was a young mariner, I believed them to be as close to paradise as it is possible to get on this earth."

"You're not an old man, Abe," Barret said. "You'll sail again."

"Perhaps." Abraham's reply was a heaved sigh. "But for the present, I'm tied to a desk in an effort to build a future for my family. Once I've got my business secured and my grandsons toddling about Peacock House, then I'll be free to go adventuring once more."

His expression changed then, from one of nostalgic longing to one of good humor. "Enough wishful thinking." He clapped his hands to bring order to the situation. "Colin, your wife's trunks are aboard, and the *Maris Stella* is about to cast off. Bid her farewell and let her and Barret be on their way."

I looked up at my husband, the immediacy of my departure making my heart flutter with a mixture of loneliness, trepidation, and, strangely, excitement. Colin must have seen the first of these emotions mirrored in my face.

"Farewell, sweet Starr," he said, his voice hoarse. Suddenly I was in his arms and we were clinging to each other, desperate in our last minutes together.

"I love you, Starr," he muttered against my bonnet. "Don't give up on me."

I could not answer. My throat was too painfully tight.

"Let her go, boy." Abraham, who had been near enough to hear Colin's words, spoke coldly. "She'll be waiting for you in the spring, a much more manageable creature than she is now."

"This way, Mrs. Douglas." Captain Madison swept out an arm to indicate the waiting gangplank. Colin released me, and I turned away from him.

"Farewell, and try to behave." Abraham handed me over to the captain. Barret Madison wasted no time propelling me up the plank to the deck.

I looked down over the bulwarks at Colin. Suddenly he was Darcy—Darcy who'd been parted from me, surrounded by plans for a future that was never to be.

Panicked by the analogy, I would have fled back to him had not a seaman, at that moment, raised the boarding plank. As Captain Madison's mate bellowed his master's orders to scurrying sailors and they hastened to cast off the great ship's moorings, I swung on the ship's commander.

"Let me off! Let me off at once! I can't leave my husband!"

"Control yourself, Mrs. Douglas, or I'll be forced to once more confine you to my cabin." Captain Madison looked down at me in ill-disguised contempt. "I have work to do. I can't have an hysterical female rushing about my decks."

Defeated, I quieted, and he continued, "I would advise you to smile and wave a fond farewell if you truly care for the lad. It would be cruel to leave him with a final memory of tears and ravings to carry him through a long, cold winter."

I saw the truth in his words. I went back to the rail and raised a gloved hand in farewell to the handsome, distressed-looking young man on the pier. With a supreme effort, I forced a smile across my trembling lips.

"God bless you!" Colin yelled as the ship slid out into the current. "I love you! I'll come for you!"

Then we were beyond hearing as the great ship, caught by winds and the river's swift flow, moved away.

"I've only one sleeping cabin aside from my own." Barret Madison returned to my side. "It's not luxurious, but you'll have to make do. The *Maris Stella* is a cargo vessel, not an elegant passenger ship."

"Yes, I recall your aversion to human cargo." I cast him what I hoped was a demeaning glare before turning my attention back to the diminishing village of Pine.

****

The night was a cold, crisp, star-sprinkled beauty. I came up on deck to find the *Maris Stella* gliding southward. Only the sound of her bow piercing the wavelets and an occasional creak of the boom or flap of canvas broke the peace. A male voice I recognized was singing softly in French. Turning, I saw Captain Madison, a dark silhouette alone at the helm. Forward, a solitary seaman kept watch.

I walked to the rear and joined the master.

"I didn't know a captain actually took the wheel of his vessel," I said.

"On nights such as this, I often do," he said, breaking off from his song. "It gives a man time to reflect."

"Reflect on what? I believed you and Jared Fletcher were men of action, not contemplation."

"On the contrary, ma'am, I often contemplate my situation in life. For instance, tonight I've been thinking I should have been master of a vessel like this thirty years ago during the war. What a privateer this lady would have been! And I'd have become rich, not merely a Douglas servant."

"I would hardly call you a servant," I said. "As master of a fleet the size of Abraham Douglas's, you're a good deal above that status. I think it must be wonderful to be in command of even one vessel. If I were a man, I should have become a master mariner like my father. He owned his own vessel and ran blockades and carried out secret missions for the Prime Minister. After he died, people said he was a rogue and a pirate, but it wasn't true. He was brave and honest, a true patriot."

My voice broke as I recalled the slurs on my father's reputation and how they had hurt my mother and me.

"Then your father truly was…?"

"I've already told you. Captain Morgan Reynolds," I said proudly, thrusting out my chin and taking a deep breath to chase away the tears threatening to spill down my cheeks.

A silence followed, punctuated only by the flapping of canvas, the creak of the boom, and the soft splash of the ship slipping through the waves. I thought of my father, commanding his *Sea Starr* on a night such as this. Had he perhaps at times been lonely for my mother? Or had the thrill of racing through the waves under wind-billowed canvas been enough to make their long separations worthwhile?

"Would you like to take a spell at the wheel?" Captain Madison aroused me from my reflections with the unexpected offer. "Morgan Reynolds' daughter should know the feel of a ship beneath her hands."

"You'd let me guide your *Maris Stella*?" I couldn't believe his offer.

"Come here." He stepped to the left to make way for me.

Amazed and excited, I obeyed.

"Place your hands so. Hold tight. There. Now, steady as she goes." His strong, brown hands placed mine on the wheel, then slid away to leave me alone at the helm.

At first I was tense and awkward, struggling against the rudder's pull. I could feel the tug of the great ship beneath my hands. The rise and fall of the deck beneath my feet became her breathing. Gradually I began to relax and lose myself in the utter thrill of it. The wind was at my back, the *Maris Stella* lived, and for the moment I was her master.

The night, the sea, the stars, the great ship…all about was magic. For the first time I understood what drew men like Barret Madison and my father to this life, why it enthralled them as surely as Colin's music and Randall's medicine encompassed their lives.

For an enchanted time, I held the great vessel on course. Even when my arms began to ache and the wind freshened, making my task more arduous, I could not bring myself to relinquish the wheel. I had fallen in love with sailing.

A sudden gust hit the canvas above me with a force that made the tall sails snap and the booms groan. The *Maris Stella* leaped and lurched. I was all but dragged from my feet by the force sent up from her rudder.

For a moment I feared I'd lose control. Then those familiar weathered hands closed over mine and held both the ship and me steady.

"Easy as she goes, matey." He chuckled, his chest against my shoulders as he stood behind me. "You've done well. I didn't think a little girl like you could hold her as long as you did. Put on another sixty or seventy pounds, build up your biceps, and there'll not be a mariner north of the equator better."

He was teasing, but there was also a note of genuine admiration in his voice. I blushed under his praise and was glad it was night.

As the ship once again settled to a moderate pace, I became aware of his nearness, of his powerful body pressed against my back. I could not move without rubbing against him. I shivered.

"You're cold," he said, moving aside to free me. "You'd best go below before you catch a chill."

"Yes," I said, stepping away. "Yes, perhaps I'd better. Thank you, Captain, for letting me discover the magic both you and my father have known."

****

Late the following afternoon, a storm broke over the *Maris Stella*. I lay in my bunk and clung to its sides as the great ship, buffeted by the tail of a tropical hurricane, pitched and bucked over mountainous swells. I wondered if I'd live to see Colin again.

When night came, I did not undress for bed. I knew sleep would be impossible. Bells clanged to announce the changes of watch, rigging creaked and groaned above the roar of wind and surf, and often the voice of Captain Madison's mate bellowing urgent orders echoed into my cabin. Exhaustion eventually took its toll and, in spite of the heaving ship, I fell into a doze.

I was awakened in the dark hours shortly before dawn by a commotion in the companionway outside my cabin. I staggered to my feet and steadied myself across rolling floorboards to open the door.

Barret Madison, in dripping oilskins, stood in the companionway, one of his sailors cradled in his arms. The man was moaning, the water running from his drenched body red with blood.

"Dear God!" I gasped. "What happened?"

"He fell from the rigging," the captain said. "His left arm is badly torn. I haven't a man I can spare to see to him."

"Bring him in."

Barret stripped the man of his wet, bloody clothing and rolled him, groaning in agony, into my bed.

"Have you any laudanum?" I asked, fetching a sewing kit Rose had insisted I bring with me and recalling the drug he'd given Colin.

"Here." He pulled a small flask from inside his dripping coat.

"Dose him as heavily as you dare." I pulled white thread through a needle. "Then get out of those oilskins and help me."

"Help you do what?" He forced the liquid between the sailor's lips.

Indicating the injured man's frightened stare, I shook my head. No need to further distress him. He'd soon be beyond caring.

"Captain," he rasped. "If I die, send my pay to my missus. She's got four young ones and another is on the way. She'll be needin' a fancy dress to catch herself a new man."

"You're not going to die, Jim." Captain Madison's words brooked no denial. "Abe's own daughter-in-law is going to see to that, aren't you, Mrs. Douglas?"

"Of course I am," I said with a good deal more confidence than I was feeling. "You rest and leave everything to me."

"You're as pretty as one of God's own angels, ma'am." The injured man looked up at me, his eyelids already drooping from the effects of the drug. "If you say you'll heal me, then I believe you." Then he was unconscious.

"What are you going to do?" The captain pulled off his oilskins.

"Sew his arm back together before he bleeds to death." I tried to sound matter of fact, but my fingers were shaking as I knotted the end of the thread. "I saw Cook do it once when I worked in the scullery in England. A kitchen boy fell on some ragged glass. She saved his life by using her sewing kit to close the wound. Now do as I say. Knot this towel tightly about his upper arm. It will slow the bleeding and keep the wound clear enough for me to see what I'm about. Then fetch clean sheets, towels, and water. And a bottle of rum. I'll need alcohol to cleanse the wound."

He didn't question me further. Instead he moved swiftly to obey. When he was once again at my side, he held the sailor's ragged flesh in place as I stitched it together. Several times I feared I might faint but told myself a man's life depended on me. I must not weaken.

Finally it was finished. Barret helped me wash and bandage the arm. The bleeding had stopped and the man's breathing, although labored, was regular. I stood and drew a deep breath.

"Now all we can do is hope and pray," I said.

"And get you out of here," Barret said gently,

looking about at the bloody rags, sheets, and bowls of water. "I'll have one of my men clean this up once the storm abates."

He took my arm and led me out of the room and along the companionway to his cabin. I was too emotionally spent and physically exhausted to protest.

Once inside the warm, clean room, I felt the nerves I had held in check for the past hour shatter. With a trembling sigh, I sank down on the edge of his bed and covered my face with my hands.

"Drink this." I looked up to see him holding out a glass half full of liquid. I obeyed, then choked as it scalded its way to my stomach.

"Brandy," he said, patting me on the back. "Wonderful for frazzled nerves. Now let me get you out of that drcss."

"No!" I caught his hands as they went to its buttons.

"I'm not going to hurt you," he said, his voice so gentle my eyes flew to his face in surprise. "How could I? You're as strong and brave as you are clever and beautiful. A man would have to be pure scum to take advantage of such a woman…a woman a man such as Morgan Reynolds would have been proud to call his daughter."

His words placated me with their sincerity. I stood still and allowed him to open the buttons, then pull the bloody, wet dress over my head. When he'd finished, he went to his sea chest, took out one of his own white linen shirts, and dropped it over my head. It laced at the throat and hung to my knees. Then he led me, clad in my strange nightshirt, to his bed and tucked me between soft, warm quilts. .

“It’s all right,” he murmured, taking my icy fingers and raising them to his lips. “Rest. You’ve been as courageous and resourceful as anyone should ever have to be.”

He bent forward, placed a kiss on my forehead, adjusted the covers about me, then left me alone with the memory of his actions both warming and confusing me.

Chapter Ten

The Academy turned out to be a somber structure of gray stone, owned and staffed (save for a cook and a servant girl) by one Mrs. Elvira Lambert. The mistress was a full-bosomed widow of middle age, prim, strict, and unrelenting in her bustling effort to transform ignorant young women into acceptable wives for affluent men who'd fallen victim to pretty faces and shapely bodies combined with minds and manners unsuitable for the social circles of their wealthy spouses.

Aside from myself, the academy had only two students at that time. Tuition and board at Mrs. Elvira Lambert's Academy for Young Ladies were expensive, Becky and Sarah, my fellow pupils, informed me. Only the very wealthy could afford the cost.

In the weeks that followed, Becky, Sarah, and I were aroused at 5:30 a.m. and, shortly thereafter, put to our studies. We learned social graces, table settings, grooming, appropriate clothing, and manners for all occasions. Mrs. Lambert also attempted to give us a basic appreciation of the arts and to instruct us to an elementary knowledge of French.

My knowledge of music amazed our teacher. The first time she sat down at the piano in the drawing room, she played an uninspired version of a concerto I recognized immediately.

"Now," she said when she had finished. "I'm sure none of you recognized that piece, but perhaps after several months…"

"Bach," I said.

"I beg your pardon, Mrs. Douglas?" She turned to me in surprise.

"The selection was composed by Bach," I said.

"That is correct," Mrs. Lambert sniffed disdainfully. "But how could *you* possibly know?"

"My husband is a pianist," I said proudly.

"Then you must study music with a will, madam." Mrs. Lambert threw back her shoulders and looked down her nose at me. "Nothing pleases a gentleman more than to have his lady well versed in his interests."

"Yes," I agreed, but soon found I was studying French with equal enthusiasm.

****

On Christmas Eve, Mrs. Lambert came into the drawing room, where we three young ladies were reading, to announce I had a visitor.

"You may receive him in the parlor," she said, stepping aside for me to precede her from the room.

"Did he give his name, ma'am?" I laid my book aside and stood.

"He did," she replied. "Now come along."

Knowing further questions would antagonize her, I went out of the room and down the hall, aware of her critical appraisal of my every step. I wondered if I were progressing to her satisfaction, and then I was at the open parlor door. Inside, his back to me as he warmed his hands at the hearth, was a tall, blond, broad-shouldered young man I recognized joyfully.

"Colin!" I rushed into the room.

He turned to me, and I flung myself into his arms. "Oh, Colin, it's so good to see you!" I choked as I clung to his fur-collared greatcoat. Tears escaped my eyes and trickled down my cheeks. "I've been so lonely without you!"

"Starr, I'm sorry," he said, his voice trembling. "If I could have prevented it, I never would have allowed my father to send you away."

"I know." I blinked back my tears and forced a smile as I looked up at him. "But it's been for the best. I'm learning to be a wife you can be proud of." I spun away from him that he might inspect my changed appearance. "Haven't I improved? See how I've learned to put my hair up. No more wild curls or bits of ribbon."

I paused. He was smiling.

"You look wonderful," he said. "But then, I've always thought you did."

I blushed under his praise.

"I've come to spend the Yuletide with you," he said. "I have a room at the King's Inn."

"Oh, that's wonderful! But couldn't you stay here? I have my own room, and…"

He touched my cheek with his fingertips. "It's best this way, Starr."

Embarrassed by his admission of his lack of desire for me, I turned away and went to the piano by the window. "I hope you've been practicing," I said.

"I haven't touched a piano in weeks," he said. "I've been working in the bush. After you left Pine, Father sent me back to the woods. He said I was getting soft, that it wasn't surprising I hadn't been able to make you pregnant, since I was in such poor physical condition.

He said if I wanted to be able to succeed with you when we went to the Caribbean in the spring, I'd need to do manual labor. He sent me out to his most notorious timber boss, Moonlight Jake. The brute came by his nickname honestly. If there's moonlight enough to see by, he works his men at night as well as by day. My hands are so sore, I doubt I shall ever play again." He held out them out, scarred and bruised.

"Colin," I breathed, tears of compassion stinging my eyes. I caught his hands in mine and kissed them. He laid his cheek against my hair and sighed.

"Play for me now," I said softly. "I know you can."

"If it would please you," he said, shrugging out of his greatcoat. "But don't expect a polished performance."

He sat down at the keyboard. For a few moments, he stared down at it, flexing his fingers and rubbing his wrists. Then he placed his hands over the keys and squared his shoulders.

At first he ran his fingers over simple scales and exercises. As dexterity and confidence returned, he struck out on one of his own compositions. Soon the house was resounding with his exquisite, masterful touch.

He played and I was placated, caressed, and finally lifted by the magic. When he paused and the last note had drifted into oblivion in the quiet house, a small but heartfelt ripple of applause made us both turn toward the doorway. Mrs. Lambert and my two fellow students stood on the threshold, delight mirrored on all three faces.

"That was magnificent, Mr. Douglas." Mrs. Lambert advanced into the room. "Mozart, was it not?"

"No, ma'am." Colin got to his feet and smiled at her in his appealing, unabashed manner. "It's one of my own compositions."

"Amazing," she breathed, her eyes bright. "Mr. Douglas, you are a gifted gentleman. You appear to have awakened an appreciation of fine music in my young ladies, something I've failed to do in the past months. I wonder"—she paused pensively—"will you be stopping long in Halifax?"

"A couple of weeks at least, ma'am," he said. "I plan to be with my wife at Christmas."

"Of course," she nodded. "Would it be too great an imposition if I asked you to play for us occasionally?"

"I'd be honoured, ma'am." Colin bowed.

"Excellent!" She flourished her hands at the two young women in the doorway. "Run along now, girls. We must allow Mr. Douglas time with his wife. Good day, Mr. Douglas. We'll be eagerly awaiting your next concert in our little academy."

"Well." He shrugged boyishly after they'd gone. "Perhaps I should also leave. Will you have supper with me at the King's Inn tonight? I can come for you at seven, if that would be convenient."

"I'd like that," I said. "It's rather like living in a nunnery here, in spite of the fine clothes and bric-a-brac. It would be most pleasant to go out."

"Most pleasant?" Colin grinned at my stilted speech.

"Oh, all right," I laughed. "It would be loverly."

He took my hand then, sobering.

"Don't change too much, Starr," he said, looking into my eyes. "I like you just the way you are." He bent from the waist and kissed my fingers. Then he gathered up his greatcoat and left.

I went to the parlor window and watched him hail a passing cab. As he drove away, his words echoed in my mind: "I like you just the way you are." Perhaps there was hope for our marriage after all.

Sarah burst into the parlor. "Starr, he's an Adonis!"

I turned from the window, surprised at her exuberance.

"Who?" I asked innocently as Becky followed her into the room.

"Why, that beautiful man you married!" Sarah cried. "My James is rich and I love him, but Colin Douglas is a prize! I tell you, I could take that man in rags and be happy forever."

"He *is* very handsome, Starr," Becky said shyly. "He has a fine face and beautiful blond hair."

"Don't act the lady, Becky," Sarah prodded her with an elbow. "Don't pretend you didn't notice that tall, lean body with its broad shoulders and flat belly. He looks as firm as a rock. Is he, Starr?" she teased, nudging me, her eyes dancing with mischief.

"Sarah, please!" Becky was chagrined at our friend's outspokenness. "Don't mind her, Starr," she continued gently. "She's teasing."

"Teasing, like hell!" Sarah laughed boisterously. "My James is a rough diamond and your Jonathan is a wealthy milksop, but we each love them with all our hearts for the good men we know them to be. Starr, here, has simply gotten icing on her wedding cake. Her man is the best-looking thing I've seen in years!"

I would have been lying if I'd replied I hadn't been aware of Colin's blatant good looks, but this was the first time I'd been exposed to other women's frank opinion of him.

The realization came to me in a rush. I must have been mad to allow Colin's father to send me away from him. Pine had a number of comely young ladies who probably viewed my husband as did my companions. And what about his former love? Who and where was she?

Disconcerted, I walked across the room and let the piano cover fall over the keys with a bang. I would not be separated from my handsome husband again.

As soon as Sarah and Becky left me alone, I hastened to find Mrs. Lambert and tell her of my husband's invitation. Her permission was necessary. She allowed no one to leave the house without her consent.

"I have no objection," she said when I made my request. "Mr. Douglas appears to be a fine, cultivated young gentleman. I might even make an exception to one of my cardinal rules," she continued, lowering her voice and looking furtively about to make certain Becky and Sarah were not within earshot. "And allow you to spend the…er…entire evening at the King's Inn with him."

"You mean the night?" I could barely believe my good fortune. "Oh, yes, please. It would mean so much to me, to us."

"I normally do not permit such…conjugal visits. The families of the young men whose brides are entrusted to me for improvement prefer not to risk…complications before they're satisfied with the results of my work."

"You mean pregnancies," I said.

"Yes, if you must be so indelicate." She sniffed.

"Your young man, however, appears too much a gentleman of refinement to allow any such unfortunate occurrence. Thus, I'm prepared to risk giving him a night alone with his wife. Return after dinner and pretend to retire. I'll let you out again at eleven. There will be a carriage waiting. I'll readmit you at six tomorrow morning. Don't be tardy."

I flung myself at the woman and hugged her. She gasped in surprise.

"Oh, thank you, mum," I cried, releasing her. "God bless you, mum."

"Really, Mrs. Douglas, you must try to curb your exuberance," she said, straightening her collar. "And correct that terrible grammar at once, or I shall change my mind. Now go bathe, and dress your hair. You have scant time to make yourself presentable."

"Why are you allowing me this liberty?" I'd started from the room but turned back, seized by suspicion. Was this some trick designed to have me dismissed in disgrace from her academy? The woman had no soft place in her heart for me.

"That boy you married is a musical genius," she said. "He should be denied nothing that might inspire him. I'm sure, being a young man, he is inspired by his wife. I therefore consider it my duty to the world of music to send you to him tonight."

Thinking Colin's music must indeed have magic powers, I dashed toward the stairs. I was in such high spirits, I could not feel resentful as I heard the woman mutter something about wondering how a talented man like my husband had gotten himself married to such a feckless creature.

I dressed in my finest, a blue velvet creation

trimmed with deep flounces of snow white lace, piled my hair into a soft halo of curls about my face, and threw about my shoulders a cape that matched my gown and was lined with silver fox fur. As I drew the hood over my coiffure, I looked into my mirror and smiled. If Colin Douglas did not find me desirable tonight, he must be an unusual young man indeed.

****

As we were finishing our dinner at the King's Inn later that evening, I told Colin of Mrs. Lambert's offer. The carefree happiness that had underscored our evening vanished from his face.

"That was kind of Mrs. Lambert," he said, unfolding and refolding his napkin. "But I think it best you return to the academy for the night. I'll come for you tomorrow. We'll go for a sleigh ride."

"Colin, you don't understand," I said, leaning eagerly across the table toward him. "We must try to complete our marriage. I don't want to lose you, and I fear I will if..."

"You'll never lose me, sweetheart," he said his confidence returning as he put his napkin aside and took my hand to kiss my fingers. When he raised his head, he smiled. "I need you, I love you. I can't imagine my life without you as my companion."

"Companion, Colin? I'm your legal wife."

"You think you can't hold me without intimacy in bed?" Colin's tone was incredulous. "Sweetheart, you've kept me alive since we met, since Darcy's death. You couldn't send me away if you wished."

"Colin." I looked into his clear blue eyes, not knowing how to proceed.

"Look," he continued, drawing a small velvet box

from his pocket. "Open this and see if you still have doubts of how I feel toward you." He put the little container into my hand.

I raised the lid and gasped. Inside, a large sapphire surrounded by a starburst of diamonds glistened from its setting in a gold ring.

"Colin, it's beautiful."

"Do you really like it?" he asked, boyishly shy and grinning.

"Of course! It's magnificent."

"I'm glad." He took it in one hand and the fingers of my left hand in his other. "Because I'd like you to wear it as a wedding ring. Will you?" He paused and looked into my eyes. "Please?"

"Colin, it's much too fine," I protested. "A simple band would have been proof enough."

He slid the extravagant jewel onto my finger and raised it to his lips. "With this ring I declare you my partner in life," he said, his voice husky with emotion. "With this ring, I seal our bond of mutual affection and trust."

****

Later, when Colin left me at the door of the academy and drove away, I waited only until he was out of sight, then hurried back into the street. I hailed a cab and headed back to the King's Inn.

After a footman at the King's Inn who'd seen us having dinner together had identified me as Mrs. Douglas, the hotel clerk gave me directions and a key to Colin's room. Trembling with anticipation and apprehension, I mounted the stairs.

Moments later, I eased open the door of Room 14 a few inches and slid inside. I was careful to let as little light as possible intrude. I didn't want to awaken Colin before I'd set my plan in motion.

Once the door was closed behind me, I tiptoed across the room to stand by the bed. The quilt-swathed figure silhouetted in the glow of a fire dying on the hearth did not stir. I almost sighed aloud with relief. I bent and removed my fur-lined leather boots.

A moment later, cloak, gown, undergarments, and stockings joined them in a discarded heap on the floor. I pulled the pins from my hair and shook it loose about my shoulders. Then, clad only in a thin silk-and-lace chemise, I bent over the form in the bed and carefully pulled the covers from his shoulders.

"Colin," I said softly. "Colin, darling…"

The rest of my words died in my throat as raven-haired Barret Madison rolled sleepily to face me.

"What are *you* doing here?" I gasped.

"Might I not ask you the same question, madam?" he asked as he struggled up on one elbow. "I don't remember inviting a lady to pay a midnight call this evening."

In the shadowy gloom, groggy from sleep, he hadn't yet recognized me. I could escape before he learned my identity. I grabbed up my gown and struggled into it.

"There's no need for such haste, ma'am," he said, a jesting tone invading his voice as he came fully awake. "Although you were uninvited, you're not unwelcome."

The dress fastenings fumbled out of my fingers. I grabbed my cloak, flung it over my ill-donned gown, pushed bare feet into my boots, and made a dash for the door.

The captain was quicker. He leaped catlike from

the bed and was between the exit and me before I could reach it. In the darkness beyond the reach of the fire's weak light, his hands seized me and I was pinned against the wall and kissed with arousing thoroughness.

I floated, swirled, my solar plexus sending out shafts of incredible pleasure. He thrust his tongue into my mouth over mine and I lost touch with reality. Was this love? Or lust? I didn't care which it was. I only knew I wanted more…and more.

But as he brought his body full length against mine and began to pull the cloak from my shoulders, I came to my senses. Slashing down my burning passion with strength-sapping effort, I wrenched away from his demanding mouth.

"Come, now, missy, don't be coy," he chuckled. "Let's get to the purpose for which you obviously came. I assume you're a Christmas gift from one of my friends. Captain Fletcher, perhaps? Good for Jared."

"Let me go, you filthy bastard!"

My curse brought him to a halt. As my outer garment fell to the floor, he gave a sharp intake of breath.

"Starr! Sweet Jesus!"

His arms fell from me, and I collapsed against the wall, gasping for breath.

"What in God's name are you doing here?" he muttered.

"What are you doing here?" I cried. "The desk clerk told me this is my husband's room."

"Colin couldn't sleep because of the noise downstairs," he replied. "He found my room at the rear of the inn quieter. We exchanged lodgings."

"*You* brought Colin to Halifax, didn't you?"

"Yes," he said. "We sailed out of the Miramichi through shell ice hours before the final freeze. I brought Colin to you, and Jared and Caroline to attend the Nova Scotia Governor's Ball. Randall was too involved in the political struggle for a mail contract to come with us…or, at least, so he said."

He crossed the room and struck a match. The room brightened as he lighted a lamp, and I saw his blatant virility in all its power as he was revealed to me, naked except for a pair of form-hugging undertrousers, his dark hair tousled from sleep. Barret Madison physically and emotionally stirred me to the quick of my being.

"Why did you come to Colin at this hour? Did he invite you?"

"No… Yes… That is…" I could not conjure a fitting reply.

"Starr, sweet princess." His fingers touched my flushed cheek with great tenderness. "You came here to seduce Colin, didn't you? He hasn't made love to you yet, has he?"

Strangled by his compassion, my bitter reply died in my throat. Tears slid down my cheeks.

"Hush," he soothed against my hair as I broke down, sobbing. "I know. I understand. You were terrified by a sexual attack, and Colin's desires lie elsewhere."

"What am I to do, Barret? Colin's father is pressuring us to have a child, but Colin won't…can't…make that a possibility. I don't know if I could let him…if I love him in that way."

"Starr, look at me and be honest." He held me out from him and gazed into my eyes. "Isn't some of your confusion attributable to what is between you and me?

It's time we faced reality, my love."

"Yes," I whispered. "I don't understand, but yes."

"It's simple. We're in love and have been since we met aboard the *Maris Stella*. Denying it at first was a matter of false pride and mistrust on my part. You were, after all, from the steerage. Then suddenly you were married and it was too late, as it will now forever be too late."

He turned away and took a cigar from a box on the dresser. At the hearth, he bit off the cigar's tip and spat it into the fire, then took up a burning bit of kindling, and lit the tobacco. "At first I told myself that, in spite of the fact that you may or may not be Captain Morgan Reynolds' daughter, you were a mercenary little whore, and I set out to harass you out of Colin's life. Then, on the way to Halifax, you saved my seaman's life and I saw another side of you…that night as I tucked you into my bed, I admitted the truth to myself for the first time. Your actions on that night made me respect you for the person you truly are and made me realize that I was in love with you. I also realized it was an impossible obsession. You are my best friend's wife."

The truth of his words broke over me. I tried to return to his embrace, but he shook his head. "I love you, too, Barret."

"Hush," he said, putting a finger to my lips. "Remember Colin, remember his gentleness, his caring. Can you hurt him?"

I sank down on the edge of his bed, covering my face with my hands.

"You said you love me," he said, going to put a log into the fire. "I believe you. That entitles you to know the truth about me." He walked away from me, across the room, then turned back. “I’m a bastard in the true meaning of the word, love. My father never married my mother. He deserted her long before I was born. She was a French governess on one of France’s Caribbean islands. When her employer learned of her condition, he cast her out. She was forced to make a living as a singer and pianist in one of that island’s brothels. I was born there and grew up in it.”

“Barret, I had no idea. When I called you…that name…I had no idea. I’m so very sorry.”

“Don’t be.” He hurled his cigar into the flames with a vehemence that denied the calmness of his words. “My mother was an exceptional woman. She remained a kind, loving person who gave every ounce of her energy to raising me. She taught me to read and write, to sing and play piano and guitar, the only knowledge she could provide to me as a means of making a living one day. When she died the year I was ten, I thought I would die, too.”

”I understand.” The sharp pain of remembrance in my chest told me I did.

“But I didn’t.” He drew a deep breath and continued. “I recovered and took her place, entertaining the clientele in the grand salon with my music. I passed my adolescence in an atmosphere most children never even know exists. Whores were my friends, a madam named Maggie my surrogate mother. Other children sneered at me in the streets, boys of my own age shunned me as a whorehouse bastard and whoremaster of prostitutes. You may well imagine the scars such a life left on a young boy. Until I met you, I never thought I dared expect love from a decent woman. But you’re an exceptional woman, like my mother. You look at people with your heart."

In the flickering firelight, his face appeared emotionless, but a glisten of sweat on his upper lip betrayed the pain he was suffering.

"Even if you were free, you could not bear to let me touch you, knowing what I've just told you," he said, his voice gruff with emotion. "I've lain with whores since I was sixteen, Starr."

I stood and went to stand before him. His jaw twitched with a nervous spasm, and his eyes were hot and moist.

"I'm the victim of a sexual attack, as you're aware," I said. "I know how eternally dirty a person can feel. I also know love can wash away those feelings. If I were free, if it were not for Colin, I would not hesitate to make love to you, to love you body and soul."

"You're a generous woman, angel," he muttered, his voice gruff with emotion. "Now I must take you back to the academy before we do something we'll regret."

He took my face between his hands and leaned forward to kiss my forehead.

"Barret!" I grasped his fingers. "Is this to be all we shall ever have? A knowledge of our love, and that it can never be?"

"You know it as well as I. If we loved Colin less…but we don't and never will." He released me and handed me my cloak. "Hurry. Lingering will only prolong the pain."

****

It had begun to snow. Huge, soft flakes as gentle as a chick's down floated to the earth amid a hush in the still, after-midnight air as we left the inn by a rear door and made our way through an alley to a back street.

An excruciating, burning ache like a hot knife blade seared through my body and soul and made each breath a painful necessity. Love shouldn't hurt so badly. It wasn't fair, it wasn't fair.

And then the shot rang out.

Like cannon fire in the silent night, and as blasphemous as Barret's half-yelped curse of anger and pain that seemed to accompany it, the explosion rent the cold air. He staggered and fell against me.

"You've been shot!" I gasped as his weight forced us to our knees.

"Get me on my feet." He struggled to get up. "Whoever fired that shot at you will try again."

"Me?"

"Remember Colin's beating? You and your husband have a vicious enemy, sweet princess."

Together we staggered to our feet. With him leaning against me, we made a crooked lunge around a corner and into an alleyway. In the shadows we paused, gasping for breath. Barret fell back against the clapboards of a shop.

"Are you badly hurt?" I asked, clutching at the arm he held across the front of his body to hold his injured shoulder.

"I have some lead in me." His words were calm but his breathing harsh. "I'm going to need your help, love. You'll have to get me to a doctor who'll remove this damned bullet and ask no questions."

"Of course," I said. "But is he a good doctor? If his claim to fame is simply that he doesn't question his patients, then I don't think…"

"My darling innocent," he breathed in

exasperation. "You're Abe Douglas's daughter-in-law. It's past midnight. We're on our way from my bedroom. It would all look rather shabby if that story got about. But I do need a doctor, and I can't get there alone."

****

The doctor's house was in a disreputable-looking section of the city, not far from the docks. Shuttered and dark, it sent a wave of foreboding over me the moment we paused before its scarred, weather-bitten door.

"Keep your hood up and your face hidden," Barret muttered. "Mrs. Colin Douglas must not be recognized here with me in the middle of the night."

A dwarfish, bent, stubble-faced creature wearing thick, eye-distorting spectacles, a stained white shirt, and unbuttoned black vest opened the panel a crack and asked in a grating voice who came to his door at that ungodly hour.

"Captain Madison," Barret snarled. He had grown excruciatingly heavy against me; his breathing ragged and shallow. "Let my lady and me in at once, you vile little butcher."

"Ah, so you've finally been forced to bring me one of your ladies."

The door fell wide ajar, and we were admitted into a poorly lit room furnished with a crude plank table and a rough sideboard filled with jars, knives, and pans. The place stank of human sweat, carbolic, and other odors I dared not let my reeling mind identify. From behind a curtained door at the rear, a woman sobbed softly; a man, his voice often breaking with emotion, was trying to console her.

"She's a young one, Captain," the weird little man peered into my hood in the lantern light with those grotesquely glassed eyes. "They always fare best. Take off your clothing, dolly, and climb onto the table. The captain will be taking you home within the hour."

I looked up at Barret in horrified confusion.

"I'm not looking for an abortion," he snapped. "I've got a bullet in my shoulder."

"Ah." The gnome sighed in disappointment. "Well, then, help him undress, dolly."

"Slowly, my love." Barret grimaced as I started to slide off his greatcoat. Beneath, his shirt was crimson. I cringed as I saw the dark hole in its shoulder.

"Help him up on the table, dolly," the little man ordered. As I obeyed, he went to the sideboard and selected an instrument.

"Lie down," he ordered, as he returned to where Barret sat on the table's edge. "Let us get to it."

"Very well." Barret bent with an effort and took a small, black gun from a pocket inside his boot. He forced it into my cold fingers. "Point this at him. If he makes the slightest wrong move over me with that knife, kill him. Understand?"

I nodded, the horror of the place and the immediate future making me dumbly obedient.

Barret stretched out on the table. The strange little creature proceeded to tie him to its sides with leather thongs. Then he sliced the bloody shirt from the man's body with a few deft strokes of an ugly-looking knife.

"It's not pretty, Captain," he said, peering at the wound. "It'll take a deal of work." He returned to the dirty sideboard to bring a liquor flask back to the table. "Take a good swallow, my lad." He raised Barret's head with a gnarled hand. “You’ll need it.”

Barret obeyed, choking and cursing over it.

“Get a good hold on yourself, dolly.” The doctor looked over at me and grinned sadistically when Barret’s eyes grew heavy-lidded. “I wouldn’t want you fainting and becoming unable to protect the good captain while he’s at my mercy.”

“Never fear,” I heard myself replying confidently. “I’m not about to give you a chance to let your scalpel slip.”

“Tough little wench, aren’t you?” he jeered. “Dressed like a fine lady though you be, I’ll wager you’re only another of Madison’s whores. Well, watch this and show your mettle.”

The knife went into Barret’s oozing shoulder. The captain jerked and bellowed an oath. I fought nausea and giddiness as I steadied the tiny, cold weapon at the doctor.

****

A half hour later, the weird dwarf wiped his crimson hands on a towel. Leaving Barret barely conscious from shock, pain, and loss of blood as he lay sprawled on the table, he came around the crude bench to squint up at me in the lamplight.

“Well, dolly, it’s done,” he rasped. “Now whether he lives or dies is up to you. What happened? Did your father, or perhaps your husband, catch him in your bed? You both have the look of having dressed in haste.”

“None of your damn business!” I snapped, although my knees seemed barely able to support me and my stomach was ready to relieve itself of its contents.

“Of course, of course,” he chuckled, rubbing his

hands on a filthy towel. "My fame rests upon my discretion in such situations. Due to your lack of preparation for this visit, however, I fear neither of you has about your person coin with which to pay me. And I do not grant credit." He paused, then touched the fur of my hood with a bloodstained hand. "But, now, this pretty thing would just about cover my charges."

I lurched back from him and snapped the gun to a level of his head. "Stay away from me," I hissed.

"Don't get excited, dolly," he chuckled, but backed away. "I was merely offering a suggestion." He returned around the table to leer at me over Barret's prostrate body. "But," he continued—and suddenly he was holding a long scalpel poised over the captain's heaving chest—"I can't let you leave without paying. If you choose to shoot me instead of making good your debt, I'll fall across your lover and sink this useful little tool three inches into his belly. Without immediate help, he'll die in minutes."

Cold sweat ran over me. "Take the cape," I said, reaching to unfasten it.

"Ah, no," he said, his expression evil in the half-light of the dirty lantern. "When you spun so charmingly on me a moment ago, I saw something more valuable and more easily disposed of on your pretty person. I want the diamond-and-sapphire ring you're wearing as a wedding band. Obviously it means little to you or you wouldn't be here with this whoremaster. Hand it over, dolly, and you may stay warm this night."

"You despicable little cur!" I spat, my fingers tightening on the gun. "I love my husband!"

He shrugged and made a move as if to plunge the

knife into Barret's belly.

"No!" I tore the glittering ring from my finger. With an oath of contempt, I flung it across the plank floor into a dark corner, where it winked tauntingly up at me from among the filth.

"That was wise, dolly." The weird little man lowered the scalpel. "Now take him and get out. He'll be vomiting soon—they all do—and I don't want him fouling my surgery."

****

We entered the King's Inn by the same rear entrance we'd used to flee the hotel two hours earlier and were able to make our way unobserved to Barret's room. As we reached his bed, the last of his strength deserted him and he tumbled onto its covers with a deep groan.

"Barret…"

"Take my clothes off, angel," he muttered. "Get me into bed before I catch pneumonia. I've got to get better in time to make that January voyage for Abe."

With strength I would not have believed I possessed, I managed to roll him out of his greatcoat and get his head upon the pillows. Except for a heavy swath of bandages about his chest and shoulder, he was naked to the waist. We'd left his blood-soaked shirt in the surgery.

"Now my boots and pants," he instructed. "Get me under the blankets."

I pulled off his boots, then hesitated.

"It's all right, my love," he said, looking up at me with feverish eyes. "Unbuckle my belt and open my trousers. I'm too cursed weak to be aroused."

I put my fingers to his bare waist and opened the

buckle. Shortly I had him naked and beneath the blankets.

“Thank you.” He pulled the blankets to his throat and shuddered.

“You’re cold,” I said, and went to the fireplace to build up the flames languishing there. When it was blazing I returned to the bed.

“Barret, don’t die. Please don’t die…not now…when we’ve finally found each other.” I caught his hand and pressed it to my cheek.

“Starr, I’m a little drunk and a bit off center with pain, but I have to talk to you,” he said, his voice barely above a rasping whisper, his eyelids heavy. “You and I have walked on dangerous ground this night. We’re attracted to each other much too strongly. We must not allow ourselves to hurt Colin. We have to…to kill the feelings between us before we do something we’ll regret.”

“Barret, I feel warm and safe when I’m with you,” I blurted, rash from raw nerves and fatigue. I put a hand to his clammy cheek. “To fall into your arms and let you hold me and—”

“No!” he barked, struggling up on an elbow and away from me, his eyes bloodshot, sweat beading his face and chest. “Remember Colin! And go…now!”

Seeing the wisdom in his words, I turned and fled. I caught a cab and returned to the academy in a predawn darkness as black as Gethsemane and nearly as disheartening.

Mrs. Lambert seemed satisfied that my disheveled appearance was simply the result of a night of conjugal activity, but she clucked her tongue as I scurried past her and up the stairs to my room.

"And I thought Colin Douglas was a gentleman," I heard her mutter.

Once alone in my room, I shed my clothing, pulled on a nightgown, and scrambled into bed. There I lay curled up in a fetal position, trembling, shivering, realizing my life was a shambles. I was married to a dear, sweet man who'd been nothing but kind and generous to me, yet I was hopelessly and forever in love with his best friend.

****

Colin came to the academy at 10:00 a.m. the next morning. His expression was one of deep concern.

"Barret was shot late last night," he said softly when Mrs. Lambert had finally left us alone. "He won't elaborate on the circumstances. They're not important anyway. What matters is that my friend is very ill. Will you come with me while I see to his care? I'll understand if you refuse. Visiting a wounded man is hardly an ideal way to spend Christmas morning."

"Of course I'll come," I said. Although I was plagued with guilt, I desperately wanted to see Barret again.

With Colin's promise to return later in the day to play for the inmates of the academy, Mrs. Lambert allowed me to go with him, ostensibly for a holiday luncheon.

My husband hurried me out to the waiting cab and we drove in haste to the inn.

****

"Barret?" Colin moved to the bed, and the man lying there with quilts up to his waist opened his eyes. They were bloodshot and glazed, a day's growth of dark stubble covering the lower portion of his face.

"Colin." He tried to pull himself up on his pillows. "Merry Christmas, my friend."

"How are you?" my husband asked.

"Sore as hell." The captain grimaced. "But I'll be ready to sail within a week. I have to make that voyage to London. If I don't, Abe won't have a snowball's chance in hell of getting that mail contract."

"Forget the contract and London," Colin said. "Rest and get well."

"You're a good friend, Colin, but not much of a businessman." Barret rolled on one side and took a small flask I recognized from his nightstand. With a shaking hand, he raised it to his lips. He swallowed some of the reddish-brown liquid, then fell back onto the pillows, breathing hard.

"How much of this have you taken?" Colin picked up the container and frowned at its depleted contents. "You always said a person should be very careful of this concoction."

"I'm in a deal of pain, brother," Barret muttered, closing his eyes. "Don't preach. Not now."

"Very well. If that's what you want. Now, look. I've brought Starr for a visit." Colin tried to lighten the mood. "She was concerned when she learned of your accident. She's brought you a basket of food."

"That's kind of you, Mrs. Douglas." Barret rolled his head in my direction, aware of my presence near the door for the first time. "But what I really need is someone to help me from this damned bed for other bodily functions. I tried to get up earlier but passed out in the attempt."

"Perhaps you should leave, Starr." My husband flushed to the roots of his hair. "I'll meet you in the lobby."

"Of course," I said. "Good day, Captain. I wish you a happy Christmas and a swift recovery."

When my husband rejoined me, he sat down by my side with a shame-faced grin.

"Forgive Barret his crudeness," he said. "I'm afraid he'd taken too much laudanum to be aware that he was offending a lady. I'll send you back to the academy in a cab. I'll rejoin you shortly, but at present I must fetch a reputable doctor for Barret. Last night he went to the only surgeon in town who takes late-night patients without asking questions. I suspect he got that wound in a fight over a lady and didn't want to tell anyone who might make report of the circumstances to the authorities," he said, lowering his voice. I shifted in my seat. "The man who attended him is little better than a butcher. His wound was crudely treated."

"But won't this doctor you're about to fetch ask questions?" I asked.

Colin shook his head. "He's a good man. The welfare of his patients always comes before his curiosity. I'll order you a cab. The sooner I take care of Barret, the sooner we shall be free to go on our Christmas sleigh ride."

He took my hand, raised it to his lips, then stopped. "Starr, where's your ring?"

"Ring?" For a moment I was aghast. But it was only for an instant. Then, turning actress like my mother, I gasped, in well-feigned dismay, "Oh no! I've lost it! It must have come off when I removed my gloves." Hot shame burned me as I mouthed the lie.

"Love, don't look so distressed," he made me further despise myself by replying. "It was a gaudy bauble. Tomorrow I'll buy you a string of pearls I saw in a shop on Barrington Street. They're much more tasteful than that ostentatious sapphire Barret and my father insisted I purchase for you."

"Captain Madison helped you choose the ring?"

"I'd never purchased jewelry for a lady, and I asked him to help me with the selection of your gift." He grinned nostalgically. "Barret has been with me the first time I did almost anything important. I had my first sea voyage aboard a ship under his command. He taught me sailing and navigation. He showed me how to take the best advantage of the slightest breeze. He also taught me to ride." He smiled reminiscently. "He and Ben Smith took the place of a father too involved in his business to have time for an incompetent son." He paused, then chuckled. "I made my first visit to a tavern in Barret's company. He nursed me over the brawl I got into that night and the hangover the next morning. I smoked my first cigar in his company, and…"

He hesitated.

"And had your first lady?"

"No! Starr, I swear to you I never…"

"It's all right, Colin. I never expected to marry a celibate man."

"Starr, please! Because Barret has known a lot of women and I'm his friend, it doesn't mean I've been like him in that way."

"Hush," I soothed, rising. "Go and get a doctor for your friend. I'm eager to be off on our sleigh ride."

****

On New Year's Eve, Colin and I had been invited to attend a ball held in honor of the governor of the province. I was delighted. There would be music and dancing, and I would have an opportunity to wear a new gown I had recently acquired. I would also wear the beautiful strand of pearls which had replaced the sapphire ring.

On the night of the ball, I was astonished to discover Captain Madison had come with Colin to escort me. His recovery had either been swift or he was strong in conquering his pain. As I descended the stair, both men arose from where they had been seated in the parlor with Mrs. Lambert. Colin, handsome in evening attire, came to me as I reached the foot of the steps, his face bright with admiration.

"You're beautiful," he said, taking my arm and kissing my cheek. "That peach-colored gown is perfect with the pearls. Barret?" He turned to the captain. "Isn't my wife beautiful tonight?"

"Tonight and every night," he said, coming to join us. "If you haven't already noticed her loveliness, you must be blind, sir."

"Let me assure you, Captain, I'm far from sightless," Colin retorted. "I often see things I believe you'd rather I didn't."

Was Colin referring to the captain's interest in me? I couldn't bear it if my husband discovered the truth. Glancing at the ship's master, my heartbeat quickened. Captain Barret Madison in evening attire was a charismatic man, a man who would forever be at the center of my heart.

I tried not to recall our mutual confession of love, but failed. I longed for him, wanted him with body and soul. Every day without him was a burning torment I would have to bear for the rest of my life.

"I'll get your wrap." Colin brought me back to the

present.

"I'll show you where it is, Mr. Douglas," Mrs. Lambert, always eager to have Colin to herself, volunteered.

As the captain and I waited alone in the foyer, I turned to him.

"Why did you come with Colin? It can only make things worse."

"Perhaps," he said. "But you need protection." He flashed open his coat and I caught a glimpse of the small pistol secreted in an inner pocket.

"Surely that's not necessary."

"Surely it is," he replied. "Have you forgotten Christmas Eve?"

"No, but…"

"Hush." He stopped me. "Here comes Colin."

****

During an intermission midway through the evening, the orchestra leader came over to where Barret, Colin, and I were seated. His round, bright face was flushed with pleasure as he stopped before us.

"Herr Colin Douglas, is it not?"

"Yes, sir." Colin stood and bowed. "This is my wife, Starr, and my good friend Captain Barret Madison, master of the *Maris Stella*. Please join us."

"Forgive my boldness in approaching you, Herr Douglas," the maestro said, as he accepted my husband's offer and Colin signaled a waiter to bring more champagne. "But I heard you play in Vienna last year. I was deeply impressed. Tonight, when I saw you here, I thought to myself, 'Wilhelm, you must ask that young man to play with your humble orchestra. It would be a rare and wonderful experience for this assemblage to hear such genius in command of a piano.' "

"You're very kind." Colin flushed at the praise. "But I haven't practiced in some time. I'm afraid these good people might be disappointed by my performance."

"Never!" The maestro was emphatic. "Yours is a great gift. It does not diminish. Please. I would be most grateful."

"Go ahead," Barret urged him. "You know you'd enjoy having an audience again."

Colin hesitated only a moment longer. Then he stood.

"Excellent, excellent." Wilhelm Kroisenbacher beamed. "Come, come, I will introduce you."

With a resignedly good-natured shrug to Barret and me, Colin straightened his cravat and smoothed his vest. "I hope I don't embarrass you," he said.

"You won't," Barret assured him.

A few moments later we watched as Maestro Kroisenbacher returned to the dais and tapped the podium with his baton. When all was quiet, he cleared his throat and spoke.

"Ladies and gentlemen!" He beamed. "I am most honored and privileged to present to you, as a special guest pianist, a young man who was the toast of Vienna before he was yet twenty years of age. I give you Herr Colin Douglas, the most gifted and unique young musician I have ever been fortunate to encounter."

A light sprinkling of applause accompanied Colin as he joined the maestro and bowed first to the assemblage, then to the orchestra. These people did not know Colin's talent and were expecting a performance inferior to the one they had been enjoying under the baton of Herr Kroisenbacher. They possibly knew of Colin as his father's son, a young man involved in shipbuilding, timber export, and international trade. They probably imagined Herr Kroisenbacher had turned his piano over to him only in hopes of securing a large financial contribution from the Douglas enterprises to help support his group of itinerant musicians. Wealthy patrons were courted by men of the arts.

The orchestra leader smiled, nodded, then conferred softly with his musicians as Colin seated himself at the piano. I waited breathlessly as my husband got the attention of the orchestra. Then he put his fingers to the keyboard and the first notes of a famous waltz filled the ballroom.

In a matter of seconds the entire group was mesmerized by my husband's masterful performance. Transfixed by the genius of the handsome young musician, the guests made no move to dance. Instead they listened with rapt attention.

"Come." Barret took my hand and drew me to my feet. "We must dance. We're unlikely to get such perfect accompaniment again."

"He's wonderful," I breathed, as we glided out across the dance floor, my full skirts swishing softly in time to the melodic sounds.

"He's a genius," Barret said matter-of-factly.

I wondered what Abraham would think of the son he'd dubbed a failure if he could see him at that moment. Holding an audience spellbound with his music, Colin Douglas was a tremendous success. I could only conclude Herr Kroisenbacher had spoken the truth when he'd called my husband the toast of

Vienna.

The music took a sweeping upbeat. Barret swung me gracefully about until my skirts billowed and my feet barely touched the floor. His arms strong and possessive about me, the pulse of the romantic music surging in my soul, I was overcome by the rightness of it. I closed my eyes to the crowd watching us. There was only the exquisite beauty of the music and the erotic sense of Barret's lean, powerful body tantalizingly close to mine. The excitement of the moment and several glasses of excellent champagne erased the inhibitions of reality.

A gush of cold air on my skin made my eyes fly open to discover Barret had waltzed me out onto the dark, glassed-in side porch of the manor. Unheated and without lamps or candles, the sunroom brought a shiver washing over me.

Barret had obviously planned this move, for once we were out of sight of those in the ballroom he flung my cloak about my shoulders. He'd had it ready on a chair. Then he drew me into his arms.

"I'm sailing at dawn," he said, kissing my hair. "I had to see you alone one last time."

"No!" I pulled away from him and put my fingers to his lips.

"Hush, my love." He stilled my outburst. "I must go. And even if I didn't, what is there for me here? I would have to go on loving you, watching another man share your life. Another man I call my friend, my brother. No, sweet angel, it's best I go and let the fates decide my future."

"Barret, come with me now!" I was desperate, wild, impetuous. "We'll go to an inn where no one knows us! We can have one night, one magic night…" Half-mad with despair, I gripped his arms and begged.

"Angel, don't. I'm only flesh and blood. If you weren't a little drunk, and if I didn't respect you for the wonderful woman you are, if I didn't love Colin, and if I didn't know how you would loathe us both in the morning…"

He caught me in his arms and crushed me against him so savagely it seemed he was trying to merge our two bodies into one. Then he released me, kissed my forehead, and strode off into the darkness.

I was cold, so cold not all the feather quilts and hearth fires on earth could make me warm. I turned and fled back into the ballroom.

As I rushed through the open doors, I collided with my smirking sister-in-law.

"Well, well, little sister," she smiled slyly. "Giving our commodore a warm send-off, were you? Generous of you, I'm sure, but I'm not certain our father-in-law would view it in the same way."

Chapter Eleven

"Let's run away, Colin."

I made my startling proposal when we returned from a sleigh ride the following afternoon. Astonished, my husband halted the horse and turned to me.

"Run away? Where would we go? What would we do?"

"We could be itinerant musicians." I rushed ahead with my idea when I saw he was willing to hear me out. "There's a dearth of entertainment in this country in winter. Your father would never find us among the small villages and lumber camps of this province. Say you'll agree! I cannot tolerate your father's pushing and shoving at us any longer."

And, I continued in my heart, I cannot bear to sit passively in that academy and await the news that Barret Madison has been lost at sea.

"Of course, Starr!" He startled me by agreeing when I paused for breath. "It's a wonderful idea! We can do it, I know we can."

"Of course we can," I echoed. "Together we're invincible."

"Yes." He flapped the reins to start the horse. "I believe we are. And your idea comes at a perfect time. I was concerned about returning home. You see, Father didn't send me to spend Christmas with you. I knew Barret was sailing for Halifax before the river froze, to be ready for his New Year's voyage to London. I asked him to allow me to stow away. I'm already a runaway."

"Oh, Colin, you're delightful." I laughed, clutching his arm and giving it a squeeze. "Now we can really begin our life together."

****

At midnight that same night, I stole out of the academy dressed in boy's woolen breeches, fur hat and coat, and high-laced leather moccasins which Colin had provided. My most practical clothes, along with a couple of elegant gowns I deemed suitable for performing, were packed into the carpetbag I carried.

Colin, in the rough homespun of a woodsman, his guitar slung on his back, was waiting for me with a pair of saddled horses behind the school. We rode off into the sub-zero chill of a star-sprinkled night.

Confident we could make good our escape, I had left Mrs. Lambert a note pinned to my pillow. She was not to worry, I had written. My husband and I were going away to be alone together. It would be days, perhaps weeks, before she could get word of our defection to Abraham Douglas in Pine.

For several weeks Colin and I met with success both in our escape attempt and our efforts to survive by our talents. Winter after Christmas in this country was a hard, bleak time. Inns, taverns, and even logging camps welcomed any form of entertainment that would ease the tedium of grueling cold and backbreaking work.

Colin came into his own during those early days of our escape. Given the position of the man of our small family and therefore my protector, he became self-confident, ready to meet any challenge to our wellbeing or safety.

His newly found self-assurance was demonstrated one bitterly cold January night when a drunken lumber man attempted to grab me during a performance. Within seconds, Colin's fist had connected with the man's bearded jaw and sent him sprawling across the floor.

As two of his fellows moved in to revenge their fallen friend, Colin planted his feet squarely apart and thrust aside his frock coat to reveal a pistol stuck in his belt, a knife hanging in a scabbard beside it.

"The lady is my wife, gentlemen," he said. "I insist you show her proper respect. Come, my love. I think it's time we left these people to their own forms of entertainment."

Putting me behind him, he backed us out of the room. I was trembling with delighted excitement. This was all part of the adventure, and I was reveling in it.

We continued to travel and perform through the months of January, February, and most of March. Sometimes we received only bed and board for ourselves and stabling for our horses; other times, a collection taken among the audience yielded coin. We were happy, free, and prospering…until Colin caught a chill.

It happened late one afternoon during the last week of March, after our horses had plunged through the shell ice of a river near Truro, Nova Scotia. We were soaked to the waist. By the time we'd found a tavern willing to take us in, it was pitch dark and bitterly cold. As we made our way upstairs to the room the landlord had offered, Colin was shaking uncontrollably.

"Get into bed and I'll bring you a hot drink," I ordered him. "Rum, if I can get it, with lots of butter."

"But we promised a show," he protested, as I removed his jacket and shoved him down on the bed to pull off his frozen boots.

"*I* promised a show," I reminded him of my exact words to the landlord. "A low-cut gown, a few up-flips of my skirt, and he'll never notice you're missing."

"Starr, no! I hate when you…flaunt yourself for money."

I unbuckled his belt, opened his trousers, and pushed him back on the bed to strip him from the waist down.

"Flaunt myself? Poor baby, just look at yourself!" I tried to tease him as I pulled off his clothes.

"Dear God, Starr!" He grabbed a quilt and quickly pulled it over his nakedness.

"Sweetheart, I'm joking." I bent to kiss his flushed cheek and was appalled at the fire in it. "Rest. I'll put on a little show, then bring us up a nice, warm dinner. And I promise, I won't flaunt myself…unnecessarily."

"Starr…!"

"Teasing, love, only teasing. Rest."

When I returned to our room after a successful performance, a tray of hot venison stew, biscuits, and tea in my hands, I found Colin feverish. He ate only a little of the meal before pulling the quilts to his throat and rolling up in a ball, shuddering with chills. I built up the fire in the small stove in the room, pulled off my dress, and joined him beneath the covers.

"Hold me, Colin," I said. "Let me warm you with my body."

He obeyed, and soon, lulled to sleep, he settled against me.

****

Colin was worse the next morning. When I awoke in what I took to be pre-dawn darkness, I found our bed damp with his sweat. His face had a ghastly pallor, his breathing labored and rasping.

"Colin," I said sitting up and touching his burning shoulder. "Colin, love."

"Mother," he gasped, arousing and staring up at me. His face was wet with sweat, his lips dry and cracked. "Mother, I don't want to go back to the timber camp. Tell Papa…please tell Papa."

"Colin, it's me, Starr, your wife," I said. "Wake up, love. You're dreaming."

But he grasped me with fiery hands and continued, "Mother, he hates me…he hates my music. Let's leave him. We'll go to your home in Vienna." Then his grip relaxed, his eyes closed, and he fell back, unconscious, onto his pillows.

I sprang from the bed to dress in shirt and breeches. I must get a doctor. Surely there must be one in the area. I pulled on my fur-lined moccasins in the faint glow from the embers winking out through the stove's drafts.

Not wanting to arouse Colin, I tiptoed to the door, coat and hat in hand, and tried to open it. It did not budge. I wrenched at it. I had to get out; I had to get a doctor. Colin could be dying!

My best efforts failed. I stumbled to the window and threw aside the heavy tartan draperies. I found it shuttered and secured from outside. Colin and I were prisoners.

Panic gripping me, I ran back to the door and pounded on it. "Let us out! My husband is ill! I must fetch a doctor!"

My fists were smarting when a key turned in the lock and the door swung open. It let in a flood of light behind the big Scotsman who was the landlord. Two of his stable hands stood behind him.

"Thank God!" I breathed. "My husband is ill. He needs a doctor."

I tried to rush past them, but the landlord caught me by the arm.

"You'll no be goin' anywhere, lassie," he said. "You and the lad are to remain our guests for a few days."

"What? Why?"

"You and the lad are fugitives." He shoved me back inside. "I saw a notice in Halifax last week offering one hundred pounds' reward for the apprehension of one Colin Douglas, blond-haired, blue-eyed, six feet tall, twenty years of age, believed traveling with his wife, a honey-haired lass of eighteen. You two fit that description to a T, so I'll just be keepin' the pair of you until Abe Douglas sends someone to identify you and make good his offer. I've already sent word to his agent in Halifax that I have you both in my custody. Now it's just a matter of time before I'm a much richer man."

"How dare he!" I was outraged. "How dare he offer a reward for our capture! We're not criminals, nor his property. You have no right to hold us."

"Abraham Douglas is a wealthy, powerful man." The Scotsman shrugged. "He can do as he pleases."

"If you must hold us," I said, seeing no way out, "at least get my husband a doctor. If you don't see to his care, he'll die before you can collect your reward."

"Lassie, there's nay a doctor for miles. My boys

will tend him as best they can. After that, he either lives or dies. It's the best I can do."

****

For the next four days Colin and I were held prisoners in that locked and shuttered room. The landlord and his men brought us hearty meals, fresh linen, and hot buttered rum, and saw to our other needs. We were waited on, almost pampered. Our jailer wanted us in good condition when Abe's envoy arrived to collect us and pay him.

I did not consider an escape attempt. Colin had grown worse, far too ill to travel, and I would not leave him. Often he was delirious and cried out for his mother or Barret.

Finally, on a blustery March afternoon, the Scotsman came to take me down to the common room.

"A gentleman sent by Abraham Douglas has come to fetch you," he said as he led me down the stairs. "Master of the old man's fleet, he says he is."

I caught my breath at his words and then was on the threshold of the common room, facing Barret Madison.

"Mrs. Douglas." Those two words warned me against familiarity.

"Captain," I replied, holding my head high, although I longed to rush into his arms, weak with relief that he was safe. "So you've come to drag us back."

"Aye, madame. I've already paid this good man for his trouble. Now take me to your husband. I want to be on our way as soon as possible. This day is working itself into a spring blizzard frenzy. I have no wish to be caught abroad in it. Mr. Colin is unwell, I understand?"

He took my arm and headed me toward the stairs.

"We'll not be requiring any further assistance, landlord," he said over his shoulder to the Scotsman, who had made a move to accompany us. "I'll take charge of the two of them from now on."

"Barret." Colin's fever-cracked lips moved with an effort as he recognized his friend. "Take...Starr... home. I'm too sick...to care...for her...any longer."

"I've come to take you both home, brother," Barret said, his tone gentle and reassuring. "I have horses and a sleigh outside. Now," he said, sitting down beside Colin on the edge of the bed. "What is it?"

"My chest." Colin choked. "It hurts...to breathe."

"How could you have allowed this to happen?" The captain swung on me, gray eyes as cold as the day.

"I didn't know he'd get sick."

"Didn't know? In God's name, girl, where is your common sense? He had pneumonia only a little over two years ago, just before his mother died. You can't be so ignorant as not to know that once a person has had that illness, he's forever vulnerable to it."

I should have recalled his telling me about his illness; I should have guessed it had been pneumonia, although he'd never actually named it. I should never have allowed him to be in a position where he could contract it again. Oh, dear God, how could I bear the guilt if he died?

"I can't breathe," Colin gasped. He looked up at Barret. "My chest pains."

"You need rest and a good doctor," Barret said. "I'll see you get both. Starr," he turned to me, his tone moderating from that which he'd previously raked over me. "Get your belongings together. We're leaving."

****

The drive back to Halifax was a bitterly cold act of madness. All through the blustery late afternoon and halfway through the harsh night that followed, Barret drove the powerful team he'd brought to collect us, drove with unrelenting savagery. When they dared slow their pace or faltered in a drift, he arose from his seat to crack his whip over their steaming flanks and roar curses until they once more floundered forward. Like a man obsessed, he kept the sweating horses moving, accepting nothing but their most valiant efforts. In the rear of the sleigh, wrapped in furs and drugged with laudanum, Colin slumbered.

I kept my peace until one of the horses fell in a belly-high drift. Barret rose and brought the whip down on the animal's sweating rump. The mare screamed and stumbled, trembling, to her feet.

"Stop!" I grabbed his upraised arm as he prepared to strike her again. "She's exhausted! If you don't rest this team, they'll never get us to Halifax."

He paused and lowered his arm.

"You're right," he said, and leaped from the sleigh to throw robes over the wet horses. Leaving them standing heaving for breath, he rejoined me. For a few minutes, we sat in silence. Then I spoke.

"Was your voyage to London a success? Did Colin's father get the mail contract?"

He shrugged. "Who knows how such decisions are reached. The governor is still undecided. Are contracts awarded on proof of ability? Or on government patronage? I only know I gave it my best effort. Now it's up to Randall." He paused and heaved a weary sigh. "I lost two of my men in the process."

"You mean they deserted?" I asked, amazed.

"Surely no one would dare desert the Commodore of Abraham Douglas's fleet."

"No, I mean lost…dead. They froze to death chopping ice from the rigging to keep the *Maris Stella* from capsizing with the spray frozen to her masts. Abe's proof of ability had a very high price tag."

"Barret, I'm sorry." I felt his pain and regret as if it were my own. I put my gloved hand on his arm.

"Don't," he muttered, pulling away. "I've been at sea for weeks, with only men as companions. I have needs, Starr, fierce needs after weeks of celibacy. To be touched by you, of all people, makes them even worse."

I nodded. Tears trickled down my cold cheeks.

"Starr, don't, please. You'll break my heart, *chèrie*."

"Drive on, please." I swung away from him and assumed my role as Mrs. Colin Douglas, loyal wife and haughty prisoner of the womanizing Captain Madison. "I do not wish to have my reputation sullied by being caught abroad and, for all practical purposes, alone with you at night. Let us get to Halifax as quickly as possible."

"Aye, Mrs. Douglas, ma'am," he responded gruffly. "The sooner I'm rid of you and your invalid spouse, the better."

He jumped from the sleigh to take the covers from the horses, and I pulled the buffalo robes more snugly about me. The heavy wraps did nothing to prevent sharp, piercing ice crystals from forming about my heart.

Chapter Twelve

"You did a rash thing in encouraging my son to forsake his responsibilities," Abraham said as I stood before his huge mahogany desk a month later. "You realize that now, I presume?"

"No," I said defiantly. "I did what I thought best for both of us. My only regret is that we did not succeed."

"Damn you!" he roared. "The only reason I tolerate your impudence is in the hope you'll one day pass some of that indomitable spirit on to Colin's children. God knows they'll need all they can get."

He came to stand before me, his thumbs hooked into his vest.

"Colin is recovering, but he's still very weak," he said, his tone cooling. "And you're still slim as a reed and will remain that way for some time, as a result. I believe you're quite content with that circumstance."

"That's not true."

"Shut up, you piece of baggage!" He leaned toward me—and for a moment I thought he meant to grab me. "Shut up and do as I say, or I'll have you thrown so far out into the wilderness not even God Himself will be able to find you."

I could barely prevent myself from cowering before his fury. I knew he meant every word. I didn't speak.

“That’s more like it.” When I failed to retort, he turned and walked away.

At a window he paused and drew aside a lace undercurtain to look out at the village. His village, I realized, feeling his power.

“Randall says Colin will need rest and a congenial climate to recover fully,” he said, his gaze on the river flowing cold and black between shores still edged with melting April ice. “When he can travel, I’m sending the two of you to an island in the Caribbean. I have a pleasant cottage there. You’ll enjoy the climate. It relaxes the inhibitions and arouses natural urges. I’m confident you’ll return to this house pregnant.”

“Mr. Douglas, I *love* Colin,” I said. “He doesn’t have to give me a child to strengthen our relationship.”

“Damn it, girl!” He swung on me, his face reddening. “I don’t care about sentimentality and philosophizing—I want a grandson. Now go to your husband and try to help him back to whatever pretensions to manhood he once had.”

With as much haughty dignity as I could muster, I strode out of the room. Once beyond the office door, I collapsed against the foyer wall, my knees too weak to support me. I understood why strong men cringed before my father-in-law and were made to feel both hatred and respect for him

****

“He ordered us to have a child, Colin,” I said as I came to the bed in a white silk nightshift that same evening. “He said we must.”

Colin, lying on his back beneath the covers, moved uneasily in chagrined agitation. “Do *you* want a baby, Starr?” he asked. “Do you want *my* baby?”

"I love you, Colin. I could love your child."

"But do you *need* a baby to hold us together?" he asked, looking up at me with harried eyes.

"No." I slipped into bed beside him. "We care for each other, we enjoy each other's company. I'm content. Are you?"

"Yes," he said, looking up at the ceiling and blinking rapidly. "Yes, I am. Don't ever leave me, Starr. I need you."

"Colin, don't distress yourself." I touched his cheek. "I've said I'm content, and I meant it."

"But I've seen the way men look at you," he said. "And I ache in my heart to please you as…Barret could…as Jared pleases Caroline."

"You know about Captain Fletcher and Caroline?"

"Of course. We're a troubled family, my beautiful wife. Do you often wish yourself free of us?"

"No, I love you as the brother I've never had. You've given me caring and tenderness beyond any obligation."

"Thank God for you, my lovely Starr," he breathed, and drew my fingers to his lips. Then he broke down, coughing. I held him and soothed him and, shortly, he drifted off to sleep.

****

"You and Colin will leave on Friday next, aboard the *Linnet*," Abraham informed me when he summoned me to his office in mid-May.

I stifled an audible sigh of relief. I had feared being shipped off aboard the *Maris Stella* with Barret Madison.

I was packing that evening when I heard someone at the piano in the drawing room. My heart caught and stumbled over the staggering notes. I knew who was making that valiant effort. As I started downstairs, I wondered how to proceed. He would need comforting after his garbled recital, and I must somehow find the words to provide it.

I paused in the drawing room doorway. A low fire on the hearth struggled to dispel the spring chill and encroaching gloom. In the bleak May twilight my husband sat alone at the piano. He wore a white linen shirt and black trousers. A blanket was draped about his shoulders in defense against the cold to which he'd become acutely sensitive since we'd been returned to Peacock House.

He started a new composition, a beautiful nocturne, but completed only a few bars before his fingers tripped and fell over the melody. Frustrated, he raised his hands and crashed them down upon the keys.

"Colin, no!" I rushed forward and caught his wrists as he was about to once again smash his fingers into the ivory.

"I can't play, Starr," he yelled. "I may as well be dead. Darcy is dead, I'm back in this house, and I can't play!"

"No." I shook him, trying to bring him out of his temper. "You'll play again. You're still recovering from a brutal illness. Wait until you're well. And we are escaping from this house." I lowered my voice. "Once we're on that Caribbean island, we can book passage to Vienna. Your father will be too far away to stop us this time."

"Do you think we could?" He looked up at me, his expression one of naïve, childlike expectation. "If only I could believe…"

"Believe," I said with a confidence I was far from feeling. "This time we will be free."

He drew me down onto his lap and into his arms to hold me in a trembling embrace.

"I will believe," he breathed. "I must. Otherwise, I will die."

"Now, play." I kissed his cheek and extricated myself from his embrace. "I know you can."

"Yes." He flexed his fingers, grimaced, and replaced them on the keys. "Yes, I can."

The music was slow, faltering at first, but it was a start. I folded my hands and smiled. Yes, Colin would play again.

Then a slight sound from the doorway made me turn. Captain Madison stood on the threshold watching us. Our eyes met for a moment, and he winked and nodded approvingly before moving away unnoticed by my husband, who was already engrossed in his music.

I left Colin absorbed in his practicing a half hour later and returned to our bedroom to finish packing. Rose had gone, leaving my cases neatly in order. With a sigh, I sank down in a chair to rest. It was then I heard voices in the office below. Reverend Prescott, Abraham, and, surprisingly, Mary Constable were having a discussion.

"I do not want to marry Captain Fletcher," Mary pleaded, her voice trembling. "Please, Mr. Douglas, sir, don't insist!"

"Think about it, my girl." My father-in-law's tone was authoritative. "He's well-to-do and a handsome beggar, to boot. You could do much worse."

"Abraham, please listen to the child," Reverend Prescott was imploring. "I'm sure Captain Fletcher will have no part of an arranged marriage, either."

"I caught him fondling my daughter-in-law!" Abraham shocked me by booming. "He'll do exactly as I say or lose not only his present command but his master's ticket as well. I will not have him drawing Randall's wife into adultery to satisfy his physical needs."

"Abraham, please!" Reverend Prescott implored. "There's a young woman present. We must speak accordingly."

"Don't worry about me, Reverend." Mary spoke up, her voice hard with anger. "I was aboard the *Maris Stella* when Starr Reynolds seduced Captain Madison and convinced him to allow her to share his cabin for a fortnight. Captain Madison is a good, kind person, but he is a man, and that creature knows all the tricks. If you force me to marry that…that womanizing Captain Fletcher, I shall tell Mr. Colin the truth about his bride."

"Why, you despicable bit of baggage!" Abraham raged. "How dare you threaten me! Get her out of here, Adam, before I forget myself and strike a woman. Captain Fletcher is too good for such a lying bitch. Rose!" he roared out into the hallway. "Fetch Captain Madison. Immediately!"

As I listened to Mary and the minister leave and heard Abraham bellow for Captain Madison, I was ill with fear. By the time Barret had joined my father-in-law, the older man seemed to have regained his self-control and could speak civilly once more.

"Barret, a disturbing accusation has been laid against you," he said. "Mary Constable has told me you took Starr as your mistress for the crossing from England. Did you?"

"No." The reply was crisp. "I thought about it. I even gave her my cabin for a couple of weeks and fondled her a few times. But she rejected my advances. And I wasn't about to take her by force. I like my ladies ready and willing."

"I thought as much." Abraham chuckled. "I believe you. No matter what your other vices, you're no liar. Now tell me, when you fondled her, did you find her to be a virgin?"

"Sweet Jesus, Abe! I said fondled, not examined. I never got so far."

"Good. Very good. Did she seem attracted to you, did she try to seduce you, anything to indicate she was loose or had a yen for you?"

"She shoved me away. Take that as your answer."

****

I couldn't sleep. Many things were troubling me. Aside from Mary Constable's accusation, I'd made a wild promise to Colin in an effort to raise his spirits. Now I lay uncomfortable and disconcerted in our bed while he slumbered by my side, no doubt with visions of Vienna dancing through his head.

He stirred and muttered in his sleep, "Cold."

"I'll get another quilt," I murmured, and arose.

When I'd spread it over him and he'd settled with a contented sigh, I stood a moment looking down at him, then went to gaze out the window at the huge moon rising over the river.

How could I manage the escape to Vienna I'd promised him? Maybe Barret could be persuaded to help. No, I couldn't ask that of him. Abraham would ruin him if he dared to take his son away again. I had to find some other way.

****

A raw April wind was sweeping over the docks, as we waited for our trunks to be stowed away aboard the *Linnet*, when Barret Madison galloped Lucifer onto the pier. Randall, mounted on Bach, rode close behind him.

They had come to bid us farewell, I thought, as I stood between Colin and his father, my fur-lined cloak keeping the cold at bay, my leather boots protecting my feet from patches of lingering snow and icy puddles. In three weeks Colin and I would be on a Caribbean island, living in Abe's cottage, under orders to bring about a pregnancy. I looked up at Barret Madison and my heart skipped a beat. How could I become pregnant from another man when I was in love with him?

"I thought you were going to miss your ship." Abraham addressed the captain. Startled, I glanced up at my father-in-law.

"Never fear." Barret swung to the ground and handed Lucifer's reins to Randall. "My sea chest was aboard at dawn."

"Barret is accompanying you," Abraham explained. "Last week Andrew MacDonald saw fit to steal the *London Lass* from her anchorage in this very river. He claimed he'd purchased most of her shares before he left my employ and that she was rightfully his. I disagree, and since I still hold her ownership papers, I have the law on my side. Barret, with the help of Jared's crew, is to seize the *London Lass* where I've been told she lies at anchor in the Caribbean and bring her back to me, loaded with guano. I'll not be defied, nor denied what is rightfully mine, you see, my dear." He looked meaningfully at me.

"Barret." He turned to the captain. "Pack the *Lass*'s

holds well with those bird droppings. Supervise her loading personally and, as you do, keep in mind that holds are meant for cargo and not as hiding places for your employer's errant son."

"Father, that's not fair," Colin protested. "I forced Barret to take me with him to Vienna the spring Mother died, and to Halifax at Christmas."

"And just how did you force him, my lad? Did you torture him with your guitar? Or jam his fingers in your piano?"

"I'll bring the guano." Barret ended the argument. "Now let's get on board."

****

We had been at sea almost three weeks and were entering warmer climates off the Florida coast when the drama that was to entirely alter the course of my life began.

A sailor had brought a tray of wine and cheese to our cabin shortly after I retired there following dinner. I recalled having told Colin such fare must be reserved for special occasions and wondered why he had requested the treats on this particular night.

I had just finished bathing when Colin joined me. He had a glass of brandy with Barret and Jared each evening after our meal, to give me the privacy of our room for my toilet. On this particular night, he returned slightly inebriated and began to undress.

It was the first time I had seen him intoxicated since our wedding night, and I was nonplused as he stripped off his jacket, vest, and shirt without reaching for a dressing robe as he normally did.

"Starr, I know my father has threatened you with banishment if you…if we don't have a child," he said.

"I can't risk that happening." He tugged at his belt and staggered close to the built-in bed where I sat curled up in a rose-colored silk wrapper. "Tonight I will be your husband," he slurred, towering over me. "Tonight I will give you my baby."

"Colin…"

"Damn it, Starr! It's our only chance." His eyes reflected his desperation. "I can't fight my father. And God knows we'll never succeed in eluding him." His voice softened to near pleading as he knelt beside my bed. "Please help me! Please help us stay together. I'll be gentle. And when the baby comes, I'll stay with you through your labor. Starr, I'm begging you. Don't refuse me!"

"Colin, you don't have to do this," I said, reaching out to stroke his tense cheek. "I'm not afraid of your father. All I care about is your happiness."

"I know that, Starr," he said. "But I also know what you've already suffered, how cruel and comfortless your life was—Darcy told me much more vividly than you did—and now I want you to have all the luxuries you deserve. I want you with me forever. And if our having a baby together will accomplish that, then we'll do it." He released his belt and dropped his trousers. "I love you, Starr," he said, his voice full of emotion. "Believe me, I do."

He moved to a chair, pulled off boots and socks, then came to join me on the bed, clad only in his skintight undertrousers. With trembling fingers, he undid the sash of my wrap and slowly, looking nervously into my eyes for approval, opened it.

"You're very lovely," he murmured, lowering his gaze when I made no move to stop him.

"I love you, Colin," I whispered, my heart pounding so loudly I could barely hear myself speak. "If you think fathering a child will keep us as you wish..." I put my arms about his neck. Slowly and gently he pushed me back to lie on the bed beneath him.

"Starr, oh, God, Starr," he moaned, and he was trembling. He drew himself over me, his body tense and shuddering.

He fumbled with the fastening of his drawers. In an effort to encourage him, I kissed his sweat-damp forehead. I could feel no fear of this awkward boy who was my husband, only pity at his desperate attempt to make love to me.

"Help me, Starr," he begged. "Help me. I can't..."

He moved over me frantically, his efforts breaking out sweat over his chest. He slid himself between my legs and thrust against me.

"Colin, sweetheart, we've got all night," I soothed, feeling his anxiety. "Let's just lie quietly together, and after a time you'll be able to."

"No, no, I have to...now...now," he choked, increasing his efforts. "Now..."

A burst of cannon fire stopped his torrent of impassioned words. The *Linnet* shuddered beneath us. From the decks above came the sudden sound of running feet, accompanied by an angry cacophony of sailors' voices.

"What was that?" Colin turned in my arms as, startled, I pulled my robe around both of us. A moment later Barret Madison burst in upon us.

"Pirates!" he yelled. "Stay below and keep quiet! With luck, we'll be able to fight them off."

"I'll come with you." Colin was scrambling from

the bed, closing his undertrousers.

"No!" Barret's single word was an undeniable command. "You aren't yet strong enough to make yourself anything more than a liability. Stay here and be a comfort to your wife. She's as white as a ghost. And for God's sake, put some clothes on. If we're overcome, you'll both be raped."

He left as abruptly as he'd entered.

"Miserable cur!" Colin spat, reaching for his clothes. "Belittling bastard!"

"Colin, pirates do rape women prisoners, don't they?" I asked. Captain Madison's words had flashed a terrible memory across my brain. "Please don't let them rape me, Colin! I couldn't bear it."

"Oh, my poor angel!" he breathed, forgetting his annoyance in concern for me as he took me into his arms.

He drew his long legs, knees bent, onto the bed, and I huddled between them, my head against his bare chest. He stroked my hair and murmured, "Hush, hush," as the sounds of the brutal fight erupted above us.

Then we heard them breaking open cabin doors as the marauders made their way down the passageway to our cabin. Savage shouts and scuffles over the division of the spoils in each room marked their progress. Finally they were outside our very door.

"Colin, please, please don't let them rape me!" I clung to him, mesmerized with terror. "Swear before God you'll kill me yourself before…"

Before I could finish my sentence, the door burst open. I huddled against my husband's chest as the marauders, their features hidden behind black hoods, surged into the cabin.

“Well, well, what have we here?” one of them laughed. “A pair of young’uns matin’? Come, lad, let us see your bitch.”

“I’ve money,” Colin replied with astonishing control, but beneath my ear his heart was thundering. “Take it and go. Leave my wife alone. She’s…with child.”

“Laid her good, did you, boy?” the burly leader spoke again, a vicious chuckle in his throat. “Well, I’d like to look at this pregnant wench of yours. Perhaps she’s not yet too ungainly to give us sport. Give her here, lad.”

“God damn you!” Colin leaped to his feet. He swung at the black hood who’d made the suggestion, but a second pirate came at him from the side. Before Colin’s blow could touch the leader, the second man’s fist had sunk deep into my husband’s belly. Colin roared in pain and sank to his knees, clutching himself.

I remembered the knife Colin had brought to the cabin with our lunch. Lying between the wine and cheese, it winked at me in the lantern light. As the pirate leader came toward me, my fingers inched slowly toward it.

“Why, she’s a right comely little wench,” he leered. “And her belly isn’t swelled a bit. Either the lad is lying or she’s not far gone. She’ll make sport, and that’s all we care about, right, lads?”

The others roared their approval, but as the towering hulk reached for me with huge, hairy hands, my fingers closed over the knife. Like an enraged feline, I lunged at him, screaming and lashing out with the weapon. Taken by surprise, he stumbled backward and all but fell.

My first stab found its mark deep in the flesh of his left thigh. He yelled in pain, then brought up his hand to slap me across the face. The blow sent me reeling back against a wall beam with a nauseating flash of blinding pain. Dazed but still conscious, I crumpled to the cabin floor.

"Vicious little whore!" I heard him rasp. "Take her to the deck, lads. We'll teach her manners!"

I was thrown over a hard, broad shoulder and carried from the cabin.

On deck, the pirate dropped me to the planks. As the fresh salt air revived me, I became aware of Colin, his hands shackled behind him, kneeling beside me. His face was a ghastly shade of gray, but he was crouching over me, his concern concentrated on me.

"Starr, sweetheart!" he choked. "Are you all right?"

"God damn your miserable souls to Hell!" I recognized Barret Madison's voice as my throbbing head cleared. "They're only children! Leave them alone!"

"Now, *Mr.* Madison, would you go denyin' us what gossip in Pine says you've already had the pleasure of?" Groggily I rolled my head to see a huge, familiar form towering over Colin and me, legs planted wide apart, arms akimbo, blood dripping from the wound I had inflicted in his forearm.

Beyond him, I saw Barret and Jared Fletcher tied, backs to the mainmast. Barret's face in the light of swaying lanterns was a monument to outrage. Jared's subdued crew, with many injured among their number, had been herded against the bulwarks aft, guarded at musket point by black-hooded pirates.

"The lad says she's carryin' his brat!" the pirate roared. "But if the stories told be true, it's more likely *Mr.* Madison's leavin's she's got in her belly."

At the remark, raucous laughter erupted. Colin lurched to his feet.

"Filthy, vicious scum!" he yelled. "Rotten, miserable liars!"

A musket barrel caught him along the side of his head. With a yelp of pain, my husband was sent sprawling face down, unconscious, onto the deck.

"Swine!" Jared's voice rose in fury. "Rob the ship and get the blazes off her! Leave Colin and his wife alone!"

"Leave them alone?" The sailor I'd stabbed sneered. "The bitch tried to kill me. I'll have a bit of her in payment before I leave this tub."

He yanked me to my feet. My head groggy and throbbing, I staggered and would have collapsed back onto the deck had he not caught me to him. The stench of his unwashed body and his breath reeking of rum and stale tobacco made my senses reel with horrific memory. Mad with terror, I looked up into his masked face and recognized the small, mean eyes of Simon, the overseer.

"So this is old Abe's prized daughter-in-law," he said, his voice trembling with the ecstasy of conquest. "Fling me into that pigsty he calls a jail, will he? By God, I'll show the old bastard what I think of him and his fine family!" He flung me to another sailor. "Throw her to the deck and part her legs. We've earned a little sport!"

"No!" I screamed. "No! Colin, help me!"

But my husband could not come to my aid. He lay

semi-conscious on the planks.

"That'll do!" A big, barrel-chested pirate appeared from out of the darkness near the stern. "There'll be no raping of young girls. She and her husband will be cast adrift in a lifeboat, with Captain Madison to navigate for them. If he can row as well as he can coerce, they should reach an island due west of here by midday tomorrow. We'll keep Fletcher and his crew here to sail this trim beauty for us."

The man's Scottish accent aroused another memory. The hooded pirate captain was Andrew MacDonald, the man Abe had removed from command of the *London Lass* and whose ship Barret had been on his way to confiscate.

I had little time to marvel at my discovery. The reprimanded sailor made a lunge at his commander from behind, a cudgel in his hand. He brought it down on Andrew MacDonald's scull. MacDonald, with a grunt of pain, sank to the deck.

"Now, me lads, hold her down," Simon returned his attention to me, dripping blood and holding the bat. "We'll show Mr. Madison how to use his whore."

Barret gave a bestial roar. All heads turned to see the captain rip free of his ropes with seemingly superhuman strength. Then, wrists crimson with blood, he leaped to the deck, his face a portrait of unbridled rage.

"Take on a man, you piece of stable droppings!" he snarled, circling Simon like an attacking wolf. "Let's see if you've got even a semblance of guts in that fat, filthy body."

"Bastard, whorehouse leavin's," Simon rasped, and lunged at Barret.

The pirates moved back to give them room. This

was a fair fight; they would not interfere.

The savage battle seemed to last an eternity. First Simon, then Barret would appear to have the upper hand. Both men became bloody and battered. Barret had ripped Simon's hood away and the former overseer's ugly face began to show the results of the pummeling he was receiving. Barret's countenance was blood-streaked from a cut above his right eye.

Finally, locked together in savage embrace, they staggered to the bulwarks. For one heart-stopping moment it appeared Simon would be the victor as he choked Barret over the rail. Then, with a great roar, the captain freed himself, grabbed Simon, and flung him bodily over the rail.

Below, in the water, there was a splash, a few desperate screams, a thrashing about, and then a horrible silence.

"The sharks be quick tonight," one of the pirates said. "What with him bleedin' like a stuck pig, they'd get him in seconds."

"It be the blood," another agreed. "They smells it quick as sin. Now let us get to the sport Simon wanted. Madison be spent. He'll give us no more trouble, and it wouldn't be right to let the old fella die for nothin'."

"Barret!" I scrambled across the bloody deck and into his arms as he leaned, heaving for breath, against the rail. "Barret, kill me, please kill me before…"

"That'll do."

Unnoticed in the excitement, Captain MacDonald had regained consciousness and risen to his feet. Now he pushed his way to the center of the group and took command. "There'll be no raping of women aboard any ship I command. I may be an old man, but I'm still fit enough to take on any one of you lot."

The sailors shuffled uneasily.

"Very well. Prepare a boat with food, fresh water, and blankets, and lower it over the side. Captain Madison, with the boy and girl, is about to leave us."

Within minutes Barret, Colin, and I were in a dinghy about to float away from the *London Lass* and the *Linnet* into the blackness. A dull thud announced a gunnysack hurled from the ship into our small craft.

"You'll find a compass, chronometer, and sextant among the supplies, Captain," Andrew MacDonald's voice came out of the darkness above us. "They'll let you navigate to that island, if you're half the mariner you profess to be."

"Obliged, Andrew." Barret's response reeked of sarcasm. "I'll remember your kindness when next we meet."

****

The two ships became black silhouettes in the distance. I was left to huddle against my wounded, semi-conscious husband while Barret rowed, his wrists raw from rope cuts.

All that night and next morning we drifted, Barret rowing intermittently and fighting to keep our course due west toward the promised island. By noon Colin and I were sunburned and parched. Barret would allow us little water. We needed to conserve, he said. I saw the wisdom in his words, but in my discomfort, I hated him for his domineering attitude.

At midday the captain pointed westward. Colin and I, dozing in the stern, followed his outstretched arm. At first I dared not believe what I saw. Then, as my eyes told me I could not be mistaken, I cried out in joy. The currents were moving us slowly but certainly toward a green rise in the sea. We were moving toward an island. Barret's navigational skills had saved us.

The water shallowed as he rowed our skiff closer to the island. A coral reef inhabited by infinite varieties of colorful fish could be seen beneath its hull. The turquoise water made the lessening depths appear a place of enchanted loveliness. Colin and I stared down into the exotic beauty of the sea, excited by its magnificent scenery.

"It's a wonderland!" my husband exclaimed. I believe he was feverish from the sun, his wounds, and lack of water. He looked at me with hot, bright eyes. "The water can't be more than four feet deep beneath us. I'm going to pull this boat ashore." The next instant he'd leaped out of the dory and was chest deep in that benign-looking tropic sea.

"Colin, get back in the boat!" Barret yelled. He dropped the oars and stumbled to my side to reach out and grab him by the shirtfront.

"Leave me alone, Barret!" he snapped, shaking off the captain's hands. "I'll have us ashore in no time."

"Colin, don't move. Don't disturb the water!"

Barret's fist clutched again at my husband's shirt, but it was too late. Out of the corner of my eye, I saw the pair of fins piercing the blue-green surface in the dory's wake. I had heard of sharks, but until that moment I'd never seen one. I screamed and pointed.

Barret saw them, too, and gave a mighty pull at Colin's shirt. The thin garment rent under his hands. Colin, still unaware of the danger, broke free. The next instant his mouth opened in a horrific roar of shock and pain.

He screamed, clawing at Barret's outstretched arms. The water about him became stained an anemic red. Barret leaned far over the edge of the boat and managed to get his arms about Colin's chest.

"Help me!" he yelled at me. I flung my arms about his waist and together we pulled. Soon, although it seemed like hours, we had Colin back on board. Gasping for breath, I sank to my knees and gazed in horror at my husband's legs. His trousers were shredded rags with crimson rivulets of blood pouring through the tatters.

"Barret…" I turned him.

He shot me a glance that ordered me to control myself as he knelt beside Colin.

"Barret…" My husband's body twitched with shock and pain.

"Try to lie still," Barret's words sounded remarkably calm. "We'll be ashore soon, and I'll dress your wounds."

He reached into the provisions given us by Andrew MacDonald and took out a small flask. It contained a familiar reddish-brown liquid.

"Drink this," he said, putting the bottle to Colin's lips. "It'll help."

My husband obeyed. The jerking spasms slowly ceased, and he lay still, his eyes glazed.

The boat drifted slowly, at a snail's pace it seemed, toward the shore. The oars which Barret had used to row us this far lay useless across the gunwales. To further disturb the water would draw more sharks, Barret said. Our small craft could not withstand an attack of an entire school.

Finally we were in water Barret deemed too

shallow for sharks. He lowered himself out of the boat and pulled it ashore.

Once our craft had been beached, the captain climbed back into the dory and lifted Colin into his arms. My husband started and moaned, but the laudanum had removed his consciousness to a place beyond the reach of most of the pain. He lay against Barret's chest, his eyes slits beneath fallen lids.

Leaving a horrifying trail of red dots behind them, Barret carried him over a beach of white sand. I followed, thinking how strange the sand did not feel hot beneath my feet, thinking about my filthy person, thinking about anything but Colin and the horror of his wounds.

Barret laid my husband beneath a palm tree. "Give me your underwear," he said grimly, turning to me. "I need white cloth to dress these gashes."

I hesitated.

"Dear God, woman, your husband is bleeding to death!" he barked. "This is no time for modesty!"

He knelt beside Colin, and I began to unbutton the blue linen dress Captain MacDonald had allowed me to don before being set adrift.

****

Colin was dying. Barret and I sat beside him beneath the gently swaying palm fronds and watched his life ebbing as the day waned. There was nothing we could do. As the beach grew dark and the horizon alone stayed bright with a rainbow sunset, my husband opened his eyes and looked up at me. He was incredibly young and innocent in that moment. I put my hand to his burning forehead.

"Starr," he rasped.

"Don't try to talk," I begged. "Save your strength."

"No," he said. "I must. Where is Barret?"

"Right here, brother." Barret moved closer to allow Colin to see him without turning his head. "I won't leave you."

"You are my friend, aren't you, Barret? You'd do anything for me?"

"Rest, lad." Barret's voice was gentler than I had ever heard it. He brushed blond curls back from my husband's wet forehead.

"Barret." With a grimace of pain, Colin grasped at Barret's shirt and drew him near. "Take care of Starr. Don't let my father send her away. Do what I couldn't do for her. Make love to her, Barret. Give her a baby my father will believe is mine."

"You're feverish," Barret said, hiding the shock I was certain Colin's bizarre request must have given him as fully as it astounded me. "Don't say things you'll regret."

"I won't regret my words. Promise me, Barret! Promise me you'll take care of my wife. Promise me you'll sleep with her." He was begging as his eyelids drooped slowly shut. He was sinking fast.

"I promise," I heard Barret mutter.

A slight smile tipped Colin's lips. "Thank you," he whispered.

His face contorted in a spasm of agony. His fingers clutching Barret's shirtfront turned into white-knuckled balls. When it was over, he exhaled long and exhaustedly. It appeared all the strength had drained from his body. A moment later, his expression brightened and he smiled up in astonished delight at something he appeared to be seeing beyond me. His hand released Barret and fell to his side. His eyes closed.

"Colin!" I screamed as the full realization came to me. I flung myself across his chest, sobbing. "Colin, don't leave me!"

"Starr, no." Barret was taking me from my husband's body and drawing me against him as he crouched beside me. Half-mad with grief, I fell against him and screamed out my pain and despair.

He let me air my sorrow. Finally, sheer exhaustion brought an end to my tirade, and I lapsed into a troubled sleep.

When I awoke it was morning. I found myself wrapped in a blanket, on a bed of palm fronds. A few feet away Barret Madison sat, his back against a tree, his face buried in his hands.

He was weeping.

****

We laid Colin to rest in a shallow depression on a grassy knoll near our landing site, then covered his grave with stones. Trembling with grief, I knelt to pray beside the rocky mound. Barret stood behind me, his face like chiseled stone.

Through a mist of tears I heard again in my soul my young husband's wonderful music while images of the two of us as we had once been washed through my mind. I saw us riding our horses through meadows rich with sunshine and wildflowers, huddling beneath the limbs of a lofty white pine when a summer storm caught us abroad on foot during a fishing expedition, running barefoot in the shallows of the river, enjoying his music in the drawing room in a peaceful twilight, struggling for an orange in the parlor, and even sobbing over lost loves in each other's arms.

I recalled him as he had been with the servants and workers in his father's employ, as he had always been with me…compassionate and understanding. Dear God, I prayed. Care for him tenderly as he cared for me and for everyone his life touched.

"Come." Barret moved forward, bent, and took my arm to draw me to my feet. "We have work to do." His fingers beneath my elbow trembled.

****

We built a lean-to of palm fronds, grasses, and stakes near a sheltered lagoon that first day. Then we set out in search of food and fresh water. Fortunately we discovered the island abounded with fruits Barret knew to be edible, and there was a spring of fresh water within easy access of our crude shelter.

Much to my relief, we encountered no evidence of dangerous wildlife or hostile natives. The island appeared to be inhabited mainly by a vast variety of birds. In places its rocks were plastered with guano, which Barret kicked from his boots in disgust.

"We'll survive," he said, as we returned to our shelter, our arms full of fruit.

"How long do you think it will be before we're rescued?" I asked, leaning back wearily on the palm leaves we'd used as flooring.

"It probably won't be any time soon." His pessimism startled me. "Jared's course had veered off the usual shipping lanes just before we were attacked. I questioned him about it, but he told me I was wrong, that we were on a normal course toward the Caribbean."

"Are you saying we're so far from the shipping

lanes we might never be found?"

"Never is a very long time." Barret flexed work-raw hands. "I'm simply saying I think it could be weeks, maybe even months, before a ship passes this way. Our best plan of action is to settle ourselves as comfortably as possible and wait."

"Very well." I sat up stiff and prim. "This island seems relatively safe and amply supplied with the necessities of life. We can survive for as long as we must in order to be rescued."

"Survive, most definitely." His tone took on a more optimistic note. "And much more. Starr, I was raised in these islands. A place like this can be paradise. Life in the Caribbean can be a glorious experience…sensuous and exciting. I'll teach you."

"I don't know… If only Colin were…"

"Starr, don't. We can't allow ourselves to dwell on him. If we do, unhappiness will destroy us both. Now let's get some rest. We've had an arduous day. Tomorrow I'll teach you to fish in the lagoon. The entrance is too shallow to allow sharks or any other dangerous marine life to enter."

I lay down on my palm frond bed and he drew a blanket over me. Before going to his own mattress on the far side of the hut, he brushed my forehead with a kiss.

"Sleep well, princess," he murmured, and moved away into the deepening twilight.

****

I awoke as the first rays of a magnificent Caribbean morning crept in under the blanket-draped doorway of our hut. Stretching like a contented feline, I rolled to look at Barret and discovered he was gone from his bed.

I got up and went outside. Shielding my eyes against the huge tropic sun rising into a clear blue sky, I looked toward the lagoon and saw him swimming toward shore. When he struck bottom and stood, his powerful chest and shoulders glistened in the sun. He waded toward shore, and as he came into the shallows, I choked. He was naked.

I hurried back into the hut. The sensations coursing through me had to be indecent. My husband had been dead only a single day. The sight of another man's naked body should not so soon set my pulses racing, my body stirring.

But could it be wrong? Barret Madison was not just a man; he was the man I loved, the man who'd said he loved me.

"Good morning."

I turned to see him silhouetted in the doorway.

"What *are* you wearing?"

"It's called a loin cloth," he said, moving into the hut, naked except for a brief bit of white cloth about his thighs. "The natives find it the most practical garment a man can wear in these climes. I agree. Only Caucasian prudery keeps whites in the region from adopting it. And since there are no prudish Caucasians about, I see no reason why I shouldn't wear it. Does it offend you?"

"No," I faltered.

"And I have another reason for choosing this kind of dress," he said, going to squat native-like near his bed to pick up a piece of fruit from the pile we'd gathered the previous day. "We must save our civilized clothes for the day we're rescued."

"But what can I wear?" I asked, looking down at

my dress. “Even though I’m not a prudish Caucasian, I can hardly adopt your style of garment.”

“There is a length of sheeting among the supplies left us,” he said, then paused to bite into a ripe, juicy fruit in his hand. “”Bring it to me and I’ll show you how to fashion a sarong such as the native women wear.”

I obeyed. He laid aside his breakfast and, with a few deft slashes of his knife, cut the cloth into several lengths.

“Take off your dress,” he said, rising to stand before me, cloth in hand. “I’ll show you how to wrap this about yourself securely for comfort and ease of movement.”

“No!”

“Starr, you have to trust me.” Exasperation accented his words. “I slept only a few feet away from you last night. I could have come to you. You were exhausted and hurting and vulnerable. Sleeping with you would have been easy…if that was all I wanted. Now take off your gown and let me teach you to be a native.”

Slowly I unbuttoned my dress and let it slip to the ground. I wore no underclothing. It had gone to become bandages for Colin. As I stood naked before Barret, he paused, his gray eyes filled with repressed desire as he stood staring at me.

Then he reached out and swept a length of cloth about me. Several deft wraps and a couple of strategic tucks later, I stood bare-shouldered in a white garment that ended just above my knees and fastened beneath my armpit. Feeling suddenly free and uninhibited, I unpinned my hair and let it fall down my back in a tangle of waves and curls.

"You're very beautiful…too beautiful." He backed away from me and looked me up and down, rubbing his palms on his thighs. I sensed the gesture was an unconscious attempt to keep from reaching out and touching me. My heartbeat, already much faster than normal, raced away like a wild horse before a violent gale.

This isn't right. We should be mourning Colin with all our souls, not lusting after each other.

He broke the spell by drawing a deep breath and rubbing a hand over his stubbled chin.

"You're going to have to get used to living with a bearded man. A razor wasn't among Andrew's bounty."

"You don't sound much concerned that he is responsible for our predicament," I said. His return to normal conversation had made it possible for me to get myself under control…with an effort.

He shrugged. "In his position, I might have been tempted to do the same thing. Taking a man's command from him can make him bitter and vengeful. Now, enough of the past. Eat your breakfast." He tossed me a piece of fruit. "This is delicious. Later I'll teach you to fish in the lagoon."

****

For a week we retained a chaste, brother-sister relationship, but the atmosphere between us was as acutely charged as black clouds bearing an intense lightning storm. At night I often lay awake well into the hours of darkness, longing to go to him, longing to feel the comfort of his embrace, longing to satisfy my curiosity about the joys of shared lovemaking with the man I loved, who had declared himself in love with me.

I'd hear him move on his bed of palms fronds and knew that he, too, lay sleepless, probably struggling to keep those same powerful desires at bay.

Eight days after we'd arrived on the island, Barret brought matters to a head. Arms laden with a great bouquet of wild orchids, he returned from the jungle late that afternoon and laid them in front of me.

"What's this?" I asked, looking up in surprise. I'd been sitting in front of our hut, preparing fruit for our evening meal.

"I've come a-courting," he said, dropping on one knee.

"What?"

"I should like to be granted the privilege of courting you." He spoke earnestly. "I've never courted a woman before, and I'm not sure how to proceed. My previous relationships have always been born out of pure sexual need."

When I stared him, stunned to silence, he continued, "I had to wait until my face and wrists healed, to prevent my being physically repulsive. Then I remembered gentlemen I've known have asked permission to court a lady. I thought a gift might render that permission more readily granted. Am I correct so far?"

A ghost of a grin twitched his lips, but he was rubbing his hands together, and I could sense his discomfort.

"Permission granted." I smiled. "The flowers are beautiful. Thank you." I picked one from the pile and fastened it in my hair.

"My pleasure." With his relief obvious in his face, he reached forward, took up a bit of fruit, and began to help me with supper preparations. "After our meal, will you walk with me on the beach? Since there are no soirees or balls to which I may escort you, I think it might be the next appropriate step in our relationship."

****

For the next three evenings, Barret took me walking on the moonlit beach. On the fourth evening, as we paused before re-entering the hut, he put his hands on my shoulders and asked, "May I kiss you?"

I nodded. His mouth, warm and strong, gently covered mine. Cautiously he enfolded me into his arms, against his hard, scantily clad body. The sensuous tenderness of the moment flashed through me. I couldn't remain detached and ladylike one moment longer.

"Starr, no! It's too sudden." He pulled away and held me at arm's length.

"I love you!" I cried. "I have for so long. Don't keep me in this limbo any longer."

"You mean we can be together…now? But I've been told respectable women need months of courting…weeks of…"

"For a man of the world, you know remarkably little about so-called respectable women. We're flesh and blood, too. We have needs and desires…"

"Sweet Jesus!"

He scooped me up in his arms and carried me into the hut. There he laid me on his mat, among his blankets, then straightened and for a moment stood looking down at me.

"I love you," he said, gray eyes smoldering with desire. "I've never known any feeling like it. It fills up my senses, my soul. But I have to know…was Colin ever able to make himself your lover?"

"Barret..."

"Please, Starr. I have to know!"

"No, never," I breathed, my heart pounding impatiently against my ribs and wondering why he'd chosen this moment to question me about my relationship with my husband with such obvious vehemence. "He tried...in the meadow where you came upon us, and then aboard the *Linnet*...as you saw. But he never...could."

"Hush." He lay down beside me, gathering me to him and stroking my hair. "The past is past, and I despise myself for asking. But I had to know. I had to be certain."

"Barret," I whispered as I slowly released my sarong's fastening, "there will always be only you."

"Yes," he muttered. "There will be only me from this day forward. And I vow there'll be no others for myself. No matter what has gone before, this will be the first true lovemaking of both our lives...the first time we've been in love and made love."

He opened my sarong and let his gaze move over me. The gesture in the twilighted shelter was as sensuous as if he'd been touching me with his hands. My breath caught in my throat.

"Barret..." I whispered. He took my hand in his and placed it on his loincloth.

"Take it off," he said, his voice deep with emotion, when I tried to flinch away. "Take it off and see if you're still willing to make love with me."

When I hesitated, his hand went to cup my chin, to raise my lips to his in a kiss that was at first tender and gentle, then probing and forceful. As I became lost in its passion, his hand went to my breast. My senses whirled out of control, and my hand on the scrap of cloth that was his only garment pulled it free.

His patience that night was amazing. I felt no fear, no panic, no revulsion. Only ecstasy as he made love to me—at first gently, then, as I responded, with a seductive passion I could never have imagined. Simon and his brutality slid from my mind.

A skillful lover, well schooled in the art of satisfying a woman, he rejoiced in my inexperience, in my delight of all he had to offer and teach me, and in what I gave so uninhibitedly to him.

I was a child, a neophyte in the art of lovemaking, and in the days and nights that followed Barret proved an enthusiastic and talented teacher. Together we blended innocence and experience, honesty and desire, body and soul, to achieve total fulfillment.

I was happy as never before, and Barret told me he felt the same. Free at last to live a life together, we swam naked by moonlight in the lagoon and foraged for food and building materials during the day. I grew tanned as a native, my unbound hair a tangle of curls about my shoulders and down my back. Barret became bearded and bronzed by the sun. We were Adam and Eve, he jested, and so we named our island Eden. Freed of pasts of which we did not speak, uninhibited in love, and living in a veritable paradise, we were that first couple.

****

We had been on the island about five weeks when I awoke one morning to find Barret gone from his place beside me. It wasn't unusual. Often he arose early to swim or fish or search out fresh treats for our breakfast.

I stretched lazily and smiled. I was happier than I'd ever been, happier than I'd ever dreamed of being. I understood what had been missing in my marriage to Colin. I also knew that all the wealth and mansions in the world could not replace what I now possessed.

I sighed contentedly. Barret and I had it all…food, shelter, and most importantly, freedom and love. There was only one more wish we could cherish and perhaps some day bring to reality, the product of our love, our very own child.

I knew Barret envied family ties, although he never admitted it. His reference to his employer's sons as brothers, his closeness to Marie and her family because of his French blood, and his own lack of relatives, all painted a picture of a man longing for roots.

A baby! Barret's baby. I put a hand to my flat belly and suddenly realized that I had, by two weeks, missed my cycle. Was it possible? I sat up and re-calculated the days. Yes, I was definitely, undeniably late. And only yesterday I had experienced an unusual revulsion against breakfast.

I smiled and lay back slowly, my hand still on my stomach. I was pregnant! How wonderful! I tried to picture the joy on Barret's face when I told him. Our very own baby, conceived in love and born on this glorious island. We would teach him to read and write, and sing, and speak his father's mother tongue. He would grow up strong and wise and brave and gentle like his father.

I could not wait any longer to tell Barret. I got up, slung my sarong about me, and hurried down to the beach, where I found him weaving a basket in which to carry fruit. His broad, tanned shoulders were toward me as I went quietly up behind him and knelt to slip my arms about them.

"Ah," he grinned, leaning easily back against me. "My love. Did you sleep well?"

"Of course." I stroked his hair and kissed his temple. "Barret…"

I let my gaze wander out to sea. And it was then I saw the sails of the ship that would rescue us.

I did not have a chance to speak further, for at that moment he saw them, too, and leaped to his feet to wave his arms.

****

Soon a long boat was rowing in toward us. We'd dressed hastily in the clothing we'd saved for the occasion, and now we stood on the beach as respectable-looking as possible with Barret's heavy beard and my wildly unkempt hair. I knew I must tell him about the baby before our rescuers arrived.

"Barret," I said, looking up at him. He stood, legs apart, a hand shielding his eyes as he watched the approaching craft.

"Barret," I repeated, when he failed to respond. "We're going to have a child."

"*What* did you say?" He swung to face me..

"I'm pregnant," I said, smiling. "We've made a baby with our love. Isn't it wonderful?"

"Wonderful!" His face registered outrage. "You let me lay with you while you knew you carried another man's child? My brother's child? And now you try to convince me it's my baby in your belly? And Colin encouraged you in this deception! Sweet Jesus, betrayed by the two people I cared for most in this world!"

"Barret, it *is* your baby! You have to believe me. Colin and I never…"

"Liar!" he snarled. "Your child can't possibly be mine. I'm sterile—have been for years."

Chapter Thirteen

Within an hour we were aboard the *Atlantic Lady*, our rescue ship. Already carrying a full cargo of guano from neighboring islands, she'd been on her way up the American coast scouting out new prospects for future voyages. Her captain decided to forego further exploration and deposit Barret and me on a nearby island, one settled by the English, before proceeding farther north.

"A woman aboard a cargo ship has always been bad luck for me," the burly, gray-haired master declared. "The sooner we land you safely, ma'am, Abe Douglas's daughter-in-law though you declare yourself to be, the better I'll feel."

"I agree, Captain," Barret said caustically.

He turned and strode away, leaving another thorn in my already aching heart. But then, I should have expected nothing more. As soon as we'd boarded the *Atlantic Lady*, he'd alienated himself from me, ignoring me or calling me "Mrs. Douglas, ma'am" whenever he was forced to acknowledge my presence. He avoided being alone with me, keeping himself in the presence of one or more of the seamen, allowing me no opportunity to speak privately with him.

This estrangement did not stop the mariners from drawing what to them seemed the obvious conclusion concerning our days on Eden. They nudged each other and pointed at us with leering grins.

I tried to accept the situation with grace and dignity. By the time we reached the island to which the *Atlantic Lady* was taking us, Barret would have realized he'd been wrong about his physical condition. He would find a clergyman, and we would be married. Or so I struggled to reassure myself.

When we docked at Del Ray Island, the English family of a wealthy plantation owner, on learning I was daughter-in-law to powerful Abraham Douglas, took me in. In the flurry that followed our arrival, I lost track of Barret. When I was settled in the plantation mansion, I inquired after him.

He'd vanished, I was told. He'd disembarked from the *Atlantic Lady* and disappeared into the dockside crowd. No one had seen him since that time.

Alone and pregnant, ill with despair and morning sickness, I didn't know how I'd survive. Please, God, I begged, don't let him go on believing I deceived him, that this is not his child I carry.

****

Within a month the *Maris Stella,* under command of Jared Fletcher, arrived at Del Ray to fetch me. The pirates had released him and his crew on an uninhabited stretch of Florida coast, he explained, then scuttled the *Linnet*. After several days of struggling through the swamps, he and his men had managed to reach a settlement. When there had been no news of Colin, Barret, or me after they'd managed to return to Pine, Abraham had given Jared command of the Douglas fleet.

When Jared asked about Barret and Colin, I could only tell bits of the truth. Colin was dead and Barret had vanished. I could not bring myself to confide in him regarding my condition.

****

Back in the Douglas household, I became overwhelmed with an ever-increasing panic. Widowed and now deserted by my lover, I didn't know what was to become of me if the truth about my pregnancy became known. Ill with apprehension, I watched the days slide by, hoping for a miracle that would somehow extricate me from the situation.

Then one morning, as I came down to breakfast, a wave of giddiness overwhelmed me. The last conscious memory I had was of toppling down the remaining three steps and crying out in pain.

****

When I returned to consciousness, I lay in the big featherbed I had once shared with Colin. The room was darkened and those around me spoke in whispers.

As I became able to focus on faces, I saw Randall bending over me. Behind him stood Abe, Gram, and Caroline.

"Hello, little sister," my brother-in-law said. "How do you feel?"

"Weak and sore," I said becoming aware of pain in my back and left shoulder.

"You took a nasty fall," he said. "But you're going to be fine. After a few days' bed rest, both you and that baby you're carrying will be right as rain." He patted my hand reassuringly. Then he and Abraham left the room.

When the men had gone, Gram sat down on the edge of the bed.

"So you're to have my great-grandchild," she said,

taking my hand between her wrinkled palms. “That’s wonderful news.”

“Is it really?” Caroline came to stand by the bed, arms akimbo. “She was alone on that island for weeks with Barret Madison. And we all know his reputation with women.”

“That will do!” Eyes snapping, Gram arose and faced the woman. “Starr is not to be harassed.”

Abraham returned.

“Leave us, ladies,” he instructed. “I wish to speak to my daughter alone.”

They obeyed, Gram casting me a reassuring, conspiratorial wink, Caroline’s expression one of utter contempt.

When they’d gone, Abraham seated himself on the edge of my bed and looked at me with penetrating gray eyes. Did he suspect the truth?

“So you’re to present me with Colin’s child.” He startled me by beaming. “Thank you, young lady. Bear a healthy lad with none of his father’s weaknesses, and I’ll see to it you and your boy rule this valley when I’m gone.” He took my hand. “I always knew the right woman could make Colin act like a man.”

He stood and began to pace, rubbing his hands together. “Now that I’m to have a grandchild, I must plan accordingly. I must expand my enterprises immediately. This autumn I will go to England and secure more credit to advance my endeavors.”

“Mr. Douglas…” I began. I knew I should tell him the truth. It was wrong to allow him to believe the child was his son’s.

Then the part of me that was my mother, ready to do anything to secure a safe, comfortable life for her child, surfaced and I knew I wouldn't.

"Father." Abraham smiled. "I want you to address me hereafter as Father. Having conceived my grandchild, you have become a true daughter to me." He leaned forward and kissed my forehead. "And I overheard Caroline's innuendo. Let me assure you I have no such doubts about the child's paternity. You see, Barret Madison and I have an agreement, and I know him well enough to be confident he'd as soon rot in hell as go back on any promise he made to me."

I recalled their conversation earlier, a conversation in which Barret had assured Abraham that any child I bore would most definitely be his grandchild, and was appalled. Barret *had* broken his promise.

"Rest." Abraham was leaving the room. "Nothing must endanger the baby you carry. It's my hope for the future, my dream of a dynasty to come."

He left. My duplicity was underway. But now I understood Colin's insistence, on his deathbed, that Barret sleep with me. Pregnant supposedly by my husband, I would be able to remain in the comfort and luxury of Peacock House; my child would inherit Colin's legacy.

****

During my pregnancy, Randall became my solicitous companion. He came to my room each morning when Rose informed him that I was suffering from morning sickness. He dismissed the maids whose fluttering, he knew, increased my agitation. He held back my hair as I retched over a basin. When I would fall back on the bed, sweat drenched, he'd bathe my face with cool water and brush damp curls from my forehead.

"This baby is very important to me, little sister," he said one morning after I had had a particularly brutal bout of vomiting. "It will be the child I shall never have."

"How can you say that?" I struggled up on an elbow. "You and Caroline are young. There's still time."

"No." He squeezed excess water from a cloth into the basin of water by my bed, then pressed me back against the pillows to apply it to my forehead. "I contracted a simple child's illness on our wedding trip. As a result, I'm sterile."

"Randall, perhaps you're mistaken," I said. "Perhaps…"

"My father has sent me on a number of humiliating visits to various physicians," he said. "You see, the wedding trip, which I didn't want to take, was his and Caroline's idea. He forced it upon me. As a result, I suspect he carries at least a small measure of guilt. Perhaps if he'd let us stay here at Peacock House he might have had at least one grandchild…before we discovered how greatly we detest each other."

****

Then came the awful night I thought I would lose my child, and I realized what the baby I carried truly meant to me. It had been a brutally hot August day. I had felt feverish and short of breath since morning. Randall insisted I keep to my bed and tended me himself in the stifling bedroom where even the drawn curtains could not keep out the fierce heat.

At suppertime he brought me a tray with a light meal, but I could force down only a few mouthfuls. Even the milk which I usually drank in quantity tasted unpalatable. After the first sip, I set it aside. It tasted odd. I assumed it was souring due to the heat of the day. Exhausted, I fell asleep, the tray on my bedside table.

I awoke in the darkness of a still, sultry midnight to horrible pain and drenching perspiration. When my sleep-befuddled mind could focus, I realized I was having contractions. It was too soon, far too soon. I knew my baby would die if he were forced from my body now. As a ragged bolt of lightning stabbed across my room, a cry of fear escaped my lips…fear for the life of my child. Clutching my stomach, I struggled to my feet and stumbled into the hallway.

"Randall!" I gasped, beating on the door of his room. "Randall, I need you!"

When he opened it, clad only in undertrousers, I was in a heap on the floor.

"Starr!" He knelt to gather me up into his arms. "What is it, little sister?"

"I'm losing my baby!" I choked. "Randall, please help me! Don't let it happen!"

I huddled against his naked chest.

Suddenly Caroline was before us in a dressing robe, her eyes flashing with rage.

"My God, Randall, she's pregnant with another man's child." she flared. "What's wrong with you?"

"Get out of my way, Caroline," he ordered with an authority I had never before seen him demonstrate. "She came for my help. She thinks she's losing the child."

Through hot waves of pain I saw the anger fade from Caroline's face and an expression of evil elation slid into its place.

"How unfortunate," she purred, and moved

gracefully aside with a mock curtsey to allow us into my room.

Randall started to put me into bed, but I clung to him. “No, no!” I pleaded, our encounter with Caroline reducing me to a mound of defenseless fear. “Hold me, Randall. Please hold me.”

“Of course.” He sat down in a large rocking chair in a corner. “Caroline, light a lamp and fetch Gram,” he ordered the woman who’d come to stand in black silhouette on the threshold.

“Of course,” she mocked him, and left in a rustle of silk.

“Don’t cry, little sister,” he soothed as I sobbed against his chest. He settled himself and drew my nightshift between us and down over my legs.

Shortly Gram entered, nightcap askew on her white hair, a dressing gown wrapped haphazardly about her.

“Light a lamp, please, Gram,” Randall said. “Caroline didn’t bother to do it.”

When she had done his bidding, the old lady turned to look at us again. “Put her in the bed, Randall,” she said.

“No, no!” I begged, clinging to the strength and warmth of my brother-in-law’s body. Beneath my hands, he felt like Barret. I needed to be reminded of the man I loved, the father of the baby I was losing. A bolt of lightning illuminated the room, and I cried out.

I felt Randall’s hand on my belly as he did a cursory examination.

“You’re having contractions,” he said. “That doesn’t necessarily mean you’re about to go into genuine labor. The baby feels strong. He’s fighting for his life. You must, too. Try to relax. Sometimes these pains stop as quickly as they begin. Breathe deeply."

"Lay me in my bed," I choked. "There's no hope of saving my baby."

"You won't lose the child," he reassured me, brushing my forehead with a brotherly kiss, his hand still on my belly. "The baby is at rest now. His struggles are over."

Reassured by his words, I huddled against him. Shortly before dawn the pains ceased. Gram mixed me what she termed a sleeping potion, and I drifted into an exhausted slumber. I roused slightly, when Randall again checked the baby, to hear him discussing the incident with Gram in whispers.

"Someone put it in her milk," he was saying. "I'd know its scent anywhere. It's a miracle it didn't succeed in causing her to miscarry."

"But who?" Gram's voice echoed concern as she adjusted the covers over me.

"Someone who fears Father having this grandchild," Randall replied. "Gram, we must guard Starr and her baby every minute. We mustn't give this killer another chance."

I drifted into a troubled sleep filled with weird dreams of Gram preparing one of her potions while Ben Smith, his face contorted into a mask of evil intent, looked on. Tired of Abe's grasping ruthlessness, they were plotting to prevent his obtaining his most desired possession…a grandchild.

****

The following day I awoke near noon to find Randall seated beside my bed drinking a cup of coffee. On a nearby table, a large pot indicated the extent of his consumption in his efforts to stay awake. A stubble of beard covered his gaunt jaws beneath bloodshot eyes, but he was sober and alert.

"Good morning." He smiled. "Feeling better?"

"Yes, thanks to you."

"Don't thank me. You and that tough little person you're carrying did it all. Are you hungry? You should eat something."

He went to ring the bell for the maid.

"Randall," I said as he returned to his seat and poured himself another cup of black coffee. "How does a man know he's sterile?"

"You mean me?" he asked. "I've already told you. I had a child's disease as an adult."

"No, I mean how can a person otherwise know."

"Mainly because his relations with women produce no issue," he said. "Starr, who are you talking about? Not Colin?"

"No, not Colin." I paused, then blurted, "Barret."

"Barret!"

"He told me he was, but he…"

"Fathered your baby," Randall finished. "I knew from the moment we discovered your pregnancy. Colin certainly…" His voice trailed off, and he smiled. "You're in love with Barret, aren't you?"

"I loved Colin, I…"

"Yes, but you weren't *in* love with him, nor he with you. You cared deeply for each other, but there was no magic between you. There is between you and Barret, isn't there?"

I lowered my eyes and tears trickled down my cheeks. He understood. He was in love with his girl from the fish sheds.

"I told him I loved him and that I was going to

have our child, and he said…he said he was sterile, and that…the baby had to be Colin's, and that I was a liar and…" I was sobbing too hard to continue.

Randall eased himself onto the edge of the bed and gathered me into his arms. "Did Colin ever penetrate you?" he asked.

I shook my head against his white-shirted shoulder. "Never. Only Barret, only Barret."

"Then Barret was wrong about himself."

"But he's never had a child, and I know he's slept with other women…lots of other women." I was trembling.

""Whores," he said with a naturalness that startled me. "Prostitutes and sluts who know all the tricks to prevent pregnancy or how to get rid of it as soon as they discover their condition. Barret was raised in a brothel. Those are the kind of women he felt at home among. Until you came along. Starr, you're the first woman who gave him a fair chance at fathering a child, and he did. Barret Madison is no more sterile than that oversexed stallion of his."

"But why did he say he was?" I was totally confused now.

"He must truly believe he's physically incapable of producing a child," Randall said. "Barret never lies."

"Why would he believe such a thing?"

"Perhaps he was injured at some time, or he may have contracted a brothel disease reputed to cause sterility." He shrugged. "God knows he's had a rough life. Anything might have happened to him."

"But he's wrong!" I said. "Randall, some day I must find him and convince him he truly is my child's father."

"Yes," he agreed. "But until then, we must keep up the ruse that this is Colin's baby. It's the only way I can keep you in this house, under my care."

****

As I recovered from my ordeal, I mulled over Gram and Randall's words about murder. Had I heard them correctly, or had it been an hallucination induced by pain and Gram's sleeping draught? As I watched the two of them in the ensuing days, I became convinced it had been a real dialogue. Like guards, one of them was constantly near me. When I was unable to dine with the family, one of them always accompanied my tray from the kitchen. At night, they made certain I locked my bedroom door.

I grew furtive. I caught myself eyeing others in the household with suspicion. With fear growing to horror within me as my ninth month dawned, I thought of confessing to the family that my child was not the long-awaited heir but the offspring of one of Abe's captains. Then my child would be safe from the murderer who was intent on his never drawing breath.

He would also be born into degradation and poverty, a sailor's bastard of a woman people would only too easily brand an adventuress and an adulteress. I had too much of my mother's blood in me to allow our present security to be thrown away. I remained silent.

****

Alone, Randall delivered Barret's child at the height of a February blizzard. Abraham had gone to England three months previous, as he had said he would, to obtain increased financing for expanding his interests. Gram was ill with another of her increasingly frequent bouts of indigestion, and Caroline refused to come near me.

As I lay in the bed I had once shared with Colin, Rose and the housekeeper hovered nervously about. It was obvious they did not share my confidence in Randall's ability to deliver my child safely.

"We should have sent for the midwife before this storm set in," I heard Mrs. MacDonald mutter to Rose as Randall positioned me for the birth.

"Try to relax." He ignored them and rolled up the sleeves of his white shirt. "Breathe deeply. Don't fight the pain. Ride it like a wave that crests and breaks and is over. Mrs. MacDonald, Rose, please leave us alone."

Misgivings mirrored in their faces, they obeyed.

"Talk to me, please," I begged, as he bent my knees wide apart. "Tell me about yourself, Randall. Tell me your hopes and dreams. It will take my mind off the pain."

"My dreams, sweetheart?" He smiled sardonically. "Well, once upon a time I dreamed of being a doctor, a really good doctor who could give the people of this community the medical attention they deserve. I went to medical school with shining visions of a future with a respected practice, a loving wife, and a host of happy sons and daughters.

"But somewhere along the way, the dream cracked and fell apart. I found myself to be an attorney and politician, forced to do the bidding of a ruthless father. As for the loving wife and babies…"

I interrupted him with a scream of agony as a great, excruciating cramp leapt through every inch of my body.

"Oh, God, Barret, where are you?" I cried,

desperate in my misery. "I need you!"

"Breathe deep," Randall instructed gently. He looked at my body. "Bear down. Now! We almost have a baby." Sweat had broken out on his forehead and upper lip, but his eyes and hands were gentle and in control.

"Again, Starr," he encouraged, perspiration trickling down his face. "Just one more push."

I drew a deep breath, thought of Barret and how we'd been on the island, and found renewed strength. I pushed and writhed and moaned and, with Randall's hands guiding, I was delivered of a son.

"He's beautiful," I breathed, looking into the cherubic face of the baby Randall finally placed in my arms.

"Yes," he agreed, looking down at us. "Babies are beautiful miracles. You and Barret have been blessed."

****

My baby was six weeks old when he experienced his first taste of Abraham Douglas's wrath. It was early morning. I had finished my breakfast and Rose had brought little Colin to me. Propped up against satin pillows, I was nursing him when my father-in-law entered the room. I had been dreading his return from England, fearful that he might see Barret's features in my child's small face. I withdrew the baby from my breast and covered myself.

"That's not necessary," Abe said, coming to stand beside the bed as Colin began to whimper. "A grandfather should be permitted to watch *his* grandson nurse."

The strangeness in his voice and expression unnerved me. He was not the thrilled grandfather I'd expected him to be. He carried his riding quirt and kept slapping it against his high, polished boot, a gesture I'd come to recognize as being indicative of his being in an agitated state.

"Well, go ahead," he said shortly, and I became terrified as he moved to tower over me, his face flushed. "Give the child your breast. Make him as contented as you made his father."

I opened my gown and put the baby to my nipple. As he settled to suckle, I looked up at the big man beside my bed.

"You are incredibly beautiful." His voice trembled with an emotion I recognized as outrage. "Why weren't you able to arouse my son? Why?" The last was a roar as he cracked the whip against the covers near my knees.

"What…what are you saying?" I shuddered, putting a hand over my baby's head.

"This wasn't the first time you were pregnant, was it?" he rasped, sweat breaking out on his upper lip. "You had an abortion last Christmas Eve in Halifax, didn't you? You had Barret Madison's first bastard taken out of you, but you got caught here in this house with the second! Oh, I know you tried to lose it. I've heard of your 'illness' in July. But you failed, and this time there was no dockside butcher to help you!"

His big hand shot out and he pulled me bodily from the bed. Little Colin toppled from me and fell screaming among the sheets. Terrified, I stood before the raging dictator. When he raised his quirt to strike me, I cowered against the bedpost.

"Papa, in God's name, stop!"

Randall burst into the room and inserted himself

between his enraged father and me.

"Get out of my way, Randall!" Abraham ordered amid my baby's screams. "This bitch has deceived me! She's gotten rid of the first of the bastards my good Captain Madison gave her, and now she's tried to foist this whelp off on me as my grandson. I will see her punished."

"Strike her and I swear I'll reveal every underhanded scheme you've ever engineered, to the governor himself."

Abraham froze. Father and son faced each other, pale with rage.

After what seemed to me like an eternity, Abe lowered his whip and spat on the carpet at my feet.

"Get out!" he snarled. "Take your sailor's trash and get out. You'll never see your lover again, I can assure you. He's done with you since you've proven stupid enough to get yourself in a family way twice with his leavings."

He took something from his pocket and threw it at my feet. I gasped as I recognized the ring I had used to pay the doctor in Halifax.

"I returned by way of Halifax," he said. "That disgusting little butcher brought this to me and tried to blackmail me into buying it back. He said he'd learned who the girl with Madison had been on Christmas Eve, and that he would disgrace my family by telling the governor all the sordid details if I didn't purchase the ring. It disgusted me to the point of vomiting to know you'd used my son's wedding ring to pay a butcher to rid you of a piece of sea tramp's lust."

He turned and strode from the room.

****

An hour later Randall, wearing a fur coat, hat, heavy-laced moccasins, and thick gloves, carried my child swathed in blankets down the winding staircase to an entry ablur with familiar faces. I followed, a small bundle of possessions clutched in my arms. As my father-in-law had predicted, I was leaving Peacock House as ragged and penniless as I had entered it. Only now, I had a baby.

As we reached the bottom steps, Gram came forward, kissed my cheek, and touched the baby fondly. "God be with you, my child," she whispered, tears bright in her eyes. She swung on Abraham, who was standing by the door. "And may He somehow forgive you, my son, for this infamy!"

She moved out of our way, and I saw Caroline sneering at me from the parlor doorway. Richly gowned, her hair perfectly dressed, she was a vision, the obvious center of Jared Fletcher's attention and admiration as he stood behind her, newly arrived from the overland journey from Halifax with Abraham.

"Don't forget to come back, darling," she purred to Randall. "Remember, the quickest way to get rid of trash is to throw it on the river ice and let it flow out with the other debris in the spring."

Ignoring her, Randall walked to the door his father had thrown wide open for us, and strode out to where Abe's shabbiest single-horse sleigh waited.

"Where are we going, Randall?" I asked as he clucked the horse into motion.

"To a place where you'll be well cared for by a beautiful, loving woman my father refers to as a fish shed slut," he said between set teeth. "I'm taking you to live with the woman I love, Bridgit O'Brien."

"I'm glad." I adjusted the slumbering Colin in my arms. "I'll feel comfortable with anyone you love, Randall."

"My father committed a brutal act when he threatened you and your son," he said grimly. "I'll care for both of you in Barret's absence."

"Randall, I love you," I whispered, my voice catching over the lump in my throat. "You truly are my brother."

"Thank you, love," he said. "Try not to judge Bridgit and me too harshly. If I could, I'd marry her tomorrow."

****

"Are you sure you're comfortable, Starr?" An hour later, Bridgit O'Brien adjusted pillows about me as I lay with Colin in a white spool bed in the second of two small bedrooms in her cabin a half mile beyond Darcy's house.

"Quite comfortable," I said, looking up at the pretty, auburn-haired young woman beside my bed. "Please don't fuss over us, Bridgit. You've been extremely generous in taking us in."

"I'm glad to have company." She smiled. "It's been lonely since Kevin died. And tonight, with Mary off tending Mrs. Prescott, who's ill again, I'm especially glad to have you and the wee lad with me."

"Bridgit, love, if I had my way, you'd never be lonely again." Randall slipped an arm about her shoulders and drew her close.

"I know, darlin'," she said, patting his hand, the one on which a wide gold wedding band gleamed in the lantern light. "Starr, please don't think ill of us. We truly love each other."

"I know you do." I looked at them, at their love, and recalled how Barret and I had been together.

"You'll be with him again, Starr, I promise," Randall said, sitting down on the edge of the straw mattress and apparently guessing my thoughts.

"Of course you will." Bridgit supported him as she pulled the patchwork quilt more snugly about me. "But now you must rest. I'll build up the fire, and we'll pass the night snug as bugs in a rug. I wish I had a larger house, that you might not be squeezed into this tiny cubicle with this darlin' wee laddie."

"Bridgit, love, you have only to say the word and I'll have workmen here in the morning to build you the biggest, finest house…" Randall began, but she stopped him.

"Naught of that talk, my boyo. We've already been through all that nonsense. I'll not be givin' people any call to say I'm your whore who exchanges her favors for your money."

"Bridgit, please…"

"Randy, love, be a good lad and close your mouth on the matter. Good night, Starr. May flocks of angels guide you to your rest."

She and Randall left me alone. Warm and comfortable, I snuggled Colin close to me. I was exhausted, but the excitement of the past hours kept me wakeful. I heard Randall draw a protesting Bridgit into the adjoining bedroom.

"Randy, love, no. Starr will hear."

"Sweetheart, she understands," he muttered. "How often do we have such a chance, with Mary away?"

I fell asleep to the sounds of their lovemaking, loneliness for the father of the baby in my arms all but breaking my heart.

The next morning I awoke late to hear a woman's voice humming softly in the next room. Sunlight streamed in a window. I guessed it was near midday. Then, with a shock, I realized Colin was gone from his place beside me. I struggled to my feet, wrapped a quilt about me, and hurried to the bedroom door. The scene in the next room amazed me.

Mary Constable sat in a rocking chair by the hearth. My baby, swaddled in blankets, lay in her arms. The young woman was humming as she rocked the child. Becoming aware of my presence, she turned to face me.

"He was fussing, but I hated to awaken you to nurse him," she said. "You looked so tired. Bridgit has gone to work at the fish sheds. It's always the season for some kind of fish. But I, of course, since Captain Madison left, have no employment. I could not bear to work with Captain Fletcher, knowing the intentions Mr. Douglas had for him and me."

"But I thought…"

"That I hated you, despised the good fortune you apparently had had as a result of wayward behavior?" She adjusted Colin in her arms. "I've had time to change my opinion since those days; time to hear how you cared for a young husband you couldn't possibly have loved; time to hear of your courage in defending him from a great brute in the shipyards; time to learn of your faithfulness in spite of the love that was between Captain Madison and yourself. Under those circumstances, I doubt I would have been as strong. I remember how it was when Kevin and I were in love, you see."

"You know about Barret and me?" I gasped. "How?"

"I worked with him for several months," she said. "After he rescued me from that unthinkable marriage proposal, I trusted him and he came to rely on my integrity. He told me often, but not directly, of his feelings for you. The look in his eyes said it all, whenever you were mentioned. He's a kind, strong, generous man. I owe him a deep debt. If I can begin to repay it by helping to care for his lady and his son, then I shall do so with a glad heart."

****

I lived with Bridgit and Mary for more than two months that winter. They were sincere, compassionate young women, and I developed a sisterly affection for both. Bridgit particularly delighted in helping me care for Colin and constantly extolled the baby's prowess in growth, strength, and intelligence.

"I swear, Randy, he's the finest lad I've ever seen," she declared one evening late in March when Randall arrived to find her rocking little Colin in a chair by the fire. "Starr and Captain Madison have been blessed, indeed."

"Bridgit, darling, I know you love children," he said, dropping on one knee before her. "I'd give you one of your very own if I could. Dear God in heaven, you know…"

In the flickering light of the gently crackling fire on the hearth, his expression ached with tenderness. I feigned absorption in the tiny garment I was mending, but I could not avoid hearing.

"I know, my darlin', I know," she whispered, her eyes swimming with tears. "But the good Lord has seen fit to grant us a bit of Starr and her captain's joy. We must content ourselves with that."

"Oh, love, I've come to take even that from you," he said, looking up at her. "Jared has located Barret. Starr must go to him."

"Barret's been found?" I cried, falling to my knees beside Randall and clutching his arm. "Where? When? Is he well?"

"He's on the small French island in the Caribbean where he was born," Randall said, rising and drawing me to my feet with him. "Starr, according to reports Jared's received, he's not well."

"Has he a disease? Was he injured?" My words tumbled over one another in my excitement.

"Not exactly." Randall held me by the arms and looked deeply into my eyes as he struggled to find the right words.

"Tell me!" I cried. "For God's sake, tell me, Randall. Don't keep me in this limbo."

"He's become addicted to laudanum…opium," he said. "He's been living in the brothel where he grew up. The madame, an old friend of his mother's, is caring for him."

"Oh, sweet Lord Jesus!" Bridgit gasped. "Starr, you must go to him at once. You must bring his baby to him and make him want to live again."

****

The next morning Randall told his father he must make a voyage to the Caribbean aboard the Douglas's fastest available ship. The governor had asked him how quickly a letter from Pine could reach the Caribbean aboard a Douglas vessel, and Randall had said he had rashly declared within seventeen days. Now he must prove his word by going himself in that time.

At first Abe was appalled at his son's foolishness. His fastest ship, the *Maris Stella,* was in drydock being readied for a voyage to England. .

"We'll take the *Winsome Witch*, the ship that was to have been Jared's if Barret had returned to master the *Maris Stella*," Randall said. "She's swift and light, if a trifle fractious, but I'm sure Jared can handle her."

On the night of May first, Randall and Jared smuggled my baby and me aboard the *Winsome Witch*, the ship that had been christened on the day I discovered Jared in bed with Caroline.

I came up onto the moonlit deck one night a week into our voyage to find Jared himself at the helm. A single sailor stood watch near the bow. Aside from the seaman, the captain and I were alone.

"A bad habit I picked up from Barret," he grinned when I joined him. "A captain should never be seen at the wheel himself. It does, however, give one an opportunity to reflect, as Barret used to say."

"And what were you reflecting upon tonight, Captain?" I asked.

"On many things." He smiled vaguely. "For instance, I was just now thinking how much like a beautiful, eager, yet rather unruly woman this *Winsome Witch* is. She's trim and fast and exciting, yet sometimes she seems determined to try me, to dare me to control her." He shrugged and laughed lightly. "I'm being fanciful, too fanciful for a ship's master. If my men were to overhear me, I'd have a mutiny on my hands."

He's thinking about Caroline. I turned back to my quarters. *He's wondering if he will ever be able to control her.*

****

"I should like to see Captain Barret Madison," I said, holding Colin in my arms.

The address to which Jared, Randall, and I had been directed was on a street lined with taverns, inns, and large, shabby houses whose shades were tightly drawn. At midday, beneath a scorching tropic sun, all was quiet, but at night I felt certain this district exploded with life and all the pleasures it could offer human flesh.

The middle-aged woman who'd opened the door peered out at me suspiciously. She clutched a ruby-colored silk robe over her ample bosom, rings glittering on her softly wrinkled fingers. Her auburn hair was a mass of disheveled ringlets, she reeked of cheap perfume, and the paint on her sagging cheeks appeared to be a remnant of the debauchery of the previous night.

"Who are you, and what do you want with Barret?" she asked, her voice hoarse from the sleep I'd interrupted.

"I'm Starr Douglas," I said. "This is my child, Colin. Captain Madison is his father."

"Starr!" she exclaimed, coming fully awake. "Come in, come in. Thank God you're here."

"We'll wait for you outside," Randall said. "Once you've had your reunion, Jared and I will join you."

The woman drew Colin and me into the shadowy recesses of the house and up a flight of thickly carpeted stairs with such haste I had only a glimpse of the interiors through which we passed. I scarcely had time to gather an impression of dark reds and golds, of overly ornate, crowded rooms, heavy carpets, and pungent scents mingling with the odors of stale cigar smoke and liquor.

As she hurried me along, the woman talked rapidly.

"A friend of his found him unconscious in the street a month ago," she explained in a hushed, slightly breathless voice. "He'd taken too much opium; he's become addicted. He kept mumbling my name, so the man brought him to me."

She halted me with a heavily ringed hand at the foot of a second flight of stairs, narrow and uncarpeted, that led upward to a closed, white plank door at their zenith.

"The first week was pure hell for him," she said, looking into my eyes. "He screamed and raved like a lunatic from need of more of that cursed drug. His friend had to restrain him and tie him to his bed lest he injure himself. On the eighth day, he quieted and fell ill with a raging fever. My ladies and I were kept a-running to keep him alive, I can tell you. Now all that has passed, but he's thin and weak, a ghost of what he once was. Do you still wish to see him?"

"Yes."

"God love you, dearie, you're all he said you were," she whispered, tears filling her tired eyes. "His friend, the man who found him and brought him here, is with him now. He's cared for him most of the time."

We went up the stairs, and she opened the plank door and thrust me into a small, austere, white cubicle. A single gabled window curtained with snowy gauze let in enough light for me to see the man lying on the narrow cot against the far wall. A washstand and a ladderback chair were the only other furnishings in the small cell. A big man who'd been sitting hunched in the chair stumbled to his feet at my entrance.

The woman shoved me forward. "Go to him," she said, her harsh voice soft with emotion. She shut the door and left us.

I started forward, Colin clutched in my arms, then stopped as, in the dim light, I recognized the man standing by the bed. Captain Andrew MacDonald looked at me in utter astonishment.

"Mrs. Douglas." The two words were a harsh intake of breath.

The person beneath the patchwork quilt and ivory sheets stirred at the sound of his voice.

"Andrew, who is it?" he muttered.

I moved to the couch and looked down at the man who rolled to face me. Barret Madison, bearded, naked to the waist, stared up at me. His dissipated countenance and red-rimmed, sunken eyes shocked me. I could barely believe he was same man whose life I'd shared on Eden.

"Starr!" he breathed as he recognized me. "What are you doing here?"

"I've brought your son," I said, my voice cracking over the words.

"My son?" He wet dry lips with his tongue. "No, it couldn't be. I couldn't…have a child. Not after…"

"You have a child," I said kneeling beside the low bed to let him look into Colin's sleeping face. "Look at him. Colin Barret Douglas is our son."

I explained all Randall had told me about male sterility, Barret's own case in particular. When I'd finished he stared up at me for a few moments. Then he looked down at the child in my arms. As Colin awoke and the gazes of two pairs of gray eyes met, I saw realization dawn in those of the man.

"Sweet Jesus," he breathed, struggling up on one elbow. "Is he…are you…are you both all right?"

"Take it easy, laddie," Captain MacDonald urged, easing him back into the bed.

I nodded, unable to speak over the lump in my throat. Of course we were all right, now that the three of us were together, my heart cried.

****

"Why?" I asked Andrew MacDonald later, when Barret slept. "Why did you help him? I thought you hated him."

"Not the lad himself, only Abraham Douglas and all that man stands for," the grizzled seaman said gruffly. "When I found Captain Madison lying in the street, drug addicted and near dead, I had to help him. We're both mariners, both victims of Douglas's ruthlessness.

"He kept mumbling Maggie's name, so I brought him here and learned his story. I couldn't desert him then. When he'd recovered a bit, he told me he'd sold his soul into hell and wanted to die. I had to fight to keep him alive. I couldn't let Abe Douglas claim another victim.

"But now you're here and you have his child. All will be well. I'll be leaving. I hope someday you'll be able to forgive what I once did to you and him and the boy. I'll end my days here in the Caribbean running short junkets with my lovely *London Lass*, free at last."

"On the night of the attack on the *Linnet*, you saved us, took our part when things looked blackest," I said. "I can only be grateful."

"And for casting you adrift?" he asked. "I did a despicable thing, done in irrational outrage, which I shall always regret. I allowed others to encourage me into evil retribution against innocent people. Even taking that pig Simon aboard was another's idea. But enough. Where are you stopping? I'll help you get the captain to your lodgings."

"I'm living at my father-in-law's cottage," I said. "It was fortunate Barret happened to have been found on this island where we have a house to go to…or, at least, as Randall Douglas's guests we do. He and Jared Fletcher are with me. I'll go below and tell them we'll be down directly. Then you must come to supper with us."

"Yes, Andrew." Barret awoke and enhanced the invitation.

"I'll see, laddie, I'll see."

Leaving Colin with his father in the narrow bed, I hastened down to inform Randall and Jared of my success. When I returned to the garret moments later, I was surprised to find Barret's rescuer gone.

"Where is Captain MacDonald?"

"He left." Barret was involved in staring down at his son with such tenderness it warmed my heart. "He said he was no longer needed."

Together Barret, little Colin, and I went slowly down the narrow stairs and through the garish house. As we passed doorways, a number of half-dressed women emerged to follow us to the front entrance. I longed to be out of the place, away from its tawdry sensuality, and shuddered inwardly when I thought of the child Barret growing up in such an unhealthy environment.

As I was struggling to open the front door for Barret, who was leaning heavily on my shoulders, the madame who'd admitted me to Barret's room, now wearing a black, low-cut silk gown, stopped us with a glittering hand on his arm.

"Good luck, love," she said, blinking back tears. "I'm sorry I had to put you in that cell, but since you weren't a paying customer I couldn't give you a room my ladies needed."

"It's all right, Maggie," he said hoarsely. "My mother and I spent many good years in that garret. And without its shelter this time, I would have died in the street." He looked into her painted, haggard face and smiled. "I'll be fine now. This is Starr, the woman I told you about. The child is our son. I'm going to live with them."

"Well, then, all the best, my pet," Maggie gave him a hug. "Lise would have been happy to see you with a family of your own. You've been like a son to me all these years, but this isn't a fit place for you to call home. Take care of him, my girl. He's always been a good lad."

As we made our way to the waiting cab, now with Jared and Randall's help, I understood why Barret had sought solace in Maggie's establishment. Maggie, the madame of that house of ill fame, had loved him as a mother. And for all her less-than-admirable lifestyle, she appeared to have greater capacity for true affection in even one of her heavily ringed fingers than Abraham Douglas had in his entire body.

Chapter Fourteen

We returned to the cottage where Jared, Randall, and I had deposited our belongings before going in search of Barret. Once seated on the wide, open verandah facing the sea he loved, Barret revived. He shared a bottle of wine with the two men while I settled Colin for the night.

Through an open window, I could hear them talking, even laughing at times as they spoke of successful voyages. It did my heart good to hear Barret restored to the man I'd known him to be, even though I realized all three men were carefully picking their topics of conversation. None were ready to get into deep and potentially troublesome subjects at the moment.

By the time I rejoined them, Randall and Jared had gathered up their belongings. They would be spending the remainder of our stay on the island at an inn in the village, they declared.

"That's not necessary…" I began to protest, but Randall silenced me with a finger to my lips.

"Yes, it is, sweet sister." He smiled. "You and Barret need to be alone together…with your child."

"Well," I said, turning to face Barret after they'd gone. In spite of the ravages of his recent illness, he was still a devastatingly handsome, virile man with commanding presence. I was suddenly as shy as a virgin bride before him.

"Well," he repeated, leaning back in his chair and stretching out his legs. "It seems I have much to apologize for."

"Yes," I agreed, leaning against one of the verandah's supporting pillars.

"Where do you want me to begin?" He looked over at me, gray eyes cool and steady.

"By saying you still love me. By asking me to marry you. By becoming the legal father of our child."

"Very well. Of course I still love you. It was the thought of giving you up, of never having you as my wife, that drove me to lose myself in drugs."

"And the possibility that you'd slept with your best friend's already pregnant spouse?" I knew I was being cruel, but I had to strike back, to get the pain he'd caused me out of my mind.

"Yes, that, too. Starr…" He looked away from me. "You must understand how it appeared to me…when I believed I was sterile."

"Yes, but Barret, when you denied me, left me…" My voice broke, and I turned away, unable to continue.

I heard him rise from his chair and come to stand close behind me. Then his hands were on my shoulders, his cheek against my hair.

"I'll never leave you again," he said huskily. "I swear before God. That is"—he turned me to face him—"if you'll agree to be my wife."

"Yes, Barret, oh, yes."

"Excellent. But tonight I refuse to wait for a church and a priest. We've been apart too long."

With amazing strength he gathered me up into his arms. In the last rays of an exotic tropical sunset, he carried me inside to bed.

****

The next morning, over breakfast, Barret informed me of his startling decision.

He was going to take me back to Pine, where we would be married by the priest in the Catholic church, Little Chapel of Jesus. Afterwards we would settle in the village.

"Surely you can't be serious! Abraham controls the entire valley, and he despises both of us. You'll never find employment. If we went to Halifax, you could obtain a command. Your reputation as an outstanding master mariner is…"

"Destroyed," he said. "Since Abe saw to it that I lost my master's ticket, I've been an opium addict and lived in a whorehouse. My reputation, as you call it, is in ruins. I have to start to rebuild from less than nothing, and Pine is where I've chosen to do it."

****

We sailed back to the little New Brunswick village with Jared and Randall at the end of the week. With our ship docked at Pine, we remained aboard until everyone else had disembarked. Then, under cover of darkness, Barret, Colin, and I made our way furtively ashore to find the appointed spot where Randall had left Lucifer and Lady, with Colin's guitar tied to her saddle, in readiness for us. Together we rode to Darcy's cabin.

We discovered Jared had chopped wood, lighted lamps and a fire, and prepared the stable for our horses. Mary and Bridgit had left coffee, a pot of stew, and two loaves of fresh bread waiting with a note of welcome. The rooms had been cleaned, the bed made up. There was nothing left to do but ride to the Little Chapel of

Jesus to be wed.

We were married shortly before midnight in the reverend hush of the little log church deep in the forest behind the village of Pine. Randall and Bridgit served as witnesses, while little Colin waited in his basket at the rear of the chapel.

As we knelt before the big, kindly priest and said our vows, Barret slipped a narrow gold band, supplied by Jared, onto my finger. Afterward Randall, Mary, Jared, and Bridgit came back to the cabin with us, and we celebrated our joy with them over several bottles of excellent champagne supplied by Randall. Then they left and we were alone as husband and wife.

****

The next morning Barret got up early and announced he was going to see Abraham to seek employment. He was like a new man, confident and bold—the master I had once known, revived again.

"I'll be a ship's master again in a matter of months," he said. "Abe can't afford to hold a grudge against me. He needs me in command of the *Maris Stella*, with those mail contracts looming in the near future. Jared is a good man, but he's no commodore. I'll be back in the old man's good graces in no time."

"Don't be mad." I scrambled from the bed and began to pull on my clothes. "If you dare to go near Abraham Douglas, he'll have you crucified. This is no small grudge he holds against us."

"Do we have any coffee?" He went to the hearth to begin to build up a breakfast fire.

"Very well. Since you're determined to carry out this madness, Colin and I will go with you," I said, fastening up my gown. "We're family. If Abraham decides to punish you, he'll have to punish all three of us."

An hour later we stood on the verandah of Peacock House and waited while an astounded Rose went to inform Abraham of our presence.

Shortly, the entrepreneur came striding to the door, his face red-purple with rage.

"God damn you, sir!" he roared at Barret. "How dare you bring this tramp and her bastard to my home. Filthy fornicator! Remorseless traitor! I should blow your head off."

"Starr is my legal wife," Barret replied evenly. "I would be grateful if you would refer to her and our son civilly." There was a static hiatus as the two men faced each other. Then Barret continued, "I want my job back, Abe."

I couldn't help but admire my husband, even in those moments of what I considered insanity. Bold and unflinching, he faced the heavily breathing despot and exuded perfect command both of himself and of the situation.

"You never change, do you?" Abraham said, when his breathing allowed him to reply. "You're still as bold as brass and twice as hard. You realize you broke your word to me in fathering a child on Colin's lady, and yet you have the unmitigated gall to stand here before me and request employment that you might house and feed the bitch and her whelp."

I saw Barret's hands knot into white-knuckled fists at his sides, but still he controlled himself.

"Well, sir, I have only one position available," Abraham continued, an expression of cold, vindictive pleasure coming over his face. "It's one as an ordinary seaman on one of my guano carriers. The job requires scraping droppings from rocks and piling it in the holds, then unloading it again when the vessel docks. As I recall, you had a strong distaste for such labor."

He started to close the door, but Barret's hand shot out to halt it.

"I accept," he said.

****

A week later, Randall came to visit. He was alone in a carriage filled with bags and bundles, and jumped down from the driver's seat to greet me with alacrity when I ran out of the cabin to meet him.

"Randall!" I cried in delight. "I'm so glad you've come. We've missed you."

"And I you, sweet sister," he replied. "But newlyweds need time alone, I've been told. Where's Barret?"

"He's working in the stable," I said, taking his arm and drawing him toward the rear of the house. "Barret, look who's come to visit," I called as we came to the door of the small log stable.

Barret emerged. He was dirty and sweating, his cheap, mended clothing clinging to his body. I wondered what my husband, once a veritable fashionplate, must be feeling as he stood before his handsomely dressed and groomed friend.

Pity and guilt stabbed at me. His wretched state was my fault. If I had not come into his life, he would still be Abraham Douglas's swashbuckling lieutenant. As God is my witness, I vowed, I will one day, before I die, see him once again dressed in the finery he enjoys.

With our help Randall unloaded the carriage. He had brought food and blankets for little Colin, he said simply, but the abundance belied his casual description. He was providing a beginning for all three of us in a way he'd determined would be least offensive to Barret's pride.

"Starr and my son need these things, Randall," Barret surprised me by accepting the supplies. "I'll repay you when I'm able. Presently the best I can do is to express my gratitude. Abe has denied us credit in the village. I was beginning to think I would have to sell the horses to provide for my family, no matter how badly I'll need them to plow a garden in the spring."

"You plan to farm?" Randall's eyes widened.

"It'll help provide us with food." Barret shrugged. "My wages on a guano ship won't be enough to sustain us."

"Dear God, Barret!" Randall threw the bag of provisions he'd been lifting from the carriage to the ground in disgust. "How can he be so vindictive? Go to the man, face the old blackheart with the facts! Tell him the truth about yourself! And"—he hesitated—"about Colin."

"Never!"

"Damn it, Barret, I delivered that little boy you're so proud of. I care about him and his mother. Don't let your son grow up not knowing who his family really is. Don't let him think of you as a guano shoveller."

"Never," Barret repeated and snatched up a bundle to carry into the cabin.

****

In early November, Barret came into the cabin and shut the door on the wind and snow. His shabby clothing was crusted with sleet and his face was haggard from cold.

"We sail at first light," he said, pulling off his mittens. He removed his boots, then went to the fire to hold cold, callused hands out to its warmth. He had been working as a groom in Abe's stable while he waited for the voyage.

"If you leave for Cuba now, you won't be back until…"

"Spring," he said pulling off his coat and hat.

"Barret, you can't leave me alone all winter. Colin and I need you."

"It's the only job I can get in this village," he said, dropping into a chair by the hearth and leaning forward to flex his work-sore hands in the heat. "If I take this voyage, I may get a bo'sun's position in the spring. You won't be the only woman spending the winter alone with her child. Johnny Kelly has signed on, as well. He needs money, too…money his work in the steam pit can't provide in winter."

"And if I won't agree? I'll take Colin and go to Halifax if you leave me again."

"No!" He was on his feet and towering over me, his face dark and incensed in the firelight. "You'll never leave me. You'll never make Colin grow up a bastard like me!"

A sickening warmth enveloped me. I passed a hand over my eyes in an effort to steady myself.

"Starr, sweet Jesus! Starr, I'm sorry."

He was beside me, steadying me, his face contorted with concern.

I looked up at him, lightheaded and nauseous.

"Help me to bed, Barret," I murmured. "I feel ill."

He gathered me up in his arms and carried me into the cubicle we called our bedroom. Once I was on the bed, he knelt beside me.

"I'm sorry, Starr," he muttered. "I didn't mean to frighten you. But I have to go. I have to win back Abe's trust."

****

Shortly after Christmas, Colin fell ill. Our supply of dry firewood had dwindled to an alarming level, and I was trying to conserve by letting the fires burn low at night when my son and I were wrapped up in our bed.

Colin, however, had developed a skill common to many babies, that of kicking off his covers. One night in early January I awoke to hear him breathing with a fearful, rasping sound. I scrambled from my bed and rushed to his crib. He sounded like another Colin I remembered—another Colin who had been subject to life-threatening bouts with pneumonia.

I struggled into my clothing, my boots and cloak. Outside a blizzard raged, but I was heedless to its dangers. My baby needed a doctor. My baby needed Randall.

Rose answered the door of Peacock House in response to my desperate beating upon it.

"Rose, my baby is ill!" I gasped, clutching Colin inside a frozen shawl. "I must see Mr. Randall at once."

Caroline, resplendent in a flowing gown of warm tangerine velvet, suddenly appeared beside the staring maid.

"Well, well," she gloated. "A beggar. Close the door, Rose. We don't give handouts to tramps."

"You arrogant bitch!" Gram's voice snapped across my failing strength and aroused it to one more effort. "Get out of my way! Let the child inside at once!"

In a haze of exhaustion and relief, I saw the old lady reaching out to draw me into the warmth and light of the great house. “Randall,” she called. “Randall, come here at once!”

As she slammed the door on the elements, Randall appeared at the top of the stairs.

“Carry the child to my room, boy,” Gram ordered, looking up at him. “He’s ill. You, there, girl.” She snapped at Rose. “Take my granddaughter to her old room and get her dry clothing and hot food.”

After the slightest hesitation and a furtive glance at the glowering Lady Caroline, the young woman bobbed a curtsy. Randall took Colin from me. Relieved of motherly responsibilities, I sagged against a wall, the last of my strength leaving me in a gush.

****

It was dawn when Randall came to see me as I lay in bed in the room that had once been Colin’s and mine. He smiled as he sat down on the edge of the bed, and I knew my son would live.

“He’s over the crisis,” he said. “But he’s still very weak and will need my care for some time. I’ll tell Father you’re both to remain here until I deem it safe for you to leave.”

“Thank you. What would I do without you, my dear brother?”

“Rather, what would I do without you, sweet sister.” He smiled again and bent to place a kiss on my cheek. “You’ve brought love and joy and indomitable courage into this house of cold ruthlessness and insensitivity. I’ll always love you. You give me the support and affection I’ll never get from the woman I married.”

"Why *did* you marry Caroline?"

"When I learned my father had paid Caroline's impoverished gambling parent, Lord Newton, to send out his titled daughter to be my wife, I was outraged," he replied slowly. "I swore I wouldn't capitulate again…not after giving up medicine for the law to satisfy him. On the day her ship docked, I took a carriage and drove to the wharf, determined to reject the lady and send her straight back to England on the next ship.

"I was late arriving. All the other passengers and most of the crew had left. It was growing dark and there she sat, stiff and prim and all alone, on a pile of deal, wearing a threadbare dress and a cloak at least ten years out of fashion. In her hands, she clutched a tattered portmanteau. She looked so destitute and brave and alone, my heart went out to her. I could have sent a rich, glittering lady packing. I could not reject the shabby, shivering young woman I found on that pier."

"So you married her out of compassion…as Colin married me." The similarity of the situations was undeniable.

"I suppose," he said. "But Colin was lucky. He married an angel. I, on the other hand, married a succabus."

"Succabus?" I asked.

"A female creature that lures men into her bed and then puts their souls into hell. Caroline certainly did that to me. On our wedding night, she refused to allow me to touch her. She teased and frustrated me until I became drunk. I don't recall making love to her." He walked to a window and pushed aside the curtains to gaze out into the beginnings of a gray winter's morning.

"When I woke, I found our sheets bloodstained and Caroline sobbing in a chair by the window," he continued without turning to face me. "Fighting a deuce of a headache and nausea, I struggled out of bed and went to her, but she shoved away my attempts to comfort her. She called me a great drunken lout who'd forced a virgin through a night of pain and degradation no decent woman should ever have to endure."

He turned back toward me, his face pale and grim, a nervous tick afflicting his jaw. "I was on my knees, apologizing for God only knew what, and begging her forgiveness, when I saw the small cut on her arm. Suddenly it was all crystal clear. My father believed he had purchased me a virgin bride. What I'd gotten was a woman of experience…experienced enough to have gotten me drunk and then feigned virginity with a blood-marked bed. I was incensed." He strode to a chair by my bed and sat down. "Hung over and disillusioned, I grabbed her. I called her a lying slut. In spite of her screams and struggles, I forced her into the bed. I was…raping her, when Father burst in, Burt and Harry close on his heels. Those two apes pulled me from her and dragged me from the room while Father set about comforting her. Her! The bitch! The deceitful, pernicious bitch."

"Randall, I'm sorry," I said. I recalled Colin's similar ruse on our wedding night. My young husband had lacked the guile to devise such a scheme on his own. "Did you tell Colin?"

"When Burt and Harry dragged me from Caroline, I was naked," he said without embarrassment. "They couldn't leave me standing in the hallway, so they thrust me into Colin's room. Poor boy! I'll never forget the expression of shock on his face as he bolted upright in his bed. He was only fifteen, too young to fully understand the situation, and had I not been distraught to the point of madness, I would not have elaborated. But I did, in glowing, obscene detail, as I struggled into some of his clothes and vomited in his dressing room. Then I left. I was gone for over a month, drunk in Halifax for most of it. I was penniless and ill when Barret found me and brought me home."

He began to search the pockets of his coat and vest. "I need a cigar."

"There's none in this room," I said. "Colin didn't smoke."

"Yes, yes, of course. My brother had few of my vices."

"Randall, you don't have to tell me all this." I could feel his pain and wanted it to stop.

"No, actually I do," he surprised me by replying. "Telling someone, someone kind and generous of spirit, is just what I need right now. It relieves my soul, much as Barret claims confession in his church restores his."

"Very well." I pulled myself upright against the pillows. "I'm listening."

"Then came another infamy." He leaned back in his chair and resumed his story. "As soon as I was well, Father insisted Caroline and I take a wedding trip to show the village we were reconciled. I hated the idea but was too beaten at that point to fight. In Boston, I contracted a child's disease. Being a doctor, I knew what it did to an adult male. As I lay in that hotel bed, sweating with fever, I knew I would be sterile when I recovered."

"Randall…" I tried to think of words of comfort,

but none came.

"Quite a love story, isn't it, sweet sister?" He headed for the door. "Thank you for having the courage to listen…and the heart to accept me as I am."

After Randall left, I fell into an exhausted sleep. When I awoke, a cold January sun was piercing into the room where I lay. Outside, the wind howled as it buffeted the windows with drifting snow and wailed down the chimneys.

"Awake at last."

Abraham Douglas's voice startled me. I turned away from the window to see him seated in a chair near the door. He got stiffly to his feet and came to tower over me, his shadow large and dark as it fell across the sunlit bed.

A sick feeling welling in my stomach, I wondered what he wanted, how long it would be before he threw my child and me out of his house again.

"Randall informs me you brought your child here ill with fever," he said. "He's also told me the boy is strong and resilient and will soon be right as rain."

What new infamy is the man building up to?

"It is now apparent I will never have a natural grandson." He went to look out the window, his back to me, "Therefore, I will legally adopt your boy and raise him as my own flesh and blood."

"You'd take my child?" I couldn't believe what I was hearing.

"You will stay in this house and mother him until he reaches twelve years of age," he continued, as if I hadn't spoken. "At that time I will send him abroad to be educated. After he leaves, you may either take a generous cash settlement and depart or remain here as housekeeper. There is only one further condition. Neither of you is ever to see Barret Madison again."

"This is insane. I won't deny my son the right to know his father."

"I advise you not to be hasty." Abraham moved closer to the bed and spoke softly in the cold threatening way he used when he was deadly determined. "Presently your boy is penniless, with no prospects. As my legal grandson, he will become a powerful, wealthy man when he matures. You yourself will be comfortably settled for life. Forget about Barret Madison. He's a whorehouse tramp. He'll never be able to give either of you a decent future. Think, my girl. Think of your son, if not of yourself."

"Why do you want *my* child?" I asked, recovering sufficiently to question him. "Surely there are many so-called penniless bastards in this valley you might adopt."

"Ah, yes, but not with his bloodlines. His father, for all his infamous beginnings, is the strongest, cleverest, most resourceful man I've ever known. Barret Madison is tough and wise in just the right proportions. And you, my girl, are bright, beautiful, and fearless. Furthermore, both of you were in excellent health at the time of his conception. This child could not have come of a better mating."

"Like horse breeding. Get the best stallion to cover the best mare."

"Exactly." Undeterred by my analogy, he said, "Now, there's another alternative I can suggest to my first offer." He moved nearer the bed to tower over me. "If you feel you must be with Madison, I'll give you a sizable cash settlement and the *Maris Stella* immediately, on condition you both sail out of this river never to return or see your child again."

"You must be insane. How dare you suggest we sell our child for a ship and a bit of money!"

"Ah, but not just any ship." He smiled satanically. "The *Maris Stella*. You forget that Frenchman you married loves that ship like a mistress, has loved her for much longer than he's known you, and your child. He might not see my proposition as such an unworthy compromise. After all, he apparently produces issue as easily as he spews forth French. You can give him another child. His beloved ship? Ah, now that's an entirely different matter."

****

Colin was very ill. Randall decreed he would need a warm environment and an abundance of good food in order to recover. He told his father the child must remain in Peacock House for the remainder of the winter.

Abraham agreed without protest. When Randall continued by saying that it would be best if I was kept close by to reassure the child, however, Abraham's eyes glinted with malicious intent.

"Of course she may stay near the boy if it's in his best interest," he said. "I will, however, insist she pay her way. They need a scullery maid in the kitchen."

I knew I could not refuse. My son needed the care and amenities Peacock House could provide, and I had to be near him. Swallowing my outrage, I set to my task of scrubbing pots and pans.

****

It was a bitterly cold night filled with harsh, gusting wind and high, swirling eddies of loose snow that, at times, blotted out the stars and moon riding high in the subzero January sky.

I sat by the big iron stove in the kitchen of Peacock House, a shawl about my shoulders, my feet swathed in woolen stockings, and wished there would be news, any news. Randall had been missing since midafternoon of the previous day. It was nearing three in the morning and searchers still had found no trace of him.

Even Caroline had gone out at dusk, dressed in men's trousers, fur hat, and greatcoat, to search the immediate vicinity for him. Looking like a strange little man, she'd returned a half hour later crusted with snow, her face hidden behind a scarf. She'd had no success in her search, either, she said, as she stripped off her odd outerwear before the parlor fire.

Randall had been drinking heavily before he left the house. He'd quarreled with Caroline and gone to be with Bridgit. Ordinarily I'd have applauded his decision, but the temperature had been well below zero, with a flesh-freezing wind lashing the bitter air into a life-threatening force. I'd pleaded with him not to leave the house.

"I have to go, Starr," he insisted, pulling on his fur coat and hat. "It can't be any more bitter outside than it is inside this house."

"Randall, please be reasonable," I begged. "Come to my room. We can talk."

He paused and looked down at me, his haggard face gentle and compassionate. "You're all I could wish for in a sister," he replied. "But I must go. At this moment, I need more comfort than even you can offer. Please try to understand."

"Randall, please…"

"I can't stay near her another minute, Starr," he said, his jaw working with a nervous tick. "I found a powder among her things just now, the prime ingredient of a potion that causes pregnant women to miscarry. Do you realize what that means? It was my wife who put that poison in your milk last summer. She tried to murder Barret's child!"

"Randall, no. She couldn't."

"Oh, but she could and did. I've told her I'm divorcing her, that I never want to see her again. She's a witch, and neither my father nor threats of the eternal damnation of my soul will keep me in this Hades of a marriage a minute longer. I'm going to be with Bridgit. Tomorrow I'll come and fetch you and Colin. You mustn't remain near her any longer than necessary. If it weren't so cold, I'd take you with me now."

"Randall…!"

He touched my cheek gently with a gloved hand. "Be very careful, sweet sister…until tomorrow." Then he'd turned and gone out into that awful cold. He hadn't been seen again.

I was startled out of my reflections by a disturbance at the front entrance. I flew from my chair and into the front hallway to discover the reason for the commotion. A group of fur-swathed figures, headed by Jared Fletcher, were carrying a snow-crusted body into the house.

"Randall!" His name flew from me just as Abraham, Caroline, and Gram hastened out of the parlor.

"We found him only a few hundred yards from this house," Fletcher said, pulling off his frozen mittens. "He's suffered a blow to the back of his head, and he's lost a lot of blood. The snow around him was crimson with it."

"Is he still lucid?" Caroline asked quickly.

"Yes," Jared said as the rescuers followed Abraham's beckoning and carried my brother-in-law toward the stairs. "But just barely."

****

"Help me get him into bed," Abraham ordered Caroline when he, Gram, and I were alone with Randall and his wife in Randall's room.

"I…I can't!" Caroline whimpered in what I knew was only a well-feigned display of distress. "My nerves…I simply can't!" She fled in a rustle of skirts.

"Fetch Captain Fletcher, Mother," Abraham ordered. "If his wife won't help him, my commodore will."

"Captain Fletcher is treating the search party to brandy and hot food in the dining room," I said. "I'll help you."

"Undressing a half-frozen, blood-soaked man is not a fitting task for a woman," he said, turning to face me.

"I'm a married woman and I've not led a sheltered life, Mr. Douglas." I went to the bed and began to open Randall's snow-encrusted greatcoat. "Now let us get to the task before your son suffers any further."

****

I was sitting with Randall when he regained consciousness. His head was wrapped with bandages, beneath which his face held a ghastly pallor. He had not stirred in the twenty-four hours since his rescue, but when he opened his eyes I started with hope.

"Little sister," he whispered, and tried to smile over fever-cracked lips.

"Don't try to talk," I begged, kneeling beside the bed and touching his wasted cheek. "Rest. Regain your strength."

"Sweet, darling little optimist," he breathed. "You've always been there when I needed you. Never change. Barret deserves you."

"Randall…"

"Listen to me, Starr. You must tell Bridgit…tell Bridgit I love her…more than life itself. Tell her we shall be together, as I promised. Tell her I will marry her."

He began to cough. I could only hold him and soothe him until the spasm had subsided and he fell back, semiconscious, on his pillows. He began to rave. "Someone behind me…following me… No! No! Stay back! Don't — You must be insane!"

Then he lapsed back into unconsciousness. Who had been following him? Who had he termed insane?

The following morning Randall Douglas died without regaining consciousness.

We placed him in the little stone mausoleum in the Presbyterian cemetery for burial in the spring. The entire village turned out for the funeral in spite of subzero temperatures, high drifts, and low-hanging clouds that promised still more snow.

I stood in the outer circle of mourners about the mausoleum, the cold air penetrating my shabby cloak, and trembled. Abraham, his face ashen, held Gram's arm in a viselike grip as if *she* were supporting him. The tough old lady stood erect and dry-eyed beside the coffin. Jared Fletcher, seemingly oblivious to the gossip he created, stood beside Caroline, his hand at her elbow.

Randall's wife kept her head bent in feigned grief, a heavy black veil obscuring her face. *What an accomplished actress, she who tried to kill my child.*

When the service ended, I started back toward the sleigh that had brought several of us servants to the cemetery. I glanced across the windswept graveyard and saw Bridgit standing alone beneath a gnarled, dead tree, away from the crowd of villagers who'd attended the funeral. Her face was red and swollen. A cheap black woolen shawl covered her head, but her hands, protruding from the sleeves of her shabby coat, were swathed in an elegant mink muff. I recalled Randall telling me he'd given her one for Christmas.

"Her poor little hands are cracked and bleeding from the cold in the fish sheds," he'd said, distressed at her suffering. "I must get her a decent muff. It's the least I can do."

"I'll be along shortly," I said to Rose, who was beside me. "There's someone I must see."

I left the maid gaping after me and hastened to Bridgit's side.

"Bridgit." I took her arm with all the urgency I was feeling. "I need your help. Without Randall, Colin is no longer safe in Peacock House. I know it's a great deal to ask, but will you take my boy in again?"

She nodded without the slightest hesitation. "And you'll come, too. We'll all live together once again. Randy would have wanted it that way."

"No." I shook my head. "That is too much to expect of you. Don't worry. I'll be safe. No one there has any reason to try to harm *me.*"

****

"I loved him, Starr," Bridgit said as we sat by the

stove in her cabin that afternoon, tin mugs of coffee steaming in our hands. "He was trying to find a way he could take care of all of us, you and Colin and Mary and me. He was a fine man."

"He told me how he loved you and how he longed to be free to marry you," I said softly. "On the night he was injured, he was leaving her to go to you…forever."

"Oh, dear God!" she breathed. "Why then?"

"He'd learned something about Caroline he couldn't bear," I said. "He'd learned she'd tried to kill my baby."

"The witch! The bloody, rotten witch! Small wonder Randy could stand no more! He loved children so. We should have married and had a dozen!"

She broke down, sobbing. "We could have been so happy, Starr, if it hadn't been for his meddling father and *her.* His father ordered him to marry her, five years ago. She was of a fine old English family, he said, a genuine lady of quality." She blew her nose on her handkerchief before she continued.

"I first saw him on his wedding day. My brother and I had just arrived from Ireland and were building this cabin. I remember thinking how wonderful Randy was, the moment I clapped eyes on him outside the church. If I could have such a man, all my dreams would come true, I recall thinking."

"He was as handsome as he was kind and generous."

"My brother went to work in the Douglas shipyards and I in Peacock House as Caroline's lady's maid." She cleared her throat and blinked. "Then the miracle happened. Randy noticed me. His marriage had proven no source of joy to him, and he was realizing the mistake he'd made. We talked one morning as I served his breakfast while he sat alone in the dining room. From that moment we knew there was something special between us."

She went to replenish her cup at the stove.

"Oh, we tried to deny it, both of us in fear of committing the sin of adultery," she continued when she'd resumed her seat. "But, finally, one night it happened. Declaring him a perverted scoundrel for seeking his marital rights, she ordered him from her bed. He got drunk and came to my room in the servants' quarters on the third floor. It was inevitable." She leaned back in her chair and sighed. "We were in love—there could be no further denying the fact. That night we became lovers. Though I knew it was wrong, I don't for a moment regret the fact. I swear, Starr, I loved him and he loved me. Such could not be a sin."

"No, it couldn't," I reassured her. "Love can never be sinful."

She stood and went to look out a window into a bleak, bitterly cold January twilight which was drawing itself like a shroud over the valley.

"I was never his lawful wife, and I was never privileged to bear his name or his child," she said softly, "but, as God is my witness, I loved him and I always will. If there's justice in the Beyond, I'll be his wife in eternity."

****

Leaving Colin in Bridgit's and Mary's care, I returned to Peacock House. Caroline had no reason to harm me, since I had not a shred of tangible proof against her, I tried to reassure myself. At any rate, I was wise to her ways now and would be on my guard.

I found the mansion in an uproar of bustling, hushed-voiced servants. Gram had collapsed on her arrival home from the funeral, Rose informed me in an urgent whisper. It was her heart, the maid said. Abraham was with her. The elderly Mrs. Douglas was not expected to survive the night.

"She's had attacks for years," the young Irish girl said. "She called it indigestion and kept taking the brew the Indians make from the plant foxglove as a remedy, but we knew what her pains truly were. She's been in delicate health for months but refused to admit it. The funeral today was more than she could bear. Now she's sinking rapidly."

****

Rose brought me the message near midnight. Gram wished to see me. Her ashen face stilled my questions. I knew Gram had taken a turn for the worse.

In her luxurious room, the curtains open that she might see the first gently falling flakes of the blizzard to come, Gram lay propped up on her pillows. Mrs. MacDonald, the housekeeper, was hovering nervously about and came quickly to me when I entered.

"Thank goodness you've come, Mrs. Madison," she whispered. "She's most unwell."

"I'll sit with her," I said, looking past the woman into Gram's hollow face. "You may go and rest."

"Perhaps we should summon Mr. Douglas…" The housekeeper looked doubtful.

"Obey the lass, Victoria." Gram's voice rose from bed, a gasping painful sound. "Allow me this moment alone with my granddaughter."

Still the housekeeper hesitated.

"Go!" Gram ordered, her tired old voice a harsh

grating cry in the quiet room.

"Very well. But I'll not be responsible for what happens. Good night, ma'am."

"Farewell, Victoria. God bless you."

The resignation in the old woman's words sent the austere housekeeper out of the room with a broken sob.

"Come closer, Starr." Gram moved her head wearily and tried to raise a hand to signal to me.

Quickly I went to sit on the edge of her bed.

"There are things you must know, things I must tell you before I go," she wheezed. "Are you aware my husband Josh was a privateer?"

"Yes." The lump in my throat made speaking painful.

"My Josh made his money during the war in 1812." The old woman's eyes grew vacant, lost in memory. "The war was over when we set sail for the Caribbean to settle on a little plantation he'd bought there. Abe was in his early twenties. He worshipped his father as the swashbuckling hero he truly was."

She paused to gather her breath, and I reached out to take her cold, limp hand in mine.

"All went well until we were off the Florida coast," she continued. "Shortly after midnight one moonless night, we were attacked by a French privateersman. Josh had disarmed his ship, with the declaration of peace. No match for them, we were boarded, and the Frenchmen declared us prisoners in a war they had not yet been informed was over."

She stopped, rested, then took up her story, traces of her old ascerbic spirit coming through.

"They were ruthless barbarians. They killed my husband in cold blood." She panted as memory overwhelmed her.

"Please, you must rest. You can finish your story later," I begged.

"For me there will be no later, my sweet," she wheezed. "I must tell you now. Abe had a sister…a beautiful child of seventeen, who was also with us. When Abe demanded that Charlotte and myself be set free, they beat him and bound him and me to the mainmast. My son and I were forced to watch as my daughter was violated again and again."

Her dark eyes filmed with tears and her voice shook.

"Gram, I'm sorry, so very sorry," I breathed, horrified.

"Charlotte was never a robust girl." She shuddered, then continued. "It had been because of her delicate health that we had decided to settle in warmer climes instead of in New Brunswick, which we loved. She died that night. Abe was left with an obsessive hatred of the French and all they stood for. That included their Catholic faith." She looked up at me, the fire in her dark eyes fallen to two last glowing embers. "Now you will understand…why he treats Barret as he does. It's the boy's French Catholic blood he hates, not the lad himself."

Her voice was fading.

"I understand," I said softly. "You've been brave to tell me, Grandmother. Thank you."

"Don't waste your pity on me," she wheezed. "Be sorry for Barret, who suffers still. Love and understand him, child. I entrust him to your care. He's very precious to me."

She touched my cheek. "Farewell, granddaughter,"

she whispered. Her hand slid to the quilts, her eyes closed, and she was gone.

****

Caroline, Abraham, Jared, and I gathered in the parlor after Gram's funeral. I served tea before a low-burning fire on the hearth. Abraham and Jared leaned against the mantel, hot rum drinks in their hands. Abraham had aged visibly during the past year. As I looked up at him, an involuntary sense of pity rose in me. Death was robbing him of his cherished dream of being patriarch of New Brunswick's most powerful clan.

Then Caroline spoke, and the lines of defeat and spiritual fatigue seemed to melt from his countenance.

"I'm pregnant," she said, her voice quivering. "I'm going to have Randall's child."

The mug of rum dropped from Abraham's fingers. Its contents spilled out into a wide, dark patch on the thick carpeting.

"Are you sure, girl?" he asked, hoarse with emotion.

Caroline nodded and lowered her head. Tears escaped her violet eyes and glided down her beautiful face.

"That was the reason we quarreled," she choked, dabbing at her eyes with a lace square. "He said I'd been responsible for our childlessness. He said I'd allowed myself to become pregnant simply to keep him from…from that fish-shed doxy. Did you know, Father, he was planning to leave me for her?"

She gave a shuddering sob. Abe went to her, raised her to her feet, and with a supportive arm about her slim waist began to help her from the room. Shocked by her insidious lies, I watched in stunned silence.

"You're overwrought," Abraham said gently. "You must rest, my dear. Nothing must spoil this miracle you've announced. Nothing."

He turned to me. "Pack your clothing and get out. I withdraw my offer to purchase your bastard."

When they'd gone, I rounded on Jared Fletcher.

"It's your child, isn't it?" I cried. "You put her in a family way and then you had Randall murdered! Now you'll pass your bastard off as the Douglas heir. My brother-in-law told me he'd been struck from behind. Now I know who did it."

"My God, Starr, how can you think such a thing?" he muttered. "Perhaps it is my child Caroline is carrying. What does it matter? I love that woman. I'll marry her as soon as it's decent for me to do so, and old Abe will die happy, believing he has the grandchild he's always wanted. Randall was a good man. I wish to God I hadn't fallen in love with his wife. I deceived him, but as God is my witness, I didn't kill him!"

Eyes blazing, he dashed the rum remaining in his mug into the fireplace. It raised a hissing, alcohol-scented steam into the air as he turned and strode from the room, a tall, handsome figure in a black frock coat.

My knees went weak, and I sank back into my chair. I had no proof Jared Fletcher had attacked Randall. Only the garbled, unwitnessed words of a dying, alcoholic man recalling—perhaps dreaming—a blow to his head gave my accusation any credence.

It would be pointless to tell Barret or anyone else my suspicions. Jared Fletcher was well liked and respected. My husband viewed him as a good friend. Only I, who had once seen Jared naked in Caroline's bed, heard his threats on that same afternoon, and listened to Randall's muttered suspicions of an attack could believe the man capable of killing his lover's spouse.

****

Abraham did indeed send me packing on the day of Caroline's announcement. For a time, my son and I continued to live with Bridgit and Mary. But when spring arrived and Barret's return became imminent, I took some of my friends' supply of firewood and moved back into my own cabin.

The morning Barret's ship was expected to arrive was accentuated with blustery winds and snow flurries, much too cold to bring to the wharf a baby who'd had pneumonia. I left our son with Mary while I made my way to the village to wait for my husband.

The ship had arrived early, I discovered when I got to the wharf. Most of the crew, eager to be reunited with families or a pint of ale, had disembarked. The cargo would be off-loaded later in the morning. As I waited by the gangplank, the captain, a young man of no more than twenty-one, came down the ramp and turned to me.

"You're Seaman Madison's woman?" he asked, his nose in the air.

"I'm Captain Barret Madison's wife," I corrected. The thought of my husband taking orders from this overbearing boy disgusted me.

"He'll be disembarking shortly." He ignored my retort. "Due to insubordination, he suffered an accident. Seaman Kelly is bringing him ashore."

Strutting like one of the Peacock House birds, he walked away. My heart pounding, I could barely keep myself from boarding the ship to find Barret. Injured, that popinjay had said. Good God, how severely?

Then I saw them coming toward the gangplank. Barret had one arm draped about Johnny Kelly's shoulders. In his other hand, he clutched a makeshift walking stick.

"Barret!" I cried as they reached the dock. "Oh, love, what's happened to you?"

"That fool of a captain ordered me aloft in a gale," Johnny Kelly explained. "Captain Madison knew I lacked the experience and skill for the task. He went in my place…and fell."

"I'm all right, Starr." My husband tried to reassure me, but one look into his drawn face told another story. "But fetch Randall, will you? I have a deuce of a sore shoulder and back."

As I searched my reeling mind for the words to tell my husband of Randall's death, I became aware of someone standing beside me. I turned to face Jared Fletcher, wearing a fur-collared greatcoat, his hands encased in black leather gloves. Since he'd assumed command of the Douglas fleet, he dressed elegantly and looked every inch a man of wealth and importance.

"I'll see to the captain." He stepped forward and relieved Johnny Kelly of his task. "Easy, Barret. I'll help you home. Come along, Starr. It's cold, and your husband needs warmth and rest."

As he and Barret started away, Johnny Kelly stopped me. "He saved my life, missus," he said, his eyes moistly bright. "I will never be able to repay him. He's a great man."

****

"Gram, Randall…both gone?" Barret's tone was

incredulous as he leaned forward over our table while Jared dressed his lacerated back. "Sweet Jesus!"

"Barret, let me put you to bed," Jared finished his work and was wiping his hands on a towel. "You've had a rough voyage, and now this miserable news. I know how you felt about the old lady…and Randall. But things will look better once you're rested and stronger. You've lost a good deal of blood, and…"

"And I can't even have the comfort of lying with my wife after weeks of celibacy." Barret straightened, flinching with the effort. "I'm too bloody broken up."

"Come on, my friend." Jared helped Barret to his feet. "You need your rest. I'll look in on you in the morning."

"Why?" I asked, when Jared had returned to the main room after settling Barret in bed. "Why would you help Barret, after all that's happened?"

"He's my friend," he said. "Professional rivalry aside, he's the nearest thing to a brother I'll ever have. I know you don't believe me, but I could never wish either of you any harm."

He headed for the door but added, "I gave him a dose of laudanum to ease the pain. He should rest easy for a few hours."

When I went into the bedroom, I found Barret lying on his belly between the sheets. His ragged breathing told me he was fighting a lot of pain. I undressed and went to join him.

"Barret," I said softly, sitting down beside him and touching his burning forehead with a cool hand.

"Cover yourself, Starr," he rasped. "Don't make me lust as well as ache. My hips are…" He broke off with a grunt of pain as he tried to turn his back to me.

I looked down and grimaced as I saw again the ragged tear above his buttocks.

"Barret, my love, why do you insist we stay here under the thumb of that vindictive old man? We could be happy somewhere else, somewhere there is no one to persecute us. Say we'll move away, please."

"No!" My husband's voice was a ragged command. "I will stay near him until…"

"Until what? Until one kills the other with this madness?"

"Go to bed, Starr. Just go to bed. In time you'll understand."

Chapter Fifteen

Barret was worse the following morning. When I awoke, I found our bed soaked with his sweat. His labored breathing frightened me. Although he forced a crooked smile as I put my fingers to his burning forehead, I knew he was very ill.

For the next two days I cared for him until my body and mind ached from strain and fear. Then the fever broke, and I knew he would survive.

That crisis passed, I faced another. Since Barret had been charged with insubordination, he would receive no wages for the voyage. We'd have no money with which to pay our creditors, let alone to purchase necessities of life for the present and future. I had been relying on Barret's income to pay several debts I'd been forced to incur in spite of Abraham's "no credit to Madisons" law in the village. Ben Smith, Gram's friend, had kindly paid for foodstuffs for Colin and me during the winter, out of his own pocket. Now I must repay him.

When I was Colin Douglas's wife, I had often gone to the mercantile for surprise treats for my husband, and Ben Smith had become my friend. He had seen me reduced from a careless, happy bride of the valley's wealthiest young man to the thin and ragged wife of an absent pauper husband whose child wailed hungrily in her arms.

Compassion had ached from his eyes each time I came into the store with my dwindling supply of coin. One day when I was a few pennies short, he pulled them from his own pocket and cast them before the hesitating clerk filling my order.

"Give Mrs. Madison anything she needs," he said shortly. "I'll take care of it. Her credit is good with me."

"Mr. Smith, I can't allow you to risk your position like this!" I gasped. "If Mr. Douglas finds out…"

"But he won't. Will he, Willis?" Ben looked shrewdly over his spectacles at the young clerk. "It will be just between us three, correct?"

"Oh, correct, sir, most definitely correct," young Willis agreed hurriedly.

As the young man turned away to complete my order, I looked up at the white-haired, frock-coated old gentleman and asked softly, "Why?"

"You brought life and laughter to that mausoleum up on the hill. You made young Colin happy. I've always thought of that boy as my own grandson. And you have a spirit not even Abe Douglas could crush. Most importantly, Ida loved you. 'Look after my granddaughter if anything happens to me, Ben,' she said on the day of the ship launching as you were scampering off up the hill to get her medicine. 'She means the world to me.' "

I knew I must repay this kindly man. In spite of the fact he managed the store, he was not a wealthy man. And I would need even more food now, with three mouths to feed. I must get a job. I had lost my position in the only house in the valley that could afford a scullery maid. That meant I had only one other viable skill to market.

That afternoon when Bridgit came to visit, I told her my plan in whispers so that Barret might not hear.

"Will you and Mary take turns sitting with Barret and the baby?" I asked.

"Of course we'll help," Bridgit agreed. "But where will you find work? And what shall we tell the captain if he asks?"

"I plan to ask Meg for a job at the tavern," I said. "You may tell Barret I'm sitting up with Ben Smith, who has fallen ill."

"Oh, Starr, no!" Bridgit breathed. "That's a terrible rowdy place. It's not fittin' for a decent woman…"

"Where else can I get work in this valley?" I asked. "I would gladly join you in the fish sheds if they'd hire me, but they won't. The tavern is the only place where the name of Madison hasn't been blacklisted, the only place that isn't Douglas-owned."

It was late afternoon when I entered the tavern and approached Meg, who was polishing glasses at the bar. The room was empty save for a traveler munching a steak at a corner table.

"Yes?" she asked shortly.

"I'm seeking work," I said. "I can sing and play guitar. I thought perhaps a performer might help increase your business. If no such position is available, I can cook and wash dishes. I have experience as a scullery maid."

"Barret's very ill, isn't he?" Her tone softened.

"Yes."

"He had no salary from the voyage because that miserable little excuse for a ship's master declared him guilty of insubordination, I've heard," she continued.

"You heard correctly."

"Insubordination, of all charges," Meg huffed. "And from Barret, who all but killed himself doing that old man's bidding!" She paused, then asked, "Would you be willing to do barmaid tasks when we're particularly busy?"

"Of course."

"Consider yourself hired," she said, and went back to polishing glasses.

Like my mother, who'd returned to work when my father had fallen into financial difficulties, I bathed, brushed my hair till it shone, borrowed a bit of paint for my cheeks from Meg, and went to work in the tavern.

Meg soon found it more lucrative to move me from bartending to entertaining. Business in her little tavern began to boom in spite of Abe's order of temperance in the village. Sailors readily filled my apron pockets to hear music hall ditties that my mother had taught me, laborers to hear the slightly bawdy songs Barret had sung for me, and young romantics for Darcy's love poems set to Colin's music.

Still others, not normally tavern frequenters but starved for entertainment, flocked to see me dance and sing my way through a variety of songs each evening while Mary and Bridgit sat with my son and recuperating husband.

I had been working at the tavern for a fortnight when Abe Douglas returned from Halifax. He'd left the day following Barret's return, his purpose to work on negotiations for his coveted mail contract. Since it had become known that Barret Madison was no longer his commodore, rumor declared it was slipping beyond his reach. Abe, stubborn and unrelenting, refused to heed these tales and kept hammering away at postal officials.

I was singing a slightly bawdy song and moving about among the customers in one of Meg's low-cut crimson gowns when my father-in-law burst into the hot, smoky room, Burt and Harry close behind him. With a slash of his riding quirt, he cleared the nearest table of its mugs and flasks and sent its patrons scattering.

I froze in my performance. Some customers fled; others, bolder and curious, moved back to clear a path for him. Silence fell as the last of the fleeing clientele vanished out the door. I stood alone facing the enraged entrepreneur in the smoky room.

"How dare you march in here and disturb my customers?" Meg broke the static hiatus as she came from behind the bar to face the raging man. "This is my establishment. You aren't lord and master here."

"Your so-called establishment is made of old, dry lumber, some of the first ever milled in this valley," Abe said, his voice cold, even, and deadly as honed steel. "It would make a splendid bonfire."

"No!" Meg gasped. "You wouldn't dare!" She clutched the end of the bar for support, her face blanching.

"I'm against the sale of spirits to my workers," he said, glaring at her. "The elimination of this den of iniquity would aid my move for temperance and up the productivity of my men."

He swung back to face me. "And God damn you, you bold little bitch! You'll not shame me in public again!"

He started toward me, his expression fanatical with rage. Determined to fight to the bitter end, I grabbed a bottle from a nearby table. Holding it above my head by the slender neck, I braced myself and waited, pulse racing, heart pounding. He'd raised his quirt and was about to bring it down on me when Barret's voice stopped him.

"Strike her and you die, old man."

Abe whirled and faced my husband, who stood in the doorway, a pistol leveled at him.

"Bastard!" Abe roared. "Burt, Harry…!"

"If Burt or Harry make the slightest move to stop my wife and me from leaving, or if a single shingle of Meg's place is harmed, I swear I'll kill all three of you," Barret replied evenly. His face, though pale, was wolfishly lean and threatening, the appearance of illness having disappeared into a state of controlled determination.

"Son of a whore!" Abe breathed.

"Come here, Starr." Barret held out his free arm as he kept the gun leveled at Abe. "We're going home…to bed. It's time we had another child."

He added the last words with deliberate malice, and I saw Abe flinch as though physically struck.

I went into the shelter of my husband's embrace, then backed out the door with him into the chill May night where Lucifer waited, saddled and expectant. Barret stuck the pistol into his belt and swung into the saddle, a grunt of pain betraying his appearance of strength. When he kicked his foot from the stirrup and held down a hand to pull me up behind him, I asked, "How did you know to come?"

"Jared," he said. "He brought Abe back aboard his ship, then came to visit me. He said he'd heard you were working for Meg. I didn't let him know I'd been ignorant of the fact, but pretended to feel ill to get him to leave. I knew Abe wouldn't tolerate your working in the tavern. I knew his first stop would be here. And that he wouldn't be above doing you injury."

"But why? I'm not Colin's wife now."

"You once bore the Douglas name," he replied. "There cannot be any unseemly behavior on the part of even a former member of the clan. The government officials in charge of granting contracts favor temperance and upstanding living. You, he would believe, could jeopardize his chances. Now get up here. I really do plan to take you home to bed."

****

"Get down." The words were a terse order from my husband.

We'd reached our cabin after a mad gallop from the tavern. His harsh words brooked no denial.

My feet had barely touched the ground when he kicked Lucifer into a run and headed for the stable. I staggered back from the stallion's slashing hooves.

Barret was furious with me. As we'd swept along the muddy, pitch-dark trail, my arms clasped about his waist, I'd sensed the rage seething through his body. I couldn't fathom the reason for the depths of his anger. I'd deceived him by lying about my absences, I knew, but surely he could understand the necessity of my working and the scarcity of employment opportunities.

Inside the cabin I found a single lamp burning low and the fire on the hearth dwindling to glowing embers. Neither Bridgit nor Mary was present. Startled, I rushed to the door of the baby's room and found it empty. I turned to face my husband, as he came inside.

"Where are Colin and Mary?" I asked.

"I took them to Bridgit's cabin before I went to fetch you," he said, leaning back against the closed plank door. "I wanted to be alone with you. We have much to discuss."

"Barret—"

"You couldn't wait, could you?" he snarled, looming over me. "You couldn't wait until I was well enough to sleep with you, could you? You had to go to the tavern looking for a man to satisfy your hot blood!"

"No! Barret, you don't understand…"

"Don't I, wife? I understand only too well. We were fine, Colin and Randall and me, until you came here. You're the catalyst for the explosion that rent us apart. No one else could have brought me to the point of threatening *that old man* with a gun. You put my soul in purgatory through Colin. Now you're shoving it farther into Hell by pitting me against *him*."

"He had your career destroyed, for God's sake!" I cried. "He threw your wife and child out into a January blizzard. He called you a fornicating bastard. All I've ever been guilty of is of loving all three of you—first Colin as a brother, then Randall as my best friend, and finally you as my true husband."

"You were hardly acting the loving sister, friend, and wife tonight." His eyes glinted in the semi-darkness.

"How dare you! How dare you accuse me of looking at other men. I went to work in the tavern to provide our family with food, you great, jealous brute!"

He froze. For a few moments silence reigned in the small cabin.

"Sweet Jesus, we're destitute, aren't we?" he muttered finally. "You've been keeping us…me, haven't you?"

"Barret…" I began, but could not find the words to reassure him. I could not bear the agony in his face. I arose and tried to take him into my arms, but he shrugged away like a petulant schoolboy and went to look out the window into the darkness.

"So this is what I've come to, what he's reduced me to," he muttered. "A whorehouse bastard who can't even provide for himself, much less his family."

"Barret, no! My mother helped my father when he needed financial assistance…"

"Your father never lost his master's ticket or his ship."

"Come to bed," I pleaded. "We'll talk in the morning."

He pulled a quilt from our bed and started toward the door. "I'll sleep in the stable," he said over his shoulder.

Chapter Sixteen

Lucifer stumbled in the torn earth, shied, and half reared in the harness. Barret roared at the frustrated stallion as he struggled to keep the plow upright. Watching from the cabin window, I felt a surge of compassion for the horse and man trying to prepare the rough field for planting. Both were unfit for the task. Both were free spirits, not drudges to be bound to monotonous tasks like tilling the soil.

Looking at Colin playing on the plank floor I had scrubbed to whiteness, I reflected that if it were not for my child and me, they would not have come to their present position. Little Colin and I had adjusted to life in reduced circumstances, but then, I had only briefly lived in an environment of wealth and privilege, while Colin, being malleable in his extreme youth, had barely seemed to notice the change in his surroundings. Perhaps my son and I were meant for a simple existence. I looked again at Barret and Lucifer fighting their way up the field. Perhaps I was more mule than refined saddle horse.

In the paddock beside the hovel we called a stable, Lady stood watching the stallion work. Due to her more even temperament she'd been the first animal Barret had put before the plow.

After a half-day's valiant effort, the little mare had pulled up lame and spent. Her deteriorating health, as well as the fact that Barret believed she was carrying Lucifer's foal, caused him to abandon her and take up the stronger but highly volatile Lucifer. Now, as Lady watched the pair, she whickered softly, a bit sadly I fancied. Perhaps, she, like myself, was pitying them their unsuitable task.

As I stood by the window watching my husband as he struggled to prepare the rough field he had cleared for planting between our cabin and the river, I found it difficult to believe he was the same man who had boldly captained the magnificent *Maris Stella* before raging seas, and who, impeccable in evening attire, had whirled me with confidence about a Halifax ballroom.

Since he'd become my husband, his life had not been bold or colorful. Where once he'd held a position of respect and wealth, he had become reduced to shoveling guano aboard ships and manure from stables.

Then I saw he had paused in his work and was looking downriver. I followed his gaze and recognized the object of his interest. The *Maris Stella*, her sails full of fresh breeze, had come into view. Returning from an early spring voyage to England under the command of Jared Fletcher, she cut a heart-stopping spectacle of sheer beauty, her white canvases puffed and stark against the charcoal clouds blanketing the sky.

I felt the tightness in my throat deepen and wondered how much more profoundly Barret was being affected by the spectacle of the ship he'd once commanded and loved as a living thing in the hands of another. When she'd departed two months earlier, Barret had been at sea. This was the first time he'd seen his beloved vessel sailing without him.

With the raw wind whipping his dark curls back

from his face, he stood rigidly straight and watched transfixed, Lucifer's reins looped about the shoulders of his shabby woolen jacket. Below mended breeches, his boots were mud-caked. The scenario lashed at my heart. Unable to bear it, I turned away.

When I returned from settling Colin in bed that night, Barret was sitting at the table, his hand clasped about a half-empty rum flask. He ate his meals with Colin and me but still slept in the barn with the horses. This was the first evening in days he'd lingered after supper, and I'd thought he was going to rejoin his family. The flask killed my hopes of a reunion.

Outside, a cold, hard rain was turning the newly plowed field into an unworkable sea of mud and drenching the baby's laundry where it hung on a cord between two trees. Tomorrow I'd have to bring it all inside and dry it painstakingly about the hearth while Barret stood in the stable doorway, restless and annoyed because of his delayed farming.

"He's asleep," I said, sinking into a chair by the fire and taking up my mending. "He's so beautiful I could gaze at him forever."

"Too beautiful to have come from me," Barret muttered.

"Are you doubting his paternity?" I asked sharply.

"No, of course not," he said, shaking his head. "I will never understand how any man can look into the face of his biological son and fail to recognize him in his heart. That's not what's eating my innards tonight." He took a long drink from the flask, wiped his mouth with his hand, and coughed before continuing.

"Today, as my *Maris Stella* sailed past, I saw myself for what I truly am for the first time…a destitute bastard who can't even provide a decent living for his family."

"That's not true, Barret! You're richer than Abraham Douglas will ever be. You have the one thing all his money cannot buy—a son, a beautiful healthy son. In fact, Abraham was so desperate for our child he tried to adopt him—even buy him—when you were away."

"He what?" Barret's bellow told me I had gone too far in my efforts to placate him. Forced to explain, I told him as gently as possible of Abraham's proposal.

"So he used me for stud service," he growled when I'd finished. "Produce issue, then get back to my stall."

"He withdrew the offer when he learned of Caroline's pregnancy."

"Little does he know she's carrying Jared's brat." Barret laughed harshly. "Sweet Jesus!" He slammed his palm down on the table. "Abe Douglas used every last bit of me before he threw me out."

"Barret, love, no!"

He ignored me and took a long drink from the flask. Then he began to sing softly, the lyrics coarse and bawdy.

"Barret, stop it!" I cried, rushing to kneel before him.

"Don't you like my song?" he muttered, his words slurred from the liquor. "I was paid to sing that ditty many times a night when I was a youngster, while a half-naked whore bounced me on her knee or sat with her arm draped about me at the piano. I sing it often, as I lie alone in that barn out back. It serves to remind me of who I am."

He pushed me aside as he rose and went to stare

out the window into the blackness of the night, the flask clutched in his hand.

"Barret, I'm so sorry, my love," I murmured.

"Go to bed, Starr."

He strode out into the night.

****

When I awoke the next morning, the valley lay shrouded in a heavy fog. An eerie silence hung over the place. Not a single bird sang, not a single branch creaked. It was as if life stood suspended, waiting for God only knew what. The atmosphere chilled me to the bone.

I dressed and went shivering into the outer room of the cabin to look out a window. Barret was nowhere in sight. Nor was he anywhere on our property, my following quick perusal revealed. My stomach was churning with apprehension when a knock sounded on the door. I opened it to find Meg swathed in a shawl, her face pale and drawn.

"He's at my tavern, Starr," she said. "He arrived there late last night. He was so drunk he could barely stand."

"Come in, Meg," I said. "You're shivering. I'll build up the fire and make coffee."

"Starr, I must confess I dreaded coming to see you today." She stepped inside, removed her shawl, and shook beads of moisture from it. "I had to trust my instincts that you truly are my friend and that you'd believe me. I wanted you to hear it from me. There was a bunch of rabble in the street who saw Barret banging on the door of my tavern—it was past closing—who saw me let him in. I had to get to you before the village gossip. I know he grew up in rooms above a kind of tavern. I think he felt that, in coming to my inn, he was in some strange way going home."

"What did he say?" I asked, my hands trembling as I swung a pot of water over the fire.

"He was like a man torn apart. He began shivering and trembling as if he'd caught a great chill. His clothes were drenched from the rain. I…I helped him undress and put him into my bed. I stayed with him until he slept, and then I went to another room for the night.

"Starr, I admit we were lovers before he met you. But last night there was nothing between us. You're my friend. No matter how I felt, how I still feel about Barret, I wouldn't, couldn't do anything to hurt you. He loves you."

"I believe you, Meg. Sit. Please. I'll make us some breakfast. Then I'll go collect my husband."

"That won't be necessary."

Meg and I turned toward the door to see Barret framed in it. Against the swirling fog, he was a dark, towering silhouette.

"I'll be leaving," Meg arose and drew her shawl over her dark curls. As she started to move past Barret, he caught her by the arm.

"Thank you," he said hoarsely. He placed a gentle kiss on her forehead before she moved away from him and, with a backward glance at me, moved out into the mist.

"Meg told you?" he asked, closing the door.

"Yes."

"I'm sorry," he said, rubbing his forehead with callused fingers.

"I know," I said.

"Sweet Jesus!" he breathed, going to sink down on

a bench at the table. "I feel worse than I did during my first bout of seasickness."

"Barret, I think it's time you told me the truth about yourself."

"What truth?" He grimaced.

"About your connection to the Douglas family. It's more than simply as their employee. I've seen you accept abuse from Abraham as you'd take from no other man, and care for Colin and Randall with every ounce of your strength. That January voyage to London on behalf of the Douglas Enterprises was far beyond what any employee would attempt for his master. Barret…" I hesitated, fearing to voice what had occurred to me in the night. "You often referred to Colin as a family member. You arrived in this valley the year before he was born."

"What in God's name are you suggesting, Starr?" He turned to face me, his expression one of utter astonishment.

"Are you… Were you Colin's father?"

"Sweet Jesus, woman, you're asking if I laid with Abe's wife?"

"Barret, you were extremely protective of Colin. You also left this valley the same day his best friend Darcy Pod was killed. Perhaps Darcy learned the truth about Colin's parentage and Abe ordered him silenced. I recall how you were once ordered to interrogate Simon. Perhaps he also ordered you to silence Darcy. You were always obedient to him."

"Dear God, have I behaved as such a depraved barbarian that you would believe me capable of such atrocities?"

"Barret…" I stammered, not knowing how to

proceed.

"Captain! Starr!" Bridgit O'Brien burst into the cabin without pausing to knock. Her hair was disheveled, her eyes wild. "Abraham Douglas has failed! His creditors are about to force him into bankruptcy. The news came on the *Maris Stella* yesterday, and this morning it's spread among the villagers. They're rioting and declaring they're going to hang Mr. Douglas for bringing ruin to the valley!"

Barret jumped to his feet and reached for his pistol. He shoved it into his belt and started toward the door.

"Barret, where are you going?"

"I have to help him, Starr." He strode out into the fog.

"Bridgit, stay with the baby!" I cried, grabbing my shawl. "I must go with him."

The village was a hot sea of rage-distorted faces as Barret and I ran toward Peacock House. The gray mist could well have been steam rising from the heat of their anger.

My heart pounded at my ribs, but I knew I must follow Barret. His fate must be mine.

As we reached the edge of the yelling, fist-shaking mob gathered about the mansion, the door of the house opened and Abraham, lordly as ever in a fine coat and spotless linen, stepped out onto the verandah.

"What's all this?" he asked. He spoke in a pleasantly condescending tone as one might address an unreasonably angry child. "I swear, you'll frighten my maid servants into ruining my dinner if you persist in behaving in this fashion."

"Never mind your dinner, you old miser!" a man in front yelled. "You've ruined all of us, you and your moneylenders in London. We'll starve, thanks to you!"

"Come, come, Jim." Abraham drew on his deep reserve of charm. "We're a long way from ruined. Who's been spreading such evil rumors? I'll have him drawn and quartered."

"It was your commodore, Captain Jared Fletcher," someone shouted.

"Jared…?" Abraham took a quick step forward. As he moved, the shot rang out.

Out of the tail of my eye, I saw Jacob Carruthers, the man whose farm Abraham had repossessed on the morning of Colin's beating, near the middle of the crowd, holding a smoking pistol.

My father-in-law clutched his left breast, his face contorted in pain, and staggered backward to slump against the house front. The fog had hidden the gunman from his keen eyes.

"Get him!" a voice yelled. "Hang the lying old bastard!"

Before anyone could mount the steps to obey, Barret vaulted over the verandah railing and stood, legs astride, arms akimbo, between the advancing mob and Abraham.

"Go home," he ordered. "Don't compound your troubles by adding the murder of a Queen's Magistrate to them."

"He ruined us, Captain, as he ruined you," a man yelled. "You were his commodore, his house guest. Now you live in a log shack and shovel guano to keep your wife and baby fed. Let us have him! We'll make him pay."

"Pay for what?" Barret asked, unmoving as a rock. "For building this town and its industries? For providing jobs for all of you when you arrived from the old countries, half starved? For supporting your church and starting a school for your children? For trying to bring a semblance of law and order to a near wilderness? And all with the borrowed capital those bankers in London are now recalling. It appears to me you've benefited more than he has; you've all had the pleasure of the cash and credit, with none of the responsibility of owing thousands."

A noticeable change washed over the crowd as Barret was speaking. When he'd finished, it was silent.

"Go home," Barret repeated. "Open your eyes to the other opportunities of this valley. Timber and ships aren't its only products. The soil is good. The river and bay are teeming with fish. The government is looking for men to build roads and railways. Soon there's to be a steam navigation school in Halifax. You can learn this new method of transportation. The fate of Douglas and Sons need not be yours. This house and this family alone will suffer the full consequences of those decisions made across the Atlantic."

A low muttering of agreement broke out among the crowd. Gradually it began to disperse. As soon as the way was clear, I rushed to join Barret. He was bending over Abraham, who'd slumped farther.

"You were most eloquent, Judas," the older man muttered, bitter, his eyes glazed with pain. "Is that how you managed to seduce my son's wife?"

"Why, the ungrateful old…"

"Enough, Starr." Barret was gathering the older man into his arms and rising to his feet. "Open the door and help me get him into a bed."

****

"Traitor!" Abraham's voice rose in a raw whisper as Barret seated himself on the edge of his bed in the huge master bedroom of Peacock House. "You should have let me die. I prefer death to an obligation to a villain."

"Abe, listen to me." Barret leaned close to him, his face grim with concern. "It's not over. We can get you away before that crowd has time to get liquored up and regroup. In a month or two, when tempers have cooled, you can return, and we'll help you rebuild your empire."

Abraham's labored breathing was harsh in the silent room. The servants and Caroline, like rats deserting a sinking ship, had fled.

"*You* help me rebuild!" he rasped. "You, who fathered a child on Colin's wife when you swore not to touch her? Bastard, lying son of a gun…"

"Take that back!" Barret suddenly snarled. "My mother was no ship's whore, and you know it. She was a decent little French governess who fell in love with a vessel's twenty-four-year-old master, a captain who left her destitute, to bear his child in a brothel. I promised you that any child Starr bore would be your grandchild, and I've kept my word. Colin Barret Douglas-Madison *is* your grandson."

"What!" Abraham struggled up on an elbow and faced Barret. "What are you saying…?"

"I'm the child you fathered on Lise LeClerq, the woman you refused to marry because she was a French Catholic," Barret roared, and jerked the crucifix from beneath his faded shirt. "Remember this? You gave it to her! She wore it always."

"No!" Abraham fell back on his pillows, his eyes

rolling. "No! As God is my witness, I never knew Lise bore me a child. I swear!"

"Well, now you do. My mother was forced to become a whorehouse entertainer in order to survive and provide for her child. That life was a living hell for a decent, God-fearing woman."

"You're Lise's son?" Abraham stared at the crucifix. "Why did you never tell me?"

Barret's anger turned to reticent nervousness. Looking down at his callused hands, he hesitated.

"Well, come, boy, tell me."

"Because I was afraid," he said finally. "Afraid you'd deny me. Or hate me. Or shun me as the bastard I am."

"Dear God!" Abraham's eyes filled with tears. "All these years I've longed for a son such as you. Tell me of Lise. And yourself."

Tears slid down his cheeks. For the first time I saw Abraham Douglas for what he truly was, an old man beaten by a world he had battled all his life, an old man who had seldom dealt fairly with others and now was being handed what must be for him the most crushing blow of all.

"She died when I was ten," Barret said. "After that, I made a living playing piano and singing in the same brothel where she'd worked."

"Go on, my boy." Abraham's hand shook as he reached for Barret's.

"One night after the tavern closed, I went for a walk to clear my head of the smell of smoke and liquor. A bunch of drunken sailors decided to make sport of me. When I fought back, they beat me, then left me barely conscious in the street.

"A young sea captain on his way back to his ship found me. I was too badly beaten to walk, so he carried me to his ship, lying at anchor in the lagoon. He took me with him when he sailed with the tide the following morning. He kept me in his cabin and tended me with his own hands."

He paused and looked down at me. "Starr, that young captain was Morgan Reynolds."

"Oh, Barret! You knew him? What was he like? You must tell me, later."

"When I recovered, Captain Reynolds gave me a position on his ship." Barret went to splash brandy from a decanter on the bureau into a ready glass. "My mother had told me my father's name and that he was a colonial from New Brunswick. It was relatively easy to find you, Abe, once I had a means of transport. You'd already become a man of wealth and position, well known throughout the province." He took a long swig of the fortified wine before he continued. "I managed to place myself in the employ of one of your ship's masters. I hid the crucifix when I was on land. I didn't want you to recognize me by a trinket. I wanted you to recognize me with your heart and soul. And although she never once told me outright, Gram soon recognized me. She had a perceptive soul as well as a shrewd mind."

"Mother knew?" Abraham was astounded. "And she never told me?"

"She knew how I felt, what I wanted from you," Barret said. "She was willing to let me have my way. I was her grandson, too, and she loved me."

"Did Lise ever marry?" Abraham asked, after a profound silence. "Is that how you came by your surname?"

"No," Barret said. "I invented the name Madison to avoid your recognizing LeClerq. Do you know"—he choked—"Do you know I lived on ale and stale bread for weeks at a time? Do you know I was often drunk before I was thirteen because I had nothing but tavern leavings on which to survive? All the while, in Pine, my brother Randall was growing up pampered and warm and safe."

"I never knew," Abraham whispered. "As God is my witness, I never knew. Now I'm to be punished. Barret, I'm sorry, so very sorry, my son. I always had a weakness for beautiful French women. I should have followed my heart and married Lise. By trusting my head and listening to my prejudices and marrying Christiana, I only made three people miserable…six, if I'm to count my sons. Even when I was granted a second chance at true happiness with Marie, I was too great a fool to recognize it. I might yet have had another child, a child conceived in love. I am not yet incapable, you realize. Marie and I…a child…it would have made up for all I've missed in my life. But she went away…and died of some shantytown disease. Dear God, I've had so much—and yet so little."

He lapsed into unconsciousness. Shocked and shaken, Barret and I stared at each other. Marie had been carrying Abe's child and my father-in-law had never known.

"He must never know," Barret muttered, guessing my thoughts. "It would serve no purpose now."

Chapter Seventeen

As the day drew on, Abraham's condition worsened. Barret and I took turns sitting with him while the other rested or ate. I thanked God for Bridgit, who cared for Colin during our vigil.

Outside, the town was in riot and we dared not attempt a return to our cabin, even had we wanted to do so.

In the early part of the afternoon, as I sat beside him, Abraham awoke.

"Water," he rasped over fever-parched lips.

I put a cup to his mouth. As I replaced it on the bedside table, he spoke again.

"Starr, you've been…a blessing to my sons, all three of them. You made their lives tolerable, while I made them living hells. I thought you simply a lovely, seductive child whose only possible use to me was as a producer of grandchildren. You've proven you're a strong woman, not afraid to face the realities of life. On the night Randall died, I saw you for what you truly are—a mature, strong, and compassionate woman who'll make a success of her life and family. You're a remarkable woman, much like my mother. You'll survive and make what's left of this family thrive."

He paused for breath, then continued, weakening with each labored word.

"When I'm gone, all that is mine—all that is left of

what was mine—will be Barret's. My will is specific: My entire estate goes to my son who produces my first grandchild. Write it down, child. Write that on my deathbed I do acknowledge Barret Madison as my eldest son, father of my first grandchild, and my rightful heir. Write, child, write! There's not much time left."

Hastily I found pen and paper and did as I was bidden. When I'd finished, I read aloud what I had put down, then held his quaking body as he signed the statement.

"Witness it, witness it now!" he implored.

Seized by a fit of coughing, he was forced to stop speaking. I did as he asked, my own hand shaking as I signed. When the spasm subsided, he was much weaker, and I saw fear in his face. He knew the end was near.

"I must tell you something else," he rasped, barely above a whisper. "I must confess. It was I…who shot Darcy Pod."

"You…!" I gasped. "But why?"

"He…I believed he deserved to be shot," he wheezed. "But not now… Not now! As God is my witness, I'm sorry. The boy did not deserve…"

His voice trailed off as he lapsed into a coma from which he did not awaken. I now knew who had killed Darcy, but not why. The mystery had simply been deepened by Abraham's confession.

Late in the afternoon, Barret and I left Peacock House. Abraham Douglas's body lay shrouded in a sheet in his great master bedroom. Barret and I would go to the cemetery, dig a grave, and then return for his remains.

As we started down the drive, Barret's arm draped about my shoulders, a shrill whinny from the stables made us both whirl.

"Lucifer!" Barret exclaimed. "What is he doing here?"

In the same breath, he was running in the direction of the cry.

When he burst into the barn, I was close behind him. Jared Fletcher struggled to lead the black stallion from the building. The horse, harnessed to a loaded wagon, was prancing and snorting. Seated at the reins, wearing a ruby-colored velvet traveling suit and peacock-feathered hat, was Caroline Douglas.

"Sweet Jesus, man, get away from that animal!" Barret roared.

"I've seen you make him behave as docile as a kitten," Jared said, releasing the foaming, wild-eyed stallion to face Barret. "I can do anything as well as you, given a chance. Didn't I take over your ship and your fleet?"

"You looted the house, didn't you?" Barret said indicating the loaded wagon as Lucifer, left in peace, stood pawing the planks beneath his hooves. "Now you're planning to run off while the town is in too great an uproar over Abe's failure to notice."

"Get out of my way, Barret," Jared ordered. He jerked a pistol from his belt and leveled it at my husband. "Move aside while Caroline and I leave or, I swear, I'll shoot you where you stand."

"Yes, I believe you would murder a man you once considered your friend, all for that piece of adulterous trash," Barret said as he drew me clear of the entrance with him. "But don't take the stallion. He'll kill you both."

"Don't try to scare me off, Barret." Jared moved back toward the animal. """He's the fastest, strongest horse in this valley. He'll take us farther and swifter than any of Abe's nags."

He flung up his free hand to grab Lucifer's bridle. The sudden movement snapped the horse's thin restraint. Eyes showing white with outraged indignation, the animal roared and rose onto his hind legs between the wagon's shafts. When his front hooves came down, they knocked the gun from Jared's right hand.

"Jared, help me!" Caroline, her face ashen, was on her feet, pulling on the reins.

The woman's shrill cries incensed Lucifer beyond his endurance. Ears pinned, teeth bared, he bolted. As the wagon flew past Jared, a wheel struck him in the chest. With a cry of pain, he was smashed down to the plank floor.

The stallion galloped from the barn at an angle, in such a way that the other wheel caught on the edge of the door. Caroline's shattering scream was to be the last utterance of her life as she was flung headlong against one of the stable's supporting timbers.

"Take me to her," Jared Fletcher, broken and bleeding, begged Barret as he knelt beside him.

"She's dead, Jared. You don't want to see her as she is now."

"Please, I'm begging you!" Jared tore at Barret's shirtfront with bloody fingers. "I sold my soul into hell for her, and I want to see her once more…just once more… Barret, she's carrying my child!"

"All right." Barret gathered his friend up in his

arms and carried him to where Caroline lay face down in a pile of fodder. Scattered about her was an array of jewelry, money, silverware, and coins from Peacock House.

"Caroline, love," Jared moaned as Barret placed him beside her. "Oh, sweet love!" He broke down, sobbing. With ragged fingers, he reached out and turned her face to him.

She had hit the beam with terrific force. When Jared rolled her toward him, all that was left of her bewitching beauty was raw, red pulp.

Jared managed to mouth her name before he lost consciousness.

Barret carried Jared into Peacock House, and together we stripped him, placed him into Caroline's bed, and washed and dressed his wounds as he regained his senses.

"I couldn't believe she tried to cause Starr to miscarry, or that once she was safely pregnant by me she'd kill her husband." Jared's words shook. "After I discovered she'd hired Simon to maim Colin Douglas, I got her to promise there'd be no more bloodletting. "When she discovered Marie was pregnant, curious as a cat, she worried the girl until she confessed it was Abe who'd fathered the child. Caroline feared Abe might marry the girl and have another avenue to an heir that would take his fortune even farther from her grasp than it already was, so she won the girl's confidence and gave her a potion to produce a supposedly safe miscarriage."

"I saw them together on the road one day," I recalled. "Oh, God, she killed Marie and her child as surely as she tried to kill my baby."

"And Ida," Jared further revealed. "She substituted another medicine for her foxglove potion. She'd overheard Barret and Ida talking on several occasions, and she'd become convinced Barret was in some way a Douglas. The only one who seemed aware and in danger of exposing the fact was Ida. She decided it would be best if the old lady did not live too much longer…especially when she discovered she herself was pregnant. And I did nothing to stop her."

He tried to move, but pain overcame him, and he sank back with a groan.

"Rest." Barret laid a restraining hand on the man's shoulder. "You can talk later."

"No!" Sweat breaking out over his forehead and upper lip, Jared Fletcher was desperately insistent. "You must listen…now! When we devised the plan of the pirate attack in the Caribbean, I charted my course carefully in order to have the attack occur near a habitable island. I knew guano ships would eventually pass by. I only wanted you to remain there long enough to cast doubt on Starr's fidelity. With your reputation with women, Barret, Caroline chose you to be the third of that party. I never knew until today, until she ordered me to take her away or be implicated as her accomplice, that she'd murdered her husband."

"She murdered Randall?" My breath caught in my throat.

Jared began to cough wretchedly. Barret took up a towel and wiped the sweat from his forehead.

"I couldn't believe what was happening on the *Linnet* when those barbarians began to molest Starr," he wheezed. "I think Caroline instructed Simon to violate her to cast doubt on the paternity of any child she might have. She didn't confide that fact to me."

"Do you know if she hired Simon to shoot Starr in Halifax?" Barret questioned.

"She must have, although she never told me so," he rasped. "She was probably afraid Colin and Starr's being together again might result in a pregnancy. I do know Simon followed you that night and saw where you went. He later told that dockside butcher who Starr really was. Simon even assured him that if he would say he performed an abortion on her, they could blackmail Abe Douglas the next time he came to Halifax."

Minutes after, as Jared was drifting off into unconsciousness, he clutched at Barret's arm and spoke with great effort.

"I loved her, Barret," he wheezed, sweat pouring over his face. "You must believe that to understand what I did. I wanted to be her husband and I wanted to be Abe's commodore, and all they both did was use me until there was nothing left inside me, not decency, not even loyalty to a friend. They destroyed me, Barret. But they couldn't destroy you. Don't let them. Swear to me you won't let them…"

His lacerated fingers dug deep into Barret's flesh.

"I swear," Barret said. "Now rest."

"No, no, I must finish my confession!" He broke off, choking, then continued desperately, "Do you know why I spread the news of Abe's failure in the village? He accused me of being responsible. He said I'd mismanaged his fleet, that you wouldn't have made the mistakes I had. He said one of the major reasons his creditors in London had foreclosed was because they had learned Captain Barret Madison, who'd made that celebrated January crossing, was no longer in command. I couldn't stand it, Barret. I'd worked my guts out for that vicious old man, and that was how he repaid me. So I played Judas. And all because of a woman who used me for stud service."

Jared's eyes were closing. "I loved her, and I killed her," he whispered. "I wanted his respect, and I betrayed him." His eyes shut. An hour later he was dead.

****

Shrouded in encroaching dusk and thickening mist, Barret and I buried Jared and Caroline in a common grave in an obscure corner of the Presbyterian cemetery.

"The villagers wouldn't approve of our burying them here, if they knew what they'd done," Barret said, leaning wearily on his shovel. "But since Jared truly loved Caroline, laying them to rest together can't be wrong. I'll see to it that Bridgit is placed beside Randall when her time comes."

"Yes."

"It's been a long day." Barret slipped an arm about my sagging shoulders. "Tomorrow, when the rioting quiets, I'll return to Peacock House and take care of burying…Father."

Together we turned toward the village and in the same instant saw the unearthly glow piercing the fog.

"My God!" Barret breathed. "They've set fire to Peacock House. Father will be burned!"

Flinging the shovel aside, he started down the darkening trail at a full run.

"Barret!" I cried, pursuing him. "Your father's dead. There's nothing you can do for him now."

But he had outdistanced my words. All I could do was race down the misty trail behind him. I had not yet found the courage to tell him his father, on his deathbed, had confessed to murder.

****

The village was a bedlam of enraged, drink-reddened faces and savage roars. Many of the rioters carried lighted torches and flasks of rum. Several drunken horsemen, careless of the safety of pedestrians, were galloping foaming, wild-eyed horses through the melee.

Looters had already smashed the windows from all Douglas buildings save the mercantile. The shipyard, too, was undergoing pilfering. I didn't pause to think about it. I had to find Barret.

As I ran past an alley between the Black Horse Inn and a shop, I heard a muted scream. Glancing into the shadows, I saw Meg, her dress torn from one shoulder, being held against a plank wall and mauled by a massive sailor. It was not a night for any woman to be abroad alone in Pine.

I grabbed a broken plank from a doorframe and rushed to her aid. A well-placed blow took the brute to his knees, and a second rendered him unconscious. For a moment, Meg and I, breasts heaving, stood over his inert body. Then I flung the board to the ground and took off at a run toward Peacock House.

"Starr, no! You must go home! It's not safe!" Meg screamed after me, but I ignored her and raced up the street toward the flaming mansion.

A great crowd had assembled in the dooryard. I saw Jacob Carruthers at the head of the mob, laughing as the manor burned.

"I shot him, and I'm glad!" he bellowed. "Now I'm watching him burn! Abe Douglas took the land that was my living from me. My baby starved and my wife died of misery. Now he's tasting the kind of Hell he made for so many others!"

"Starr!" I whirled to see Bridgit pushing toward me through the maddened crowd. "Captain Madison went into the house. Make him come out! The roof is about to collapse!"

I burst through the circle of celebrating humanity and rushed into the heat and smoke billowing from the front entrance. Great tongues of flame burst out of the upper-story windows, timbers snapped and groaned, and suddenly, with a mighty cracking, the roof caved in.

"Barret!" I screamed as a great blast of heat burst out upon me. I staggered backward, away from the inferno.

A tall, broad-shouldered figure carrying a body in his arms appeared in what was left of the doorway. Seconds later, my husband collapsed beside me, the back of his shirt in flames, the body of his dead father clutched in his arms.

The house, with a final roar, split apart and thundered into a fiery heap that would smolder for days before it finally gave up.

****

The following morning, when hangovers and exhaustion from the night's debauched catharsis had cooled outrage and passions, Barret and I set out to bury his father.

Alone, Barret dug in the hard, resisting earth, sweat drenching his face and chest. He would not allow me to help. His back beneath a thin, worn shirt was a raw mass of burned and oozing flesh, but I could not stop him.

Gradually townspeople began to trickle up the hill to encircle the yawning hole and the sheet-swathed body beside it.

"Old Abe wasn't all bad," I heard someone murmur. "He got us a church and a school, and he threw the best launching parties this side of the Atlantic."

Several came forward to help Barret lift the bundle that had been Abraham Douglas and lower it into the earth.

"Farewell, Father," Barret said, as he straightened up. His jaw flinched with a nervous twitch, his expression as iron.

"Father!" The murmur rippled through the crowd.

"Abraham was Captain Madison's father," I said, my voice shaking, as I turned to face the villagers. "Thank you for coming. Now perhaps we should leave him alone with his grief."

The astounded group turned, one by one, and walked slowly back the way they had come, whispers and murmurs of amazed discussion marking their departure. Leaving Barret alone with the man he had finally been able to call Father, I followed.

At sunset Barret came home. I was sitting by the hearth rocking Colin to sleep when he entered our cabin and knelt before us.

"I love you," he said hoarsely. "I love you both so much. I realize now that it is the three of us who are my family, and I'm ready to devote myself to our future together."

The next morning, Barret and I walked through the ragged remains of the village. The Douglas offices and shipyards resembled spent battlefields. A half-built ship had been ripped apart in its slip in the shipyard and lay canted on one side like a massive, vulture-stripped carcass. The doors of the buildings along the main street hung open, many on a single remaining hinge. Windows had been shattered. Papers and records from Abraham's offices scuttled about the muddy ruts of the street whenever a breeze wafted through the devastation, including mortgage agreements and indenture files destroyed forever. Many in the valley would have their first genuine taste of freedom.

The mercantile alone stood unscathed, a monument to the kindnesses of Ben Smith. The old man stood in the doorway and shook his head sadly as we passed. The town he'd founded with such high hopes was in a shambles.

"Our legacy," Barret said wryly, as we paused to survey the damage. Last night I'd told him of his father's deathbed will. Suddenly a breeze, warm in spite of the heavy gray cloud cover, touched my cheek with soft, reassuring fingers.

"Barret, look!" I breathed, as my gaze fell on the river.

"Sweet Jesus!" Barret muttered.

Riding at anchor beyond the sadly tattered, wharf-moored Douglas fleet, the *Maris Stella* floated proud and unviolated.

"Your legacy, Captain," I said, taking his arm.

"*Our* legacy," he said, looking down at me with bright, eager eyes. "Let's go out to her. I need to feel her beneath my feet today."

****

The following morning, Johnny Kelly drove up to our cabin, a large blanket-swathed cargo in the back of his farm wagon.

"Welcome, Johnny," Barret said, as we came out of the cabin together to greet him. "How are your wife and daughter?"

"Heather and little Starr are in fine fettle, Captain," he said leaping down from the high seat. I recalled how Colin had gotten Randall to attend the baby's birth. "I've brought you and your wife something I saved from the fire the other night," he continued, climbing back into the wagon. He swung back the blanket to reveal Colin's piano and bench.

"How?" Barret asked in amazement as he went forward to examine the instrument.

"I knew what it meant to him," Johnny said shyly. "Once, when I went to the house with a message, I heard him play. I told him how fine his music was, and he said, 'It's my life.' When I saw the house in flames, I knew I had to save what he'd loved best. I smashed those glass doors at the side of the mansion that led into the room where it sat, threw its bench atop it, and shoved it on its wheels out onto the verandah and down the steps. I fear I may have damaged it somewhat, but it couldn't be helped."

I rushed to the bashful young man and threw my arms about his neck.

"Thank you so much, Johnny. Barret and I will treasure what your kindness and bravery have saved for us."

Johnny helped Barret shove and maneuver the heavy instrument into our cabin, then left.

When we were alone, Barret ran his hand over its polished wood.

"He loved this thing," he said. "He used to say it was an old and trusted friend who helped him hold onto what he loved most when he felt his whole world slipping away from him. Before his mother died, they'd sit together on its bench while he played and she sang. He told me that as a child he'd kept his most treasured toys inside its bench. He said he'd believed they were safe because they were with his friend."

He bent and tried to raise the seat's lid.

"It's locked," he said, surprised.

He took a knife from the sideboard and pried the delicate lock. When it gave, he lifted the cover to reveal musical scores, all written in Colin's carefully detailed style.

"Sweet Jesus!" he breathed. "This is where he kept his original compositions."

He removed several, closed the lid, and seated himself at the keyboard.

"Magnificent," Barret breathed when he paused in his playing a half hour later. "Even on this instrument that desperately needs tuning after the abuse it's suffered, it's obvious these are the works of a genius."

I put my arm about his shoulders, too moved to reply. The music Barret had played had been the creations of a man of great talent.

"We must have them published," Barret said. "Colin's music belongs to the world. I'll take them to Vienna, where they'll be most appreciated."

He arose and dropped to one knee to reopen the lid and again examine its contents. On the bottom of the bench chest lay a sealed envelope addressed to me.

"Open it," Barret said, placing it in my hands.

I did as he instructed and read aloud.

My dearest and most beautiful friend, Starr, I will be dead when you read this...each day suicide seems more and more the only answer to my mangled life...but I cannot go in peace until you know the truth; the truth which is not that you were undesirable, but that you, even in your beauty, were only undesirable to me. My sexual preference does not run to women, my darling, you see. My father has called me a demented pervert, but I cannot help myself. Today, by the river, I tried, oh, dear God how I tried, but even if Barret had not interrupted us, I know I could not have made myself your lover or fathered a child. I loved once and fully. My lover was Darcy Pod.

"Dear God!" Barret breathed as he read over my shoulder. "He wanted you to know, after all."

My eyes had blurred with shock. What was this madness? Darcy and Colin—lovers? Dear, dear God!

Finally I regained my courage and read on.

We both loved you as a dear sister, Starr, Colin's words continued. *But my music and his poetry bound us together in body and spirit. We cared for each other as I realize Barret cares for you. Barret knows of my preference. He's tried to understand. Please do the same, Starr. And when I'm gone, marry Barret. He's a truly good man who will give you a man's love and children and all the things I can't. Farewell, sweet sister. Remember always, Darcy and I loved you as best we could.*

On an attached sheet was Darcy's story as he had told it to Colin. Early in his life, Sir Harry's son Charles had recognized his tendency. He'd taken Darcy from the mines and made him his lover. Thus was explained Charles' reluctance to marry. Through compliance to Charles' wishes, Darcy had secured my release from the mines and, later, his passage to America.

Then Darcy had met Colin. It had been their love of music and poetry that had drawn them together. Then one night they'd discovered a deeper attraction.

The story, in Colin's hand, continued:

One night my father, in searching for me, came to Darcy's cabin. In our passion, we'd forgotten to bar the door. As we lay upon the bed, he burst in. I shall never forget Father's stricken expression. Speechless from shock, he paused only a moment before he staggered like a drunken man from the cabin.

The next morning Darcy, a revolver in his hand, was found dead. His death was declared to be suicide. I knew he'd been murdered, and by whom.

I pretended nothing had happened. Father did likewise. When I married, I think he felt he'd done the right thing and had succeeded in quelling my perversities. I tried to change my ways, too. Today, in the meadow I made a valiant effort to perform properly. But I failed, as I will always fail to be aroused by a woman.

Ill with shock, I refolded the letter and handed it to Barret. In my distress, I forgot I had not told him of his father's deathbed confession.

"Sweet Jesus, Father murdered that boy!" he breathed. "He shot the lad for being different. And all my life I would have given my soul for the love and respect of that brutal old man! All those years wasted on longing to be called son—by a remorseless killer."

He went to stare out the window into the bright

sunlight of a spring day.

"The dream of having a father and a home and a family is a wonderful vision," I said softly. "That's all you ever wanted. No matter what Abraham Douglas did, nothing can change that fact."

"And my dream has come to reality," he said, turning to look into my eyes.

"You knew about Colin's…preference…all along, didn't you?" I asked.

"Yes," he said. "While we were in Vienna, he had a relationship. I confronted him and tried to convince him it was wrong. He broke down and cried. He was what he was, he said, and I either must accept him or turn away from our friendship forever.

"When he married you, I hoped he'd changed. His behavior on several occasions gave me reason to believe he had. But he hadn't. And never would. After a deal of soul searching I decided I shouldn't sit in judgment on others. I couldn't tell you," he continued. "I hadn't the courage or the words. I couldn't tell you about a world you probably didn't even know existed…a world where men made love to men."

"But Colin and Darcy, in love, sharing a bed…"

"Hush, hush," he said, holding me. "Remember Colin and Darcy as you knew them—talented, compassionate young men who loved you as best they could."

****

Two weeks later, Barret set sail for Vienna to have Colin's music published. I didn't accompany him. I told him I was needed to help the villagers re-establish themselves. That was only an excuse. The real reason was that I'd discovered I was pregnant again and didn't want to risk losing the child on a sea voyage. I kept this news from Barret. He had to go.

Ben Smith, restored as proprietor of his store, also helped the villagers get back on their feet. He advanced reasonable credit for seed and farm implements to give much neglected agriculture a chance. The valley must become self-sufficient, he declared. Its people must not rely on overseas credit or foodstuffs.

He rode to the provincial capital and spoke in Randall's vacant government seat to secure jobs for the men in building railways and roads, and instruction in the running of trains and steamships. With the assistance of the local priest, he found nuns willing to establish a school for the families of Acadian fishermen, and others who would set up a rudimentary hospital in Pine.

A month later, he was once again appointed magistrate for the valley, with Johnny Kelly acting as his constable and jailer. The house of cards that Abraham had built his wealth upon looked, in retrospect, incredibly ostentatious and superficial when compared with Ben Smith's sturdy new society.

Bridgit became manager of the fish-packing industry. She paid a fair price for catches, a fair wage in the packing sheds. Brisk and businesslike in her trim, new suits, Bridgit O'Brien was every inch the lady entrepreneur, wise and resourceful, but also compassionate and altruistic when the situation warranted.

Meg Warden continued to serve liquor in her establishment, but on certain occasions prohibited its sale and invited families, French and English, rich and poor, Protestant and Catholic, to enjoy the music and song supplied sometimes by itinerant musicians and sometimes by myself. Mary, who kept books by day for Ben and Bridgit, was always more than willing to mind Colin for an evening.

Ben Smith and we four women were setting the foundation for a solid and lasting colonial town. If Captain Barret Madison had been with us, our contentment would have been complete.

****

Barret had been gone several weeks when a lawyer arrived from England. He was a small, gray-haired man who carried a large briefcase as he walked gingerly and furtively toward my cabin through the golden leaves of late September. Apparently he was new to the colonies and was expecting some poisonous snake or other deadly creature to manifest itself in my dooryard.

"Mrs. Madison?" he asked when I met him near my front step. "Formerly Starr Reynolds, fiancée to one Darcy Pod?"

"Yes."

"May I come inside your house, madame? I believe I have news which will prove most agreeable to you."

As he spread a film of legal papers over our plank table, I poured him a cup of coffee. Then I took the place he patted beside him.

"Mrs. Madison, before he left England, Darcy Pod made a will, a very legal, very all-encompassing will," he began. "He named you beneficiary to all he owned or ever might own. The amount he left in trust for you with our firm at that time was minuscule, barely enough to buy you a gown and a pair of decent shoes. Recently, all that has changed, and we felt impelled to find you. Have you heard of Sir Charles Blackwell?"

"Yes," I said, a shudder washing over me. "I knew Sir Charles."

"He passed away recently, without issue but with a rather unusual bequest." The lawyer paused, drew a deep breath, then continued, "It appears he and your fiancé, Darcy Pod, shared a rather…er…intense relationship; so intense, in fact, that Sir Charles left Mr. Pod the entire Blackwell fortune. The most lucrative item at this time is, of course, the coal mining business he inherited from his mother. Steamboats and railways have made that commodity as valuable as gold. Now, if you've been following me, Mrs. Madison, that makes you, as Mr. Pod's sole heir, a very wealthy woman."

I gasped. Was I hearing correctly? Was Sir Harry's wealth, which my mother had died trying to secure for me, finally mine? Surely fate could not be so dramatic, so twisted.

"It's true, Mrs. Madison," the lawyer was continuing. "We've checked the details thoroughly. In such an unusual case, we must. Rest assured, I would not have made this arduous journey if I had not been certain you are the legal heir to Blackwell Mining and the Blackwell estates. Now, please do me the honor of signing these papers quickly, so that I might catch passage on the next ship leaving this wilderness."

****

I was a wealthy woman. After the lawyer left, I sat by the table and pondered how his visit would change my life. He had left me several hundred pounds in cash "to tide me over," as he'd put it, until I could take full possession and command of my mines and other interests. I could pay my bills, buy new clothes for Colin and me, presents for Bridgit, Ben, Meg, and

Mary. I could even fulfill one of my heart's fondest wishes…to see Barret dressed as he'd once been and able to enjoy the amenities of life again. I could do almost anything except what I wanted most…bring my husband instantly back home to share my good fortune with me.

My mind slid back over the years. So many things were clear now. Sir Charles had taken young Darcy from the mines to be his lover. His position as secretary had been a cover for his real purpose in the manor. I shuddered as I thought of innocent young Darcy being taken from the mines that November night and up to the manor where Charles Blackwell waited, riding crop in hand.

I recalled Darcy's condition on the day he'd told me he'd managed to have Simon driven from the estate with the hounds at his heels; the dark circles under his blue eyes, the hoarseness in his voice, flinching when I'd touched him.

Then I remembered how, later, when he'd told me of his chance to go to America, he'd called Sir Charles simply Charles. Perhaps, later, it had not been so terrible for him, perhaps he'd come to care for Sir Charles and he for Darcy. That was probably why Maude Bell had insisted on sending Darcy away. Older, shrewder, and more worldly than I at that time, she'd no doubt recognized their relationship for what it truly was. She'd seen there would be no chance of the all-important heir if Darcy remained Charles' intimate friend.

I struggled to understand such a relationship. It was easier to comprehend that of Darcy and Colin. The latter must have been as intense and satisfying to them as Barret's and mine was to us, I thought.

****

It was Christmas Eve. I put away my notes and got up from my place at the table, glad I had finished writing my life story to that date. Perhaps someday someone would read it and find some measure of interest in it.

Colin was asleep in the bedroom, Mary dozing by the fire.

"I'm going to the tavern, Mary," I said. "The musicians Meg hired didn't arrive because of the storm yesterday. I don't want the families she invited for caroling to be disappointed. I'll play my guitar for them and be back in a couple of hours, when they leave to attend church services."

"Are you sure that's wise, Starr?" Mary was instantly awake, her eyes wide with concern. "Your child is due any time. Captain Madison wouldn't want you to take any unnecessary risks."

"Life is a risk," I replied. "Captain Madison would understand I cannot disappoint these good people."

I put on my boots, fur coat, and hat, and went out into the last slowly falling flakes of the previous day's blizzard, Colin's guitar on my back.

****

Seated on a stool at the end of the bar, I led the caroling with Ben, Bridgit, and Meg by my side. Then, as the evening drew to an end and church bells began to summon the faithful, I was requested to sing "Ava Maria." Carefully I started the emotional and difficult piece, not sure how successful I would be. Suddenly, from the shadows near the doorway, a tenor voice, strong and beautiful in its support, came to steady me.

Startled, I stumbled to a pause, hardly daring to breathe, not daring to recognize it. Then he was coming toward me, still singing and looking so tall and strong and handsome in the lantern light he took my breath away.

When he stood beside me, he removed the guitar from about my neck, took up the instrument, and continued the hymn. Overcoming my joyous surprise, I joined him with overwhelming happiness. My captain was home!

****

Our second child was born at dawn that wonderful Christmas. Lovingly delivered by his own father, Randall Abraham Madison was a handsome, lusty baby, strong and robust, another fitting son for a man like Captain Barret Madison. Our next child I vowed, however, would be a girl…Lise Ida Madison…in honor of her grandmother and her great-grandmother.

As the baby nursed contentedly, Barret told me Colin's scores had met with wild approval in Vienna. Posthumously, Colin Douglas was an acknowledged musical genius. Then I told him of my newfound wealth and my plans. We would use the money to help the people of the valley. We would build roads, and a new school, and a real hospital with a real doctor. And he must take me to England aboard the *Maris Stella* once baby Randall was weaned. I must oversee the ending of the despicable conditions in the mines I now owned.

Barret smiled at me in the lantern light, his expression so full of love and caring that tears welled in my eyes. "I'll take you anywhere," he said. "I'll do anything you ask…except leave you. Nothing will ever separate us again. Now rest. I must go to my firstborn.

Colin needs his father. We mustn't give him reason to be jealous of his brother."

He kissed me and left the room. I drifted off to sleep, his child slumbering in my arms, a smile on my lips, knowing he spoke the truth.

A word about the author...

Gail MacMillan is the award-winning author of twenty-eight published books and a graduate of Queen's University. She has had articles and short stories published in magazines both in North America and Western Europe.

Contact her at:

macgail@nbnet.nb.ca

www.ingramcontent.com/pod-product-compliance
Lightning Source LLC
Chambersburg PA
CBHW070805030726

47504CB00003B/697

9781628301946